DIVIDED DESTINIES

Aaron—the son of an American father and a Chinese mother, who finds he must make the terrible choice between two worlds . . .

Melin—a daughter of wealth and privilege whose beauty is her curse as she makes the ultimate sacrifice to family duty on a bed of shame . . .

Kwanjin—a child of the Pearl who chooses to stay and fight for the future of his native land, and pays the price for joining the wrong side of the struggle . . .

Michiko—the exquisite Japanese girl whose only hope of survival is in living among people who have every reason to despise her . . .

Sung Hwa— the young man determined to best his father, but betrayed by the woman he loves. . . .

From San Francisco to Hong Kong . . . from Pearl Harbor to the Chinese mainland . . . they risked all for the promise of power, respect, wealth and l... T... ... the **joys of** su... ...nate **price. . . .**

TEMPLE OF
THE MOON

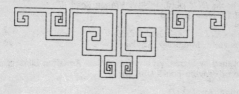

BY

Ching Yun Bezine

Ø
A SIGNET BOOK

SIGNET
Published by the Penguin Group
Penguin Books USA Inc., 375 Hudson Street,
New York, New York 10014, U.S.A.
Penguin Books Ltd, 27 Wrights Lane,
London W8 5TZ, England
Penguin Books Australia Ltd, Ringwood,
Victoria, Australia
Penguin Books Canada Ltd, 10 Alcorn Avenue,
Toronto, Ontario, Canada M4V 3B2
Penguin Books (N.Z.) Ltd, 182–190 Wairau Road,
Auckland 10, New Zealand

Penguin Books Ltd, Registered Offices:
Harmondsworth, Middlesex, England

First published by Signet, an imprint of New American Library,
a division of Penguin Books USA Inc.

First Printing, April, 1992
10 9 8 7 6 5 4 3 2 1

 REGISTERED TRADEMARK—MARCA REGISTRADA

PRINTED IN THE UNITED STATES OF AMERICA

PUBLISHER'S NOTE
This is a work of fiction. Names, characters, places, and incidents either
are the product of the author's imagination or are used fictitiously, and
any resemblance to actual persons, living or dead, events, or locales is
entirely coincidental.

BOOKS ARE AVAILABLE AT QUANTITY DISCOUNTS WHEN USED TO PROMOTE PROD-
UCTS OR SERVICES. FOR INFORMATION PLEASE WRITE TO PREMIUM MARKETING DI-
VISION, PENGUIN BOOKS USA INC., 375 HUDSON STREET, NEW YORK, NEW YORK
10014.

Dedication

To our beautiful Crystal.
Thanks for being my writing partner.
Our eternal love erases the line
that separates two different worlds.
We look forward to flying with you,
somewhere beyond the Temple of the Moon.

Acknowledgment

To Audrey LaFehr, my editor.
You planted the seed for this book,
then very tactfully helped it to grow.
May our little Chinese flowering tree
bloom beautifully in its American home.

A Special Thanks

To Frank Bezine, my husband.
You showed me that love and faithfulness
do exist in the heart of a man.
I'm glad that when tradition warned me about you,
I did not listen.

There is a Great Buddha
Living in the Temple of the Moon.
We send up our prayers
When the spring moon is full:
"May there be no sorrow on earth,
May all our dreams come true."

"Sorrow is but the other side of laughter,
Dreams must fade with the morning dew.
Disappointment will make you strong,
And tears will make you grow."
Shaking his wise head,
Answered the Great Buddha in the Moon.

PART I

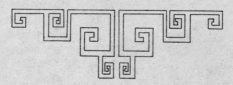

1

A FULL MOON hung over the horizon, shining from a cloudless sky and gleaming over San Francisco Bay.

A car appeared, moving alongside the water. The beauty of the moonlit ocean attracted the driver. The vehicle slowed down and stopped.

A tall man emerged from the car, walked toward the ocean. He had on dark pants and a white shirt. The wind fluttered his sleeves, tossing his jet-black hair over his forehead. As he stood facing the Pacific, the moon brightened the striking features of his handsome young face.

His eyebrows were thick and arched, his eyes deep and round. He had prominent cheekbones and a high-ridged nose. His thin lips curved up over the single dimple on his chin as he smiled contentedly like a carefree child.

Moonlight turned the ocean into a silk quilt, covering all the creatures living in the water. The waves leapt and fell vigorously, and Sung Hwa felt himself blush as he looked at the sea's motion.

Only a short while ago, the silk quilt over two naked bodies had risen and plunged in a rhythm even more fervent than that of a turbulent ocean. Sung Hwa could scarcely believe his good fortune when he thought of Judy, a beautiful American girl with hair the color of honey and eyes blue like a clear summer sky.

"Judy, I love you, and I'm going to marry you," he whispered to the sea, smiling wider, his youthful eyes glistening with innocence and passion.

Then a frown chased away his smile when he thought of breaking the news to his mother, A-lin.

Four years ago, his father, Sung Quanming, had left his wife, son, and daughter for an American woman in Hawaii. Financially A-lin couldn't complain, because in the divorce Quanming had settled with her more than generously. But emotionally A-lin could forgive neither Quanming nor Laurie, and her hatred and bitterness were centered mostly on Laurie.

"All American women are ugly," A-lin said frequently. "They have large feet, rough skin, and heavy hair. We delicate Chinese ladies wear size-three shoes, those barbarian females wear size eight, nine, or even ten. They need to shave their legs every day, otherwise their legs will look like those of a hairy beast. If you look at their faces closely, you'll see that most of them have mustaches."

Sung Hwa shook his head as he remembered that whenever his mother said those words, she glanced at her own hairless legs proudly and raised a hand to touch her face, which was as delicate as porcelain, with only a few fine lines left by age.

Sung Hwa had first seen Judy a year ago during freshman orientation, and was immediately attracted to her radiant beauty. Judy's figure was like a living hourglass, while the figures on almost all the Chinese girls he knew resembled dead doors. Who cared if Judy had large feet?

A-lin also commented constantly, "There is not

a single true lady among the American females. They wear low-cut gowns to show their large cowlike bosoms, and call those indecent gowns 'formals.' As soon as they see a man, they begin to wiggle their broad hips and bat their false eyelashes. I bet that among ten eighteen-year-olds, you can find no more than one virgin!"

The night sky remained cloudless, but a dark cloud appeared on Sung Hwa's face. Judy was eighteen, a year younger than he. And she was not only no longer a virgin, but also experienced enough and passionate enough to be his teacher in the art of lovemaking.

Sung Hwa shrugged as he said to himself, "A true Chinese groom waits until his wedding night to discover the mystery of life together with his innocent bride, but I simply do not have that Chinese virtue of patience."

He felt the warmth on his face again as he watched the ocean surging. He wished that Judy had been a virgin, but then the soft quilt that covered them would never have skyrocketed if Judy had been as inexperienced as he.

He could still hear Judy's laughing voice as she used her skilled long fingers to guide him inside her.

"Am I my poor innocent China Boy's first woman?" she teased.

"China Boy" was her pet name for him, a name he resented but didn't have the courage to stop her from using.

Once again he shook his head, trying to dispel his embarrassment. And then he made a decision. Tomorrow he would propose to Judy. And of course he would not share her pillow again until they were married. Pillowing once could be explained as the result of his wild young lust, but more than once would be an insult to his future wife.

A faint smile returned to his face as he thought that one of these days in their married life he would be able to prove to Judy that he was a powerful man, not only in bed, but in all the other aspects as well—just like his commanding father.

Staring at the rolling ocean under the brilliant canopy of a luminous spring night, Sung Hwa could see himself as a young child and his father a middle-aged man.

"Hwa-hwa, will you go away across the ocean with Baba?" he heard his father asking.

"No, Baba, I can't leave Little Sister Guai and Mama," he heard himself answering.

Tears filled Sung Hwa's eyes as he watched, still in his mind's eye, himself growing into a teenager and slipping away from his much-adored Baba. He blinked the tears away, squinted his eyes to gaze at the far horizon, and screamed out the words that had lain buried in his heart for a long time:

"Baba! Can you hear me in Hawaii? Do you know that I love you, miss you, and want to be your little Hwa-hwa just like I used to be? I'm sorry for making you angry! I should have never befriended Mama's lover, Moa Lau. And I should have never skipped school to play Mah-Jongg with them. I did many things to make you dislike me, Baba, and I'm sure your disappointment in me is the reason you no longer want me."

He bowed his head, and then added in a low, apologetic voice, "You see, Baba, I was only a child then, and it was so much easier to be a bad child than a good one."

He felt the hot tears pouring from his eyes, rolling down his face, which was chilled by the night

wind. He was ashamed of being a crybaby. He
raised his hand to dry those tears, then forced
himself to smile at the moonlit horizon.

"Baba, you'll be surprised to see me at your
doorstep, bringing with me a beautiful American
wife. Your wife and mine will get along fine, and
you and I will be close again."

Smiling confidently, he turned and left the Bay.
He drove through the quiet city, reached Post
Street, and stopped in front of a narrow two-story
house near Chinatown. The garage looked like a
crouching turtle, carrying on its back the rest of
the building, which was shaped like a tightly
packaged bundle. As he parked his car, he missed
his childhood home, a big ranch-style house built
by his father on several acres in the hills outside
of San Francisco.

His mother had gotten rid of all the things that
could be traced back to Sung Quanming, except
her two children. As soon as the divorce was
final, she had fired all the old servants, sold the
grand house with all the furniture in it, given all
of Quanming's remaining things away, and married Moa Lau. They had moved then, to a new
home that was very close to Moa's tailor shop,
amid all the sights and smells, the noise and bus-
tle of Chinatown.

Hwa walked up the stairs, past the master bedroom, pictured his Mama and Moa lying in bed
together, and felt a knotting sensation in his
stomach.

At fourteen he had enjoyed the lazy company
of Moa. But at nineteen he found his stepfather
disgusting. Each time he saw the aged tailor putting those cigarette-stained fingers on his mother,
he wanted to scream:

"My mother and father may never have been
happily married, but still, she belonged to him,

and you have no right to soil what is Sung Quanming's! Watching you hold Mama is like seeing
an emperor's art collection dirtied by the hands
of a drunken peasant!"

In front of his sister's room, he stopped at the
closed door, wishing that there were a closeness
between him and Guai so that he would have
someone to talk to and wouldn't be so lonely.

At sixteen Guai had inherited their mother's
look of a little mouse, but was much more clever
than A-lin had ever been as a young girl. Guai
was cold and pragmatic. She knew about her own
plainness, and never expected any of the tall
handsome boys to pay attention to her—which
had been the mistake made by A-lin when she
fell in love with the handsome Quanming.

Guai waited patiently, keeping her observant
eyes on the boys from good Chinese families who
were intelligent and hardworking but homely.
She left school after finishing the eighth grade,
knowing that she could be an ideal wife to the
right man without further education. She taught
herself to shop cleverly, to give firm orders to the
servants, to invite the right people to parties, to
frown at the poor and smile at the important and
influential. Her frosty nature made her remote
from her brother. She never needed him, and
never cared that he might need her.

Hwa raised a hand, soundlessly ran his fingers
over the tightly closed door to his sister's room,
then walked away, knowing that a door always
would stay closed between them.

Before entering his own room, Hwa glanced at
the open door of an empty room at the end of
the hall. His maternal grandmother, Mrs. Wu,
had died a year ago. Her husband had been a
rich man, and she had left all her money to Hwa.

Sung Hwa had never valued his wealth more

than he did right now. As he undressed, he thought of Judy's fabulous home on Nob Hill. He whispered to the lovely image of her that filled his mind and heart at all times.

For the next few hours he turned and twisted in bed, dreading the confrontation with his mother when morning came. He knew that besides her own loathing toward the female white race as a whole, she would tell him that with a white woman as a wife he would immediately be cast out of the Chinese circle and viewed as an outsider from then on.

Hwa knew that Mama was right. This was 1937, but for a Chinese boy to marry an American girl was cause for all Chinese to shout, *"Ah-ya!* Our ancestors are crying in their graves; the blood of our descendants will never be pure again!"

Hwa tried to comfort himself. He said in his thoughts while gradually drifting into sleep, "If Mama disowns me for marrying Judy, and if the entire Chinese population in San Francisco starts to throw rocks at me, I can always take Judy to Honolulu to live with my Baba."

Sung Hwa awoke a few hours later, remembering that this was the most important day of his life. He jumped out of bed quickly and left the house while everyone else was still asleep.

He wanted to buy a ring that was good enough for Judy, a ring that was unique and unavailable in the white men's jewelry stores. He drove slowly around Chinatown, searching for an antique shop that was open at this early hour.

He braked for the bony dogs that were digging into the garbage cans that lined the streets, and felt sorry for the drunk, the sick, and the homeless, who were white, black, and oriental, wavering their way along the littered pavements.

He passed a small restaurant named Yung Fa, a closed prostitution house called the House of Wan, and the deserted Sung Wu Company that had, at one time, belonged to his family. He recognized the immense difference between Chinatown and Nob Hill, and began to understand why Judy said to him repeatedly, "I like my China Boy, but I hate Chinatown! How could a man so handsome and tall and intelligent also belong to such a filthy, dingy, and backward environment?"

Hwa wondered: Was he a part of Chinatown? He wasn't sure. He did not feel truly Chinese, but he knew he wasn't American either.

He entered the antique shop, and his eyes were caught by a large ruby ring surrounded by small diamonds.

"It came from Thailand," said the aged hunchbacked and yellow-toothed shopkeeper. "It used to rest on the delicate fingers of one of the king's favorite ladies-in-waiting. The beautiful woman plotted to run away with her handsome lover, packed all her valuables, and placed them in his hands. She was caught and beheaded. He ran away alone to the Land of the Gold Mountains, sold her jewelry, and married a good Chinese girl."

Hwa didn't believe the salesman's story. No man could be that heartless and forget that easily. If Judy and he were in the situation of the unfortunate Thai lovers, he would remember her forever and never marry. He paid for the ring without bargaining.

Driving toward Nob Hill, he whistled a happy tune, thinking how lucky he was. After admiring the most beautiful girl in college for over a year and doing all sorts of chores for her when opportunity allowed, he had finally been invited to her home last night. When she asked him to stay after the party, he was thrilled. He was certain then that she loved him as much as he loved her. It was lucky for both of them that her parents were in Europe and there had been nobody but the servants in the house.

He reached Nob Hill and stood with a thumping heart, looking at the impressive mansion. He was insulted when the butler kept him waiting outside the door and went upstairs to ask Judy's permission to let him in.

"You'll treat me quite differently when I become your young lady's husband," Hwa said under his breath to the arrogant servant's back.

Judy was propped up by several pillows, sitting in her canopy bed with a tray on her lap, drinking coffee and reading the morning paper's society section.

"Good morning, my sweet China Boy." She smiled at him without putting down the paper. "Did you forget something?"

"No, darling," Hwa answered, and went to sit on the edge of her bed. He leaned forward to kiss her, but she turned her head to one side. His kiss landed on her cream-covered cheek. He was surprised by her lack of warmth, then realized that she must not be fully awake yet to respond to his affection.

"Judy, I have something for you," he said, smiling positively, knowing for sure that at the sight of the ring her attitude would change.

She sipped at her coffee and watched him take the silk pouch out of his pocket, then open it with pride. Her expression didn't alter when she saw the sparkling red stone.

Hwa was surprised, but told himself that she must consider the ring as no more than an ordinary gift. He blamed himself for being so stupid.

He quickly got off the bed and got down to one knee. "Judy, I love you. Will you marry me?"

For the next minute Judy continued to drink her coffee, glancing at the ring casually, looking now and then at Hwa in his kneeling position. When she saw the sincere expression on his face, and the way he offered the ring to her with both of his arms stretched like a humble worshiper before a goddess, she couldn't conceal her amusement any longer.

One corner of her mouth curved up in a taunting smirk. She laid down the cup and pushed away the tray and the newspaper. She studied Hwa long and hard, trying to find out what had possessed this young man whom she had thought at one time to be clear-minded.

When she spoke, her voice was hard and cold. "My grandparents built this house on Nob Hill. My parents are proud of the old money in our family and the fact that there is no other race but pure white in this neighborhood. I am my parents' only child—wilder than they wish me to be, but I still resemble them in many ways, especially the way I think."

She paused, and her clear blue eyes swept over Hwa sharply. "Sung Hwa, I am white, and you are yellow. Have you not noticed the difference? Do you not know that no one in this world would want to see us married, including me? That interracial marriage is not even legal?"

Hwa's stomach gave a sudden strong lurch. He stared at her, his face paled, and cold sweat broke out on his forehead. He could hear the word *Heon-jeo* ringing in the air, echoing in his ears, overpowering Judy's voice, filling the room and expanding into the whole universe. *Banana!* A pitiful creature with yellow skin and a white heart!

"Judy . . ." He faltered, his voice trembling. "Last night . . ." He groped for words but failed.

Judy shrugged. Her lacy pink strap slid down one of her beautiful shoulders, revealing the mark left there from Hwa's love bite. "What about last night?" she asked, staring at him innocently.

Hwa felt a bucketful of icy water being dumped on his back, sending a chill over his entire body, making his skin crawl and his teeth chatter. "You . . . what we did last night . . . is not something that you would do with just any man! You felt for me . . . and I thought—"

Judy cut him off impatiently. "Of course I don't go to bed with just any man. I'm a good girl, and don't you forget it!"

She laughed softly. Her voice was as crisp and clear as a silver bell rung by a chilly winter wind. "As a matter of fact, you are my very first China Boy."

She arched an eyebrow, looking at him sideways, saying slowly, provocatively, "Of course I feel something for you. Ever since I first laid my eyes on you, I wanted you like I wanted to have a taste of those exotic Chinese drinks. You know, the kind that come in tall glasses with cute little umbrellas."

She paused, shrugged, then stretched lazily, raising her arms over her head and revealing more of her ample bosom. "Honestly, you were not bad. Clumsy and ignorant, of course, but with possibility."

Hwa watched her, shaking uncontrollably. His upper teeth sank into his lower lip, drawing blood.

She giggled, lowered her arms, but didn't bother to pull up the quilt. Her full breasts heaved from underneath the thin lingerie, and her dark nipples danced like two little mushrooms. "You proved to me that whatever I've heard about Chinamen is not true . . . not in your case, anyway."

Hwa struggled to get to his feet. He almost fell, and had to put a hand on the bed for support.

Judy placed a scarlet-nailed hand on his shaking arm. "You don't have to give me the ring. I don't like rubies. My father has bought me so many rings that I don't have enough fingers to wear them. And if you promise never again to let silly ideas such as marriage enter your head, we can have more fun like we did last night."

She squeezed his arm and winked at him mischievously, "You are rather well-built for a race known to be small. With practice, you'll be a pleasure."

Hot tears burned Hwa's eyes, but he used all his willpower to keep them from spilling over. He freed his arm from her grasp with a jerk. He saw her hand drop to the silk quilt, and her bright red long nails sparkled in the daylight, each nail a sharp sword piercing through his heart as he remembered how she had used those experienced slender fingers to guide him into her. He felt sick. He turned abruptly and fled the room. As he descended the stairs, he heard her laughing, as if greatly amused by a silly clown.

He sped out of the Nob Hill area, drove blindly on the newly constructed highway. He heard his own voice shouting above the sound of the wind blowing strongly outside the open windows of his sports car.

"I hate American girls! Mama was right all along! Why didn't I listen to her? I hate all the white devils! They *are* devils instead of human beings, and that's why my ancestors gave them their fitting name. I wish I had not been born in this country!"

Through the open windows, the odor of hot

grease, raw fish, and old garbage nearly gagged him. He looked and found himself once again in Chinatown. He drove slowly, looking for a sense of belonging, but could find none. "Judy was wrong. I am not a part of this district. To the people of Chinatown who are native Chinese from the Pearl River, I'm as much an outsider as I am to those living on Nob Hill."

The image of his own people glaring at him and calling him names served like salt on the wound. He was angry not only at the white race but also at everyone in Chinatown. He would never go back to Judy's place for the ruby ring he had left behind. "It's the tuition for what I learned about girls in the USA!" he said through clenched teeth.

He imagined what his mother's expression would be if he should tell her about his experience with Judy. He trembled. No, he would never tell Mama. But sooner or later he would have to go home and face her. Like all mothers, A-lin was quick to detect her son's trouble.

Hwa could also see the looks on the faces of the Chinatown people when they discovered that he, the son of Sung Quanming, had been made a fool by an American girl, a white cow. No, he could not meet anyone eye to eye. His misery and humiliation were written clearly on his features, and his people were so clever they would notice at a casual glance.

He must escape from San Francisco. He must go somewhere far, far away.

He almost ran over a woman holding a basketful of palm leaves. He slowed down and noticed that around him, almost all the people were carrying the same kind of long leaves tied into bundles, and sweet rice, and other things for the celebration of the May Festival. It was the fifth of May, according to the lunar calendar.

Suddenly he remembered the story told to him by his father.

Centuries ago, in China, there lived a poet named Chu Yuan. He wrote about the agony of his kinsmen, described their pain and sorrow. His poems were well-loved, and his fame grew, until one of his poems offended the emperor and he was ordered to die. On the fifth sunrise of the fifth moon, Chu Yuan threw himself into the River Ming and drowned. The people of China didn't want his spirit to go hungry. They used palm leaves to wrap up sweet rice and meat, then steamed the small bundles and threw them into the Ming River. These rice bundles became a popular food called *Jeo-tze*, and the people in China ate it every year when the spring moon was full.

Hwa heard once more his father's voice. "In China there are many festivals, created to lighten some of the pain we must endure every day. Now I am far from China, but when I'm depressed I always think of China and the harsh life of the Chinese people. It works like magic. I immediately stop feeling sorry for whatever I don't have in life, and feel grateful for what I do have."

All of a sudden Sung Hwa knew what he must do. He would have to put up a big fight with his mother before she would give him her consent, but surely she would not deny him a trip to their homeland.

2

A BUS FROM the west side of Oahu Island stopped near Waikiki Beach. Among the many exiting passengers was a young girl in a pink kimono. She had an oval face, round eyes, a delicate nose, and a small mouth. Her long hair was thick and black, tied behind her neck with a red scarf and adorned with a red flower. He skin was tanned from working in the sugarcane fields, and because of that she was considered a peasant.

Michiko Ikeda was only sixteen. She had been in Hawaii just six months. Her original home was Hiroshima, Japan, where life was difficult. Her three older brothers had died when they were children. In the summer of 1936 a labor trader came from Kure, a town near Hiroshima, to recruit workers for the sugarcane plantation in Hawaii. It didn't take Michiko's father long to decide to quit his low-paying job in a machinery shop and move his family to Hawaii.

On the crowded ship, the Ikeda family met a family by the name of Yamada, from Kyoto. Jebu Yamada was nineteen, three years older than Michiko. All the male passengers on the ship followed Michiko with their eyes, but she had eyes only for the handsome Jebu. While their parents talked, Michiko and Jebu exchanged shy glances at first, then short sentences, until endless words were pouring from their full young hearts.

Jebu had told Michiko proudly, "My father is a sculptor, very creative. He likes to develop his own style instead of following tradition, and because of that he is not well-received in Kyoto and we are not rich. A few months ago a wealthy Chinese came to Japan looking for an artist to design jewelry and statues for his coral factory in Hawaii. His name is Sung Quanming. He liked my father's work very much, hired my father, and gave me a job in his factory."

When the ship docked in Honolulu, the two families exchanged addresses before parting. The Yamadas were met by their employer and driven to Ewa Beach. The Ikedas were taken by an unfriendly plantation foreman to Waianae, a town on the west side of the island. The older generation didn't have much time to visit one another, but Jebu went to see Michiko often, and invited her to see him frequently.

Michiko walked toward the beach, remembering how unhappy her parents were about her catching a bus and traveling across the island to see Jebu. They would rather that she stayed home when she was not working, to help her mother with all the domestic work.

Michiko looked at the beach. A long ribbon made of sand curved softly to circle around Diamond Head. Above the dormant volcano's flat top, the night sky was brightened by a full moon. Moonlight clothed the palm trees with silver, turning them into dancers in glittering costume. The wind blew gently, and the dancers swung their arms gracefully, following the rhythm of the ceaseless tide. She liked the beautiful scenery of Hawaii. Unlike her parents, she was seldom homesick for Japan.

Tonight she had accepted Jebu's invitation to come to the beach to join him, his parents, and

Mr. and Mrs. Sung Quanming for a picnic under the spring moon. The moon's magic power was recognized by the native islanders, as well as those whose original homes were in the ancient lands of the Orient.

Chinese, Japanese, Koreans, and Filipinos—all worshiping the spring moon on the same beach. Michiko watched them burning incense, lighting red candles, and offering the Moon Buddha red flowers, fresh fruit, and a variety of food favored by people of dissimilar origins, such as steamed rice, ginger-spiced fish, and flour buns filled with red beans.

She searched until she found a group of five people sitting around a low folding table behind a row of flowering trees. She was glad that they hadn't yet noticed her. She would like to calm down first. A Japanese lady should not be seen with her face red, her hair tossed by wind, and her forehead moistened with sweat.

Standing behind a bush, Michiko admired Laurie Sung, a Caucasian woman in her forties, busy arranging a large bouquet of flowers. Her white skin was tanned to the color of bronze. Her red hair was bleached golden by the sun. She was wearing a yellow muumuu that looked white in the pale moonlight. A flower lei adorned her neck. "I hope I will look as good when I'm her age!" Michiko murmured.

Michiko looked at Sung Quanming, Laurie's husband. His handsome face was deeply suntanned. It contrasted with his silver hair, creating an effect much more forceful than that of any good-looking young man. His body was lean and solid, his back straight and shoulders square.

Michiko remembered Jebu's words: "Mr. Sung used to live in San Francisco, where he was a powerful man. He moved to Hawaii a few years ago, established an import-export business, then expanded his trade into many fields, including hiring deep-sea divers to bring coral out of the Pacific, then turn it into beautiful jewels and art objects. He is much more than a businessman. He and his wife formed a school for the islanders to develop special skills that are related to the island culture. Mr. Sung is very influential on this island." Wearing shorts and a colorful shirt, Sung Quanming sat cross-legged, talking vigorously to the next man.

Looking at Heroshi Yamada, it was easy to think of him as a common man. He was slightly built, in his early forties, but his slouched shoulders and stooped back made him look much older. People would change that opinion when they looked at Heroshi's eyes. They were bright and penetrating, and shone with intelligence.

Looking at Mr. Yamada's clothes, Michiko laughed and quickly raised a hand to cover her mouth. In spite of the warm weather and the sandy beach, Heroshi had on a dark blue formal kimono. Jebu had said that when his father decided to come to Hawaii to make a better living, he had also decided to take his culture and tradition with him forever, everywhere.

Michiko glanced at Kiko, Heroshi's wife. The woman had a petite body and a small pretty face. She was a year younger than her husband. Wearing a gray kimono decorated with white butterflies, she sat on her heels, busily arranging two bowls of fruit and moving with the poise of a noble lady.

Michiko turned toward Jebu and her heart drummed. She had fallen in love with him on the ship, and had grown to love him more each day. Jebu had grown two more inches in six months, and was now a head taller than his father. He

was helping his mother with the food and trying
to hide his unhappiness at the sight of the
seaweed-wrapped rice. He had developed a great
fondness for bread, milk, and red meat. His appetite was not the only thing that had become westernized: he was wearing shorts and a Hawaiian
shirt instead of a kimono.

Michiko walked gracefully toward the five people. They welcomed her, and she communicated
with them in stilted English, the universal language of Hawaii.

Jebu blushed as he greeted Michiko. Kiko and
Heroshi treated her with more reserve than did
Quanming and Laurie. Michiko bowed to every-
one, then started to help Kiko pour the rice wine.
As she worked, she compared Quanming with
Jebu, thinking that Quanming was like a lord and
a shogun, while Jebu was a young samurai serv-
ing under the master.

"Quanming, will you pick some more plumerias for me?" Laurie asked her husband. She had
already placed a bouquet of the yellow-centered
white flowers on the mat when she noticed Mrs.
Yamada's disapproving frown. "I think I've chosen the wrong color. Please find me some red
ones for good luck."

Michiko perceived it right away. So, this was
the American approach. A wife had the right to
order her husband around!

"I'll get the flowers for you, Mrs. Sung," said
Jebu, jumping up immediately and heading
toward the other side of the beach.

Quanming's eyes followed the young man with
great affection, then turned to Heroshi. "How did
you raise such a wonderful son? He is clever,
hardworking, and most polite."

Before Heroshi could answer, Kiko turned to
Quanming and bowed deeply from her sitting po-

sition. "Jebu ordinary boy," she said in heavily
accented English. "Very common. Not worthy of
good words." She bowed again, and her face almost touched the sand. But when she looked up,
a proud mother's happy smile was sparkling on
her face.

Quanming laughed. "Japanese mothers and
Chinese mothers are alike. When people pay com-
pliments to their children, they feel obligated to
deny. When I was Jebu's age, my mother was
very proud of me. But in front of people she always insisted that I was nothing but a common
boy."

Jebu returned with a bunch of plumerias, gave
one to Michiko to add to her hair, the rest to
Laurie. Laurie began to rearrange the bouquet
with the red flowers. Kiko continued to lay out
more small dishes of food and order Michiko
around. Heroshi and Jebu knelt comfortably, facing Quanming, and the three men talked about
the world situation.

Quanming said with a sigh, "My country is divided into two. Chiang Kai-shek established his
capital in Nanjing, and Mao Tze-dung took his
men to Yenan."

Heroshi shook his head. "And my Heavenly
Emperor has lost his control over the military
leaders."

Jebu asked innocently, "Mr. Sung, is it true that
the Japanese have occupied a large part of
China?"

Quanming didn't answer. He liked Heroshi as
one of the most intelligent men he had ever met,
and respected the Japanese artist for his great talent. It embarrassed him to let his friend know
that he knew what the Japanese had done in the
northeastern part of China.

Heroshi noticed Quanming's embarrassment and

smiled at him reassuringly. "I am not responsible
for the Japanese military invading China, any
more than you are for the actions of the Chinese
warlords. No matter what happens on the other
side of the Pacific, you and I will always be
friends."

The men were interrupted by Laurie. "We are
here to honor the spring moon. Can the three of
you stop talking about the war?"

Kiko was shocked. How could Laurie tell the
men to change their topic of conversation? If Kiko
did something that unreasonable, Heroshi would
be furious. Poor Mr. Sung, stuck with such a
woman!

"My son's wife must be all Japanese!" she
hissed at Michiko, making clear that if the girl
should become a Yamada, she was not going to
follow Laurie's example.

The old woman smiled at Quanming kindly,
wishing to erase some of the humiliation the poor
man had received from his barbaric wife. "Mr.
Sung, would you like to do us the honor of saying
the first prayer to our Moon Buddha?" she said,
giving Quanming a box of matches.

On the low table stood a red candle as thick as
a baby's arm. To set the candle aglow was to call
Buddha's attention to the beginning of their
prayers. Quanming struck the match, and the
men began to talk to Buddha. When they finished, it was the women's turn. They prayed for
peace, good health, and happiness. No one asked
too much; both the Chinese and the Japanese
were humble people.

After each had prayed in turn, Laurie looked at
the beautiful young girl and remembered something Jebu had mentioned. "Michiko, have you
been going to the night school in Waianae?"

"Yes, Mrs. Sung, I've been going there three

nights a week, learning English, typing, and bookkeeping," Michiko answered. "My parents don't mind, since we don't have to pay anything. But I'm afraid I'm learning rather slowly, because I'm usually very tired after a whole day's work in the sugarcane field."

Laurie looked at her husband. Quanming understood the unspoken suggestion. He said, "Michiko, why don't you come and work for me? I can always use an extra clerk."

Michiko's face glowed with happiness. "Mr. Sung! How kind you are! I will not disappoint you, I promise. I don't know much about bookkeeping yet, and I can only type slowly, but I'll improve quickly. I'm a rather fast learner." She turned to Laurie, put her arms around her. "Thank you, Mrs. Sung, for making the suggestion with your eyes. Your husband is such a good man. He listens to you in everything, right? All husbands should be as good as he, I think!"

Michiko glanced at Kiko from the corner of her eye, ignoring the older woman's fury. She looked at the happy Jebu and said, "I'll give my notice tomorrow. My parents will be happy for me, I hope."

On the other side of Oahu Island, the waves of the Pacific Ocean touched the Hawaiian shoreline softly, sighing their good-byes to the fading moon. They welcomed the sun with cheerful whispers as the glowing red ball rose from the eastern horizon. Not far from the ocean, the small huts in Waianae gradually became visible, like many porcupines resting under the swaying palms.

An ear-shattering siren broke the peacefulness at exactly five A.M. The plantation workers streamed out of their little huts, wearing coolie hats, long-sleeved shirts, and long pants that were tucked into high rubber boots. Around each person's neck hung a chain with a small brass disk, on which an identification number was stamped. The disks were called *bangos*, and all the workers hated wearing them.

They carried nothing on their backs, and their lunch boxes were light. But they walked with shoulders hunched and backs bent, as if the weight of a mountain were thrown upon them.

"I'm humiliated by this dog tag!" said one man in Japanese, taking the brass disk in his hand as if to crush it within his fist. "We are from the cultured lands where a name means everything to a man. Why do they call us by numbers? In Japan even prisoners are allowed to maintain their family names."

Beside the Japanese walked a young Chinese man. There was a language barrier, but no communication problem. Pulling the chain angrily, the man said in Cantonese, "Hawaii is known by my people as the Fragrant Land. I came here to make money for my starving family, but not to become a dog!" In order to make his friend understand, he barked, then shook his head. "In China, when a man is stripped of everything, he still can be proud as long as he has his honorable name!"

Michiko Ikeda walked among the long procession of workers, heading toward the sugar plantation. She no longer looked as she had on the beach, wearing her beautiful pink kimono and flowers in her hair. Under the straw coolie hat she wore a red scarf that covered most of her face, showing only her bright dark eyes. A pair of dark green pants were tucked into her black rubber boots, and the sleeves on her brown shirt were long, so that only her fingertips were exposed. Carrying a small lunch box in one hand, she raised the other to pull on the shameful tag. "Today is the last day I'm called by a number! Tomorrow I'll never see another luna!" she said proudly.

Luna was the Hawaiian word for "foreman." For every hundred plantation workers there were three lunas, riding on horses, using long leather whips to keep the workers in order. The female workers were like little mice, counting each day as a day of blessing if they survived the claws of the luna. A particular luna had cornered Michiko several times in the remote corners of the field, when she was collecting cane stalks. He had also tried to run her over with his horse more than once when she was by herself chopping and hoeing weeds.

"When tomorrow comes, I'll never be afraid again," Michiko said to herself, and smiled at her future.

At the entrance of the cane field stood a small temple built with bamboo. The Spanish and Portuguese workers passed it without pausing; the Chinese, Japanese, and Filipinos stopped at it and knelt. Michiko got down to her knees and peered in at the statue of Buddha with great respect. The large wooden statue had long ears that reached the shoulders, and a fat face broadened by a dimpled smile. Around the Buddha's neck someone had tied a red scarf, an offering that guaranteed a wish would come true.

"Dear Buddha, you owe me your protection," Michiko said to the statue. "When you came to Hawaii many years ago, you sailed with my people. Over the Sea of Japan, the ship was hit by a storm. The captain ordered my people to throw all the useless things overboard. In order to keep you, one of the men threw his worthless daughter into the roaring water." Michiko closed her eyes and concluded her prayer quickly. "Since that poor girl died for you, please protect me from the hands of the *luna* for only one more day!"

For the next five hours, under the glaring sun, the men cut the ripe cane and the women collected it, while the children, the aged, and the sick chopped and hoed weeds. When a loud siren sounded at half-past ten, the workers sat wherever they were and ate quickly. Fifteen minutes later there was another piercing siren, and the lunas came on horseback to rush all the workers back to their duty.

Michiko had just swallowed her last bite of seaweed-wrapped rice when she saw the luna's horse. He came toward her, and she stepped quickly to one side to escape the horse's hooves. But he kept coming, and there was no place left for her to go but to run ahead. She had taken off her scarf to eat her lunch, and had not had a chance to put it back on. She had rolled her sleeves up, and now her arms were bare. Her exposed face and arms flared up the luna's desire; he chased her vigorously. When she was forced to run into a field where the cane was uncut and the weeds not cleared away, the tall grass cut into her face, and her arms and hands were sliced by the sharp weeds that stood in her way.

The big middle-aged man was a mixture of Chinese, Japanese, Filipino, and Caucasian, but he had no sympathy for the people of any of his many origins. He was determined to get Michiko before the day was over. It was easy for him to ride through the wild field, his legs protected by thick leather boots. He laughed when he saw the beautiful face of his target streaked with blood and tears. He gave his tall horse a kick, and drove the animal closer to the frightened young girl.

Michiko fell at the edge of the plantation, next

to the Buddha's temple. Both her parents and the other workers were far away, and her screams couldn't be heard. She fought with all the strength she possessed, but besides scratching the foreman's face, she accomplished little.

"Buddha! Help!" she cried when the big man climbed on top of her.

"Please, Buddha! Where are you?" she yelled when her clothes were torn off.

"Aren't you going to save me, my merciful Buddha?" she screamed when he entered her.

"Buddha!" she sobbed when he was gone and she was left bleeding beside the temple. She lay helplessly on the ground, staring at the fat Buddha's smiling face. She watched the red scarf flapping in the wind, thinking about the young girl thrown into the ocean for this wooden statue, and the people who had offered the scarf for a favor. "We sacrificed for you. Why didn't you come to my rescue?"

The workers left the plantation at four P.M. The huts once again occupied by their owners. Women cooked and children played, while the men gathered under the palm trees, talking and drinking their rice wine from tiny cups. The door to the Ikedas' hut was tightly shut, but Michiko's soft sobbing could still be heard. No one paid any attention to her cries; every family had its problems, and according to the Japanese culture, it was polite to pretend that they never heard what they were not supposed to hear.

Michiko had managed to come home without being noticed, and waited for her parents to return. When she told them what had happened, Mr. and Mrs. Ikeda listened calmly. When Michiko finished, her father got up from his kneeling position and walked toward the window. He

stood silently for a long time as Michiko continued to cry and his wife continued to sigh deeply.

With his back turned to Michiko, he said to his
wife, "There is only one thing for her to do."

With tears rolling down her cheeks, Mrs. Ikeda
rose from the floor. She went to the wooden
trunk they had brought from Japan and took out
a white cotton kimono. She returned to kneel
once again beside her daughter, and placed the
garment on the young girl's lap. Controlling her
emotion with all the willpower she had, the
mother said with composure, "This was meant to
be your bridal gown. Go bathe yourself and put
it on."

Michiko bowed while kneeling, then stood up
and took the kimono with her. There was only
one room in the hut. She went to the corner that
was separated by a paper screen. A dresser, less
than two feet tall, stood against the wall. A cushion embroidered with a white crane was the only
other piece of furniture. Michiko laid the kimono
on the cushion, then left her corner.

She glanced at her parents and saw her father
standing facing the window with his back straight
and head high, a picture of determination and
courage. Her mother was kneeling in front of the
Ikeda family plaque—a wooden slab with the family name written on it—crying silently, trying un-
successfully to match her husband's bravery.

*They expect me to be as fearless as they, and I
mustn't disappoint them*, Michiko said to herself,
leaving the hut with a small wooden bucket that
was the Ikedas' bathtub.

She walked toward the water pump, past many
other plantation women. They smiled and talked
to her, politely ignoring her swollen eyes. She answered as well as she could. No one knew what
shame had befallen her, not yet. But the foreman

would brag about his victory, and everybody would know. Then the others couldn't continue to pretend that they didn't know Michiko's misfortune, and the Ikeda family wouldn't be able to pretend that nothing had happened.

She filled the bucket with water and carried it back to the hut. Squatting behind the screen, she washed herself thoroughly with a cloth. She then put on the white kimono and knelt in front of the low dresser. With many hairpins she piled her long hair into a high dome. A beautiful face looked at her from the mirror, a face fresh with youth. "It's a shame to die at sixteen," she whispered to her own image, watching the tears roll down her cheeks. She would never become Jebu's wife now. He would never want a soiled girl.

A thought very much against tradition occurred to her. It was so shocking she dropped her comb. She stared into the mirror and asked herself in a low murmur, "Even if Jebu doesn't want me, don't I have a right to live for myself?"

There was only a small window in this corner of the hut. But the sun managed to shine in, casting its red glow on Michiko's face. She looked out the window and saw a piece of blue sky and two white birds flying high.

Maybe I should try to go to Jebu and explain what happened, she thought while looking at the beautiful world outside her window. *If he wants me to die, then I'll consider it. But if he should wish to have me alive, not as a wife, of course, but as a maid to wait on him and his future wife . . . well, I'll hate that woman, but I wouldn't mind being alive..*

Her thoughts were interrupted by her mother. "Your father wants to know if you are ready," Mrs. Ikeda asked without looking at Michiko.

Michiko got up. She wanted to share her thoughts with her mother. But before she could say anything, Mrs. Ikeda said without lifting her eyes, "You must obey your father's words quickly. Please don't keep the spirits of our ancestors waiting."

Michiko bowed her apology to her mother, then followed Mrs. Ikeda to the family plaque. She cast her eyes obediently on her feet, while her heart drummed with indecision.

"Kneel!" her father said, and she obeyed, out of her habit of a lifetime.

In front of the plaque, two swords, one long and one short, rested on a horn rack. Mr. Ikeda took the short sword in his hand, pulling it from the sheath slowly. "The Ikedas were not always poor. Many generations ago, we were samurais. The most honorable death a samurai could have was to commit hara-kiri. Had you been a son, you would have deserved that great honor."

Mr. Ikeda's eyes brightened with pride as he went on, "When a man commits hara-kiri, he is allowed to use the short sword to stab himself in the lower abdomen, and his best friend is honored with the mission of chopping off his head with the long one."

He looked away from the long sword, turned to the short sword in his hands, and then continued with regret. "Since you are but a female, you must die in a much more humble way." He sighed, then gestured to his wife, "Tie up her legs so she can cut her own throat with the short sword . . . it's a pity that the long sword will never be used."

Mrs. Ikeda bowed her head and left. She came back with a white scarf more than three yards in length, then knelt beside her daughter. While dying, no matter how brave the spirit was, the body would be tortured with pain. The girl's legs must be tied together so that while struggling,

she wouldn't kick around and show her under-
garments and take her last breath in a disgraceful
position.

Michiko looked at her mother with disbelief.
Mrs. Ikeda's face was bloodless, and her lips were
trembling. But with tradition as her guide, the
woman was ready to use her own hands to tie up
her only child and help to end a precious life.

In wonder Michiko looked up at her father.
His lips were a tight line, and his eyes showed
deep sorrow. However, with the family honor as
his beacon, the man was certain that he was
doing the right thing in giving the sword to his
daughter.

Suddenly Michiko dropped the sword and pushed
her mother's hands away. She turned to her father and bowed deeply. "Please allow your
worthless daughter to have her last wish," she
said.

"Hm?" Mr. Ikeda frowned unhappily.

Michiko got to her feet in a hurry. "I would like
to die with a fresh flower in my hair," she said,
knowing that according to tradition, her last wish
must be granted.

After a brief hesitation Mr. Ikeda stamped his
foot on the floor. "Go!"

Michiko bowed to her father once more, then
turned to her mother. She would have liked to
give her parents a farewell embrace, but didn't
dare. If she showed any emotion, they would become suspicious—her people were proud of being
emotionless in events such as this.

The fragrant plumerias grew on the other side
of the beach. Michiko took the long skirt of her
kimono in her hands and kicked off her slippers.
She ran on her white socks with parted toes, and
felt the wind blowing through her wide sleeves.
She felt like a bird flapping its wings, fleeing from

two hunters who loved her but wished to see her dead. She knew that they were watching her from the door. Seeing her running as fast as she could, they would nod their approval and say to themselves that they had raised a good daughter who was eager to gather the flowers that would adorn her death of honor.

The beach rose into a hill, and the sandy soil was rich with dirt. A row of tall flowering trees stood on the other side of the hill, and Michiko could smell their sweet aroma. She raced forward and soon saw the many trees, each blossoming in a different color. Pink, white, red, and yellow petals radiated in the island sun, urging her on.

She ran through the budding trees. The flowers fell on her in the soft breeze. The white plumerias bloomed on the last tree and were the ones she was expected to gather. When she was under the white flowers, she glanced over her shoulder to make certain that she was out of her parents' sight, and then kept running without stopping.

3

THE SPRING MOON was full and bright. It turned the sky into a shimmering canopy hanging over the South China Sea.

The rocky coastline of Hong Kong curved to embrace many small harbors. On the low land, shabby huts, like insignificant ants, swarmed together to form countless fishing villages. Two thousand feet above them, atop Victoria Peak, mansions rose like dark giants shrouded in shining capes. Behind one such home a gazebo stood at the edge of the cliff with six pillars supporting a tiled roof.

On the stone bench sat a boy, his short hair and pajamas fluttering in the soft wind. The moonlight revealed his face—his features had the dark coloring of a Chinese and the deep setting of a Caucasian. At fourteen, Aaron Cohen was tall and thin. Like a young tree reaching for the sky, all the limbs were but long sticks that carried no meat.

He looked down at the fishing boats. Each boat was a black silhouette enhanced by a pinch of yellow light that cast zigzag reflections on the water.

Four years ago, when his family had first arrived in Hong Kong from San Francisco, they took a trip to his mother's hometown, Jasmine Valley. Aaron had watched the village women making fishing lanterns, gluing oil paper to thin bamboo sticks tied into cylinders. As the night fell, a stream of fishermen would carry these lanterns in their hands, walking slowly toward the Pearl River, which flowed near their homes. The lanterns were placed at the bows of their boats to lure the fish, and each fleck of the light glistened with a humble prayer whispered from the lips of a worried village woman.

"Great Buddha, please don't let the Dragon King's daughters take my man."

The story of the Dragon King's daughters was like one of the many other tales told to him by his mother, reflecting the difficult life lived by the poor of China: The fishermen had to take the fish from the Pearl River, the Dragon King's domain. The King sent his many beautiful daughters to the surface of the water, tempting the men with their red coral lips and long seaweed hair. With each storm a few men would drown, and their waiting brides would bring their spirits to the King as payment for the fish the men had taken.

Aaron sighed and whispered to the unseen fishermen on the remote boats, "Your life is so different from mine. I am half Chinese, but I know almost nothing about you and your world."

Aaron's father, David Cohen, was a successful businessman. He had started with one jewelry store in Hong Kong four years ago, and now had branches all over the peninsula, and was expanding into the New Territory and mainland China. Aaron's mother, Meiping, was involved in many charity organizations. Aaron and his sister, Rachel, had been well-protected all their lives. The school they attended on the Peak was the most prestigious in Hong Kong. Lessons were taught in English, and the majority of the teachers were British. As a result, Aaron could neither read nor write in Chinese, although he could speak the Pearl River dialect he learned from his mother.

Aaron looked up at the splendid moon and remembered another of his mother's Chinese stories. She had told him that when the spring moon was full, it had the magic power of making all earthly wishes come true.

"I wish to travel through China someday, to see every town and every province, to be among the people, and to understand where I came from." He made his wish as he left the gazebo, but only the Chinese half of him was willing to count on the moon.

Aaron pushed open the front door, walked softly on the marble floor. He ascended the steps. Past his parents' room, at the end of the hall two doors stood facing each other. He turned the doorknob and entered Rachel's room. He and his sister were so close that no knocking was ever needed between them.

A neatly kept room lay bathed in moonlight. All the pink was bleached away by the magic illumination. The curtains and the bedding seemed white, while the white furniture and carpet became silver. Aaron tiptoed toward the bed, his heart filled with pride as he looked at Rachel.

"My sister is the most beautiful girl in Hong Kong . . . or maybe even the whole world!" Aaron said, smiling at the thought.

As she slept soundly on her side, Rachel's long ebony hair spilled like black water over the pillow. A thin quilt covered her slim body, and only her face and shoulders could be seen. Her cheeks were pink, her lips moist and red. Her eyelashes were two tiny black fans now resting on either side of her delicate nose, shielding her large almond eyes. She was the image of a lovely bud about to bloom into an exquisite flower.

Aaron remembered his mother saying with worry in her eyes, "When Rachel was born and my friends came to the hospital to visit us, we made such a big mistake. Like fools, we bragged about Rachel's beauty. We caught ourselves and took back our words immediately, of course . . . we all claimed that she was ugly and worthless. But I've been worried ever since then. I hope that no evil spirit heard us, and waits in the dark corners for a chance to take Rachel away."

Aaron shook his head. He couldn't understand the Chinese fear of showing too much joy lest the gods become jealous and take the source of joy for themselves. He wasn't worried. He knew that no evil spirit would have the heart to take away Rachel, the most precious gem in the eyes of her parents and her brother.

He left her room tiptoeing, went across the hall to his own room.

He gasped at the mess. When he couldn't sleep and had gone to the garden, he had left a lamp on, shining on the chaos all around. Clothes, books, records, shoes, and crinkled papers covered every inch of the floor. He picked his way through the room toward his bed, wondering why Yin, the young maid, never complained. Was it because Yin was Chinese and a poor orphan? The poor of China took life as it was, and were always grateful for whatever lot they were given.

"I want to understand the people of China!" Aaron threw himself on the bed, lying on his back. He folded his hands under his head and wondered about the vast land of his mother's birth.

Beside the window and on the dresser, a porce-

lain pig caught Aaron's eye. Its fat body was well
fed with money that he received on birthdays and
other occasions. He had no need to spend it, as
he never lacked for anything.

In Aaron's imagination the fat pig gradually
changed into a charm for a bracelet, yellow and
shining. It was the head of a Buddha, less than
an inch high in solid gold. Its eyes were two chips
of diamond, sparkling and animating the face.

"Mama's birthday is coming soon," Aaron said
to himself, and jumped off his bed. He reached
the dresser and grabbed the porcelain pig. He carried it to the bathroom and wrapped it in a towel.
He used the heel of a leather shoe to pound on
it until it shattered. He unwrapped the towel and
took the money from the many pieces of broken
porcelain. He counted it and smiled—it was more
than enough for the gold charm.

The fragrance of wild jasmine in the deep valley
intensified with the heat of the early-summer sun.
It reached the many villagers standing around the
newly dug grave.

Aaron sniffed deeply, smelling the flowers. He
felt the wind blowing softly and saw the pink and
white petals falling from the fruit trees, dancing
in the breeze. This was his first encounter with
death. His grandfather had died suddenly on the
day before his mother's birthday. Aaron had had
to give the gold charm to his mother on the train,
when he, Rachel, and Meiping were on their way
to China for the funeral. His father was too busy
to leave Hong Kong.

Aaron looked at the crowded graveyard. Everyone had known his grandfather, and most of
them had been customers in Yung's Tea House.
Some still owed the old man money for wine and
food. Aaron wondered if these people were here

to bury a dear old man or to look at Meiping, one of their own, and her two half-American children.

The villagers didn't keep their opinions to themselves. Being true natives of the Pearl River, they didn't believe in lowering their voices. Listening to them, Aaron wished that he couldn't understand Cantonese. Their words painted him a portrait of his mother in her rich splendor, and he liked that. Their statements confirmed his opinion of Rachel, and he was very proud. But their comments also forced him to look at himself more objectively, and he didn't like what he saw.

"Meiping is not young anymore, but she doesn't look as old as a Jasmine Valley woman looks at her age. It seems that she still has all her teeth . . . it's unbelievable what wealth can do!"

"Her daughter is beautiful . . . for a mixed-seed. The girl doesn't look real. She looks like a picture. How old do you think she is?"

"About sixteen, the same age as Meiping when she left the village for America. But Meiping was never as gentle as her daughter. Meiping fought with her father every day, never showed the poor man any tenderness. Look at this sweet young girl: she is crying over her grandfather, but at the same time holding her mother's hand and whispering comforting words."

"Meiping's son is more like her when she was in her rebellious youth. There are no tears in his eyes. He seems a little sad, but very bored. I don't think he really cares that his grandfather is dead. His mother's tears didn't bother him either. I think he is ready to leave the village and go on with his adventure to some other part of China. Did you see Meiping frowning at her son? I don't think she's happy with him at all."

"Why is Meiping's white-devil husband not

here? A man is expected to be at his father-in-law's funeral, even if he is white!"

"Meiping told her stepmother that the white man has to stay in Hong Kong to run his business. Clever man! He needs to make more money for his wife to spend . . . look at those urns!"

There were two iron urns in the graveyard, filled with the paper items to be burned. The villagers looked at them with envy, wishing that someday they too could afford to die as lavishly as Yung Ko, the lucky old man.

The coffin was lowered into the ground, then covered with a small mound piled over its top. Mrs. Yung and Meiping picked up the two young willow shoots that lay waiting beside the grave, and started to plant them. The willows would take the places of the wife and the daughter of the deceased, to stand beside the grave and to keep the dead company. When the wind blew and the willows swung their graceful branches, the dead would feel his wife and daughter reaching for him with their soft arms, embracing him lovingly.

After the willows were planted, Meiping and Mrs. Yung went to the urns. The paper men were burned first—they were Yung Ko's servants. The paper women were burned next—they were Yung Ko's concubines. Paper wagons and horses were turned into ashes—Yung Ko must go visiting places in the other world, though he had never liked to travel when he was alive. A many-roomed paper house was set aflame, together with a pile of paper furniture—Yung Ko was now the master of a well-furnished mansion. A large deck of paper clothes was torched, and several suitcases were cremated—Yung Ko had never liked fancy clothes in the world of the living, but in the world of the dead he would be the best-dressed man. The most important item was incinerated at last—bundles of paper money blazed so that Yung Ko could buy respect and love from other Chinese spirits.

Ashes filled the sky, like black butterflies flying chaotically. Now the mourners were eager to leave. They all knew that Meiping had paid several village women to cook in the Yung's Tea House for the feast that, according to custom, must follow the funeral.

Aaron cast a farewell glance at his grandfather's grave. He took his mother's arm and heard her whispering to the dead, "Good-bye, Baba. This time it's your turn to go on a long journey. I'll be thinking of you every day, just like you thought of me when I left you for the Land of the Gold Mountains."

Aaron went to his grandmother, and listened to Mrs. Yung's tearful words. "Old man, have fun with the pretty ladies I burned for you. When I join you, your fun will be over."

Aaron walked between his mother and grandmother, with Rachel following them. They climbed into the waiting wagon. None of them noticed that the charm Aaron had given Meiping had fallen to the grass-covered ground.

When Meiping discovered that the little Buddha was missing, she was very upset. "It's from my son. I treasure everything from my Aaron and Rachel. I even saved all the baby teeth the two of them lost. I have the first drawings of theirs from kindergarten. I simply must find that little Buddha!"

They looked everywhere in the teahouse, then went back to the graveyard. They searched every inch of the ground, but couldn't find the charm.

Meiping's face was white, and there was fear in her eyes. "It's very bad luck to lose a Buddha."

She turned to Aaron apologetically. "I know I promised we'd go to Beijing and many other places after your grandfather's funeral, but now we must cancel the trip and go home."

"No, Mama!" Aaron took his mother's arm and shook it hard. "Please don't cancel it, please! There are too many superstitious old sayings in China. How can you believe them? I bought you the charm. If any bad luck should come of it, it should fall on me alone. Oh! I hate Chinese sayings!"

The next moment, Aaron's voice was covered by those of Meiping and Mrs. Yung.

Mrs. Yung shouted loudly, glancing at all the dark corners in the room, "Evil spirits everywhere, please don't pay attention to this ignorant boy. He is half white devil and doesn't know what he is talking about. If bad luck must fall, let it fall on me. Do whatever you want with this lonely old woman, but please leave the young boy, the honorable son of a good man—although he is a white devil—alone!"

Meiping stamped her foot on the floor. For the past four years she had lived the life of a rich lady. But when things didn't go right, the elegant lady of Hong Kong quickly became the village girl she used to be. "*Due-na-ma!* If my charm was swallowed by a dog, may the beast soon become a plate of stew. If the gift from my son was stolen by a thief, may the worst luck fall on the bastard or the whore!"

Aaron and Rachel looked at each other and tried not to laugh. Like their father, they had learned to be quiet when Meiping was angry.

"*Ah-ya!* How could we forget?" Mrs. Yung gasped.

"What?" Meiping asked, still fuming.

"The worst luck does not fall on the one who

loses the Buddha, but the one who steals it. That's why in temples all over China the valuable statues of Buddha, some coated with gold, are never removed, even when times are extremely hard." The old woman winked at Meiping.

"That's right," Meiping said, smiling at Mrs. Yung conspiratorially. According to the old beliefs, a person could fool the evil spirits by directing them whichever way he wished them to go.

The two women quickly changed the subject. Aaron and Rachel had no idea what was going on. They knew that Meiping and Mrs. Yung were playing a Chinese game, but they didn't know the rules. They were only happy that the trip to Beijing was not canceled.

4

Autumn 1934

IN SOUTHEASTERN CHINA, in the province of Kiang-si, the Ching-kong Mountains rose majestically under the radiant moon.

The silver beams colored every inch of the land with a hue of tranquillity, concealing the more than 130,000 Communist party members, now gathered under the full moon's light to discuss whether to kill or be killed.

The night air was cool. Campfires were built in the valley surrounded by many barracks. Each fire was shared by a cluster of men and women in baggy pants and dark shirts. One of the larger fires was circled by five party members—Li Kwan-jin, Wong Chung, and three others of higher rank than they.

Li Kwanjin was twenty-two, the youngest of the five. It was his duty to keep the flames going, and as he added more wood to the fire, he smiled to himself, then whispered to his former teacher, Wong Chung.

"According to Communist theory, we must denounce the old. Based on our principle of equality, all the party members are but fellow comrades. Yet when I'm with the older party members and those who outrank me, I always end up as the servant boy. How do you explain this incongruity?"

Wong Chung gave his former student a look of warning. Wong Chung had tried to teach this boy since they were together in a small fishing village called Willow Place, and often had been proud of the clever boy. But to demand true equality with the hard-line party elders? To ask that a concept be carried out word for word? Wong Chung shook his head and glared at Kwanjin disapprovingly, doubting the younger man's intelligence.

The fire glowed on Li Kwanjin, revealing his striking good looks. He had inherited from his father the broad shoulders of a Pearl River fisherman, and received from his mother the delicate features of a Willow Place woman. Most arresting was the fearless twinkle in his young eyes. It pained Wong Chung to know that Kwanjin's daring thoughts behind those eyes must be erased if he wished to live until his smooth face wrinkled.

"Chiang Kai-shek's men are closing in on us, calling themselves the 'Bandit Extermination Campaigners.' They have surrounded us with rings of small concrete fortresses, and are gradually tightening the rings. We are now captured in a giant squeeze. We must choose either to break the lines or to hold our ground—both are extremely difficult . . ." said one of the elder comrades, purposely leaving his statement unfinished to avoid any possible doubt about his loyalty to the party.

"The Red Army is not sufficiently equipped to carry out either operation," said another old and wise comrade, expressing both tact and caution. "But no matter which operation we choose, with Chairman Mao as our great leader we'll be led into victory, just like the weak and helpless creatures of the night are always led out of the darkness by a red shining sun."

Kwanjin couldn't help but laugh. The others glared at him. He bowed his head and added more wood to the already roaring fire.

The third-ranked comrade cleared his throat. "I imagine our wise and brave Chairman will lead us away from the Ching-kong Mountains, instead of into a direct fight with Chiang's men. The old saying goes: At times, the best advance is a retreat."

Li Kwanjin couldn't keep his lips sealed any longer. He looked at the others one by one, then raised his young voice. "A retreat is to run away. To advance will mean victory. The two are completely different. Why can't we simply admit that we are too weak to fight with the Nationalist Army and must run for our lives?"

The others looked away from Kwanjin, pretending they didn't hear him. If they acted as if they had heard his words, then they would be obliged to report his statement to the official who kept a detailed record of any possible disloyalty to the party.

When the moon faded and the fire died down, people began to leave the valley and return to their barracks. Kwanjin saw his mother, Leahi, with her head bowed and shoulders sagging, walking beside her new mate, Sen. Her misery was so obvious that his heart ached with guilt for having persuaded her to enter a second marriage.

Leahi's unhappy marriage had been the first ray of light upon Kwanjin's blind devotion to party doctrine. Soon after that, Kwanjin began to look at everything with his eyes open wide instead of accepting it on faith. As a result, he had discovered injustice, corruption, greed, and cruelty. He dared not mention his troubled feelings to anybody but Wong Chung. But whereas his mentor used to explain everything thoroughly and rationally, now all Kwanjin received from Chung was either a warning look or a severe admonition.

"If you don't want me to turn against you, you must stop criticizing the party," Wong Chung said.

"I value your friendship. But I can't help it if I sometimes think the party is wrong," Kwanjin said stubbornly.

Before autumn turned into winter, the Communist party's bases in the Ching-kong Mountains were destroyed. The Communists were forced to leave the Kiangsi province and flee toward the northwest.

The night before leaving the mountain, behind a thin closed door, Li Kwanjin and Wong Chung sat beside their packed bags and shared a bottle of rice wine.

"It's going to be an impossible journey." Kwanjin lifted his chipped cup and drained the remaining wine in one gulp. "The order says we're going northwest, traveling through the barren and uninhabited regions. We'll have to cross many rivers on foot, carrying our heavy supplies on our backs. First, the turbulent Yangtze, the River of Endless Tears, and then the forceful Yellow River, the River of Eternal Sorrow." He looked at his former teacher. "Tell me, how can the old and the weak, the children and the sick, survive the trip?"

Wong Chung looked away from Kwanjin, refilled both wine cups. "We'll be equipped with the Great Chairman's wisdom, and we'll be able to go through deep water and hot fire without being harmed."

"*Due-na-ma!*" All the Communist party members were ordered to speak Mandarin, the national dialect, in an attempt to achieve language uniformity throughout China. But Kwanjin cursed in his native Cantonese just the same. "That's dog shit! How many times have we talked about the absurdity of Christianity and laughed at its carpenter named Jesus who walked on water? Are you asking me to be as stupid as the Christians?"

Wong Chung drank his wine without looking at Kwanjin. "The River of Endless Tears . . . and the River of Eternal Sorrow!" he murmured. "Even the rivers in China have sad names." He looked at his protégé meaningfully. "When people are eternally and endlessly fed on tears and sorrow, they need to grasp some kind of hope. Chairman Mao is our only hope, you must admit."

Kwanjin closed his eyes, going through his mind the rulers listed in his history book. When he opened his eyes again, his expression softened a little. "I guess you are right. So far, Mao Tzedung is the best leader we've ever had. He did help our people fight for food, homes, and freedom from the merciless landlords and warlords. The others never did anything but take the meager belongings away from the weak and the poor."

Kwanjin drained his second cup of wine. "But I still don't see why Chairman Mao and his party can't be criticized. Criticism leads to improvement. As long as we have the good intention of improving our nation, why must we either shut up or lie?"

"Because . . ." Wong Chung stopped. He looked at the closed door with fear in his eyes.

A year ago the Chairman had encouraged the children in the Ching-kong Mountains to form the "Teams with Long Ears." It was now unsafe for people to talk openly even in their private rooms. On the other side of the closed doors children could be listening with their long ears, memorizing the conversations without understanding them, then repeating them to the authorities half-accurately. Many careless people had been punished severely, and now the rest lived in constant fear.

"It's almost dawn." Wong Chung raised his voice and shouted at the door. "A bright day will soon begin! I can't wait to start the wonderful long march under the superb leadership of our magnificent leader! Long live our Chairman Mao!"

Kwanjin stared at his teacher, then hissed, making a sound that was either a chuckle or a sigh. "My Great Buddha! This is worse than falling out of love with a girl! I've liked girls, found faults in their characters, then admitted my infatuation. But with communism, when I find faults with it, I'm told to continue pretending that I'm still madly in love!"

He remembered the disappeared party members and the sad looks on the faces of their families. He thought of his mother. He stopped talking. Following his teacher's gaze, he looked at the door, felt a chill race down his back, then immediately hated himself for being afraid.

When dawn came, Kwanjin, Wong Chung, Leahi, Sen, and more than 130,000 others left the Ching-kong Mountains.

They walked for the next 370 days, covered six thousand miles, carrying on their backs food, clothing, guns, printing presses, and limited medicine. They trekked through eleven provinces, and passed the two deep rivers, plus numerous swamps and snow-covered mountains.

They were not supposed to take anything from the villagers they encountered. According to

Chairman Mao's words, "Not even one piece of thread or one tiny needle." But as they marched through the villages, hunger drove them to rob the impoverished farmers and fishermen. When the villagers had nothing to offer, the marchers frightened them into killing the water buffalo that were needed for farming, the pigs and hens saved for festival days, and even the dogs that were the children's pets.

In his comrades' behavior Kwanjin saw his idealistic dreams crumble.

They were attacked often by the local warlords and Chiang Kai-shek's soldiers. Many comrades were killed, and the survivors underwent dramatic changes. Their quiet voices became loud, and their warm glances turned cold. Gentle attitudes were replaced by rudeness, and all the softness in their natures gave way to cruelty.

Many of the marchers fell sick and perished. Kwanjin's stepfather, Sen, caught pneumonia and died. Leahi had never wanted Sen as a spouse, even after he was forced on her by her honorable son, who believed, at the time, that no woman in the commune should live alone. She walked alongside Kwanjin, detached from the rest of the people, stubbornly putting one foot in front of the other. When she was sick, hungry, and weak, she was supported by the strong belief that a woman's duty was to obey her father, husband, then eventually her son. Each time Kwanjin looked at his mother, he realized how strong a little village woman could be.

They reached Yenan in October 1935, but only 20,000 of the 130,000 marchers were still alive. Mao Tze-dung quickly made Yenan the Communist capital and started to reorganize. With the death of many of the elder party members, a group of much younger leaders emerged. Wong Chung was one of them.

"We need to build a strong base in this cave city." Wong Chung looked at Kwanjin carefully. "We need tough and resourceful workers to be in charge of many projects. You're only twenty-three. But if you can manage to keep your big mouth shut and all your negative opinions to yourself, then I'll appoint you as my youngest junior party leader."

Kwanjin thought of the benefits that would come with the appointment. The higher-ranked officials ate better and lived in larger quarters. The theory was that better living conditions would make the leaders healthier and more capable of guiding the general public into greater victory.

Kwanjin was ashamed of his hatred for hunger and discomfort. He certainly would like to provide better for his mother and himself. He forced a smile on his face and nodded his agreement.

After the appointment, Kwanjin had many new responsibilities. He helped the people in Yenan to build homes inside the caves. He joined the others in the fields to work the impossible soil and to grow their own food. He helped to raise the chickens and pigs, and in his spare time he taught the party ideology to the new comrades.

Two years later, in one of the larger caves that was used as a classroom, boys and girls sat on the ground, looking at Kwanjin with their eyes bright and their brains absorbing, believing, and remembering his every word.

"Chairman Mao says, in order to overthrow imperialism and feudalism, our new democratic revolution consists of *two* revolutions: a national struggle to achieve liberation from foreign oppression and a class struggle to overthrow the rich and the educated, who have used their money and knowledge to oppress the peasants . . ." Kwanjin stopped at the sight of a raised hand.

A young boy, resembling a younger version of Kwanjin in many ways, stood with a puzzled expression. "Comrade Li, I'm confused," he said. "Not all the rich and educated are bad. When we go through the class struggle, how do we avoid harming the nice landlords and intellectuals?"

After a long hesitation Kwanjin decided to answer the boy honestly. "We must be very careful. Upon taking over a village, we should ask around and find out which landlord is good, and which scholar never tricks anybody. A good gardener cuts the weeds but keeps the flowers untouched. Revolution is a delicate mission if you want to achieve the best results."

The boy sat with a satisfied smile, and a girl raised her hand. She had short hair and bangs, and her young eyes were hungry for knowledge. "Comrade Li, how can we tell which western culture should be adapted because it will benefit us, and which must be rejected because it will only damage our own civilization?"

Kwanjin answered quickly. "We should definitely study the western sciences. Their medicine can help reduce our mortality rate tremendously, especially among the children and old people. There is more freedom in their art, and their music is beautiful—"

He was interrupted by Wong Chung.

"Comrade Li!" Wong entered the cave in a fury. He yelled and pointed a finger at Li Kwanjin's forehead. "You need to have your head examined! I heard your answers to both of the questions, and they are absolutely wrong!"

He pushed Kwanjin aside, took his place, and stood facing the young people who gaped at him in awe. "You must forget what was said by Comrade Li," he said, his voice shaking with anger. "First, every single one of the rich is bad, and so are all intellectuals. If we apply our principles to only some of the rich and educated people, then it's the same as letting some fish escape from a hole in our net. We'll become sloppy fishermen. Chairman Mao will not tolerate such fishermen, I can guarantee you that!"

He glared at Kwanjin, then continued, "All the foreign nations are evil, except Russia, who helps China now and then. The USA is our number-one enemy, and all the American art, literature, music, and even their scientific inventions are tainted by capitalistic greed. We must reject everything and there is no question about it!"

He quickly dismissed the class, then had a long talk with Kwanjin. He lectured his former student again on communistic doctrine, and then toward the end he asked, "What happened to you? You used to hate America, the imperialistic land that lured your shameless father away from you and your mother."

Kwanjin answered in a low emotional voice, "That was before my mother's second marriage, the Long March, and many other things that have happened in front of my eyes. I no longer hate my Baba. In fact, I think he is a very good, hard-working man. He left home to go to America as a laborer so that Mama, my grandparents, and I could live. I've matured a lot in the past three years. I've become less naive. People do have the right to grow and become wiser and change their viewpoints, don't they?"

"Not if you are a Communist, and living in Yenan!" Wong Chung said, shaking his head. After looking at Kwanjin for a few moments, his voice softened. "Perhaps you need to leave Yenan for a while. Living in caves can drive people out of their minds, and that's probably why many of the other party members have become disloyal to our Chairman. Maybe you need to go to the areas that are not yet liberated by us, to experience the bitter taste of imperialistic rule, and then you'll regain your faith in communism."

Suddenly Wong Chung's eyes were brightened by an idea.

The most dangerous mission for the comrades in Yenan was to travel to the other provinces to persuade the landlords and warlords to give their support to the Communists or to absorb more party members and bring the new blood back to Yenan.

"I'm sending you to Beijing," Wong Chung said in a firm voice that left no room for debate. "There are many college students in that old city, with idealistic dreams and the urge to rebel against tradition. I shall request permission for the mission immediately."

5

IT WAS A long way from Waianae to Ewa. By the time Michiko reached her destination, the sun was gone and a crescent moon shone proudly on a velvet sky.

"Michiko, what happened?" Jebu gasped.

Michiko stood at the door, hair hanging all over her face. Her white kimono was soiled and torn, her socks stained with mud. She stared at him for only one second, then without catching her breath asked while still panting. "Jebu, do you want me dead?"

"What?" His jaw dropped. He put his hand on her shoulders, looking at her dirt-covered sweaty face. "What are you talking about?"

She shook off his hands. He was a head taller than she, and weighed about fifty pounds more, but she pushed him away with tremendous force, then stood at a distance with her hands on her hips.

"Don't touch me!" she shouted at him. "I'm not a virgin anymore!"

Jebu had never heard any young girl use the word "virgin" before. He blushed, looking at her with bewilderment.

Without taking her eyes from Jebu, Michiko cried, "The foreman raped me! The Buddha didn't protect me! My mother was ready to tie up my legs, and my father had the family sword out of its sheath. They wanted me to gash my throat. I had to come to you and hear your opinion."

Jebu was staggered by the news, and shocked by Michiko's blunt way of letting him know. He stood staring at the girl, couldn't utter a word.

Kiko Yamada appeared from behind her son, followed by her husband, Heroshi. They had heard Michiko's every word, and were now at their boy's aid.

"Please come with me," Kiko said to Michiko, taking her by the arm. "You need to wash up and drink a cup of tea."

"But I can't go into your house if you think your family name will be offended by an impure girl!" Michiko struggled to stay outside the door. She was much too proud to impose herself on those who didn't truly welcome her.

"I'm not taking you in as a daughter-in-law," Kiko explained clearly, keeping a firm hold on Michiko's arm. If this young thing wanted to be stubborn, well, this old woman could be even more stubborn. "While Jebu is deciding whether to marry you, you can be a family friend."

Jebu recovered from the astonishment just enough to shout over his mother's shoulder, "Michiko! I shall always want to marry you, no matter what happened!"

Heroshi put a hand on his son's arm. "Only fools make quick decisions. You and I will talk things over first."

The Yamadas' house on Ewa Beach had been given to them by Heroshi's employer, Sung Quanming. There were four rooms. In the master bedroom Kiko closed the door behind her and Michiko.

"Take off your clothes," Kiko said to Michiko, pointing at the adjoining bathroom. "Then go sit in the water."

Michiko heard the commanding tone in Kiko's voice and relaxed a little. Kiko's ordering her around was a good sign. Perhaps there was still hope for her to become the Yamadas' daughter-in-law, after all.

The bathroom had been rebuilt by Heroshi Yamada, who had brought with him from Kyoto the memory of a Japanese culture that covered all aspects of life. Michiko undressed in front of a tub that was already filled with hot water. The water was kept hot all day, by a low flame. The bathroom floor was covered with tile and had a drain. Michiko stood naked on the floor, found a large ladle, dipped it into the tub, and filled it with water. She poured the water over herself and then picked up a bar of soap. It was the Japanese way to wash oneself outside the tub, then sit in the clean water to soak away the fatigue and to think deep, peaceful thoughts.

Kiko stood at the bathroom door, crossed her arms in front of her, appraising the young girl's naked body. She liked Michiko's wide hips. They were a sign of bearing good strong sons. She didn't think much of Michiko's flat chest. But except for the white cows, who wasn't flat-chested? After the first child was born, the breasts would grow, and there would be milk—she wasn't really worried. Michiko's arms were very thin; Kiko frowned. How could a plantation worker have such unmuscled arms? If Jebu married this girl, Kiko would have to make sure that her daughter-in-law was the one to carry all the heavy things, and not her precious son.

When Kiko looked at Michiko's face, her heart softened. In spite of her dirty cheeks and messy hair, Michiko still looked beautiful. A man would be pleased to come home every night to a face like that. Jebu would be glad to pillow with the body that belonged to such a face. Putting the Yamada family's seed into the womb of Michiko would be an enjoyment for Jebu, and Michiko's impurity was, after all, only skin-deep.

Kiko realized that there were not many unmarried young girls in the Fragrant Land. One as beautiful as Michiko was most rare. If Jebu didn't marry Michiko, he would have to get a picture bride, and his family would be asked to pay for the girl's traveling expenses. By looking at a picture, what guarantee was there that the girl had not already been soiled in Japan?

While Kiko was in the process of making up her mind, in the study a serious conversation took place between the father and the son.

"So, you still want to marry her, although she is impure?" Heroshi asked with a serious face and a grave tone.

"Yes," Jebu answered, then added in a low voice, "I love Michiko. I fell in love with her on the ship, and I will always love her."

"Love!" Heroshi waved a hand, dismissing the childish word. "Don't you want to know if it was her fault that the foreman violated her? Is she a flirt? There are other girls on the plantation. Why was she the one touched by the man?"

"There are other girls violated on the plantation, but none dare to say anything, I'm sure. Really, it's not Michiko's fault, I know." Jebu said eagerly, trying to control his voice so it wouldn't sound like he was arguing with his father. "When she gave notice a while ago, that horrible man had already given her reason to fear him. She is a good girl. She never allowed me to lay my hands on her. She is not a flirt. Please believe me and accept her." Jebu bowed deeply to his father. When he looked up, there were tears in his eyes.

The son's glistening tears refreshed the father's

memory. Many years ago, in a temple in Kyoto, a young artist had met a delicate girl holding a pale green umbrella and wearing a pink kimono. They fell in love with each other, but her family didn't want her to marry a poor artist who was struggling to make a living. Heroshi had felt hopeless then, and his eyes had been constantly filled with tears of despair.

Now he sighed. "Well, let's wait and see. When Michiko's next monthly sign comes, she must show the blood to your mother. As long as the foreman didn't leave his seed in her, perhaps our ancestors won't be too offended by her impurity."

Jebu bowed. He couldn't ask for more.

The next day, Jebu and Michiko visited Laurie and Quanming. Sitting in a sunny living room, Jebu told them what happened.

Laurie was furious. "Why does this happen in every country and through all ages? Why do men treat women like this and get away with it most of the time?"

Quanming quoted an old Chinese saying. " 'When someone breaks my arm, I'll hide it in my sleeve to keep my family from losing face.' I could call the police, and the foreman might be arrested. But before he is punished, the Ikeda family will be greatly humiliated."

Jebu put an arm around Michiko, lovingly and protectively. "If someday I should face that man, I'll wring his neck." He lowered his eyes. "But I can't accuse him in the court of law. My parents will definitely forbid me to marry Michiko then."

As they discussed Michiko's misfortune, Jebu, Quanming, and Laurie had expected to see the girl cry, blush, and bow her head. To their surprise, she did none of those things. She listened to them attentively, looking at each one bright-eyed. She held her head high, waiting for them to come to a pause so that she could talk.

"Rape is wrong, but so is the people's attitude." When she had a chance to speak, her voice was loud and clear. "Why do my parents want me to commit suicide? Was being raped much worse than being bitten by a mad dog? If I were bleeding from a dog's bite, my family wouldn't feel ashamed. What's so shameful about bleeding from a man's crazy desire?"

She turned to Jebu, who flinched each time she used the embarrassing word. "Thank you, Jebu, for not wanting me to die. Now all we need is to wait for my next monthly sign, which, I'm sure, will come at any time." To everyone's surprise, she tilted her head to one side and started to laugh. "Well, Jebu, to tell you the truth, I'm not sure I would have killed myself even if you agreed with my parents!"

Jebu wouldn't look at Quanming and Laurie. He was ashamed of Michiko's tactlessness. He had thought of Michiko as a delicate flower, but now realized that he had made a mistake. The fragile blossom was actually more like his father's coral art, carved out of a very strong substance.

Quanming and Laurie exchanged glances, then both looked at Michiko admiringly.

Smiling at the young girl, Quanming asked her if she still wanted to work for him.

"She'll take the job for a short while, and then become my wife. She doesn't have any other plans for the future," Jebu said before Michiko could answer.

"Wait a minute!" Michiko faced Jebu and raised her voice. "You sound just like my father!" She turned to Laurie and said in a determined voice, "Mrs. Sung, I would like to keep improving myself in every way, for the rest of my days. I'll be much more than Jebu's obedient little wife."

Jebu sighed. Laurie and Quanming laughed. Quanming winked at the young man. "A woman is a puzzle," he said, looking from Michiko to Laurie. "She looks at you with helpless tears in those lovely eyes, wins your heart, then changes from a fragile flower to a powerful tigress."

The ship arrived from San Francisco, picked up more passengers in Honolulu, then set sail for Tianjin, the harbor in north China not far from Beijing.

Michiko and Jebu stood on deck and waved at their friends and Jebu's relatives until they were but small dots on the shoreline. When Honolulu disappeared from the horizon and night darkened the water and sky, they went down to the dining room. They shared one of the round tables with other passengers and enjoyed a fabulous dinner.

"You must be newlyweds," said the Chinese woman sitting next to Michiko, in English.

Michiko blushed. She didn't think she and Jebu showed that much affection to each other in public. "How do you know?"

The woman smiled, pointing at Michiko's red skirt and Jebu's red shirt. "Young couple, holding hands, wearing red. I lived my whole life in Los Angeles, but still I am a true Chinese. Besides tea leaves, I can read many other signs."

The talkative woman told them that she and her husband, a shy little man next to her, had both been born in the States and were now going to China for the first time. "Our grandparents came to America as laborers, they sailed in the hold of a ship . . ." she rattled on.

Michiko looked around the table. It was set for ten. The seat next to Jebu was empty, the rest occupied by three Caucasians and four Asians, all much older than she and Jebu. She thought of Quanming and Laurie's generous wedding gift to her and Jebu: a round-trip ticket on a cruise ship and all expenses paid in Beijing. If it were not for Quanming and Laurie, she and Jebu would also have had to wait until they were old to afford such a journey.

Her thoughts were interrupted by the woman's nudging elbow. "I said, your husband is wearing a very unusual pendant." The old woman stared and gestured impatiently. "A head of the Great Buddha, but not smiling."

"Oh." Michiko looked at the small white coral pendant hanging from her husband's neck. "It's a wedding present from my father-in-law," she explained. "It's for both of us, but I let my husband keep it, since in Hawaii all men wear pendants."

Heroshi had carved the head of Buddha, and made it unlike the ordinary figures. Instead of laughing, it had a sad, weary face and looked at the world with a thoughtful expression. Michiko remembered what Heroshi had said to her and Jebu on their wedding day. "My son and daughter, life is never easy. When the two of you encounter hardship, remember that the Great Buddha is watching over you from heaven, and your elders are willing to do everything for you in this world."

"We are lucky." Michiko turned away from the old woman, and said to Jebu in Japanese, "The food is delicious, the dining room fabulous, the ship a moving palace. Remember the awful ship that carried us to Hawaii from Japan? I can't believe in such a short time life has improved so much for you and me. Maybe your father was wrong to say that life is full of hardship . . ." She stopped when she saw that Jebu was not listening to her at all.

Next to Jebu, a young man had just taken the vacant seat. His mouth agape, Jebu leaned forward and watched him closely. Michiko was ready to tell her husband it was rude to stare. Then she glanced at the man's face and her jaw dropped; she couldn't take her eyes from him.

The man was troubled by Michiko and Jebu's close scrutiny. He moved uncomfortably in his seat, cleared his throat, then tried to smile as he asked in English, "Is my face dirty? Did I sit at the wrong table? But this has been my same table since the ship left San Francisco." He nodded at the talkative old woman to prove that he was in the right place.

"I'm sorry," Jebu said, then turned to Michiko. "We can't help our surprise, because . . ." Jebu shook his head incredulously. He smiled at the man but continued to study the handsome face. "How can you look so much like someone we just said good-bye to? He is much older than you, but your face and his are identical."

Michiko nodded beside Jebu and explained, "His name is Sung Quanming. He is my father-in-law's best friend, so we call him Uncle Quanming. You really do look amazingly like him."

The young man's face turned white. He gazed at the young couple in disbelief. Then, as if talking to himself, he mumbled, "The ship stopped in Hawaii, where you two came on board. Hawaii . . . Honolulu . . . Baba and Laurie . . . !" He took a deep breath, regained control of his emotion, and managed to introduce himself with composure, "Sung Quanming is my father. My name is Sung Hwa."

Michiko and Jebu gasped. They had heard about Quanming's grown son and daughter by a previous marriage. They also knew that although Quanming had asked his children to visit Hawaii from San Francisco, his invitations had been repeatedly turned down. They had wondered what kind of children would have the heart to hurt a father like their Uncle Quanming, and now they were facing this heartless young man.

Their unfavorable opinion of Sung Hwa changed quickly, however, replaced by fondness. The three of them were close in age, and it was easy for young hearts to open up and communicate without pretense. Michiko and Jebu soon understood Sung Hwa's anguish. Hwa found himself persuading the young couple to tell him all they knew about his father, admitting that hidden underneath a thin layer of anger was a son's love. Once it was clear that the three of them shared a common admiration for Sung Quanming, friendship developed effortlessly.

They were the three youngest passengers among many old people. They stayed together. As the ship sailed across the Pacific, they spent most of their time on deck, sharing the sun and wind, also sharing their secrets in life. Hwa talked about Judy's cruel rejection of his love. Jebu and Michiko spoke of the vicious foreman and their defiance of tradition. The distance between the Japanese couple and the young Chinese man vanished, and an everlasting friendship began to take root.

6

ACCORDING TO THE lunar calendar, it was June, but the western calendar indicated July 1, 1937.

The thick clouds were unmoving. There was not one trace of wind. The sun was unseen, but its mighty power was definitely felt by people in Beijing.

At the entrance of the Park of the Sun Altar, a young woman dabbed at the sweat on her forehead with a white handkerchief. She had on a light blue blouse and a dark blue skirt. Her long pigtails were tied at the ends with wide blue ribbons dotted with white flowers. Her pretty face was round, her lips thin. Her name was Hu May. She was eighteen, a foreign-language major at Beijing University. As she strolled back and forth in the steaming weather, she frowned at the memory of the argument between her and her parents.

"Why do you want to work? Haven't I always given you money to buy everything you want?" her father had asked.

She had answered, "Baba, I'm not working for money. I'm taking a job to prove that I can be a useful person."

Her mother had looked at her sadly. "I can't understand you. If you want to be useful, why don't you perfect your skills in the Four Useful Things for Women?"

May had stamped her foot and answered impatiently, "The ability to play chess and musical instruments? The mastery of watercolor and calligraphy? No, Mama. They won't make me useful. They will only make me a more interesting toy for men . . . rich men, who are enemies of the people."

May could not forgive herself for putting the wounded look in her father's eyes. "Am I an enemy of the people? The Hu family have always been rich silk merchants, but we have never been less than kind to the lower classes."

May had tried to repair the damage. "Baba, I don't mean you. I mean the other rich, the filthy landlords . . ." She realized her blunder and couldn't continue. The Hu family owned land both in the city of Beijing and in the country.

"How dare you call your father a filthy landlord? Someday he will give you many acres of the land as a dowry, so your future husband will treat you nicely." May's guilt was intensified by her mother's tearful words: "You are our baby, so we spoiled you more than we did your three brothers and two sisters. As a result, you are the only one who goes to college, and the only one who wants strange things and has strange ideas. Yes, you are the only one who has truly hurt your Baba and me."

May was relieved to see a bus stopping at the park entrance, a bus which belonged to the Imperial Hotel, one of the most elegant hotels in Beijing.

The people descending from the bus were both Asians and Caucasians. Besides Mandarin, May could speak English, Japanese, and a little French. She studied the occidental faces and hoped no one was German or Italian; she did not yet know either of those two languages. She glanced at the

Asians but couldn't decide which were Korean, Japanese, Filipino, Thai, or overseas Chinese. She hoped that she could communicate with all of them.

Regardless of her parents' objection, she had been working for nearly a month now as a tourist guide. She enjoyed the work. The meager salary was unimportant. She didn't really need it. But the sense of usefulness was priceless. Her friends, who were also rich sons and daughters of prominent families, envied her.

She greeted the tourists with a smile, remembering her friends' words: "Hu May, you're almost there. First, be useful. Then, become a Communist party member and help to save our country!"

"The altar was built in the early part of the fifteenth century. Every emperor, in the beginning of spring, would come here to pray to the Sun Buddha. Our poor farmers cannot have too little sun, or their rice will not grow. They cannot have too much sun either, or their rice will die . . ."

Hu May spoke in Mandarin, then repeated the same speech twice more, first in English, then in Japanese.

She lowered her voice when she spoke Japanese. The local residents had followed the tourists around the park, and threw glances of animosity at those they thought to be Japanese. The Japanese soldiers had been stationed outside Beijing for a long time, and on their leaves often visited the city. No Chinese had liked the Japanese since the military men of Japan took away northeastern China and turned it into a puppet regime called Manchuria.

"The altar was built by feudal lords to please the emperor. The peasants carried heavy bricks

on their aching backs, nailed the large beams together with their bleeding hands. When you walk
around the altar, if you allow your imaginations
to unwind, you can hear the cries of the
laborers."

As Hu May spoke, she noticed a young couple,
both with suntanned faces, dressed in clothes of
brighter colors than the average Asian would
wear. The man wore a white pendant, the
woman a flower in her hair. Their eyes brightened
at the sound of Japanese, and they nodded in
agreement when May talked about the gulf between rich and poor.

In spite of her dislike for the Japanese, May's
fondness for the couple was born when at the
end of her speech the man gave her a friendly
smile and the woman bowed deeply to show gratitude. Tourists seldom treated their guides with
such respect; most of them considered May a living guidebook. May nodded at them, then led the
group toward the other end of the park. The
young couple and a tall handsome young man
walked beside May.

"My name is Michiko Yamada." The woman
spoke in heavily accented English. "Your Japanese is very good."

"Oh, no. You are wrong. My Japanese is very
poor," May argued as a good Chinese should
when paid a compliment.

"No. You are the one who is wrong," the
woman argued back as a good Japanese would,
forcing the compliment on the receiver. "What is
your name?"

After May gave her name, Michiko introduced
the good-looking man with her. "My husband,
Jebu Yamada, and I are from Hawaii." She then
turned to the tall Chinese man. "Mr. Sung Hwa
is from San Francisco. We met on the ship. We

had such a good time, we decided to sightsee together."

May developed an instant resentment for Sung Hwa, who wore affluence like a hide. His hands were pale and soft-looking, his fingernails manicured. He had on either cologne or shaving lotion; May sniffed the artificial fragrance and frowned. His being from San Francisco made him even more suspect. She remembered one of her books telling her the rich in America used slaves to plant cotton and build railroads.

Sung Hwa gave May a cordial bow; she returned it with a chilly glare.

"Is Beijing always this warm in the beginning of July?" Hwa asked casually.

"If you don't like our weather, you can go back to your home in that imperialistic land," May answered sharply.

Sung Hwa was hurt and puzzled. He was not used to being treated so rudely by someone he had done nothing to offend. He walked away from May without uttering a word.

"Are you engaged or married? Or are you always oversensitive when a handsome man talks to you?" Michiko asked May in a whisper. "Our poor friend Hwa is kind and polite. Why were you so mean to him?"

May stared at Michiko for a brief moment, then realized how unfairly she had acted toward Sung Hwa. "It's just that . . ." She thought for a moment, then shook her head. "I'm sorry."

"You ought to be—" Michiko was interrupted by a shout.

"Wait for me!" a young man cried in English as he ran across the park, chasing the group of tourists.

The Eurasian boy, in his teens, wore white tennis shoes and clothes and had a camera swinging over his shoulder. "Wait!" he called, pursuing the group.

When he caught up with May, he explained in British-accented English that he had arrived at the park in a hired wagon, and the hotel bus driver had pointed out May and her group from a distance. "He said your name is Hu May and you are the guide, and that you can speak English. My name is Aaron Cohen. I'm from Hong Kong. My mother and sister are still sleeping in the Imperial Hotel. I came to see the altar by myself, but I've missed the beginning of the tour . . ." He stopped to catch his breath, then smiled at each of them enthusiastically.

Jebu, Michiko, and Hwa saw the childlike quality in Aaron and accepted him instantly. As they introduced themselves and described to Aaron what he had missed in the park, May glanced at the young man and found a similarity to Sung Hwa. She told herself not to be discourteous to another rich boy, reminding herself once more that her family had never used money to hurt people, and there was no reason for these four tourists to be different from her family. Once that decision sank into her mind, May relaxed and began to enjoy the company of Hwa, Aaron, Michiko, and Jebu.

"I'm so happy to find the four of you," Aaron said, laughing like a child. "My mother, sister, and I have been using sign language since arriving in Beijing. I didn't know that in China different dialects really mean different languages. Mama speaks the Pearl River dialect, which is a branch of the Cantonese spoken by all the Chinese in Hong Kong. Rachel and I can understand Cantonese, but Mandarin is so different from it that we might as well be visiting Greece."

They laughed as they waited for the others to

reach where they were, then Hu May resumed her routine, this time in English first.

"The pine trees here are many hundreds of years old. The rock garden behind the waterfall was designed by one of our emperors who was also a poet. The pavilion next to the fall was his favorite place for gathering poetic thoughts. Many of his famous love poems for a beloved court lady were composed there. The teahouse near the exit specializes in *Jeo-tze*, the flour-wrapped meat dumplings favored by this same emperor."

When she finished, the tourists started to wander through the park on their own. Most of them ended up in the teahouse recommended by May. The small hut in the shade of an ancient pine was soon filled with customers.

Aaron wouldn't let his friends go into the teahouse. He took one picture after another, insisting that his new friends be his models. He made them pose in front of the pavilion, the waterfall, the curved bridge, and the pagoda, until his models were exhausted from smiling and nearly dehydrated from standing in the sun.

Jebu wiped his sweaty face. "I didn't know the weather in Beijing was warmer than in Hawaii. In Hawaii at least there is always a cool breeze. Here we don't actually see the sun, but behind those gray-yellow clouds a fireball is trying to melt us into nothingness!"

"I would like to treat everyone to a cup of tea and something to eat," Sung Hwa said, looking at Hu May hesitantly. "But I don't want to offend anybody."

May laughed. "I'm sorry, Mr. Sung, for the way I treated you a while ago. Yes, thank you, I'll be glad to accept your invitation."

Sung Hwa breathed with relief, then pushed

his luck a little further. "Miss Hu, if it's not too forward to ask, will you please call me Sung Hwa?"

To Hwa's surprise, the guide smiled. "All right, Sung Hwa, if you'll call me Hu May."

People in the teahouse turned their attention to the five newcomers walking in and conversing in English. It didn't take them long to tell May apart from the other four: a native of Beijing differed from outsiders like peonies from roses. In their eyes May saw her advantage—she was with four people from three different lands and able to communicate with them. She suddenly realized that she should be grateful and make the best of such fortune.

They found themselves a table. Michiko dropped into a chair and looked at the other customers' cups. "If this is an old-fashioned teahouse that won't give us any tea without first forcing us through the long, boring tea ceremony, I'll die of thirst!"

"Oh, no. Our teahouses don't have the rituals of Japanese ones," May told Michiko.

Aaron didn't sit. He glanced around and began to take pictures of everything and everybody. "This reminds me of my grandfather's place in Jasmine Valley. Greasy tables, chipped teacups, one rag per table used as a public napkin through the entire day for wiping faces and blowing noses."

Aaron focused his camera at the middle of their table, where a bunch of chopsticks was soaking in a tin can filled with oily water. "We'll eat with these. When we're through eating, we'll put the sticks back in the same water. Then next customers will use the same chopsticks over and over again, and toward the end of the day the water will become filthy. When my sister and I first saw

the napkins and chopsticks, we nearly screamed."
He snapped several pictures before sitting down.

Aaron's words made May see her own country
through the eyes of an overseas Chinese. She had
never noticed the public napkin and the overused
chopsticks before. Her first reaction was to argue
with Aaron. She held back her words. She ordered tea and *Jeo-tze* for everybody. When a large
pot of tea was brought to the table, she filled everyone's cup, then lifted her cup high.

"Aaron, Michiko, Jebu, and Hwa," she called
each one in turn. "With this cup of tea I drink to
my new friends." She sipped the hot tea. "May
all of you enjoy your visit in Beijing."

As soon as Aaron's lips touched the tea, he
screamed, "Hot! How can anyone drink this in
such weather? Please," he begged May, "will you
order something cold for me? I've discovered the
hard way that people here don't believe in ice
cubes, but there must be something other than
scalding tea!"

Aaron looked like a child about to cry. His new
friends laughed. May called the waiter, explained
to the puzzled man that Aaron wanted some cold
water, since no juice or soda was available.

"What did he say?" Aaron asked, looking suspiciously at the waiter, who mumbled as he
walked away.

"Well." May decided to be honest. "He said
only dogs and barbarians drink cold water. He
also said cold drinks will chill your intestines and
make the warm weather feel intolerable, while hot
tea will make your body warm and make you as
one with the summer season."

Aaron stared at May. "Chinese are strange
people. China is a fascinating country. If someday
I find myself drinking hot tea in the summer and
ice water in the winter, then I can legally claim

Chinese citizenship." He then told his new friends his life story, which started with a girl from Jasmine Valley who went to San Francisco and married a Jewish jeweler.

Sung Hwa told them about his divorced parents and the agony of being a son from a broken home. His frankness erased May's last bit of distrust for a rich American man.

"My train leaves this afternoon for Kwangchow. I'm going to White Stone," Sung Hwa said.

"It's our last day here too," Jebu said. "We're taking the evening train to Tianjin, then we'll sail from there home."

Aaron glanced at his camera. "What about the pictures I took of everybody? I want each of you to have a set."

Michiko opened her purse and tore a few sheets from a small notebook. She gave one sheet to each person. "Write your name and address on the sheet, then pass the sheet to the next person," she said, and began to write down her and Jebu's address on one of the papers. "We'll all become pen pals."

After they'd finished, they all smiled and jokingly linked hands over the table as if making a pact.

May repeated her apology to Hwa. "Please forgive me for being so rude to you. It was silly of me to hate you for your soft hands and manicured fingernails." May's eyes brightened and her face flushed as she continued after a pause, "It's just that the man in my dream has big strong callused hands. With those hands he will build me a home, then grow rice and raise chickens to feed me. I will follow him everywhere. Beside him I will become truly useful, and together we will save our country."

She stopped and blushed deeper. "I never said

these things to strangers before. You are so easy to talk to . . ."

She stopped at the sight of a waiter, who had brought Aaron his cold water and the rest of them their *Jeo-tze*. The waiter's eyes widened at the five people's intertwined hands.

The five friends laughed at the waiter's startled expression and withdrew their hands. Jebu rested his fingers on his pendant, then showed the Buddha to the others. "I have a strong feeling that our friendship will be blessed by the Great Buddha."

Michiko, Aaron, May, and Hwa nodded. None of them heard the voice of Buddha crying from far above, saddened by their ignorance of the fate that awaited them.

7

IT TOOK KWANJIN fifteen hours by train to reach Beijing. The party had limited money for the funding of his trip. The third-class seats were hard and narrow. By the time he got off the train he was hungry, thirsty, and exhausted.

He saw the advertisements of many hotels in the railway station, and read the different prices for rooms. He found the cheapest and hoisted his canvas bag on his back and walked in the smothering weather. His Mandarin was distorted by his Cantonese accent. When he asked for directions, people laughed.

"Chairman Mao is doing at least one thing right," he said, lifting his shirt corner to wipe the sweat from his face. "All the Chinese must speak only one language, so we won't treat every out-of-town person as a foreigner."

The hotel was three stories high. Kwanjin saw antique furniture and thick red carpet in the lobby. When he quoted the price from the ad, the porter took him through the lobby to a stairway. With each descending step, the light became weaker, the stench stronger.

They were soon in a basement with no windows. A small light bulb, covered with grease and dust and dead flies, hung from the low ceiling, giving Kwanjin the view of a big room divided by a torn curtain in the middle, with many holes in the concrete floor.

The porter explained that one side of the curtain was for women, the other side for men. All the guests shared four toilet buckets, two on each side of the curtain.

"The advertisement said I could see Tiananmen Square from here," Kwanjin said, sniffing at the unpleasant odor.

"You can, if you have a room upstairs with a window facing the square," the porter said, pointing at the folding cots piled in the corner. "Take one and set it up on the men's side, anywhere you want."

"How about sheets, blanket, and pillows?" Kwanjin asked. "And where can I go for a bath?"

"Bedding will be extra. If you want to bathe yourself, go to the public bath on the street corner," the porter said, and left in a hurry.

The day was young. Only two other men were sleeping on the men's side, in their underwear and without any sheets, blankets, or pillows. Their mouths were open, and they were drooling and snoring at the same time. Kwanjin set up his cot far from them, lay on his back, and kept his sweat-soaked clothes on. He stretched his legs and used his hands for a pillow.

As he looked at the water-stained ceiling, confused thoughts began to go through his mind.

Perhaps Chairman Mao was right in many fields other than the enforcing of a uniform language. In Yenan, nobody had much. In the rest of China, the rich were too rich, and the poor were treated like animals. Maybe it would be a good idea to collect everybody's money, put it into one large pile, then divide it equally among all the Chinese people. Possibly Wong Chung was a very clever man to come up with the idea of sending a doubting comrade to Beijing.

I've been in this imperialistic city only a few minutes, and already I know I don't belong, Kwanjin thought to himself just before drifting into sleep.

The weather was even warmer than the day before. Hu May waited at the entrance of the Park of the Sun Altar and paced impatiently.

The tour bus was late. This usually happened when some of the guests at the Imperial Hotel had no regard for time. They were rich enough to stay in a luxurious hotel, so they felt that the world should wait for them and start the tour only when they were ready. "The spoiled rich!" May mumbled through clenched teeth.

She chuckled at what she had said. "Wait a minute," she corrected herself. "Have you forgotten the friends you met yesterday? They are not poor peasants, nevertheless they're wonderful people."

Michiko, Jebu, and Hwa were gone. Aaron remained, and she had arranged to meet him, his mother, and his sister tonight in their hotel.

May's thoughts were interrupted by a commotion.

Two police had arrested someone, and the three were coming toward the park gate, followed by a crowd who were pointing and shouting at the arrested person.

"Only a fool would preach communism in broad daylight, with the Nationalist police nearby!" One man shook his head regretfully.

"One more young fool will be executed soon!" Another grinned carelessly. "One more death scene to entertain us!"

May felt sorry for the arrested one, and craned her neck to see what kind of person could be so brave but foolish. Because of the crowd, she could only glimpse a tall frame with broad shoulders. She stood on her toes to see his face as they came closer.

May saw the arrested man's face now. Her heart skipped a beat. Yesterday she had disliked Sung Hwa upon first glance, because Hwa was the opposite of the man in her dream. Right now she felt weak and faint because the man in her dream stood before her.

Walking between two police, the man held himself tall and proud. His face was the rugged face of a peasant, hardened by weather and toughened by life. His eyes were like torches, glaring angrily at a world that was beneath his dignity.

"*Due-na-ma!*" he cursed in Cantonese. With her talent in language, May could understand most of the Chinese dialects. "Take your hands off me! You walking dogs of the filthy Nationalists!"

They were directly in front of May now. She watched the prisoner struggle with the handcuffs. "No!" she screamed.

As a child, May had had a dog. He'd had dark brown fur and was a beautiful creature. He was not too friendly with anyone but May. May's family tolerated him because he was May's love; the two were bound by a special understanding. The dog followed May everywhere. One winter morning she took him to the park. When she threw a stick and the dog went to fetch it, a man came up riding a bicycle. She saw the man throw a rope around her dog's neck, then speed up on the bike. Her dog struggled to free himself, but was quickly pulled away by the man. May cried all the way home and later was accompanied by her three older brothers to visit every dog restaurant in Beijing. The last dog-restaurant owner handed her her dog's collar, which was stained with blood, and told her she was only a few minutes too late.

"No!" May screamed again. The arrested man struggled with the handcuffs, just the way her dog had struggled with the rope around his neck.

Her screams echoed through the park. Everyone turned to look at her, including the handcuffed man. When his eyes met hers, something sparkled like lightning slicing through the night sky. The crowd and the police looked from him to her, then back to him again. Everyone was waiting for her next move.

May moved slowly toward the handcuffed man, asked without looking away from his eyes, "What is his price?"

May watched the police exchange greedy looks, knew immediately that they were corrupt and could be bought with the right amount of money. She couldn't hear their whispered discussion, but after they said something to the crowd, she heard a young man shout, "That much? If he could put up such a large sum, would he be preaching communism?"

One of the police quoted her a sum.

"I don't have that much," May said, then raised a hand to undo the first button on her apple-green blouse. A solid gold chain hung around her neck. In the middle of the chain was a gold pendant shaped like a heart.

At the birth of each of the six Hu children, a chain and a locket were made by a goldsmith. The child's name was engraved on one side of the gold locket, and the drawing of the animal that represented the child's birth year was engraved on the other side. It was believed that the chain would keep the child anchored to the world of the living, and the locket would bring good health, happiness, and prosperity in life.

May kept her eyes on the prisoner as she unfastened the chain. "One of you can have the chain, the other the locket," she said, throwing the gold at the two police. "Now, give this man to me before your chief comes and asks to share in your bribery."

After the policemen released their prisoner, the crowd followed the lucky escapee and his generous savior all the way to the park's teahouse. The owner wouldn't let people come in without buying at least a cup of tea, so the crowd dissolved. May ordered tea, *Jeo-tze*, and meat buns, then did most of the talking, while Kwanjin asked questions now and then in Cantonese-accented Mandarin.

"You saved me because I reminded you of your dog?" Li Kwanjin asked, gulping the tea, then wiping his mouth with the back of his hand. "It's not very flattering."

May laughed. "It's more than that," she said. "You also reminded me of my sociology professor. When he was arrested, my classmates and I tried to save him. He was in the hands of people with much higher rank than those two policemen, and the price they asked was beyond our ability."

He picked up a meat bun and took a big bite. He looked at her intently as he listened. His eyes had the power to make her blush. She lowered her eyes, looked at his hands, then blushed deeper. Yesterday she had described to her friends the hands of her dream love. Today those hands were within her reach.

She caressed Kwanjin's hands with her eyes. Large knuckles, massive palms, strong fingers. Scars marked the backs of both hands, and calluses covered the palms. She wondered what these hands had done, and could do in the future.

He would have no trouble using his hands to build her a house and keep her clothed and fed, she knew. She wondered how it must feel to be held and loved by his hands. She fantasized that his hands were touching her skin, and her whole body trembled.

"Are you all right?" he asked.

"Yes." Her voice was barely audible. She couldn't look at his face or his hands. She stared at the greasy table.

"But you don't look all right," he persisted.

May remembered her mother telling her that a true gentleman never forced a lady to stay on the subject she tried to avoid. She smiled. Who wanted a gentleman, anyway?

Kwanjin continued. "Your face is very red, like you have a fever. But you are shaking, like you are cold. If my mother saw you like this, she would say you were suffering from sunstroke."

She changed the subject. "Tell me about your mother."

Kwanjin finished one *Jeo-tze* and took another. "My mother's name is Leahi, which means 'Welcome to Good Luck.' She married my father when she was fifteen. He was a fisherman. He went to America as a laborer when Mama was carrying me. I never saw him in my life . . ."

He told her everything about himself, talked until the park turned dark and the teahouse owner brought an oil lamp to each table. In the lamplight May looked at her wristwatch and noticed it was way past the time she had promised to meet Aaron Cohen at the Imperial Hotel. Tomorrow Aaron would go sight-seeing with his mother and sister, and May doubted if she would have a chance to see them before they left Beijing. But she could always write to Aaron in Hong

Kong and explain what had happened to her tonight.

"Li Kwanjin," she said, looking at his face in the flickering light. His eyes seemed deeper now, his cheekbones higher. The lamp heightened his features, created a dramatic effect. "You can't go to public places like the Park of the Sun Altar to preach communism. After all, Beijing is still in the hands of the Nationalist government."

Kwanjin nodded. "I know now. But I was assigned to come here and bring back to Yenan with me at least a dozen new recruits or more. I can't find new recruits if I sit here with you."

May smiled. "Now it's my turn to tell you more about myself. . . ."

She talked until the teahouse owner came to blow the flame off their oil lamp.

On July 3 May took Kwanjin to a group of young people who were having one of their regular meetings. There were about twenty of them, in their late teens or early twenties.

"This is Li Kwanjin, from Yenan," May said proudly, introducing him to everyone. "He can take us to Chairman Mao."

The young people looked at Kwanjin respectfully and began to talk. Kwanjin found himself surrounded by eager faces and anxious voices.

"You must be sent to us from the Great Buddha in heaven! We've been praying for someone like you to appear!"

"We want to do something useful for our country but don't know how. The Nationalists are recruiting new members but we don't want to work for Chiang Kai-shek, who calls himself the Generalissimo—the Commander in Chief."

"Chiang's goal is to protect himself and the rich and powerful. Mao Tze-dung is for the whole of

China and especially the deprived and the powerless. Please take us to Yenan so we can offer ourselves to Chairman Mao!"

Kwanjin listened to them, but heard his own
voice of many years ago, full of faith and eager-
ness to do some good for his country. He looked
at them, but saw the face of a Willow Place boy
turned up toward Wong Chung, looking at the
man the same way these young people looked at
him now.

He wanted to tell them how foolish it was to
thank the Great Buddha for his being in Beijing,
because the Communists believed in no Buddha
at all. He wished to let them know that nothing
was as perfect as it ought to be, not even
communism.

But he remembered his duty and the fact that
his mother was in Yenan. He erased the doubts,
and began to talk as he was supposed to, praising
the party and the Chairman. He made communism sound like a magic wand that would make
China powerful and would free all Chinese from
fear and hunger.

He talked to them repeatedly for the next two
days. He gave them the third day to pack and say
good-bye to their families. On the fourth day he
waited for them in the train station at dawn.

The first to arrive was Hu May, fresh and glowing like the rising sun. Her eyes sparkled as she
ran toward Kwanjin. She was wearing a straw hat
and carrying a small bag.

"It wasn't easy to leave home," she said breath-
lessly. "Baba, Mama, three older brothers, and
two older sisters, plus their spouses, all tried to
change my mind for me. Baba blamed himself for
letting me go to college. Mama said it's her fault
that a matchmaker was not called earlier, and as

a result I'm eighteen and unmarried. My sisters
don't think I can last long in Yenan. My brothers
want me to let them know as soon as I'm ready
to come home and they will come immediately to
Yenan to escort me back to Beijing."

She smiled at him proudly. "I turned away
from Mama's tears and Baba's anger, and here I
am, all yours!"

"May!" Kwanjin looked at her innocent face
and almost told her to go home. He knew that if
he had a large loving family like hers, he wouldn't
be able to cause them sorrow.

"Yes?" May looked at him trustingly.

Kwanjin shook his head. "Nothing," he said
with a sigh, trying not to look at her beautiful
face.

The longer he looked at her, the stronger the
desire to be completely honest with her stirred in
his heart. He had to force himself to remember
his duty and keep his mouth closed.

May didn't know of Kwanjin's inner struggle.
She rattled on tirelessly. "Mama insisted I take
the hat, so my face won't be tanned by the Yenan
sun." May put aside her hat and took from her
bag a few steamed wheat buns. "Mama also
forced me to take these," she said. "And she cried
when she said this was my favorite food but she
didn't know when she could make them for me
again."

May's voice trembled. She blinked away her
tears and pretended to be brave. She insisted
that Kwanjin share the buns with her. He accepted a bun, bit into it, and tasted not the wheat
flour but a mother's tears. With each bite he debated whether to send May back to her loving
family.

As they ate the buns, the others began to
arrive.

Out of more than twenty, thirteen showed up. They talked about the battles they had fought with their families; each told a story that was similar to May's. They had all caused sadness in once happy homes.

Li Kwanjin led the young people to the waiting train.

For the next fifteen hours, on the journey to Yenan, the young people continued to talk enthusiastically about saving China. Their faith in communism was strong and their trust in Mao Tzedung absolute. Their idealistic words made Kwanjin's guilt unbearable. He opened his mouth several times to discourage them, then closed it without saying anything.

Hu May fell asleep during the long journey. She leaned her head on Kwanjin's shoulder. Kwanjin looked at her pretty face and couldn't resist the urge of putting an arm around her. She made a soft sound in her dream, cuddled closer to him.

"Hu May," Li Kwanjin whispered gently. "Beautiful, brave, innocent May." He tightened his embracing arm. "You saved my life, and I will use this life to keep you from harm. I will protect you forever, my little May."

With his arm around May, Kwanjin closed his eyes and drifted into a dream.

In his dream he was a fisherman like his father and May a simple village woman like his Mama. The Pearl River flowed endlessly, and endlessly, life was peaceful and the words "nationalism" and "communism" did not exist.

PART II

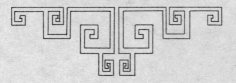

8

THE SUMMER SUN shone brightly over Beijing, heating the shallow water under the white marble Reedy Moat Bridge.

A group of tourists stood listening to their guide, a middle-aged man, speaking quickly in pure Mandarin, which sounded beautiful when spoken by the lifetime residents of this ancient city.

"It is also called the Marco Polo Bridge. When Marco Polo visited China in 1290, he fell in love with it and described it to the rest of the world in such a poetic way that the world also saw its beauty."

Aaron Cohen missed the beautiful young English-speaking guide he had met in the Park of the Sun Altar. Today's trip had been arranged by the Imperial Hotel for those who knew Chinese, and today's guide was ugly compared with Hu May. Aaron understood only a fraction of the man's endless words. He glanced at his mother and sister, wondering if they were also bored.

Meiping met her son's glance with a warning frown, saying to the young man with her eyes, "Don't you dare do anything naughty!"

Rachel nodded to her brother. "Be patient. We'll soon move to somewhere much cooler." She expressed her comforting words with a beautiful smile.

Aaron took a few steps away from the group and found a shady spot under a tree. He was no longer in the sun, but felt uncomfortable just the same. He took a handkerchief from his pants pocket to wipe his sweaty face.

His mother had been born in south China and had the ability to tolerate this kind of heat. But what was Rachel's secret? How could she be so calm and sweet and magnificent in the baking sun?

Impatiently Aaron shifted his weight from one foot to the other. Without knowing it, he took a low-hanging branch in his idle hands, tearing the leaves and throwing them aside.

At this moment he hated himself for urging his mother to continue this trip. Her treasured charm had been lost in Jasmine Valley, and except for making a few new friends, he had accomplished little in understanding his Chinese half.

"It's very difficult to become a real Chinese. I wasted almost the entire summer vacation in reaching for the impossible," he said to himself, and made a sound that was a combination of sigh and moan.

A few people turned their heads. The guide hid his dislike for this annoying boy and continued to smile and talk. "A flood in 1698 washed away the original bridge. The people of Beijing collected money to build this replica. It is seven hundred and seventy feet long and has eleven supporting arches. Please look down and find on each post a miniature lion carved out of stone."

Aaron blocked out the man's voice and imagined himself back in Hong Kong, visiting his old friends, playing tennis, swimming.

He wondered what his new friends would be doing right now. Sung Hwa, Michiko, and Jebu would be traveling. What had kept Hu May from coming to see him as promised?

"Aaron, do you want us to leave you on the street?" Rachel asked jokingly.

He returned to reality. Once more he felt the raging sun and saw the white marble bridge. He gathered his wits and answered his sister in a teasing tone. "If you leave me on the street, I'll be just fine. But you'd better be careful. Some of Chiang Kai-shek's men may come along and become enchanted by your beauty!"

Out of childhood habit, Aaron and Rachel always conversed in English. Some people heard the foreign language and cast puzzled looks at the brother and sister. Meiping tried to hush them immediately. "How many times do I need to remind you that when we are away from home you must speak Chinese?"

Aaron followed the crowd to board the bus—a way of transportation that was still uncommon in Beijing. When the vehicle began to move and the hot wind started to blow in through the open windows, he didn't feel any cooler, but at least was no longer smothered. He leaned closer to the window, looking at the streets and studying the faces of the many pedestrians and bicyclists.

His young eyes were caught by the pretty faces of the teenage girls, but his youthful heart was captured by none—it already belonged to someone. She occupied Aaron's thoughts so completely that he didn't notice the many uniformed Japanese soldiers marching toward the Reedy Moat Bridge.

Two hands shook Aaron roughly, bringing him out of his sleep.

"What is this?" he mumbled drowsily, then was fully awake.

In the light of the bedside table, Meiping stood dressed in the same blouse and slacks she had worn during the day; they were both soiled and wrinkled. Aaron had seen his mother in all sorts of moods, but never frightened like she was now. Her hair was a mess, and her eyes were wide with terror. Her lips trembled as she spoke.

"Get dressed and pack everything. We must get out of this hotel and leave Beijing as quickly as we can." With that, she turned to go. "I have to wake your sister."

Aaron sat up in bed, shouting after his mother, "Mama, what has happened?"

Meiping paused briefly at the door. "The Japanese attacked the Reedy Moat Bridge and killed many people. They are taking over the entire city."

Meiping left and Aaron continued to stare at the empty doorway. His mother's words couldn't penetrate his brain. What was she talking about? War was something that existed only in history books.

And then he heard the sound of firecrackers coming from the street. But firecrackers ought to be accompanied by cheers of happiness and cries of excitement! Why were these explosions followed by screams of panic and pain? He leapt out of bed. As he was stripping off his pajamas, he heard thumping feet, loud and heavy like the hooves of running cattle, thundering past his room toward the stairway.

"They're killing every civilian they see!" someone shouted.

"They've raped every girl in sight!" shouted someone else.

"They've burned down many houses!"

"The streets are covered with Chinese blood!"

"Chiang Kai-shek's men are not defending the city at all!"

"The warlords have packed their women and valuables and left town!"

Aaron couldn't button his shirt because his fingers were shaking so badly. He put on his pants but couldn't find a belt. He stepped into his shoes without any socks. He was throwing things into a suitcase when his mother returned, dragging Rachel along.

Rachel's face was bloodless, her eyes large with fright. She carried a suitcase with something lacy hanging out of the shut lid, and her blouse was only partially tucked into her skirt.

Aaron picked up his suitcase, then looked around to see if he had missed anything.

"Hurry!" Meiping shouted. "Forget whatever you haven't already packed. Let's go!"

Aaron reluctantly obeyed.

The stairway was a bottleneck. People moved inch by inch. Babies cried, children screamed, and all the adults yelled at the same time. Listening to them, Aaron gathered that the Japanese troops had been stationed outside Beijing ever since the Boxer Uprising. Yesterday, July 7, the Japanese had claimed that Chiang Kai-shek's men had captured two of their soldiers. The Japanese Army then demanded a search of the Nationalist Army base. When the request was denied, a clash took place right beside the Reedy Moat Bridge, and the war began.

"The Japanese looked hard for an excuse to invade China. I don't believe any of their soldiers were really missing at all!" the man next to Aaron shouted.

Another answered, "It's too bad that the Communists are in Yenan. The Red Army would fight the Japanese and protect our country, instead of retreating so quickly!"

Meiping and Rachel screamed at the same time. Aaron turned to see Meiping carrying a suitcase with one hand, holding Rachel's hand with the other. People forced themselves between them, breaking apart their linked fingers. One man shoved Rachel aside, another pushed Meiping onto her back with a small tin trunk. Aaron felt the hair on the back of his neck rise; he had never been so angry before.

"*Due-na-ma!*" He cursed unknowingly, using the very same Cantonese words his mother did when she was in supreme fury. He moved as if on a football field, shouldering his way to his mother. He took Meiping's suitcase and carried it with his own. He circled his free arm around Meiping's waist, protecting her from all the jostling elbows. He kicked the shin of the man pressing against Rachel, causing the man to buckle over in pain. Meiping pulled Rachel close to her and looked at Aaron with proud and grateful eyes. Aaron smiled. He had never attacked anybody off a ball field before, nor had he ever felt so strong and useful as he did right now.

They made their way out of the hotel door. The night was nearing its end. A crescent moon hung low in the western sky. To the east, the sky glowed red. For a brief moment Aaron thought that the sun had risen early. Then he heard his mother's quavering voice saying, "The city is on fire!"

"Mama," he turned to Meiping, tightening his hold on her, making certain that his voice was confident and reassuring. "Don't be afraid. You and Rachel have me, and I will see you both to safety."

Meiping studied her son's face in the dim light,

and tears filled her eyes. The expression on Aaron's face was no longer what she had seen for the past fourteen years. Until a few hours ago her son had been a spoiled child. Now, all of a sudden, he was a mature man. She bit her lip, leaned her head against Aaron's shoulder for a brief moment, then lifted up her chin.

The three of them held on to one another persistently, fought through the crowd, and halted a wagon. They paid the driver a fortune in advance for the short ride to the railroad station. Only one empty seat remained in the wagon, but three strangers, a young couple and their child, climbed up and joined them. The driver collected a large amount of cash from the newcomers, then piled his passengers one atop the other. The man cracked his whip and the bony horse was forced to move. The poor animal maneuvered its way through narrow alleys and crooked lanes, while its owner used his whip to chase away whoever tried to take over the wagon by force.

Again and again the horse almost ran over the dashing crowd, but the driver didn't care. The shabbily constructed wagon could fall apart at any time. Aaron sat between his mother and sister, trying his best to keep them from falling out of their seats.

It was as if they swam against the current in an ocean of horrified noise. Rachel and Meiping covered their ears, but Aaron listened bravely, holding his back straight while his face turned white. He shuddered at the sounds of torment. As he trembled, his innocent youth fell away.

They traveled through a scene of nightmare. They passed many buildings that were on fire, and saw the sobbing owners standing helplessly in front of them. Rachel closed her eyes when they saw, in the dawn's pale light, a young girl running half-naked with blood dripping down her legs. Meiping turned her head when they chanced to see, in the soft rising sun, an old woman rocking the blood-covered corpse of a young man. Aaron refused to either close his eyes or look away. He took in the scene wide-eyed, while sinking his upper teeth into his lower lip and tasting his own blood.

They were at the railroad station when the sun was high and warm. Without a word, Aaron helped his mother and sister down from the wagon. He then turned to gather their luggage, but the driver had already hurried away with the things that belonged to the six passengers. The young couple left their child standing alone and went after the wagon. Aaron started to run with them, but Meiping called him back. "I still have my purse! I'd rather lose our clothes than you!"

In Meiping's purse were their return tickets to Kwangchow and all their money. Aaron walked between Meiping and Rachel, guarding them from the deranged crowd.

They saw a warlord and his family boarding the train, shielded by a group of armed men. They also watched several young women, led by a bald man in the uniform of an officer in the Nationalist Army, moving forward in the protection of several soldiers with shining bayonets. The weaponless commoners fought to reach the train doors, and the armed ones shoved them aside.

Aaron tightened his hands into fists and hissed through his clenched teeth. "So, this is China! The warlords are taking care of their families, and the officers are tending their concubines."

He bellowed loudly like an angered animal, then started to jam through the throng. He made a path for himself and his mother and sister, until all of them boarded the train.

They had come to Beijing riding in first class, taking an enclosed cabin with comfortable sleepers and a private bathroom. They had their return tickets for the same private accommodations, but the conductor told them that their cabin was unavailable to them now. "Some powerful people have taken it, and I advise you to keep out of their way!"

Aaron wanted to go and argue with the powerful people, but his mother and sister held him down, and the aisle was so congested with passengers that he could go nowhere. Finally he had to admit that the three of them were lucky to be able to sit on the hard wood seats in the third-class car, since every inch of the floor was taken by standing or squatting people.

Suddenly Rachel screamed. She was sitting by the window, and the glass had been broken by a man from outside the train. He threw a rattan basket through the broken window, then climbed in quickly. He grinned at Rachel, showing large yellow teeth, then ran through the aisle, stepping over everybody.

"To be a Chinese is to survive in many ways!" Aaron mumbled, then said to his mother over the ear-shattering noise, "I'm glad we took this trip. It's much more educational than my school on Victoria Peak."

Meiping didn't hear her son. Over their heads there was a loud rumbling sound. They soon discovered that people were climbing to the train's roof, to hold on for the ride. The man sitting next to Aaron was unwilling to speak to the two Amerasian young people and their tall beautiful mother, so he said to no one in particular, "Well, every inch of the space inside is taken. If people don't want to stay and face the Japanese, what choice do they have? Killing, raping, torturing . . ." He continued to list the things that could happen to the people of an invaded nation.

The three of them ignored the man and waited patiently for the train to move. The sun blazed from mid-sky, and the train finally started to inch forward. People ran alongside the railroad tracks, carrying their belongings, trying to jump on. The train increased its speed, and the people were left behind. The hot air blew in through the many broken windows, and Meiping sighed with a relieved smile. "We could have been stranded in Beijing, but now, with each passing minute, we are closer to home."

The sun baked the packed-in people. Everyone was thirsty, but there was no water. "I miss the dining car," Rachel said, wetting her parched lips with her tongue. From Shanghai to Beijing they had enjoyed their many meals in the dining car, where the uniformed waiters served them a variety of delicacies.

"We'll stop at Tianjin soon," Meiping said, looking at her daughter's flushed face and the few strands of wet hair glued to Rachel's sweaty forehead. She reached over and smoothed the girl's hair with a loving hand. "There'll be food peddlers in the station, and we can buy something to drink."

On their way to Beijing, there had been food peddlers at every stop, crowding outside the windows and calling out their wares. But then they had been neither hungry nor thirsty, and besides, the food and drinks had looked both unappetizing and unsanitary.

Finally they were in Tianjin. It was only sixty-five miles from Beijing, but the atmosphere was completely different. People were unafraid of the Japanese, feeling safe and protected. The peddlers rushed toward the crowded train, selling steamed buns and sweets that swarmed with black flies. Meiping frowned, then bought some ices for herself and the children.

After the sweet, sticky ices, they were thirstier than before. When the train stopped in Tsingtao, they bought some melons that were already sliced and, again, exposed to dust and flies. They ate the melon wedges and dozed off until they heard a commotion.

The train suddenly stopped. Outside the window, a crowd gathered. People shouted loudly; some women cried and screamed. The conductor walked alongside the track, shaking his head.

"What has happened?" Aaron asked the man next to him.

The man raised a hand, slicing the side of it across his neck, smirking at Rachel and Meiping. "Two men riding on top of the train were decapitated." He rolled his eyes up and stuck out his tongue. "We passed a low bridge. The poor bastards forgot to duck. Now we must wait until their heads are found somewhere back there, for their stupid bawling widows."

The man went on to describe the details. Aaron stared at him until he heard a choking sound coming from his sister. Rachel leaned out of the window and threw up. Meiping patted her on the back, then held her tightly. Rachel cried until she threw up again. The man across from her smiled with satisfaction.

They had to go to the public toilet one at a time, so the other two could keep an eye on the unoccupied seat. They struggled through the people and reached the other side of the aisle, and then had to plead with the passengers standing or squatting against the bathroom door. Once inside the tiny room, they tried to balance themselves in the rocking train, keeping themselves from falling while squatting over a hole, through which they felt the hot air rushing in, and saw the ground passing quickly between their feet. As in all the public bathrooms in China, there was no toilet paper. If Meiping were not well-prepared, they would have been in trouble.

They passed Nanjing and Shanghai. They were starved by then. At the station of a small town, a peddler was selling steamed meat buns wrapped in old lotus leaves. Meiping bought some. The dough was gray. The meat was pink and undercooked. They bit into the buns and frowned at the funny taste. They finally reached Kwangchow after traveling more than forty hours on the noisy, smelly, hot, and crowded train.

They couldn't stand another train ride. They hired a sampan. They sat under a patched canopy, watching the man in a coolie hat standing at the end of the boat, sculling down the Pearl River.

It was early evening. The sky gradually changed its color from a blinding gold to a glorious red, and after the magnificent purple, it settled on a pale gray. A crescent moon slowly ascended the heavenly stage, in the company of a few stars. As the sky became darker, the stars increased in number, and the luminous moon drifted very close to the water. So close that Meiping and her children were certain they could reach up and touch it.

9

IN THE MIDDLE of July, Yenan was hot and dry. Li Kwanjin sat inside his cave home, looking up from his desk through a window covered not by glass, but by a sheet of oiled transparent paper.

Sandy hills surrounded the many caves. The warm wind was strong. Fine, yellow dust blew in, landing on everything. He ran his tongue over his lips and tasted the sand. It was a familiar taste that had stayed on his lips for almost two years now since he and the others arrived in the cave city at the end of their long march.

From outside the window, voices poured in.

"I can't believe I'm really here, a part of the enlightened group that will save my country!" said an eager young man.

"I love these caves! We'll have so much fun living in them until we have taken over the whole country!" said an enthusiastic young girl.

Kwanjin shook his head. The young recruits were so innocent that they were almost stupid. Yet he would hate to see them lose their naiveté and become wise. His face darkened at the realization that these faultless young people's future rested in his hands.

He looked at the stack of paper on the homemade desk. They were documents containing detailed information about the new party members, including their education, special talents, and family backgrounds.

He looked up from the name list when he heard a soft voice, "Good morning, Kwanjin."

It was May, in a comrade's baggy uniform, with her pigtails cut and her short hair combed plainly behind her ears. No matter how many times he had told her to call him Comrade Li, she wouldn't listen. A rich girl might be sincere about becoming a party member, but her sincerity couldn't change the fact that she was used to giving orders instead of receiving them. Kwanjin frowned.

His frown was chased away by the love in May's beautiful eyes. Kwanjin smiled and sighed. He had asked her to make it less obvious that they loved each other, but she had refused to agree. How could he explain that it would be easier for him to spare her from hard labor if the others didn't know he loved her?

"Good morning, Comrade Hu." He accented the last two words to remind her of the formality that must be maintained.

"Kwanjin." She ignored his warning as usual. "Come with me quickly. Something has happened in Beijing. The Chairman is ready to speak to everybody."

Not far from Kwanjin's cave, he and May met Wong Chung, shouting as he waved everyone around. "Come quickly to the meeting hall! The Japanese attacked the Reedy Moat Bridge in Beijing!"

May held Kwanjin's hand as they ran toward a large cave that served as the meeting hall. They were soon standing among the crowd, around the high-ranked officials who sat on the hay-covered ground. In the middle of the cave Chairman Mao stood like a statue, filling the cave with his powerful presence. Mao Tze-dung was not tall, but a giant among men, and had the ability to persuade the people to follow his orders even when the orders were cruel and difficult.

Kwanjin and May met their leader's impressive eyes and felt themselves shrinking in size. They had no doubt that their feelings were shared by all the other party members.

The Chairman began to speak. "The war has officially broken. We and the Nationalists have agreed to cooperate in fighting Japan. But I strongly believe that Chiang Kai-shek is holding back his best men and weapons. I know him only too well."

Mao Tze-dung smiled a chilly smile. "He will take his power and wealth to a safe place far from the front. He'll wait there, and wish for us to use all we have to fight the Japanese. Once the Japanese are destroyed, we'll be weak and vulnerable, and it'll be easy for him to come back and destroy us."

The man gave a robust laugh that frightened both May and Kwanjin. She never did let his hand go, and he didn't have the heart to withdraw it from her grasp. The Chairman continued, "Chiang, the bastard, has used the same technique many times before. He encouraged the warlords to fight with us, then sat back and watched. He attacked the defeated party, and with that technique he has won many easy victories."

Mao Tze-dung's voice hardened. "This time, we'll not be tricked by the son of a cur. We'll beat him at his own game. We'll keep the best weapons and best men right here in Yenan, saving both for when we fight Chiang Kai-shek. We'll use the new members, peasants, and the captured warlords' men to form a new force and call it the Eighth Route Army. We'll give these

men not grenades and machine guns, but
spears, sticks, kitchen cleavers, and old swords.
They'll start guerrilla assaults on the Japanese
immediately."

Chairman Mao never bored his audience with
prolonged speech. He ordered the attending party
leaders to begin organizing the new army, and
the meeting was over.

On their way out of the meeting hall, May finally let go of Kwanjin's hand. She was so excited
that she needed both hands to help her talk.

"The Eighth Route Army. I like the name. I
want to be the first woman soldier in it. Kwanjin"—she looked at him challengingly—"if you
dare to keep me in Yenan, or let me go to the
front line but assign me as a nurse, I'll never forgive you!"

"Comrade Hu, you have no idea what you're
talking about. Did you hear the Chairman's words
at all?" Kwanjin looked at May with disappointment. "Where did your intelligence go?"

May was instantly angered. She stopped walking, stood pouting. "Li Kwanjin, I am not deaf. I
heard the Chairman as clearly as you did. He said
the new members are going to the front to fight
the Japanese, and that is exactly what I want to
do."

People walked around May and Kwanjin, casting them curious glances. Kwanjin was cautious
of the children who belonged to the Team of Long
Ears, but May didn't even know of their existence. She continued to shout, "Kwanjin, I want
to join the Eighth Route Army and fight the Japanese! Don't you dare stop me!"

A severe voice came from behind them. "Comrade Li, did I hear correctly? Did our new comrade ask to join the Eighth Route Army and you
are forbidding her to carry out our Chairman's

orders?" Wong Chung looked at them with a disapproving gleam in his eyes.

"No . . ." Kwanjin answered hesitantly. "I wouldn't do such a thing, of course."

"He wouldn't do such a thing, of course." May repeated Kwanjin's words triumphantly. "If the two of you will excuse me, I want to go share my excitement with my Beijing friends. They are as thrilled as I am, I'm positive!"

Kwanjin watched May running through the crowd like a high-spirited child. "Foolish girl," he murmured. "She and her Beijing friends are spoiled brats who know nothing about real life."

Wong Chung nodded. "They are just what the party needs. Like a house, we need foundation stones. If the stones were clever, they would all want to be at the top of the house, to carry less weight but more glory. If that were the case, the house would never be built."

Wong Chung ignored Kwanjin's angry stare and continued, "I'm giving you a new task. You can forget the new recruits' jobs in Yenan. I know you have a hard time deciding who is better for clerical work and who makes a better field worker." Wong Chung chuckled. How funny and ridiculous it was, to consider the new members' future a serious matter.

He tried to keep a straight face when he ordered Kwanjin, "You will now go through the same list, and give them various positions in the Eighth Route Army. The boys will become soldiers, sergeants and captains, and the girls nurses and cooks."

Wong Chung laughed. "But if Comrade Hu May insists, then you can make her a soldier too." While laughing, he took a pack of cigarettes out of his pants pocket, lit one, inhaled deeply.

Kwanjin had never hated his former teacher as

strongly as he did right now. He imagined May's fragile body covered with blood, her lovely face lifeless behind the mask of death. He had to find a way to save her from such a fate.

With the cigarette dangling from the corner of his mouth, Wong Chung continued with his order. "Those from rich or literate families must be given the lower ranks and sent to the very front. The children of farmers, laborers, and un-educated peasants should be made officers and placed in the back." Wong Chung chuckled once again. "It's a shame that Hu May is obviously rich and well-educated."

Wong Chung walked away, leaving his laughter lingering in the air. Kwanjin looked at the back of his teacher with loathing. He wanted to go back to his cave to think, but it was time for him to teach a class.

Kwanjin walked toward the cave that served as a classroom. It was useless to send May back to Beijing, since the city was now in Japanese captivity. How could May escape? He saw the distant hills become distorted by the swirling sand as he entered the classroom.

Over twenty young men and women sat on the straw-covered dirt ground, facing Li Kwanjin with faces brightened by youth, innocence, and excitement. Kwanjin greeted them with a heavy heart, then started his lecture.

"We are forming the Eighth Route Army to fight the Japanese, following a guerrilla strategy. Chairman Mao summarized this effective strategy into four basic principles . . ." He turned to write on the chalkboard, but first glanced at the left side of the first row, where May sat.

Her face was brighter than all the other young faces. She seemed as worry-free and comfortable as a cat in a basket. She had opened a notebook on her lap and was ready to copy down his every word. She leaned an elbow on her knee, rested her chin in one hand, and held a pencil with the other. She looked at him with her round trustful eyes and smiled her beautiful smile when she saw him looking at her. It was obvious that she was no longer angry with him.

Kwanjin faced the board and chewed his lip. He made up his mind: he couldn't afford to fight the party in order to save May. He must do as he was ordered, then help May secretly.

He wrote on the board four simple lines:

> The enemy advances; we retreat.
> The enemy halts; we harass.
> The enemy slackens; we attack.
> The enemy retreats; we pursue.

As he wrote, an idea occurred to him. He put down the chalk as the idea slowly turned into a way to save May.

A crescent moon shone over Yenan, revealing two people sitting on a large rock that protruded over a cliff.

"May," Kwanjin said softly, leaning over to kiss her on the cheek.

"How come you don't call me Comrade Hu now?" May asked in a pouting voice. "If I am your May, then you should address me the same way all the time. And if I am only your comrade, then don't try to kiss me when we are alone."

Kwanjin ignored her complaint. "May, will you marry me?"

She stared at him. Moonlight veiled his handsome face. She couldn't tell what else was written in his eyes besides love and passion. Did she detect fear. She wasn't certain.

"I love you, May," he said, avoiding her eyes, looking at her lips. "I want you to become my lover . . ." He knew instantly that the party term was distasteful to May's sensitive ears. "I mean, my wife."

May stared at Kwanjin one moment longer, then threw her slender arms around his neck. She rested her face on his broad shoulder and cried. "Kwanjin! I'm so happy! Yes, I want to be your wife. I want to spend the rest of my life with you, grow old with you, and raise many children. Did you know that I fell in love with you in the park when I saw you walking between two policemen, handcuffed and struggling?"

She kissed him on the cheek, then continued to talk with happy tears glistening in her eyes, reflecting the moonlight. "You've been grouchy since we arrived in Yenan. In Beijing you acted like a country boy lost in a big city. In Yenan you became a worried old man. Sometimes I have the feeling that you don't want me here, but I love you just the same. Yes, Kwanjin, I want to marry you, very, very much! I'll write to my family to-night. I must write to my friends too, in Beijing and also those in Hong Kong and Hawaii. I can't write to Sung Hwa yet, because he is still travel-ing somewhere through China—" She would have rattled on forever if Kwanjin hadn't kissed her.

His hands took her face like a gentle breeze caressing a delicate flower. His lips touched hers like tender moonlight grazing a quiet river. "My little May, must you talk so much?" he asked be-tween kisses. "What a pair we'll make. I always get in trouble for having a big mouth, and now your mouth is even bigger than mine."

Her heart was beating fast, but she didn't forget to talk back. "If you don't like a talkative wife, then it's just too bad. You're stuck with me, Li Kwanjin, for the rest of your life!"

Kwanjin didn't answer. He held her lips with a long kiss, at the same time moving his hands from her face to her body, one hand rubbing her back, the other kneading her breast. She trembled, tried to pull away. He increased the force of his hand on her back, pressed her forward. She stopped resisting, but continued to quiver. He could feel her heart racing against the beating of his own. When they both were almost out of breath, he moved his lips away from hers and circled his arms around her. She locked her arms around him, and they clung together, listening to the night wind.

Kwanjin stood as Wong Chung sat behind a desk studying a marriage application and two files. He had waited for a long time. His feet were tired and he shifted his weight restlessly.

"I don't think the party should allow you and Comrade Hu to become lovers," Wong Chung said without looking up from the two files; one was Kwanjin's, the other May's.

Kwanjin tried to stay calm. "Why?"

"You and Comrade Hu are from different classes," Wong Chung answered quickly, still looking at the first pile. "Look at her home address: the Noblemen's Well Street. I've never been to Beijing, but I've heard that it's a street for the rich. On that street, the water from the wells is pure and sweet. The poor live on soiled bitter water, while the rich hire armed guards to watch over their wells and refuse to share them with the poor."

Wong Chung moved to the second file. "Look at you. You are the son of a fisherman who sold himself to a slave trader. You joined the party in

the Ching-kong Mountains, and survived the
Long March. You have created a few problems in
Yenan, but are still considered a trustworthy
party member . . . more or less."

Wong Chung looked up, and Kwanjin was dis-
couraged by the coldness in his eyes. "Besides the
differences in your backgrounds, I suspect the
true reason for your marrying her is more complicated than you claim."

After a pause, Wong Chung continued slowly,
throwing each word out like a hand grenade, "I
think you are marrying her to save her from going
to the front lines. Chairman Mao ordered the new
members to fight, but you're disobeying the order
by making her the lover of an old party member
so she can be spared from her duty."

Wong Chung's accusation was serious. Kwanjin
knew that Wong Chung was not going to give
him permission to marry May if he didn't put up
a fight. He took a deep breath. "Comrade Wong,"
he said, and held his head high, "I think you're
overlooking something."

Kwanjin paused. Wong Chung waited with a
crooked smile, a smile that gradually disappeared
as Kwanjin continued.

"Comrade Hu led me to her friends, and was
responsible for their becoming our newest recruits. They think highly of her. If Comrade Hu
is declined permission to marry me, their loyalty
will suffer. Since they are soon to be the foundation stones of the Eighth Route Army, can we
afford to weaken their dedication?"

Wong Chung narrowed his eyes. Hu May was
responsible for only about thirteen new recruits.
She had no influence at all. But in Yenan, anyone
had the right to accuse anyone else of whatever
crime he could invent. Wong Chung definitely

didn't want to be accused of deflating the morale of the Eighth Route Army.

He glared at Kwanjin, expressing threat with his eyes but smiling with his mouth and saying slowly, "Well, on second thought, I guess you are right. You and Comrade Hu can become perfect lovers."

Wong Chung picked up a seal, pressed it in the red ink pad, then stamped it on the marriage application. "Congratulations, Comrade Li," he said, handing the permission to his former student.

The groom stood straight and handsome in uniform, waiting for the bride to come to the mess hall. He heard everyone gasp and turned to look, and his jaw dropped at the sight of his bride.

He didn't know that May had brought with her in her small bag a red silk skirt with a matching embroidered blouse.

The wind howled over the hills, bellowing a wedding march. The song was overpowered by the raised voices of the guests saying that they had never seen a Yenan bride wearing anything more than baggy pants and a dark jacket.

Chairman Mao raised an eyebrow at the bride, and kept his eyes on her pretty face as he married the young couple. The Chairman had just taken a new lover himself, a movie actress from Shanghai. As he encouraged the newlyweds to give their best work to the party, he secretly envied the luck of Li Kwanjin.

A simple meal was served as a wedding feast, mainly vegetables and rice gruel. The only treat they had was rice wine, made by their own kitchen workers. The groom seemed nervous until many cups of wine intoxicated him and drove away his worries. The bride smiled happily, her eyes saddened for only a brief moment when she thought of her family and her friends from Beijing. None of her family could come to Yenan because of the war, and all of her friends had left with the Eighth Route Army.

The guests laughed at the groom's mother, Leahi, when she brought a chair to the center of the hall, sat, and waited for the newlyweds to offer her their kowtow. "Times have changed," they told her. "You are not living in the feudal past anymore. In this day and age the bride and groom no longer pay their respects to their in-laws."

Leahi was confused. "No kowtow? I raised a son by myself, and when he is married I don't even receive a single kowtow?" She began to cry.

May couldn't stand the old woman's tears. She bit her lip and thought. *It's degrading for one person to kneel in front of another. I cannot kowtow to Kwanjin's mother. But . . .* She took another look at Leahi's tearful face and pulled Kwanjin by the hand, led him to Leahi, and bowed three times.

Leahi felt better. She had thought May too delicate for her son, and a little too high and mighty. But since May had lowered herself to perform the bowing ritual, now she must accept May as a good respectful daughter-in-law.

Leahi rushed back to the cave. She brightened it with several red candles, then scattered a few peanuts and dates over the wedding bed, counting on the nuts to guarantee the early arrival of a grandson. For a brief moment she remembered her own wedding day, and saw in her mind another bed scattered with peanuts and dates. She shook her head, erased the sadness that accompanied the memory, and became busy. She moved her toilet things and a few clothes out of the cave. For years she had shared the same cave with her son. As an unwritten rule, when the son married, for a week his parents would sleep in a neighbor's cave to give the newlyweds some privacy.

When the night was deep, the groom and bride were alone in their cave, their spirits lifted by rice wine, their shyness all but gone. Kwanjin gathered the dates and peanuts and shook his head. "Mama will always be a Willow Place woman . . ." He forgot what he was saying when he saw his bride emerge from behind a sheet that hung from a rope stretched from wall to wall.

May had removed her red silk skirt and blouse. She was wearing a pink robe, soft and thin, like pastel-tinted water pouring over her curved body, giving her a soft glow but not really hiding anything.

The cave ground was rough. She tiptoed in the candlelight, unknowingly swaying her body sensually.

"May . . ." He stared at her, letting go of the peanuts and dates. "You are so beautiful." He felt the blood rushing from every part of his body toward one direction. "You . . . Where did you get such a robe? There is no store in Yenan . . ." He heard himself mumbling, not making much sense.

May jumped over the scattered nuts and landed on the bamboo-framed bed. The frame screamed, the bed shook. "Silk can be folded into the size of a handkerchief. I packed my wedding gown and this robe in a bag. I knew you would marry me someday." She giggled, then kicked him softly with a bare foot. "Do comrades sleep in their uniforms, or will you eventually get undressed?"

Kwanjin had never seen May's bare feet before. He grabbed the foot that had kicked him, stared at it. It was white and small, with little round toes that resembled pearls. He raised the foot to his mouth, kissed its arched back.

"It tickles!" May giggled like a silver bell as she tried to free her foot.

Kwanjin kissed her toes one by one. The music of her laughter, the view of her wriggling body, and the sound of the bed frame screeching worked together to make his already swollen manhood ache painfully.

"Kwanjin, give me back my foot, please," she said. As he held one foot in his hand, the other foot kicked out in every direction. Her legs parted, and he saw a patch of black hair like a naughty little mouse hiding in its secret nest.

"You don't wear any underpants!" he moaned, and let go of her foot. It took him less than a minute to take off his clothes, throwing them all over the cave ground. He lunged forward and landed on top of her. The bed wobbled so badly it almost collapsed.

Kwanjin moved to one side of May and pulled off her robe. The slippery garment was easy to remove. They looked at each other's naked bodies with admiration and curiosity, but also embarrassment. For a few moments they didn't know what to do.

May was a virgin. Kwanjin had had a few women, but had never combined sex with love. May waited with longing and a small portion of fear. He climbed over her with passion and tried not to crush her. He supported his weight with his knees and elbows. His bare chest covered her naked breasts, and his muscled thighs stretched over her smooth legs. He looked into her eyes, then lowered his mouth to hers.

He kissed her softly at first, the same way he had kissed her in the moonlight on top of the hill. Hunger soon drove away his gentleness. His tongue parted her clenched teeth, toyed with her tongue, reached every corner of her mouth. He then nipped her lips tenderly. She felt that her starved groom was about to devour her, but as she was bitten and sucked and licked, she felt only love, no pain. She heard herself purring like a satisfied cat, then found herself kissing and loving him back.

His strong callused hands cupped her soft breasts, caressing them with passion. The heat of his palms burned through her breasts, then sank into her heart. She closed her eyes, circled her arms tightly around his back.

"I love you, my Kwanjin, my husband. I'll love you forever," she said, her voice trembling like candlelight in a breath of air.

"I love you, my May, my wife. I'll love you eternally," he said, his words shaking like the wings of a moth struggling next to the candle's quivering flame.

It was so natural for their bodies to unite. He entered her, and they became one. He took her to the height of ecstasy, shared with her all the joy he knew.

When they were tired, they rested. When they recovered, they experienced again the miracle. His arms held her, his legs entwined with hers, his face lay against hers. They slept like twin babies in a womb, unknowing and uncaring of the outside world.

10

SUNG HWA ARRIVED in White Stone and was surprised that unlike in Beijing, now he understood every word said by the villagers.

The rickshaw pullers and wagon drivers crowded around him. "Sisan, where would you like to go?"

"Does anyone here have cars? You know, automobiles?" he asked, looking for the vehicles he had seen in Beijing and Kwangchow.

A rickshaw puller laughed. "Not yet. The rich can buy cars, of course, but they can't drive very far. We don't have any place to buy gas, not in White Stone."

A wagon driver bragged proudly, "Sisan, we don't have cars, but we do have mail delivery, and a telegraph office, and even a few radios in our village. You know, the magic box that can talk and sing and predict weather and report news. Radios are not for the poor, naturally, but the rich, like Ma Tsai-tu, do have them. There is also one in the White Stone High School, and another in the White Stone Hotel. Our village is not all that far behind the times, Sisan."

Sung Hwa smiled at the villager's pride. No wonder his father was such a proud man. "Will you take me to the White Stone Hotel?" he asked the wagon driver.

The driver picked up Sung Hwa's suitcases and

loaded them onto his horse-drawn wagon. "We have only one hotel, but it's a very nice one. Three guest rooms upstairs, and a large restaurant on the main floor. The owner is distantly related to me. Sisan, I can ask him to give you a discount. How long are you staying in White Stone?"

Sung Hwa sat on the wagon seat. "I don't know. I'll leave when there is no more reason for me to stay, I guess." He felt sad as he said those words. He had no reason to rush back to San Francisco. His mother, stepfather, and sister didn't need him. He had no cause to hurry to Hawaii either, although he had promised Jebu and Michiko that he would pass through there. His father had his American wife, and the son by a previous marriage would only be an intruder.

The wagon started to move. "Sisan is from a foreign land?" asked the curious driver.

"Yes. How do you know?"

"Sisan has the foreign air. Is Sisan from the Land of the Sun or the Land of the Gold Mountains?"

"America . . . I mean, the Land of the Gold Mountains."

The driver nodded with relief. "Good. We were visited by a few Japanese, people from the Land of the Sun, recently. We didn't like them. They seemed to be here to assess the village, preparing to take over." The man raised his voice in excitement. "*Ah-ya!* Sisan must meet the principal of the White Stone High School, my distant cousin."

"Why?"

"Because Cousin Chew can speak the foreign tongue. He went to school in Shanghai, you know, and came back with a mind full of ideas too modern for White Stone. He opened the school doors to let in the girls a few years ago, something very shocking to the townspeople. Anyway, Cousin Chew will want to talk to Sisan and ask what's going on in the white devils' land. He'll want to copy a new idea or two. But if Sisan doesn't want to see him—"

Sung Hwa interrupted the driver. "I'll be glad to talk to your cousin. I need a guide, and he just may be the right person."

In order to charge a good fare, the driver took Sung Hwa around White Stone before going to the hotel, which was very close to the train station. They passed the town square and reached the temple, old and in need of repair. An aged monk in a tattered black robe stood beside the temple wall. The driver explained, "The temple used to be in good shape and the statues of Buddha received a new coat of paint every year. The monks ate so well that they were all fat. But a group of young men came from the cities a few years ago, and called themselves Communist party members. They gathered in the temple and shouted and waved their fists and gave whoever was burning incense there a hard time. We stopped going to the temple and started to worship Buddha at our own homes. Only one poor monk is still here. He lives in a small room in the back, but continues to clean and dust the whole temple. He is my uncle's sister-in-law's nephew, who was sold to the monastery when he was little."

"Is anyone in White Stone not related to you?" Sung Hwa laughed.

"Yes, I'm not related to Ma Tsai-tu, the richest man in town." The driver pointed at a mansion some distance away.

On Ma Tsai-tu's property, behind the walls that surrounded the mansion, the night wind of summer blew softly, brushing through the trees in the garden. The birds were disturbed in their sleep, moving in their nests and chirping faintly.

A small figure entered the garden, wearing a long robe. Wind lifted the fringe of the robe and filled the wide sleeves, turning the figure into a butterfly spreading its delicate wings. Moving soundlessly, the figure crossed the garden, reached the lotus pond, and ascended the arched bridge.

Melin stopped in the middle of the bridge. She looked up at the sky, at the crescent moon. She remembered the full moon of spring. A season ago she had prayed to the majestic moon with a heart filled with hope.

Spring had shifted into summer. The forsythias died and the pink, red, yellow, and white lotus started to bloom in the pond. A marriage contract was signed between the Ma family and the family of Kao, and soon Melin would become the bride of her uncle's son.

"You didn't answer my prayer at all!" Melin looked away from the merciless moon and lowered her eyes to the dark pond. A carp jumped in the water. A frog croaked from one of the large lotus leaves. The crickets were singing all over the garden from underneath the rocks. The songs of the nightingales reached her ears from far away, perhaps from the foliage of the trees that stood on top of the haunted mountain. "Life goes on, and no one cares about my terrible fate!" Melin sighed deeply and left the bridge.

She walked aimlessly through the garden. The ground was covered with dew. Her thin slippers were quickly soaked, but she didn't care. She wandered from one part of the mansion to another, and soon paused at her parents' courtyard.

Her father was probably out. Ever since the local brothel had hired those new singsong girls from Kwangchow, Ma Tsai-tu seldom slept at home. "Mama," Melin whispered softly, facing the dark windows of her mother's bedroom. "Why do you want to make me as unhappy as you?"

As a child, Melin had thought of her mother simply as a happy fat woman who enjoyed eating. When Melin was fourteen she had caught her mother standing facing the window and looking at the haunted mountain, crying. The heartbreaking sobs that were pouring from Yoto's mouth had shocked Melin. From that day on Melin had looked at her mother in a different light, and began to understand that Ma Yoto was trying to use food as a way of forgetting her misery.

Melin shook her head and moved on. She passed the courtyard shared by her three older brothers. The oldest one, Kiang, was now twenty-four, and unmarried. Quite frequently a poor village man would come to the door and ask to see Ma Tsai-tu, saying that Ma Kiang had either coaxed or forced his young daughter into losing her purity. Ma Tsai-tu would argue with the villager and call the poor man's daughter a tramp, then agree to pay the minimum amount of money to the pitiful man. Tsai-tu would then pretend to be angry with his son, but everyone could see that he was not truly bothered by Kiang's behavior, which was not any different from his own.

Melin frowned deeply. This was 1937, but most of the rich men in China still lived in the Ching Dynasty. Her father and her three brothers, her uncle and her future husband, were all the same. Life was a game for them, and women were one of their many toys. She visualized her future husband's face: pale and wearing a stupid grin. Actually, he was not bad-looking. His father was

Yoto's brother, and in a way, he and Melin resembled each other.

Both Melin and her older sister had learned from their high-school teacher about Dr. Hu Shih, a man who had come back from America nearly twenty years ago with a doctor's degree from Columbia University. He had tried all these years to spread the western thoughts in China and to put an end to arranged marriages.

"You and your theory never reached White Stone." Melin sighed.

She stopped outside her sister's room, and her eyes teared. Her sister was home again, with a new baby. The two girls had been very close until Suelin married a man chosen by Ma Tsai-tu. Melin hated her brother-in-law. He was worse than Ma Tsai-tu and Ma Kiang. Melin knew that her father never hit her mother. Suelin's husband believed in slapping his wife around whenever she dared to complain about his many other women.

"What happened to our dreams?" Melin asked softly, staring at Suelin's closed door. It seemed only yesterday that the two girls had talked about going to Shanghai to attend the college for girls and to become students in Dr. Hu's class.

A gust of wind swept over the courtyard, carrying with it the song of the nightingales perched in the faraway trees. It was such a sad melody. Melin shivered. She could see, in the sorrow of Suelin, her own bleak future. Except that her future could be even worse than her sister's. Suelin's husband was, at least, rich. Melin's future husband's father had smoked away the family fortune through the opium pipe, and was now counting on Melin's large dowry.

Melin returned to her room. She kicked off her wet slippers and jumped back into her bed. Pull-

ing the covers over her body, she remembered
herself asking her mother: "Why do you want me
to marry my cousin when he is not even rich?"

Her mother had stared at her with such a painful look, and then answered slowly: "Melin, because I don't want you to be hurt. I know my
brother's son. In spite of all his faults, he is a
contented man. He will not leave White Stone for
an unknown world. You'll never have to spend
your life questioning his whereabouts. And he
does love you, Melin, in his own way."

Yoto had laughed then, and the laughter sounded
more like a cry. "What is love? A brief glance in
the flickering light of the paper lanterns? A quick
embrace in an old temple filled with the statues
of smiling Buddha?" Yoto's voice had become
hoarse, and a cynical smile twisted her lips. "No!
Love is to have a man by your side. May he be a
good man or a bad man, but a real man instead
of a memory." Yoto had concluded the strange
discussion firmly: "You will marry your cousin as
soon as the last year of your schooling is over."

Melin closed her eyes and a tear fell. School in
White Stone lasted through July, and the graduation took place in the second week of the following month. She was a senior in White Stone High
School. She had been chosen to represent the
graduating class by making a speech, and she had
been practicing in front of a mirror.

The speech would be the last good thing before
her marriage. After that, she could expect no
more glimpses of happiness.

Everything reached the countryside in slow motion, including the news about the Japanese
invasion.

Sung Hwa and Mr. Chew, a middle-aged man,
walked out of the White Stone Hotel, comparing

what they saw with what they had heard over
the radio.

"Unbelievable!" Sung Hwa said to the principal. "Japanese are moving south from Beijing,
taking every town and village along the coast.
Our people either run one step ahead of the invaders or stay in their homes and count on the
enemy's mercy. But I don't feel the war at all."
He pointed at the peaceful scene. "Look at the
farmers gathering their autumn harvest and the
fishermen sailing on the peaceful Pearl River.
Maybe White Stone will be forgotten by the Japanese invaders, since it is forgotten by time."

Mr. Chew shook his head. "Don't be fooled by
the sight. The farmers and fishermen can't afford
to run, so they must farm and fish as usual. I'm
sure that in the houses of the rich, things are
quite different."

One of Mr. Chew's favorite students, Ma Melin,
had mentioned recently that her father had plenty
of ways to keep the Japanese from doing him any
harm, and that everything in the Ma house was
following its schedule, including Melin's much-
dreaded wedding.

A thought came to Mr. Chew's mind, brightened his eyes. He had been born a poor boy in
White Stone, then struggled in Shanghai for a college education. He was a great admirer of Dr. Hu,
who strongly opposed arranged marriages. Mr.
Chew had watched Ma Suelin change from a
happy girl to a sad woman as the result of a marriage arranged by her father. He knew the man
who was soon to be Melin's husband. He hated
to see another budding flower wilt in the hands
of a man who didn't appreciate her. Melin's
magnificent beauty and outstanding intelligence
should be treasured by a man equal to her in appearance and mind, who could take her away

from her rotten father, feeble mother, and the rest of the spoiled members in the Ma family—someone like this tall, handsome, open-minded, obviously rich Sung Hwa. It would be very difficult to take the only unmarried daughter away from Ma Tsai-tu, but if the two young people should choose to fight, where there was love, there would always be a way.

"Will you come to the graduation in your white suit? The one you wore the first time I met you?" he asked his young friend.

"Why, of course." Hwa looked at Mr. Chew, puzzled. "Is a white suit some kind of good-luck symbol? I don't know much about Chinese culture, but I always thought that for good luck one must wear red."

"Well, you can't very well appear in a red suit, can you?" Mr. Chew laughed. "Just wear your white suit and may the Great Buddha smile at you!"

The ceremony took place on a very warm day. The auditorium was filled with people. The heat was unbearable. In his white suit, starched shirt collar, and tie, Sung Hwa wiped his face continuously with a drenched handkerchief. Sweat soaked through his shirt, and he felt miserable. He was ready to get up and leave, when someone announced that next on the agenda was the speech by one of the graduates.

"My name is Ma Melin, and I want to thank my principal and all my teachers . . ." The young girl in a white blouse and a blue skirt stood facing the audience, holding a sheet of paper, bowing gracefully.

Hwa looked at her and forgot his discomfort. She had more charm than was revealed in her bright eyes and soft lips. Her beauty was much greater than her porcelain skin and jet-black hair. Her loveliness was far beyond her fragile body and soft voice. She had a special air, an air that existed only in the painted ladies Hwa had seen on the antique scrolls that had been hidden for centuries in the treasure chests of the Imperial Palace.

He thought of Judy, who was like loud music that caught people's attention but couldn't be listened to for long. Compared with her, this girl reminded Hwa of a pure tune coming softly out of a jade flute, played near a calm lake that lay undisturbed under the moon.

Melin's speech was simple, but as Hwa listened and watched her, he forgot all his troubles and felt content with life.

"Who is she?" Hwa asked the woman sitting next to him.

"She is the daughter of the Ma family, and she is engaged to her cousin," the woman answered discouragingly. "Her father, Ma Tsai-tu, is the richest man in White Stone."

The name didn't mean anything to Sung Hwa. His father, Quanming, had never talked much about the people in his hometown. Ma Melin's being engaged didn't bother him at all. Even marriages could be dissolved, like the one between his father and mother. When the ceremony was over, Hwa went to Mr. Chew. The expression on his face already told the delighted principal what Hwa had in mind.

"The Great Buddha is smiling at you, I believe, regardless of your white suit," Mr. Chew said after Hwa stated that he wanted to be introduced to Ma Melin. "Melin's mother is sick in bed, and her father and brothers didn't care to come to a worthless girl's graduation. Her sister can't go anywhere without the husband's permission. Melin is here all alone."

At Mr. Chew's request, Melin joined her principal and Sung Hwa for tea at the restaurant in the White Stone Hotel.

Through the tea, Melin kept her eyes lowered to the cup, seldom glancing up. She talked a little to Mr. Chew, but mostly listened to her principal brag about his new young friend. She answered Hwa's questions with a simple yes or no, concealing any opinion or emotion she might have. Sung Hwa was not used to dealing with a situation like this. He was getting nowhere. When Melin went to the ladies' room to comb her hair, Hwa leaned closer to Mr. Chew.

"She doesn't like me at all! Maybe she loves her fiancé!" he said with great disappointment and hurt.

Mr. Chew laughed. "It's obvious that you don't know Chinese girls. What do you expect her to do in front of a strange man? Pick up a cup of tea and gulp it down? Look at you straight in the eye and ask a string of questions? Smile broadly to show her teeth? Laugh loudly enough to be heard? What do you take her for, a singsong girl?"

Hwa stared at the man. "Nothing you've said should degrade her in any way. Not in America, at least."

"But you are not in America. Believe me, according to our way, Melin is only behaving like a proper lady. She doesn't dislike you. On the contrary, she likes you very much, and that's why she is so careful, so that you won't think less of her. If you had any experience with a proper Chinese lady at all, you would know that the more she wants to capture you, the colder she will treat you, until there is no chance for you to escape."

Sung Hwa murmured, "I'm glad she doesn't like me a little more. What would she do then?"

Mr. Chew laughed hard. Melin appeared at a distance and he whispered, "Young man, leave it to me." He then asked, "Did you say that you only speak Chinese but don't know how to write it?"

Sung Hwa had only enough time to nod.

Melin looked even more beautiful with her hair combed and the perspiration on her forehead powdered away. She sat without looking at Sung Hwa.

"Melin, I have a request," Mr. Chew said.

"Teachers do not need to request anything from their students, Mr. Chew," Melin answered with her head humbly bowed. "Anything you wish, I'll do."

Sung Hwa was willing to give anything to hear these very same words from her lovely lips, but meant for him alone.

Mr. Chew pointed at Sung Hwa. "This nice young man is very interested in Chinese culture. He wishes to learn the Chinese calligraphy from me, but I don't have the time to each him. I've worked hard through the school year and now I want to take the rest of the summer to read some old poems of the Tang Dynasty. Melin, will you teach him, so I don't have to give up my plan for the summer?"

"I . . ." Melin hesitated. "My father will not allow me to give calligraphy lessons to a strange man."

Mr. Chew said quickly, "Your father doesn't need to know. I've already thought of a classroom for the two of you. In the deserted temple, a monk keeps all the empty rooms clean. He can be given some donation, and then he'll be more than happy to make sure that no one ever disturbs you."

The calligraphy lessons began the very next day.

Sung Hwa and Ma Melin sat at a table in a quiet room behind the temple. The monk prayed somewhere at the other end of the corridor, and occasionally banged on a small gong that produced only a soft jingle. He accompanied his prayers with the endless clatter of the "wooden fish," a hollow-centered wooden ball shaped like a fish, which reverberated with a tuneless call. "Ah-mee-tou-foo . . ." These four simple syllables, which represented a multitude of meanings and had been repeated by the Buddhists for thousands of years now, echoed in the air. The sound was like a magic medicine that purified Hwa's soul and mind. His heart was so tranquil that he forgave all wrongs against him, even Judy's cruel rejection.

The only other sounds that could be heard were the birds singing and the cicadas chanting. The world was a wonderful place and its perfection was made complete by the presence of Melin.

Now she was forced to look at him, talk to him, and answer his questions, since she had become his teacher.

"To be a true artist in calligraphy, we do not buy already-made ink," she said in a voice so gentle that he held his breath so it would linger in his ears a little longer. She used her slender fingers to lift a porcelain pot she had brought from home, together with the other things needed for calligraphy. She poured water from the pot into the well in the ink stone. She then picked up the ink stick and started to grind it in small circles, turning the water into black ink.

"You must hold the stick straight, so the end of it will not become crooked." She looked up, met his eyes, smiled faintly, then caught herself and looked down immediately. "A crooked ink stick means its owner has a crooked heart, and you must never let that happen."

She had on a pink skirt that reached her feet, and a white blouse with a high collar. Her hairpins were two little butterflies that rested behind her ears, holding her long hair back and guiding it to hang straight to her waist. Her only jewelry was two matching bracelets of white jade that clinked as she made the ink.

"Chinese calligraphy is more than three thousand, five hundred years old. The Koreans, Japanese, and Vietnamese all borrowed their ways of writing from the Chinese." She smiled once again at Hwa, and once again quickly looked down at the ink stone. "There are more than fifty thousand characters, each started as the drawing of a recognizable picture. The word 'sun' actually looks like a sun, and the word 'moon' resembles a crescent moon. 'Cry' looks like a crying face, and 'laugh' looks happy. In later years some of these characters were combined to make new words—such as putting 'sun' and 'moon' together to make 'bright,' and placing a 'woman' under the roof of a 'house' to symbolize 'safe.' There are numerous dialects in China, but only one kind of Chinese writing. If only all the Chinese people communicated by writing instead of talking, then we would all understand one another."

When the ink was black and thick, Melin spread the rice paper and showed Hwa how to make the strokes. It was necessary for her to touch his hand, and as their flesh made contact, Hwa's heart lurched. He was surprised by his own reaction to her touch, until he saw a blush

appear on her pale neck at the opening of her
collar, rising to her ears and spreading over her
cheeks. Her hands trembled. The tip of the brush
wavered and the stroke she made was a stag-
gering line.

She tried to cover her embarrassment with further instruction, driving an austere air into her
voice. "You must hold the brush straight and
make sure that the tip is at a ninety-degree angle
to the paper. You must not hold it the way you
hold a pen or pencil . . ." She stopped when he
covered her quivering hand with his.

"Don't try to act like a severe teacher," he said
softly, using the other hand to lift her chin, forcing her to look at him. "You can't scare me away.
Not now, and not ever."

She blushed deeper and didn't answer, but nor
did she look away or try to withdraw her hand.
Her hand quivered like a captured bird in his
grasp. He tightened his grip to calm the frightened bird.

"In San Francisco they call me a Jook-sing and
a Heon-jeo." She tilted her head to one side, and
her puzzled expression was so lovely that his
heart skipped a beat. "The heart of bamboo is
hollow, and a banana is yellow on the outside but
white inside. They call me that because I am a
Chinese, but there is not much Chinese culture
in me. You can call me an ignorant barbarian if
you like."

"You are not a barbarian . . ." Her voice faded
away. How could she tell him that he was the
foreign prince in white armor that the Great Buddha had sent her from heaven? What would he
say if she let him know that she had seen him
among the audience while making her speech and
had nearly forgotten her lines? Would he laugh
and run away from her if he should find out that

she had been thinking of him the whole night and looked forward to this calligraphy lesson as she had never looked forward to anything in her life?

She tried to bow her head, but he wouldn't let her. He looked into her eyes and said, "What I'm trying to tell you is that I don't know how to do things the Chinese way, your way. I have heard that in China I have to ask your permission before calling you by your first name. And I also heard that in this ancient land a gentleman must never tell a young lady how he feels about her the first time they are alone together."

He paused. The monk continued to pray, the birds sang, and the cicadas chanted. When he spoke again, his voice was sincere and truthful, just like the old monk's endless prayer and the birds' eternal song. "Melin, I love you. I want to marry you and take you back to San Francisco with me. I'll wait for you to love me and agree to marry me. If I have to, I'll wait forever."

11

AARON ENTERED THE dining room in his pajamas, holding three sealed envelopes, each thick with a stack of pictures.

The first letter was addressed to Hawaii, to Jebu and Michiko Yamada. "You were lucky to have left before July 7," he had written, then told them what he had gone through to escape Beijing.

The second was to Sung Hwa in San Francisco. "When you return from White Stone, you'll find this letter waiting for you, telling you that your friend has not forgotten the day in the Park of the Sun Altar . . ."

The third letter was addressed to Yenan, to Hu May. Aaron had received a letter from May, mailed on the day before she left Beijing. She had told him about her meeting Li Kwanjin, and apologized for not visiting Aaron as promised.

"From now on, please write me in Yenan, to this address, in care of Li Kwanjin. I am very happy, because finally I have a chance to become useful to our country," she had said in her letter. "You may be too young to understand love, Aaron, but I have fallen in love with this handsome, proud, intelligent man. . . ."

Aaron laid the letters on the dining table and pulled out a chair. He sat, leaned his elbows on the table, and rested his head in his palms. He looked at the letters and thought how wrong Hu May was about his being too young to know love.

When he had left Hong Kong for his grandfather's funeral, he didn't know love. Had it been in Jasmine Valley that he began to search for Yin's sweet smile? Or was it in Shanghai that he had felt an emptiness in his heart when unable to look into Yin's dark eyes? Perhaps it was in Nanjing that he had called Yin's name and longed to hear her voice answering him immediately. But it also could have been in Beijing, when he wanted to share with Yin the sight of the Forbidden City and then became sad when he realized she was so far away.

Aaron remembered last winter, when he had seen Wong Yin for the first time.

"I never lived through a winter this cold in Jasmine Valley!" Meiping said to the children as the three came out of the theater, standing among the crowd, looking for their chauffeur.

All of a sudden Rachel screamed, "Mama! I stepped on something! It moved!"

Aaron laughed. "So you stepped on a stray cat or a homeless dog. What's there to scream about?"

The lights outside the theater were off and the sidewalk was very dark. But then came the light of a passing car, revealing a tiny human form wrapped in torn clothes and curled into a ball.

"Kindhearted people, please don't call the police." A faint, shivering voice reached the ears of the Cohens. "I'll crawl out of your way."

The chauffeur parked the car and came forward holding a flashlight. "I'm sorry to have kept you waiting. Allow me to show you the way."

Meiping and Rachel picked their way through the littered sidewalk to the car. Aaron took another look at that pathetic little face, then grabbed the flashlight from the chauffeur. A circle of yellow light shone on a female child with two messy long pigtails. Her dirty face was badly bruised, her eyes frightened, wounded. Dried blood covered one of her ears. A handful of hair was gone from her forehead; it seemed that someone had pulled it out by force.

In the light, her trembling lips opened, crying for mercy but not really making a sound. She then raised a shaking hand to shield herself from the blinding torch and expected blow. The light gleamed on a dirty hand that was cut and scratched. Some of the injuries had developed pus, and the yellow liquid, mixed with blood, dripped slowly down one skinny arm.

Aaron and Rachel had always lived in a world untouched by the cruel hands of misfortune. When Aaron was a child in San Francisco, the struggling people in Chinatown were but a remote shadow, moving vaguely in his eyes. When he was older, in Hong Kong, the cries of the poor beneath Victoria Peak were merely the sighs of the faraway tide, murmuring indistinctly in his ears. At this moment the cruel picture of a suffering child was thrust upon him, forcing him to accept its existence. Staring at it, his vision widened and his glass dome shattered, he could never be the same again. For the first time he saw the world as a place racked with sorrow, and he wished earnestly to make it better.

"Mama," Aaron said, "we can't leave her on the street!"

Meiping gave in to Aaron's plea, and stayed on the sidewalk to question the girl.

The child answered in a small voice, "My name is Wong Yin, and I am twelve. My home is in a small village in the New Territory, across the bridge from Kowloon. My Baba died. My wid-

owed uncle wanted Mama to marry him. Mama
didn't want to marry Baba's brother, but my
grandparents said she must become my uncle's
bride because they were too poor to pay for their
remaining son to marry a woman outside the family. Mama couldn't fight them. She hanged herself
the night before the wedding. Then I heard my
grandparents talking about selling me to the landlord, who was very cruel to his servant girls. I
ran away from the village to Kowloon. I sneaked
on the ferry, and the police caught me when the
boat docked in Hong Kong. They beat me hard
for stealing a ride."

Aaron insisted on taking Yin home, and Rachel
used her sympathetic tears to help persuade
Meiping. Before the night was over, one more
young maid was added to the Cohens' many servants. From then on Aaron watched the skinny
child putting on weight, and waited for the frightened look to disappear from her moon face. Bit
by bit, the wounded kitten became a fluffy, happy
cat. Step by step, the injured girl changed into a
cheerful, pretty maid.

A pretty maid entered with a tray. "Good
morning, Sisan," Wong Yin said cheerfully in the
Pearl River dialect.

"Good morning," Aaron murmured, unable to
take his eyes from the girl's small round face,
which glowed like a full moon. Her eyes smiled
at him through dark, narrow long slits. Her lips,
full and moist, parted inquisitively to reveal a row
of white but slightly crooked teeth. She was wearing a servant's uniform—black pants and white
blouse. Her young body was like a ripe fruit, with
a deliciousness that couldn't be concealed by the
simple garment. As she bent to set the food on
the table, her small round breasts pressed against

her blouse. The sight sent a thrill of excitement through Aaron. He looked away from her chest and tried to make conversation.

"Yin . . ." he said softly while kneading his aching temples. This morning, a headache had troubled him since he opened his eyes. "What does your name mean? I don't believe I ever asked," Like many of the prestigious schools in Hong Kong, the one on Victoria Peak used English as an official language. Aaron knew very few Chinese characters or what they represented.

"The petal of a flower," the girl said, placing a bowl of oatmeal in front of her young master. "The village scholar named me, since my parents couldn't read."

"A flower petal . . ." Aaron repeated after her, then stopped. He had not been feeling well since yesterday. Last night he had slept many hours, but now he still felt tired. Suddenly, as if someone had poured a bucket of ice water over his back, he was shocked by a freezing cold sensation.

"Sisan, are you all right?" Yin watched him shiver and was scared by his colorless face and bloodshot eyes. She had never seen her young master looking so bad.

Aaron tried to nod. The mere movement of his head made him hurt all over. "Little flower petal, I think I'm sick," he mumbled in a hoarse voice, then felt the urgent need of the bathroom. He pushed back the chair to get up, but his legs were made of cotton and unable to support him. He held on to the edge of the table, but the table slipped quickly away from him.

"Sisan!" he heard Yin scream. He looked toward her and saw her face become part of a merry-go-round—Yin, the chandelier, the window, the paintings on the wall, then Yin again.

"Stand still!" he yelled, and the yelling set his

throat on fire. "Can't you see you're making me dizzy?"

He fell slowly. The last things he saw were a leg of the table and Yin's feet in black cotton shoes.

"Typhoid fever is usually caused by the *Salmonella typhosa* bacterium," said the English doctor. "It is highly transmissible through contaminated food or water. Dairy products and undercooked meats are the most common sources."

Meiping's face whitened. The ices! The melons! And the meat buns! "But it has been several weeks since we ate them," she whispered, thinking of the lost charm, wondering: had the gold Buddha been on her bracelet, would her son be ill now?

The aged doctor shook his white head. Because of his devotion to medicine, he was intolerant of people's carelessness. He had been in Hong Kong for a long time, but still couldn't understand the ignorance of the Chinese. He wouldn't have made the house call but for the fact that David Cohen was a well-known businessman and also white.

"Such sickness usually develops after an incubation period of one or two weeks. But at times it can be delayed for a few more weeks after exposure." The doctor turned from Meiping to David. "Your son must be hospitalized immediately. To confirm my diagnosis, I need to do a culture of his blood and stool, and then a few tests." He looked at the rose-colored maculas on Aaron's skin and added, "But I'm almost certain now that it's typhoid fever."

All of a sudden David looked every minute of his sixty-seven years. "Doctor, will my son be all right?" he asked in a weak voice.

The doctor shrugged. "It's hard to tell. Effective

drugs have been found, but it depends on the physical condition of the patient. I've seen the weak Chinese die of it like ants in a flood. Since your son is half white, he may be strong enough to survive." He glanced at Meiping, watching the tears streaming down her cheeks. It had to be this Chinese woman's fault, and he was angry with her. "You took the boy to some filthy place to eat your favorite food, am I right?"

"You are not right!" Meiping shouted. "We were running away from the Japanese, in a hot, crowded train . . ." She bit her lip. It would be foolish to argue with the best doctor in Hong Kong, since Aaron's life was in his hands. "I'll go pack his things for the hospital," she said, and walked away.

Three weeks later Aaron returned home thin and frail. He was tucked in bed and left alone by his family. He waited impatiently until he heard the footsteps of Wong Yin, and smiled when he saw her standing at the door.

"I knew it was you. No one else wears those soft shoes," he said, then yelled at the sight of her face. "Were you sick too? What happened to your beautiful hair?"

Wong Yin had lost so much weight that she looked almost as pitiful as she had last winter. Her pigtails were gone. Her hair was cropped so short that she could be mistaken for a boy. She inched her way to Aaron's bed, stood there twisting her fingers and looking at the floor. Trembling, in a voice low she asked, "Are you really and truly safe from the icy fingers of the Death Buddha?"

"That's one Buddha I've never heard of. He must be one of those nasty ones who will visit you when you mention his name—or so my mother believes." Aaron shook his head. "I'm out of danger, but I still need to go back to the doctor periodically for the next six months to be sure that I'm not harboring the microbes." He saw the girl's confused look, then added, "Yes, I'm really and truly out of reach of the Death Buddha."

Wong Yin breathed with relief. She clasped her hands in front of her heart, palms together, and looked up to heaven. "Thank you, Buddha, for accepting my offer. Tonight I'm going to eat some rice."

Aaron stared at her. "What are you talking about?"

She looked at him in disbelief. "What do they teach you in school? Don't you know anything at all?" When Aaron continued to stare at her, she explained, "Everybody knows that the hair of a virgin is favored by the Death Buddha, especially when she offers it to him together with a few drops of her blood. And then she must not eat anything until the person she is praying for is completely well—"

She was interrupted by Aaron. "Blood? What blood?"

Yin answered casually, "You know, take a needle, punch a hole in your finger, and squeeze out a few drops of blood. After the blood falls on the hair that's been cut off, you burn the hair and send up it to the Buddha. Actually, it's not much of an offering at all, when compared with cutting off a piece of your own flesh, boiling it in water, and feeding the broth and meat to the patient."

Aaron felt sick to his stomach as he tried to remember whether he had tasted anything funny in the past few weeks. He felt better when he recalled the simple diet he had been on.

Yin went on, "A virgin's hair will change the Buddha's mind about grabbing someone. But when the Buddha already has someone in his cold fingers, we must try the human-meat soup." She rolled up her sleeve, showing Aaron an old scar on her forearm. "My Baba was sick. Both mama and I cut ourselves. Two bowls of soup were made and set in front of the statue of the Death Buddha. The steam went up to heaven, and the cooled soup was forced down Baba's throat." Yin's eyes teared. "But Buddha didn't accept our offer. He didn't let go of my poor Baba. Baba vomited the soup and died."

"And what's this about not eating rice?" Aaron asked helplessly. He had seen his father trying in vain to understand his mother's culture. Now he knew exactly how his father felt.

"It is much more than not eating rice. I haven't eaten anything solid since you went to the hospital. I drank water and soup, leaving the meat and vegetables out. I became weak, and rather dizzy at times. But it worked." She smiled at Aaron shyly, then returned her eyes to the floor. "I'm so happy to see you home."

"I'm glad the Death Buddha didn't ask for a larger bribe from you." Aaron swallowed hard, then mumbled in English, "May there be no more ridiculous new ideas from the heads of the ignorant Chinese!"

He reached a hand toward Yin, looking into her eyes, and resumed in the Pearl River dialect, "Did you starve yourself and sacrifice your hair for me to perform the duty of a loyal servant? Or was there a better reason?"

Yin put her hand in Aaron's reluctantly. She bowed her head lower. Her pale neck was like the stem of a flower in the rising sun, turning red swiftly. The color reached her cheeks, and she tried to pull her hand away. "Well, it's more than duty, although you are my master and I am your

servant . . ." Her voice was barely audible. "You
are so good to me, and I . . . well, I would rather
the Death Buddha take me than you." With that,
she freed herself and ran from the room.

"Be sure to eat something!" Aaron shouted
after her. "And please let your hair grow!"

He was very tired. He closed his eyes and
smiled. He had no doubt now that she felt the
same way toward him as he did toward her. But
what a silly girl! When he was strong enough, he
would begin to share with her his western education. At least he knew that Buddhas never wore
wigs and therefore had no use for the long hair
of a virgin.

Two weeks later, when Aaron was able to walk
around the house with the help of Yin, Rachel
became sick.

At first she had only a dull headache, and was
able to joke about it. "Some mischievous little
monster is playing Tinkertoys inside my head,
waving a hammer continuously."

Then she became very sleepy and lost all her
energy. She stayed drowsy day and night, unable
to get out of bed. Then she began to run a fever.

The same doctor was called, and she was taken
to the hospital immediately.

Rachel's temperature kept rising for the next
few days, until it reached 105 and stayed there.
The medication that helped Aaron was not func-
tioning on her, and her temperature stayed high,
like a flame incinerating, burning a fragile flower
to ashes.

In the beginning, she could still vomit into the
tray that was held by Meiping, and was able to
use the bedpan for the constant diarrhea. Then
she became delirious, and couldn't tell her mother
her physical needs. She opened her mouth to

make gagging sounds, but there was nothing in her stomach. Yellow water dripped out of her lips, dirtied her chin and one side of her face. A rumbling sound came from her lower abdomen, and the room was filled with an awful stench. Her sheets were soiled many times a day, and when the nurse changed her, Rachel remained unconscious.

She jerked every few minutes, as her body was tortured by an invisible demon with merciless hands. Her lovely eyes were wide open all the time, but she saw nobody and nothing. Her beautiful lips opened to wail soundlessly, letting out silent screams, pleading for relief from her great agony.

"Do something!" Meiping took the doctor by the shoulders and shook him. "She is suffering so much! You must give her medication to ease her pain!"

"You should never have fed her the contaminated food!" The doctor looked at Meiping coldly. "There is nothing I can do to save her or make her feel better now."

"What do you mean?" Aaron stepped forward, clenching his fists at the doctor. "If I can recover from typhoid fever, so can my sister."

The man shook his head. "You are ten times stronger than she. She has no strength at all. I guess you are like your father, while your sister is only a feeble Chinese girl."

Aaron was ready to punch the doctor when David placed himself between the physician and the angry young man. "Please, Doctor . . ." his voice was shaking but under control. "Watch what you are saying, or I'm not responsible for my son's actions." He held Meiping tightly in his arms. He looked at Rachel and had to hold back his tears. "Doctor, only a few people in Hong

Kong are against interracial marriages, but you are obviously one of them. Please, can you just save my daughter and forget prejudice?"

Rachel's body jerked again. Her staring eyes widened in pain. Tears filled David's eyes, then streamed down his deeply wrinkled cheeks. Meiping buried her face against his chest, muffling a scream. Aaron went closer to Rachel, wishing to take his sister's place. If he had been a virgin girl, he would have cut off all his hair without hesitation. It was impossible for Rachel to take in any food now. Otherwise he wouldn't mind making her a bowl of soup with his own flesh. He now realized why his mother's people had such beliefs: when a loved one was about to be taken away by the hands of death, a person would do anything to keep the last thread of hope from breaking.

The doctor was finally touched by the family's torment. He sighed. "Well, of course I'm doing my best to save her. It's just that she was very delicate to begin with." He turned to Meiping. "Mrs. Cohen, forgive me. I should not have accused you of being careless. People do become sick, even when they are very cautious."

The doctor tried two more drugs on Rachel, but neither was effective against the disease. David, Meiping, and Aaron stayed beside Rachel all the time, watching a beautiful flower dropping its petals, a lovely butterfly flapping its broken wings. Their hearts ached, but there was nothing they could do.

A week later, with her family standing around her, Rachel suddenly regained consciousness. She focused her eyes and turned to Meiping, trying to say something, but a jolt of unbearable pain took away her strength. Her eyes began to lose their focus, and she stopped breathing.

*   *   *

"This is not fair!" Aaron screamed in the car, hitting his thighs with his fists. The funeral was over, and the Cohens were being driven home from the cemetery. "Why Rachel? Why my sister? She never harmed anybody! Why is such a perfect life destroyed so mercilessly? Why?"

David and Meiping didn't answer their son. For the first time, there was no strength left in David, and Meiping felt very old. They leaned against each other, holding hands, intertwining their fingers.

Meiping sobbed loudly. David took her in both arms, and didn't bother to dry his own tears. He felt her trembling in his embrace. Her sorrow was like a stabbing knife, adding more wounds to his aged heart, already pierced by Rachel's death.

Without looking at Aaron, David whispered, "Please. You're not helping your mother."

Aaron looked at David's sagging shoulders and felt like his father had slapped him on the face. He was suddenly awakened by the blow. "I'm sorry, Baba," he said, but couldn't find enough words to express how ashamed he was. An old man was trying to bury his sorrow and lend comfort to his wife, while a young man was complaining and crying like a baby.

It was a long way from the graveyard to their home. With each mile, Aaron grew a little. By the time they reached Victoria Peak, he walked calmly on the other side of his mother, helping his father to guide her up the front steps. Once inside the house, with her husband and son supporting her, Meiping started to walk from room to room.

In the music room she ran her fingers over the piano keys. "Rachel, please come home and play your favorite tunes."

In the dining room she pulled Rachel's chair

carefully away from the table. "Baby, please join us at each meal."

She then stumbled up the stairs and entered Rachel's bedroom. "Your sheets will be changed regularly, and a lamp will always be shining beside your window. You won't have trouble finding your way home, I hope!"

She fell to her knees, covered her face with both hands, and her words were muffled by her trembling fingers. "Baby, if there is anything else you need, please let Mama know by coming to her dreams."

Aaron and David stood helplessly beside Meiping, both crying and wishing to be more useful.

"Tai-tai, it's time for tea, and Sheo-jay's favorite cake is steaming hot." Yin appeared at the door, holding a tray. She then went to the small table and started to set it for four.

Meiping struggled to her feet. "We mustn't let the cake become cold," she said, looking at the empty chair. "You don't like cold food, Rachel."

David and Aaron exchanged a sad glance, finding it hard to share the Chinese belief. Death was supposed to be the mere destruction of the physical body, and the spirit was expected to continue in its usual existence—it would return to the loved ones every day to eat, to play, and to sleep.

Through the tea, Aaron and David watched Yin and Meiping make believe that Rachel was with them. They were grateful to Yin for helping Meiping to take in nutrition, and decided not to discourage the game.

12

WHEN THE MOON moved to mid-sky, a group of students came out of Punahou School in Honolulu.

The night classes had ended. Those enrolled were working adults interested in furthering their education. They varied in age; Michiko Yamada was one of the youngest.

She walked between two Japanese girls older than she. They were wearing western clothes; Michiko was in a soft green kimono. The three of them conversed in English.

One of them pointed at the school sign over the entrance gate. "We ought to be grateful to the founder, who built Punahou for the children of the immigrant planters."

Michiko's other friend nodded. "It was mean of the white people to discourage us from becoming more than laborers. Now we have our own school. We Asians will soon become professors and businessmen, doctors and lawyers."

Michiko said proudly, "I will become an attorney someday. When I receive my license to practice, I'll go to the sugarcane fields to tell all the girls that if their foremen should treat them viciously, they must not be afraid to report the crimes. I'll represent them free of charge."

She stopped at the first lamppost on the palm-lined street. It was the usual place she waited for Jebu.

"We'd better wait with you," one of the other girls said. "Since the war started in China, the Chinese in Hawaii have been picking fights with the Japanese." She looked at Michiko's kimono. "I don't think you should stand on a quiet street alone."

"No, thank you," Michiko said. "Jebu will be here any minute now."

Her friends were gone. Michiko looked at the deserted street and wished her husband would appear soon. He took his job seriously, and often worked overtime. Michiko never complained. The majority of the Asian immigrants worked diligently, even when they didn't like their work. She and Jebu were fortunate to be employed by Quanming. They were paid well and were doing things they enjoyed, Jebu in the coral factory, she in the administrative office.

Michiko leaned against the lamppost and waited patiently. When, fifteen minutes later, Jebu still hadn't arrived, she became a little bored. She put all her books in one hand, opened her purse, and took out three letters. She had already read them before, but she read each one once again by the lamplight.

Aaron's sister's death saddened her. She could tell from his letter that Aaron had matured a great deal in a short time. May's marriage brought a smile to her face. Jebu and she had mailed a silver plate to Yenan as a wedding present. Michiko was happy for Sung Hwa. She wondered if he would marry Melin and bring her to Hawaii to meet Hwa's father, Quanming.

"Ba-ga-ya-lu!" someone shouted from the other side of the street.

Michiko looked up and saw three men in the shadow of the palms. She knew immediately that they were Chinese. Since the Japanese had invaded China, the Chinese in Hawaii yelled *Ba-ga-ya-lu* at everyone in kimono, trying to imitate a Japanese curse word.

"It's all my father-in-law's fault!" Michiko murmured, and quickly put away the letters and grabbed her purse tightly. Heroshi had insisted that the Yamada women wear kimonos, regardless of the animosity of the Chinese all over Oahu island. *Instead of obeying him, I should have had a mind of my own!*

It was too late to blame anyone. The three men were approaching her, one with clenched fists, the others holding some kind of weapons behind their backs.

"Stop where you are, you stupid fools!" Michiko yelled. "You know as well as I, I have nothing to do with the war in China."

The one with clenched fists reached Michiko first. He pushed her hard. She tried to balance herself, but dropped all her books.

The man yelled in Michiko's face, "I guess you are as faultless as the Chinese women in all the villages. But the Japanese soldiers raped them just the same!"

Michiko stood with her back against the post. She held her purse in front of her and attempted to hide the fear in her heart. "The Japanese military men don't represent the true Japanese," she tried to explain in a quavering voice. "Especially the low-ranked men in the front line. Most of them are criminals, pardoned from death row because they were willing to become soldiers . . ."

She stopped when the lamplight glinted off the long knife held in the second man's hand. She flinched when the man waved the knife in front of her face.

The man said with deep hatred in his voice, "Your people raped our women, then used knives

like this to cut off their breasts and private parts.
My friends and I believe it is the duty of us Chinese to catch some Japanese women and give
them a taste of their own medicine."

"No!" Michiko screamed. She brought the purse
up to protect her face. "You didn't hear a word I
said! I'm not responsible for those crazy soldiers!
Not even our Emperor is responsible for them!
The Emperor of Japan tried to stop them from
invading China, but the military men have much
greater power—"

"Shut up and take off your clothes!" yelled the
third man as he revealed two clubs connected by
a short chain. He held one club and swung the
other, hitting Michiko on the head.

The pain was so severe that Michiko held the
lamppost to keep from falling. Her ears were ringing and she lost her vision. She let go of her
purse, while trying to reason with her attackers
in a voice that had become unclear. "Please . . .
come to your senses. You and I . . . are neither
in China nor in Japan. We shouldn't be . . . involved in the war. . . ."

The man hit her once more. She felt a sharp
pain on her shoulder, lost her grasp of the post,
and fell to the ground.

Vaguely she heard her husband's voice coming
from a distance.

Jebu ran toward the three men, looked at their
faces, and couldn't believe his eyes. "It's the three
of you!" He was shocked. "You attacked my
wife!"

Jebu and the three men worked together in the
coral factory. They were the divers who brought
to him seaweed-covered coral by the truckload.
He cleaned the coral, polished away the sharp
edges, then cut the large pieces to various sizes

according to the different items to be made, following Heroshi's design. He and the three of them often shared lunch, and always joked together.

The three men seemed embarrassed. The raised fists were lowered, the clubs put away, the sharp knife was quickly out of sight. They looked at Jebu, exchanged looks among themselves, and then the one with the clubs murmured, "Well, we didn't know she was your wife. All we saw was a Jap in a kimono."

Jebu was now squatting beside Michiko. "It's all my fault. I'm sorry. If only I wasn't late, these bastards wouldn't have touched you."

Jebu saw the dark spot on her pale kimono. It was blood dripping from her head. He was frightened and enraged. "What did you do to her? You hit her? With your clubs? Are you proud of yourselves? Three armed men beating a defenseless woman! So this is how you Chinese behave! You shameless weaklings!"

Jebu's words angered the three men. The many jokes no longer existed in their memory, the numerous lunches were completely forgotten.

"Now, you wait a minute!" The one with the knife raised his voice. "You better wash your mouth first. We are neither bastards nor weaklings. So she is your wife. What about the millions of wives of our people in China? Those women are beaten, raped, and cut to pieces by the soldiers from your country. We have quite a few names for you and your ancestors!"

'You Japanese are the East Sea Devils! The short-limbed monsters! The bowlegged bastards!" shouted the man with the clubs, and the clubs were raised once again.

The other man's fists were once more clenched and ready. He said, "You Japanese stole culture from China, then claimed the culture as your own. My history book tells me that your ancestors were criminals exiled by a Chinese emperor, put to sea to perish. Their ship landed on a little strip of land, and they built their lowly kingdom there."

Jebu tried to wake up Michiko but couldn't. He rocked her, patted her face gently, called her name repeatedly. She didn't move, nor did she open her eyes. Fear filled Jebu's heart. He wanted nothing more than to carry her to a hospital. He put his arms under her body, tried to lift her from the ground.

Jebu stood up slowly, carrying Michiko. But he kept arguing with the three, trying to hurt them because they had not only hurt his wife but also insulted his people. "Because of our samurai spirit, when the Japanese soldiers march into a Chinese village, they expect to see every good man defending his motherland, even if he is bare-handed and with no chance to win. The Japanese soldiers also assume that when the last man is killed, every good woman will slash her own throat before anybody else can lay his hands on her."

Jebu walked a few steps away from the three men, saying with his back turned toward them, "Anybody running for his life and begging for mercy is considered less than human in the eyes of a Japanese soldier. So you Chinese are, in the eyes of the Japanese soldiers, merely pigs who deserve to die in the cruelest ways. From what I heard, your women were raped. Your babies were thrown into the air and caught on their way down on the tips of our soldiers' sharp bayonets. And their death was the result of their own cowardliness—"

Jebu didn't have a chance to finish. His three former friends didn't allow this humiliation to go any further. They stabbed him, hit him with the clubs, and kicked and punched him.

Jebu fell to his knees, holding Michiko. He took the brutality, never had a chance to fight back, because he used his hands and his body to shield his wife as much as he could.

Two policeman passed Punahou School and saw four men fighting, three against one.

Three of them ran away at the sight of the police; the remaining one stumbled a few steps, then fell and lay unable to move.

When the police went to the wounded man, they found under his protective body the body of an unconscious woman.

The three runaways were arrested. Jebu and Michiko were taken to a hospital. When their identities were discovered, three families were notified. The Yamadas, the Ikedas, and the Sungs rushed to the emergency room, where they were told that the doctors were examining Michiko and Jebu. They lingered anxiously in the waiting room.

The Ikedas sat like two statues with downcast eyes. Mr. Ikeda's brows were knotted tightly, Mrs. Ikeda's face was white. Other than that, their worry for their daughter and son-in-law was hidden behind their pride—the descendants of samurais must not show emotion in public. Only those who knew them well could tell from his clenched hands and her tightened lips that they were in turmoil, that they loved their daughter although they had kept her at a distance since the day she ran away.

Kiko Yamada sobbed quietly on Laurie's shoulder. Ever since arriving at the hospital, Laurie had held Kiko, comforted the frightened mother with all the kind words she could think of.

"Jebu and Michiko will be all right," Laurie said again, trying to sound convincing. "The police arrived in time."

A few steps away, Sung Quanming and Heroshi Yamada stood side by side, looking out the window at a moonlit garden, exchanging hushed words.

Heroshi recounted what the police had reported. "They stabbed Jebu twice on the arms and broke several ribs. They hit Michiko on the head and shoulder but don't seem to have touched her elsewhere." He paused, then said philosophically, "If the doctors don't find any internal injuries, then the three Chinese didn't really take much revenge, when their action is compared to what my people did in your country."

"But that's different!" Quanming argued. "War is madness. Soldiers at war are lunatics. Hawaii is not a war zone, and the way the three people attacked Michiko and Jebu is unforgivable. I will fire them from my factory when they come out of jail."

Heroshi looked at Quanming for a long time, then slowly shook his head. "Have you noticed we are arguing the wrong way? Neither of us is very patriotic. You and I should try to kill each other, since all the other Japanese and Chinese seem to be doing it." He thought for a while, then said, "Between friends, three things are best left unmentioned—politics, religion, and racial differences. Shall we stop talking about the war, and concentrate on praying for Jebu and Michiko?"

Quanming nodded. They continued to stare across the peaceful garden under the moon, at a statue of Buddha that stood beside a pagoda. Behind them the Ikedas sat tensely; Kiko sobbed, and Laurie whispered.

The door to the emergency room opened. A doctor appeared in green uniform. He removed his green mask and announced to no one in particular, "Neither Jebu nor Michiko suffered any permanent injury. They are going to be fine."

The Ikedas jumped up from their chairs, ran to the doctor, put their arms around the surprised man, and squeezed him tightly.

Before the doctor had a chance to say anything to the Ikedas, the couple let go of the man, bowed deeply to him, then returned to their seats. They were embarrassed to have shown emotion. They sat with their chins touching their chests, not uttering a word. They waited for their daughter and son-in-law to come out of the emergency room, but swore silently that they would never let the children know that they had worried.

Kiko cried in Laurie's arms, keeping her face pressed against Laurie's chest, hiding her happy tears from the men. Laurie patted Kiko on the back, saying repeatedly. "They are all right. I knew they would be. I knew it all the time!"

Quanming and Heroshi, a Chinese and a Japanese, held each other in their trembling arms, regardless of the fact that across the Pacific the Japanese-Chinese War raged on.

13

SUNG HWA LEFT the White Stone Hotel holding the sandalwood Buddha given to him by his mother. He couldn't find a better gift for Melin that represented his eternal love.

He had never known that he could love so deeply, with his every heartbeat and every breath. Melin had become a vital part of his spirit and the best part of his soul. Compared with his love for Melin, what had happened between him and Judy was but a meaningless infatuation. He realized now that he had never truly loved Judy, had proposed marriage only because the two of them had shared the pillow for one night. There was enough Chinese in him to make him feel that he must carry out his moral responsibility. His pride had been hurt when she turned him down, but nothing else.

"If Melin hurts me, the injury will be fatal," he said as he walked toward the Pearl River, but he wore a confident smile.

The sun disappeared gradually as Hwa neared the Pearl. The moon, bright and round like a paper lantern, appeared on its heavenly throne, becoming more dazzling as it resumed rule over its enchanting domain. "Life is marvelous when you love and are loved by the most beautiful girl on earth. The world is fantastic when both of you know that your love will last as long as the sun will shine and the moon will glow."

Hwa leaned against a willow tree and waited patiently. Besides the old temple, the riverbank had become their favorite meeting place. "We won't be sneaking around much longer," Hwa said to two birds flying side by side to their nest. "Melin and I will fly away together just like the two of you. We'll build a lovely nest somewhere. Our happiness will exceed yours, and you and every other living being in this universe will envy us—the luckiest couple."

He caught himself and quickly added, "Never mind, I take back my words . . . we'll not be envied by anybody at all!" He started to laugh. "Well, I've become as superstitious as a true Chinese. Melin is a good teacher."

The teaching had traveled both ways. Melin had taught Hwa calligraphy and Chinese philosophy, while Hwa taught her English and western culture. They both learned quickly because his craving for Chinese manners was as strong as her curiosity about American customs.

Hwa's heart was filled with joy as he remembered the conversation between them last night.

"When we are married, our children will be experts in the enlightenment of both worlds," Hwa had said after Melin promised to elope with him soon. They knew that her father would never agree to annul her engagement and permit her to marry an outsider.

Melin had blushed at the mention of children. They had met every day in the undisturbed temple, stayed for hours closely and all alone, but never gone beyond holding hands and a kiss now and then. Bowing her head, Melin had said, "After our first child is born, we can come back

to White Stone, and my parents may forgive us
when they see the child."

Hwa looked up at the moon and dreamed about
their future. He didn't care whether Melin's parents ever forgave them. He had compared China
with America and decided that the best place for
building a love nest was not in this troubled land.
They would live far from China, and visit her parents only occasionally. He would take Melin to
Hawaii to visit Quanming and Laurie, then to San
Francisco to see A-lin and Moa Lau. Melin would
choose between her in-laws, and if she didn't
want to be close to either one, Hwa would take
her somewhere else to find a home.

"It doesn't matter where we live," Sung Hwa
said as he listened to the birds chirping in the
foliage of the willow. "Wherever Melin is, is my
heaven."

He held the statue of Buddha, rubbed its fat
stomach, and waited faithfully.

"Mama, are you feeling any better?" Melin
asked, standing beside the bed, looking at her
mother.

Yoto nodded, breathing hard. The pain in her
chest was receding, but her whole left side was
numb. "Where is everybody else?" she asked,
searching the richly furnished large bedchamber.

Melin lowered her eyes. "Well, they are busy."
She didn't want to tell her mother the truth. Everyone had been present when Yoto fainted during dinner. But Ma Tsai-tu had left hurriedly
before the doctor's arrival, and the three boys
soon followed their father's example.

Yoto understood what Melin was trying to do.
Her husband and sons were never busy; they just
didn't care. "Where is Suelin?"

Melin sighed, looking up with a frown. "Her

husband came. He snapped his fingers, and she followed him home. The bruises from his fists haven't faded from her body, but she has already forgiven him, as usual."

Yoto smiled at her daughter weakly. "She has no choice. A woman never has any choice." She pointed at the side of her bed and waited for Melin to sit. She then raised a shaking hand to touch the young woman's face. "I hope your fate is better than your sister's."

"Mama," Melin said softly. She took her mother's hand in hers, looking at the two large rings on the puffed white fingers. One jade, one ruby, glittered in the colors of good luck and happiness, contrasting the life of their owner. "Can a woman's fate be held in her own hands?"

Yoto's eyes narrowed. She studied her daughter suspiciously. "What do you mean?"

"I . . ." Melin stopped. Sung Hwa had told her to keep their plans an absolute secret. "All I meant was, if the girls in China were allowed to choose their own husbands, would Suelin have chosen a different man? Would her fate be better then?"

The mother shook her head. "No. Wisdom comes with age. The parents are always wiser than the children, and their choices are the better ones."

Melin couldn't help saying quickly. "But you and Baba have obviously made the wrong choice for Suelin."

Yoto said firmly, "We have chosen for her the best young man in our objective eyes. The rest is up to fate, which is held in the hands of Buddha." She looked out the window. The evening sky was gray. A pale moon appeared over the courtyard. "Buddha may grant a woman a fate that is much worse than having a husband who beats her."

Again Melin said without hesitation, "I can't imagine that."

"That's because you are very young and you think life should be perfect. But as you age, you'll learn differently." Yoto's voice was faint. Her eyes were on the first stars scattered dimly around the full bright moon. "Life is but an endless heartache." She closed her eyes, and her voice began to fade. "Why, a man can walk away from you, taking with him all your youthful dreams." A tear fell from the corner of her eyelid, rolling down the deep crease that marked her once smooth face.

Melin dried her mother's tear, then waited for Yoto to sink into a deep sleep. She tiptoed back to her own room, changed into a pink blouse and a white skirt, then left the house.

She was grateful for the changing times. When her mother was young, a rich girl in China was never allowed to leave the courtyard without the company of a personal maid. She walked quickly. When the sky was dark blue, the lantern moon intensified its glow, and the stars shimmered clearly, she reached the Pearl River.

"Melin!" Sung Hwa called from behind a tree. "You're late and I was worried."

"I'm sorry," Melin apologized, running toward Sung Hwa.

No one else was at the riverbank. Still, Melin looked around nervously as Hwa kissed her. In his arms, she explained, "My mother is sick. The doctor said she had a minor heart attack. My father and brothers were gone—probably visiting the singsong girls in some teahouse. Suelin left with her husband. I had to stay with Mama until she was asleep, or she would have been left with only her maid."

"Is she all right now?" Hwa knew how close Melin and her mother were to each other.

"I don't know. She can't move the left side of her body very well. But she never moves much anyway." Melin's frown was driven away by a smile. A young heart didn't stay worried for long. "The new doctor in town suggested something funny."

She went on to tell Hwa that the young doctor had been educated in the United States of America. The villagers didn't trust him because he never used anything like tree roots or lizard skins for medicine. The rich families called on him, but the women were uncomfortable with him when he did more than feel their pulses and look at their tongues.

"My mother used to trust him. But I don't think he'll be asked to make any more calls to our home." Melin giggled. "He told her that in order to stay healthy, she must lose some weight. He said that fats puts too much burden on a person's heart. He disapproved of her idle life-style. He asked her to exercise!" Melin laughed. "I can't imagine my mother moving around like a servant and eating very little meat. Why, everybody in China knows that fat is a sign of good health and prosperity. Only the starving poor are skinny at Mama's age." She continued to laugh happily in the arms of Sung Hwa, and her face glowed in the moonlight.

The moon shone on the Pearl, coating the water with its silvery beams. The soft rays made Melin's image too beautiful to be true, and Hwa had to make sure that she was more than a dream. He held her face in his hands, kissing her ardently. "Don't worry about leaving your mother," he said in between kisses, "After we are away from White Stone, we'll write to her from Hong Kong. We'll visit a friend called Aaron Cohen, then get married there. We'll write to your mother again from Hawaii, when we're having our honeymoon and visiting my father."

Hwa's voice was gentle like a whisper, but at the same time filled with strong passion. "My father will never believe you are mine. He left me when he thought I was a worthless, lazy son. It will not take him long to realize that you are a little magician. My darling Melin, you waved a golden wand at me and changed me back into the respectable, honest boy my father loved."

He looked at Melin with pride, then continued with confidence, "My father will be happy for me, until he starts to feel envious. He is successful in many ways, but not as successful as I in the most important aspect of life—marriage. He and my mother were never happy. He loves his second wife, but he'll have to admit when he looks at you that Laurie cannot compare. There is a saying: 'A person cannot be more cultured than his country.' Like China, you are a precious gem polished by a tradition that is nearly five thousand years old. But like America, Laurie is only a rough stone that is barely refined."

Melin pushed Sung Hwa away a little to look into his eyes. The triumphant glow puzzled her. "Are you competing with your own father?"

Hwa answered slowly, "Well, it is important for me to know that I am better than he in some way."

Melin thought about it, then nodded. "I suppose I, too, have always wanted a husband better than my mother's." She covered her mouth quickly, correcting herself in a hurry. "I take that back. What right do I have to criticize my father? All I meant to say was that I hope you will treat me better than my father treats my mother." When her words failed to sound right to her own ears, she stamped her foot on the ground. "My father is not bad to my mother—nothing like my brother-in-law is to my sister. But he has many other women on the side, and I'll be very sad if you should behave the same. . . . Hwa, I can't wait to start our happy life."

"My precious Melin"—Sung Hwa held her tightly against his heart—"we'll leave White Stone the day after tomorrow. I'll be waiting for you here, at sunrise. From then on we'll have our lives together, and the whole world can be jealous of our love and happiness. . . . Damn! Here I go again!"

Melin laughed in his embrace. They held each other silently with their eyes closed, anticipating their marvelous future. They heard the wind traveling through the leaves, and the Pearl River rippling on. The cicadas prayed for a delayed winter, and a nightingale sang an old love song.

Melin broke the silence as she felt something hard in Hwa's pants pocket. "Are you carrying a bag of coins?"

Hwa remembered the statue of Buddha. Still holding her, he took it out of his pocket. "I was holding it while waiting for you. Then I put it away for fear of dropping it." He gave the statue to her, "Instead of a ring, may I offer you this as an engagement gift?"

Melin held the statue with both hands, studying Buddha's smiling face. "Thank you, Hwa. A Buddha is much more meaningful than a ring, especially when he has such a happy look. He'll protect us from sorrow, and we'll be as joyful as he throughout our married life." She giggled. "But please, my Great Buddha, don't let me become as fat as you and Mama."

"My mother gave this statue to me before I left

home," Hwa said, leading her away from the
Pearl River as the night wind became stronger
and colder. "I received a letter from her this
morning. She is very worried about my being in
China since the Japanese are taking over the
whole country. I wrote and told her I'll be home
soon with a delightful surprise."

"Thank you, Hwa, for giving me this gift from
your mother. I'll try to be a good daughter-in-law
to her. When she yells at me, I'll not say one
word in return."

"I don't want you to be *that* Chinese. If Mama
yells at you, please yell right back the way the
American children do," Hwa teased as they walked
toward town. It had become chilly in the deepening night, but neither of them was ready to part.

They walked slowly, talking about their future.
When they looked around, they found themselves
a long way from the river, almost in front of
Hwa's hotel.

"Your hands are cold," Hwa said. "Let's go in
and have some hot tea."

Melin nodded. When they were in the hotel
lobby, they saw that the restaurant was crowded.
"I can't go in," she said. "Someone will recognize
me and tell Baba."

Still not willing to part, they ascended the stairway and entered Hwa's room. With the door
closed behind them, they suddenly became aware
of the fact that it was night and they were in a
hotel room alone. Both of them looked at the bed,
and all of a sudden the bed grew bigger, the colors of the bedding louder.

Melin bowed her head, blushing deeply. Hwa's
heartbeat raced like the hooves of a running bull,
his entire body heated by an unseen fire.

He held her in his arms, and she hid her face
against his chest. He ran his fingers through her

hair, breathing in her perfume. He then held her away a little to look at her face. Her eyes were bright and watering like two mysterious lakes inviting him to dive into their beautiful terrain, her lips wet and parted like a blossoming flower asking a thirsty bee to enter its sweet domain.

Hwa kissed her first on the eyes, then on the lips. There was no monk to send out tranquil prayers, to stifle his young body's hungry cry. The riverbank was out of sight. There were no passersby to threaten him with their sudden intrusion and to muffle his young heart's strong desire. He kissed her harder and held her tighter, gradually moving his burning lips from her mouth to her neck, caressing one breast, then the other.

"Hwa . . ." she whispered, her voice quavering like birdsong in a strong wind. "Please . . ."

"We'll be married in just a few days. You'll be mine as soon as we arrive in Hong Kong. Please let me have you now, or I'll explode!" He lifted her up from her feet and carried her in his arms. "I love you, Melin. To me you are already my wife, and there is no reason for us to wait."

Melin saw herself being carried to the bed. The voice of tradition nagged in her ears: "Ma Melin, you are a good girl. A good girl should remain a virgin until her wedding night."

But the same tradition also told her that a woman must obey a man, especially the man who was soon to become her husband. Obeying Hwa was easier than disobeying, because her love for him was even stronger than tradition.

She felt Hwa's firm arms around her, like a sturdy wall, blocking away the sound of protest. She didn't struggle, but buried her face tightly against his heart and closed her eyes.

She didn't open her eyes when Hwa laid her on the bed. She shut them even tighter when his hands, burning and trembling but gentle and careful, began to unbutton her blouse.

She turned her head to one side when he removed her skirt and pulled off her pants. She sank her upper teeth into her lower lip when she felt his naked body next to hers in bed. He started to kiss her on the thighs. She clenched her fingers into tight fists when he parted her thighs and knelt between them. When she felt him entering her, she held her breath. He entered her only a little, and she moaned. He stopped advancing, but didn't withdraw. He bent down to kiss her on the lips until she was relaxed, and then entered her slightly more.

"Hwa!" she called when she felt him breaking through her screen of virginity, crumbling her wall of virtue.

After a while, he was still inside her, but she no longer felt the pain. She circled her arms around him, held him tightly, and let herself move with the ancient rhythm, the waves of pleasure silencing her last doubt.

On the dresser, the statue of Buddha had absorbed the heat of the day and now encountered the cool air of night. A thin layer of moisture had formed on the Buddha's bald head. The dampness turned into drops of water, gathered under the indented eyes, then slowly fell.

14

MA TSAI-TU sat in his study with the door closed, thinking.

He was frightened for himself and his family.

To him, the two most dreaded things in life were hard work and physical pain. It seemed inevitable that the Japanese soldiers would soon rule White Stone. As a result, hard work and painful torture would befall him and his family.

In many other villages, landlords' mansions had been broken into, the men tortured, the women raped. When the soldiers were through, the rich were robbed of their wealth, driven out of their patriarchal homes, forced to roam the streets like beggars to look for work so they wouldn't starve.

For weeks, while comforting his family that everything would be all right, Ma Tsai-tu had pondered over a way to save himself and his family from such a fate. If only he could offer something to the Japanese officers and position himself on their good side. Something that the invading men would enjoy and therefore reward the giver's generosity. Something . . .

He had walked through the Ma compound, from one courtyard to another. The Japanese commander in chief would need headquarters in White Stone. Tsai-tu would offer the entire house to the man, asking only a small portion of it for himself and his family. He would make his servants the servants of the Japanese . . . but still, he needed something more.

Tonight, through dinner, he had looked across the table at his family. His sons were useless; the Japanese wouldn't take them as coolies even if he begged them. Yoto was senile and fat; the Japanese wouldn't want her unless they had extremely unusual tastes in women. Suelin had gone back to her husband's house, and all there was left was Melin.

For the first time he looked at Melin carefully, and his eyes brightened at the discovery of a piece of valuable property unnoticed all these years.

"When did my little girl become an exquisite young woman?" he had asked himself, staring at Melin, remembering her as a bony child with two pigtails and a smiling face.

After dinner he had come to his study and closed the door. He sat there debating until the full moon moved across the courtyard to the western part of the sky and the antique brass clock stroked the hour of midnight.

"What kind of father am I, should I do this to my poor little Melin?" he whispered, shaking his head.

"What choice do I have?" he answered himself, and suddenly stood from his chair.

He walked across the courtyard in the moonlight, reached Melin's bedroom. Her bed was empty, but her voice could be heard from Yoto's room across the hall. Tsai-tu had not been in his wife's room for many years now. Tradition was such a good thing when it commanded all wives who were no longer desired by their husband to move out of the husband's bedchamber and leave him with absolute freedom. He had heard that in barbaric lands such as America, a man was allowed to have only one wife, and bed only one woman at a time, or his wife could accuse him of violating the law and committing a crime called adultery. He sighed. The world was a strange place, and what he was about to do was not any more unreasonable than many other things that took place under the sun.

He stood quietly and placed an ear against the closed door.

"Mama, you look so content when you're asleep," Melin was sobbing softly. "I love you, Mama, and I'm sorry for what I did last night. At the time, I forgot what you told me all these years . . ."

Tsai-tu shrugged. What could a carefully brought-up girl like Melin do that was so bad? She didn't practice her flute as she was told to? She read a forbidden book such as *The Plum Blossoms in a Golden Vase*?

Melin's words were unclear and mostly drowned out by Yoto's loud snores. ". . . tomorrow at dawn . . . Mama . . . Kwangchow . . . Hong Kong . . . forgive me . . . Mama. Someday we'll . . ."

Tsai-tu tiptoed away. He would not disturb Melin tonight, since she was with her Mama and confessing a little girl's minor infraction.

15

ENJOYING A WARM afternoon in early spring, the Cohens were having a small tea party in the gazebo. Five people sat around the table: the three Cohens—Aaron, Meiping, and David—and two from outside the family, Wong Yin and Diana Moore.

Diana was twenty-one, tall and slender. Her light brown hair was short and straight, her lovely face without makeup. She had on a yellow pullover sweater and a pair of beige pants, brown flat shoes and white cotton socks.

Meiping glanced at Diana's shoes and socks and smiled. "I've never seen you in either high-heel shoes or flower hats. It seems that the other British ladies won't leave their homes without following such proper dress codes."

Diana smiled. Two tiny dimples appeared at the corners of her lips. "I'm not one of those high-and-mighty British ladies married to rich bankers or diplomats. I'm only a working girl receiving a meager salary from Mr. Cohen."

David laughed. "Do I hear someone hinting for a raise?"

Diana shook her head. "I'm not hinting for one. But if someone insists on giving me one, I won't turn it down."

Everyone laughed. The South China Sea roared

as it collided with the shore, far below Victoria Peak.

Diana Moore's parents were missionaries. Diana had been born in Beijing. She had traveled with her father and mother to many places, and learned several Chinese dialects. In 1934, when the Moores lived in Hong Kong and Diana was eighteen, she had applied for and received a job from David as a sales clerk. David had noticed her ability and diligence, promoted her to store manager and then buying agent. David had taught her how to select, bargain, and buy, and also the most difficult techniques of telling true gems apart from manmade stones.

Diana soon became the best buying agent David had. David treasured her, had brought her home to meet Meiping. Meiping also liked her. A few months ago, Diana's parents had been transferred to Shanghai. To both David and Meiping's relief, Diana remained in Hong Kong. Since she lived alone in a rented room, David and Meiping asked her over often.

When the laughter died down, David promised Diana. "When you return from your next buying trip, you will receive another raise."

"Thank you, Mr. Cohen. Let me think what I can do with the extra money . . ." Diana's brown eyes sparkled as she thought with her head tilted to one side.

Meiping tapped Diana on the shoulder. "If you don't mind the suggestion of an old woman, I think you should move out of that dingy room of yours in New Territory. I've visited you there only once, but once was more than enough. The neighborhood is awful. In the few minutes I stayed, several strange people came to see you. They all seemed to have some secret, and waited impatiently for me to leave."

Diana's face tensed for a second, then returned to normal. She looked away from Meiping and said quickly to David, "I'm looking forward to the next buying trip." She continued rapidly, without giving Meiping a chance to go back to the other topic, "Kwangchow and Shanghai are two of my favorite cities. And, of course, I can't wait to visit my parents in Shanghai."

David asked with concern, "How are your parents in Shanghai? Do they think it's safe for you to visit them? What did they say in their letters?"

"They are safe and sound in the International Settlement," Diana answered. "They believe the Japanese will leave Shanghai alone. They said that the Japanese are satisfied with the large portion of China in their control and don't need to invade more land. They told me to visit them at any time."

David said, "They feel about Shanghai the same way I feel about Hong Kong. I believe we are safe, because Hong Kong was ceded to Great Britain and the Japanese will never touch British-owned land."

Meiping frowned. "I don't trust the Japanese. According to the newspaper, their invasion of China has only just begun. I think you should postpone all buying trips."

Diana smiled confidently. "Don't worry, Mr. and Mrs. Cohen. I know how to take care of myself. I'm looking forward to this exciting trip . . . unless you have second thoughts about giving me a raise."

Meiping laughed but still looked worried.

Before David could say anything, Aaron raised his voice. "I envy you, Diana. You travel so frequently. I wanted to see China and understand my mother's homeland, but the war broke out, and . . ." He swallowed the words about Rachel's death. He didn't want to bring tears to his parents' eyes again.

Diana smiled at Aaron in the way of an adult comforting a child. "You have seen quite a few places." She counted on her fingers: "San Francisco, Hong Kong, Kwanchow, Jasmine Valley, Shanghai, Nanjin, and Beijing." She laughed. "You shouldn't complain."

Aaron gave Diana an angry look. "Stop patronizing me, Diana. You know as well as I, my traveling was different from yours. I stayed in hotels and went out with tourist groups, while you were on your own and dealt with the local people. But I know all about your buying trips . . ."

For the sake of impressing Diana, Aaron began to show off his knowledge.

He knew that besides buying raw diamonds from Africa, star sapphires and rubies from Thailand, and pearls from Japan, Cohen's Jewelry Enterprise also searched for already-set antique pieces from all over China and many American cities with large Chinese populations. A buying trip was considered a great success when the buyer could purchase some high-quality imperial jade at good prices.

He also knew that for thousands of years the Chinese emperors had considered the jade mines their personal property that came with the throne. As a result, only a limited amount of imperial jade had been extracted from the few mines in north China, and when the pieces were cut and polished and mounted into settings, they stayed in the hands of the few noble families. The best way for a jeweler to acquire these pieces was to go from one city to another, combing the towns if possible, to find them in the windows of pawn shops and goldsmiths' stores, sold by the rich when they were caught by the hands of misfortune.

Diana was not the only person impressed. Meiping, David, and Yin were amazed by Aaron's information.

When everyone was awed into silence, Aaron looked at his parents and said, "I want to go with Diana on her next trip."

David shook his head. "No, Aaron, I can't let you go. Diana knows how to take care of herself, but you don't."

Meiping raised her voice. "Aaron, you're not leaving home! I can't afford to lose you too!"

Wong Yin didn't want Aaron to travel with Diana at all. But she was a servant and he the master. It was not her place to stop him from going anywhere, no matter how much she wished for him to stay home.

The one who objected the strongest was Diana. "I'm not a baby-sitter," she said, then apologized to Aaron. "I'm not saying that you are a baby. But . . . well, you'll regret leaving Hong Kong. The outside world is different from Victoria Peak. Once away from the protection of the British flag, you'll be an ordinary Chinese and feel the war." She said under her breath, "Yes, there is a war."

Aaron refused to be defeated. He argued and begged his parents. After losing Rachel, Meiping and David had not been able to turn down any of their remaining child's requests, no matter how absurd. After a long debate, Meiping and David gave in. Once they granted Aaron the permission, no matter how unhappy Diana was, she couldn't argue any more.

"Diana, please take good care of Aaron," Meiping pleaded with her husband's frowning employee. "He is all we have now. If you let anything happen to him, David and I shall die." Meiping began to cry.

David said apologetically, "Diana, I know this

is beyond your duty as a buying agent. I'm not
ordering you as an employer. I'm asking you to
do a tired old man a favor." He leaned toward
her, "Please, Diana, take Aaron with you, and
protect him from harm."

Diana sighed. She looked from Meiping to
David, then shook her head. "Well, I can see that
I must earn my raise the hard way."

Diana carried a duffel bag on her back, Aaron
a leather suitcase in his hand. They both had with
them money and checks from David, and endless
instructions and orders from Meiping.

Diana seemed to want Aaron to regret his
pressing her into taking him along. She bought
two third-class tickets for the train to Kwangchow. The seats were hard wood without cush-
ions. They sat among loud, rude people with
smelly bodies. They ate a loaf of bread Diana had
brought with her in her duffel bag, drank cold
water out of a bottle she had also packed. Diana
made it clear that she wished Aaron would complain so she could send him home. She was disappointed when he took the abuse calmly.

"I enjoyed the ride," he said when they got off
the train. "When Mama, Rachel, and I ran away
from Beijing, it was much worse."

"The trip has only just begun," Diana said.
"When it becomes too rough on you, just let me
know and I'll take you to the nearest train at any
time."

The train station in Kwangchow was crowded
with people from the north. They had been
chased away from their homes by the Japanese
soldiers, carrying their babies and belongings on
their backs. They had no idea where to go from
Kwangchow. Everyone was tired, some sick, most
had lost their loved ones.

Diana and Aaron tried to make their way out of the station but were forced to stand still. They listened to the conversations of people around them.

One woman said to another, "We were hiding in a cornfield. The Japanese soldiers searched for us nearby. My two-month-old baby boy cried from hunger. I put my hand over his mouth, but still his cries could be heard. There were many others hiding with us. They forced me to put my cotton quilt over my baby's head . . ." The woman sobbed so hard that her words became unclear. "When the soldiers were gone and I removed the quilt, my baby was dead."

The other woman comforted this one, then talked about her own venture. "My husband and I walked on our feet from the north to the south. We started with my in-laws and four children. Now my in-laws are dead and three of my children have gone to Buddha. Buddha didn't protect them from either the soldiers' bullets or the scarlet fever. My husband and I have only one child now, but fortunately he is our only son. My husband said we should go from here to Shanghai because Shanghai is the gathering place of all the rich people. Chiang Kai-shek is for the rich. He will defend Shanghai if nowhere else."

The first one sighed. "My husband and I are exhausted and broke. We may stay in Kwang-chow and see what happens. If the Japanese should take over, we'll just have to live under their rules. We should have stayed home in the north and bowed to the Japanese, and tried to survive them like we've survived all the Chinese rulers. That way, our poor baby wouldn't have been smothered."

When the two women walked away with their men, Aaron said to Diana incredulously, "I didn't know things like this existed. I thought I was all grown-up after escaping Beijing and losing Rachel, but I was wrong."

Diana said, "What you heard from those two women are stories common all over China—" She was interrupted by the sudden appearance of a man.

He was Chinese, about Diana's age. He wore peasant clothes—black baggy pants and a brown shirt smeared with dirt. But he carried himself with the air of a scholar. He nodded to Diana, then gradually moved toward a quieter corner of the station.

"You wait here!" Diana ordered Aaron, then followed the man.

"I'm not interested in disturbing you and your boyfriend anyway," Aaron murmured unhappily. He watched Diana and the man maneuvering through the crowd, stopping at a newspaper stand.

Aaron withdrew his idea that this man could be Diana's boyfriend. Diana had been born and raised in China, but even when a Chinese girl met her boyfriend, she would show a certain amount of emotion. Aaron craned his neck to watch Diana, the man, and the newspaper vendor talking. The three of them bowed their heads and hid their faces, seeming to be very cautious and discreet.

Aaron saw the young vendor, also about Diana's age, give Diana and the other man each a magazine. The three then parted without looking at one another. The vendor went to wait on a customer. The other man disappeared among the crowd. Diana came back to Aaron.

"Now I know what Mama meant when she said you have strange friends," Aaron teased Diana. "She saw them in your apartment. I see them in

Kwangchow. You must have them everywhere."
Aaron grabbed the magazine from Diana's hand.
"A Chinese movie magazine! I didn't know you
were interested in this kind of junk!"

Diana took the magazine back from Aaron and
stuffed it into her duffel bag quickly. "My taste
in reading is none of your business," she said in
a stern voice. "From now on, you don't touch any
of my things without first asking for permission."

No one had ever treated Aaron this way. His
face turned red, his eyes watered. He hated Diana
right then. When they returned home, he would
talk to Baba and make sure that Diana did not
receive her expected raise.

Diana saw his tears. Her voice softened.
"Come . . ." She pulled his hand. "Let's go find
a hotel."

The hotel was on Main Street, next door to
Fong's Pawn Shop. The clerk behind the recep-
tion counter looked up from the newspaper in his
hands, studied the Caucasian girl and the half-
breed boy for a long time. "Brother and sister?"
he asked.

"You guessed it," Diana said. "He looks like
both of our parents, I look like only one. We want
two rooms."

Aaron stood in the middle of his small dingy
room, looked at the soiled sheet and pillow. He
walked around his suitcase to sit on a wooden
chair. "Diana is challenging me," he mumbled as
he glanced from the rusted washbasin to the
wooden toilet bucket. "She thinks this room will
make me go home. Well, she is wrong."

After a quick knock, the lockless door opened.
Diana stood in her old clothes and comfortable
shoes, looked at Aaron's miserable face, and
smiled. "This is the kind of hotel the average Chi-

nese stay in. If it doesn't satisfy your curiosity, I can show you much worse ones." She chuckled at the dirty look he gave her. "Well, you are the one who insisted on seeing the real China and traveling the average Chinese way."

Aaron said through clenched teeth, "I like my room just fine. I'm ready to go out with you now, to walk through the city and meet the local people."

"We can start with the pawn shop next door," Diana said. "I want to see if they have any valuable pieces."

The door of Fong's Pawn Shop was locked. Diana knocked.

"Wait a minute!" someone yelled from inside.

While waiting in the doorway, Aaron and Diana noticed the swarms of people running ahead of the approaching Japanese Army.

People had packed their belongings and carried them on their backs. Their hands were left free for holding on to each other.

Diana talked to Aaron the way a teacher would lecture her students. "These people have learned through experience that while escaping a fiasco, separation can only be prevented by never letting go. Most of them have lived through many disasters. If you listen carefully, you can hear them comparing the current catastrophe with past terrors."

"I have ears," Aaron said, "I don't need you to tell me to listen!"

Aaron saw an old man pulling an old woman who was trying to move as fast as she could on bound feet. The old man raised his voice. "When the Boxers stormed through Kwangchow, I was a young boy. It was winter, but the madmen were shirtless. They waved their broadswords at the foreigners and chopped off quite a few Chinese heads. My mother took my hand and we ran . . ."

"Look over there." Diana pointed at another old woman being dragged forward by a young man. With each step, she warned him loudly, "No matter what happens, keep your opinions to yourself. When the Ching Dynasty arrested the revolutionaries, your Baba was on this very same street. Instead of minding his own business, he said something about China's need of improvement, and they grabbed him. He was tortured and forced to admit his guilt. He was beheaded and you were born an orphan."

The woman's words disappeared in the roaring crowd. Aaron felt Diana pulling his hand. He turned and saw a young father holding his little girl in his arms and saying in a northern dialect, "You were only a baby when a warlord took over our hometown. The villagers ran in all directions. Your Mama and I took turns carrying you. Your Mama forgot to cover her face with mud, and her beauty caught the eyes of the lord. His soldiers took her away from us, and the last thing she shouted was for us to keep running. My poor baby, you're a big girl now, but we haven't stopped running!" The man switched his daughter to his other arm and continued to run.

A procession of rickshaws passed by, carrying a rich family and their luggage. It had rained, and the holes in the street were filled with water. The wheels rolled over the holes, splashing the muddy water all over Aaron. He took a step back into the doorway, while keeping his eyes on the scene.

The pawnshop door opened. A kind-faced man and a shy woman appeared. They looked at Aaron and Diana curiously.

Diana spoke to them in perfect Cantonese. "My brother and I are staying in the hotel next door.

We would like to look at the jewelry you have. May we come in?"

"You are welcome to come in. But we don't have much to show you. We have only just hidden away the better things. We must lock the door now and put shutters over all the windows."

"The lock and shutters can protect you from the Japanese?" Aaron asked, looking at the man with bewilderment.

"No." The man shook his head, answering calmly. "The Japanese are not yet here. But we must protect ourselves from the local hooligans, who will rob all the stores just before the arrival of the real enemy."

The woman touched Diana's arm gently. "Please come in instead of standing on the street. My husband is right. We've lived through enough crises to know what to do. The looters will throw rocks at the shop windows, break the doors, and then clean us out."

When the double doors were securely locked and the windows tightly shuttered, the room became pitch black. The woman lit an oil lamp and the man brought out a tray of jewelry. In the lamp's yellow glimmer Diana and Aaron looked at the pendants, rings, earrings, bracelets, and necklaces.

Diana picked up an antique brooch. The pearls had yellowed with time. The emerald glistened a transparent green. Diana said, "This is a beauty. How can you say you have put away the better things?"

The man shook his head. "When a woman's hair turns white and a pearl's glow becomes yellow, they both are worthless." He pointed at the yellowed pearls and quoted a very low price.

The lamplight shone on Diana's face. She looked soft and vulnerable. Aaron stared at her, wishing that she could look this way all the time. But all the softness and vulnerability disappeared when Diana put down the brooch and picked up another piece of jewelry to study it professionally.

Aaron ran his fingers over the rings and bracelets, visualizing some woman's pale fingers and slender arms. He touched the earrings and hairpins, imagining an unknown lady's delicate ears and thick black hair. He asked no one in particular, "I wonder what happened to her. Did she age and become poor? Was she forced to forsake her treasure because of ill health or death? Or perhaps . . ." He stopped at the banging on the door.

A mob gathered outside the pawn shop, trying to break the windows and knock the door down. They called out threatening words, and their frightening voices penetrated the thick walls and filled the room.

"My wife and I must hide in the basement now," said the man. "The two of you can either hide with us or leave through the back door that opens to an alley." He picked up the tray.

Diana paid for the brooch and quickly took Aaron back to their hotel. "If I were alone, I would go visit more pawn shops, because the merchants are willing to lower their prices when the city is in turmoil." Diana looked at Aaron and sighed. "But since I'm with you, and I've promised your parents to take good care of you, we'd better not go anywhere tonight."

Aaron couldn't sleep. He heard noises on the street. Their rooms were on the second floor. When he walked to the window, he could see several city blocks. He saw looters robbing, going from store to store. Soon they came to the hotel. He heard the hotel owner paying the looters off, and at the same time saw in the distance a wooden structure burst into flame. People screamed as they ran out of the burning building. One person was on fire. From the long blazing hair Aaron could tell she was a woman. He watched her rolling on the ground like a fireball. He didn't know he was screaming or notice his door open.

"I thought someone had attacked you when I heard you scream," Diana said with her arms around Aaron. "Are you all right?"

Aaron nodded, was ashamed of himself. He turned away from the window. "Diana . . ." He hesitated, then pleaded in a trembling voice, "Will you stay with me?"

Diana nodded, then went to her room and quickly brought back a chair. She put her chair and the chair in Aaron's room in front of the window and gestured for Aaron to sit. "I don't think we can sleep anyway," she said. "We might as well watch the war."

They sat with their elbows leaning on the windowsill, their chins resting in their hands. They watched the looters leaving the street with armloads of goods. Some owners chased after the robbers; some stood at their doors and cursed. When dawn was near, there was a brief moment of silence. The street was deserted, the air tense.

"I guess the war will begin now," Aaron said, and was proud of himself for being able to speak in a steady voice. Now he felt truly mature. "I'm ready."

Diana looked at him. "Ready for what?"

Aaron frowned. "Why do you treat me like a child? Ready for the war, of course."

"There will be no war," Diana said.

"But the Nationalist Army will surely defend

the city!" Aaron felt that Diana was insulting his intelligence.

Diana shook her head sadly. "The Nationalist Army is long gone. The weaker divisions were destroyed by the Japanese somewhere outside Kwangchow. The stronger divisions were ordered by Chiang Kai-shek to either stay in Shanghai or head for Chungking."

"Shanghai is a city of the rich that Chiang wants to protect, but what's in Chungking?"

"Chiang knows that if he can't keep Nanjin, he'll need a new capital. He has begun to send some of his men to Chungking, a city in the southwest, to establish a hiding place among the high mountains."

"How about the Eighth Route Army? I heard that they are trained by the Communists."

"The Eighth Route Army are far from here. They are somewhere near Yenan—" Diana suddenly stopped, as if catching herself talking too much.

"How do you know?" Aaron asked suspiciously. "I thought my father only taught you to tell imperial jade from green glass."

Diana answered firmly, "I don't know anything. I was only guessing. I was wrong, I'm sure."

Aaron was going to ask more questions, but stopped at the sight of the first Japanese tank.

The dawn's first light shone on the white flag centered with a red sun. Behind the flag a man's head appeared through the observation hole, glaring at both sides of the street.

"He looks just like a Chinese. If it weren't for his uniform, I wouldn't know he was an enemy," Aaron whispered, lowering himself to keep out of range.

Diana nodded. She too slipped out of her chair

and stayed low. They peeked to see more tanks
go by, followed by marching soldiers in neat rows
and officers on tall horses. All the men were
sober-faced. Their bayonets, swords, and guns
were shining and ready for use.

"Where are they going?" Aaron whispered.
"Are they just passing through, or will they stay
in Kwangchow?"

"They are going to city hall to receive a formal
surrender from the mayor of Kwangchow. The
mayor will then offer them a list of available
buildings for their headquarters. The commanding officers will take their men to these buildings,
and then the soldiers will be discharged." Diana
sighed softly but deeply. "And then the people
of Kwangchow will begin to suffer."

"Are these your guesses too? You certainly can
guess in detail." Aaron whispered his amazement.

"A buying agent needs a quick mind," Diana
said mysteriously.

They both saw a small dark object thrown out
of an upstairs window of a building two doors
down from Fong's Pawn Shop. It landed on the
sidewalk, rolled toward the center of the street,
then lay still and sent out a series of sparkles.

One of the Japanese officers shouted an order.
The soldiers quickly scattered from the object. The
next sound, the object exploded, throwing the nearby soldiers sprawling. The horses raised their
hooves and neighed, nearly unseating the
officers.

When the smoke cleared and the air was thick
with the smell of gunpowder, Aaron and Diana
saw a large hole in the street, surrounded by several dead soldiers and many more wounded ones.

"A guerrilla fighter!" Diana whispered. "I wonder . . ." She put a hand over her mouth.

The entire procession had stopped moving. The

officers shifted places in small circles on horseback while one of them shouted out his orders.
The wounded and dead were carried away toward
city hall. A group of soldiers led by a sergeant
charged into the building down the street. The
rest of them squatted and held their weapons
ready, aiming at the far-left upstairs window.

"Please hurry!" Diana prayed for the man they
were seeking. "Leave the building and join the
crowd, then disappear . . ." She stopped with a
moan. "Oh, no!"

A man appeared on the street, escorted by two
soldiers, each holding one of his pinned-back
arms. He was only in his twenties, and looked
like a college student. He didn't struggle, but his
face was colorless and his eyes burned with fury.
Behind him a middle-aged couple, an old woman,
and four children were brought out of the building. Their faces were ashen, their limbs trembling.
They begged and cried as they were kicked by
the soldiers and pushed by the sharp points of
the bayonets.

"It's my own doing!" the man who had thrown
the hand grenade hollered like a trapped animal.
"I sneaked into their house! They know nothing!
Please let them go! They are innocent—" He was
hit on the head with the butt of a rifle and fell
forward. A soldier pulled him by the hair and
forced him to a kneeling position.

Diana tried to push Aaron away from the window, but he jostled her hand away. She put an
arm around him protectively. They felt each other
shaking as they did their best to keep themselves
from screaming or making any foolish moves.

"I'm sixty-four!" the old woman shouted in a
broken voice when she was pushed down and her
clothes ripped off. "Don't you have any mercy for
the old?"

"Baba! Mama!" both teenage girls screamed when they were pinned down and stripped.

The middle-aged woman didn't make a sound. Her naked body wriggled on the ground. The soldier riding over her suddenly screamed and covered his face. She had raised her head and bitten him hard. The soldier swung his fist and the woman was knocked unconscious.

The middle-aged man stood up from kneeling. He ran toward his wife, but before he could reach her, an officer charged forward on horseback, swinging a sword.

The man's head was severed from his body and fell to the ground. For a brief moment both the body and the head continued to live separately. The headless body remained erect like a fountain, spraying red from its open neck. The bodiless head rolled toward the fainted woman, trying to comfort her with its staring eyes. Then the body folded and collapsed, and the head stopped rolling and stayed still.

The beheading of the man brought shrill screams from the mouths of the captives, then silenced them. The two boys shivered and wailed but remained kneeling. The old woman and two girls were raped by soldier after soldier, but only whimpered.

The silence was broken when the middle-aged woman regained consciousness, opened her eyes, and saw her husband's head lying next to her face in a pool of blood. She stared at it and shrieked in a voice that was inhuman.

Aaron and Diana sank their teeth into their lips, clenched their hands into fists. Tears fell from their eyes and sweat streamed down their backs. Low moaning sounds came out of their throats but were quickly swallowed.

One of the officers looked at his wristwatch, then gave an order.

"*Hai!*" four soldiers answered in unison, picked up their bayonets, and moved toward the sprawling females.

Seeing the shining blades over them, the women and girls were driven back to life by fear. They pleaded and screamed and tried to crawl away. They were caught by the soldiers' feet.

Stepping on their targets, the soldiers cut their lower abdomens wide open. They used the points of the bayonets to pull the intestines out of the bodies, like a cook using a chopstick to pull noodles out of a wok.

The soldiers left the bodies and went to the two boys and the remaining man. They raised their bayonets, then lowered them with force, aiming not at the throats or other places that would bring quick death. They stabbed the man and boys repeatedly, then kicked the blood-soaked bodies to the side of the street and left them there.

An order was given. The soldiers lined up and marched on. They passed the dead and dying expressionlessly.

Silence hung over the street for a few minutes. Then the first sound came from a shutter being removed from a window. One window was opened, followed by another. One head stuck out a window, then was joined by several more.

Aaron and Diana straightened their crouching bodies. They saw on the street one store after another opening its doors. A man walked cautiously down the street, stopping after every few steps to look around and listen. Then another man joined him, and then a woman. Within half an hour Main Street was crowded once again. The bodies were carried away, the blood was washed off the ground.

Aaron and Diana turned their eyes toward the eastern sky and saw that the sun had risen. It shone on the rooftop of city hall, where the Chinese flag was replaced by the Japanese flag.

Diana took Aaron's hand in hers, squeezed it softly. "We must go to Shanghai now," she said, "if we can manage to leave Kwangchow."

16

In Yenan, the summer wind roared over the field, shrouding everything in yellow sand.

"Left, right, left, right . . . *Due-na-ma!*" Li Kwanjin's voice was hoarse. "We've been marching all morning. Why can't you get it right?"

The thirty-some men looked at one another. Innocent grins appeared on their young faces, and they were totally unashamed. They had previously been farmers and fishermen from the Yellow River Valley. After a drought, the streams dried up, the land cracked, and the villagers starved. The recruiting men came from Yenan, promised them food, and brought them back to the cave city. After a few days of training, they would be sent to the Japanese occupied territory to fight as guerrilla soldiers in the Eighth Route Army.

A very young man raised his hand. Kwanjin nodded and the man said, "We never needed to know left from right when farming and fishing. Why do we have to know now? It won't help us to kill the Japs, will it?"

Kwanjin stared at his naive face, met his honest eyes, then looked away. He glanced at the others and saw the same simple expressions and sincere wonder. He sighed. "I guess you are right. But as long as you are soldiers, you must learn to march." He didn't have the heart to yell at them.

Like the college students recruited by him, most of these innocent peasants would soon be killed.

He saw on the feet of the men two kinds of shoes, both handmade by village women. One kind was made of cloth, the other a special kind of strong grass woven together.

"Take off your shoes!" he ordered. An idea had come to him, but he had learned to keep his instructions short and simple.

"Give all your cloth shoes to me," he said, and then gave the men plenty of time to carry out his order.

"Now give me all your grass shoes," he said, and again waited patiently.

He then told his men to come to him for shoes. First the grass, to put on their left feet, then the cloth, for the right. He examined everyone's feet and made sure that no one had put the shoes on the wrong feet. Since both the cloth shoes and the grass shoes were shapeless and flexible, they could be worn by all people on either foot. It took him a long while before every one of his men was wearing a grass shoe on the left foot and a cloth one on the right.

"Now, let's line up again," he said. "When we march, I want you to look at your feet." He gave the order and gradually increased the speed. "Grass shoe, cloth shoe. The grass one, the cloth one. Grass again, cloth again. The grass, the cloth. Grass, cloth . . . my Great Buddha, you got it!"

Li Kwanjin's method of marching was observed by many people from the remote cave entrances. It was immediately copied by all the other officers in charge of training the Eighth Route Army. In less than a month, all through China, the entire army was known as the Grass-shoe, Cloth-shoe Army.

*   *   *

Kwanjin continued to train his men. One warm afternoon the sound of marching traveled through the hills, reached the field, and captured May.

May listened as she hoed away the weeds. She smiled. Kwanjin's hands couldn't touch her body, but his voice caressed her heart. Physically they were a hill apart, but emotionally they were side by side.

"Poor Kwanjin," May murmured to herself. "I understand you so much more now."

As she raised the hoe over her shoulder, then swung it down, she thought of the similarity between the blooming of her marriage and the cultivation of vegetables on this barren land. A privileged girl married a fisherman's abandoned son and lived with him in a commune, shared a cave with his peasant mother. Hard labor kept the vegetables growing, and strong love gave life to their marriage. She thought of the love between her and Kwanjin and smiled contentedly.

The smile faded. She raised a hand to shield her eyes from the burning sun. She felt dizzy, sick to her stomach, and was about to faint.

"I need to rest," she said, and laid down the hoe.

"You don't have my permission!" A woman, who was a higher-ranking comrade, looked at her sternly.

May stepped over her hoe, approached the woman, and said to her face, "I'm pregnant. I feel awfully weak. I must go lie down or I'm afraid I will lose my baby."

The woman hissed. "Is your aristocratic body more delicate than our low-born bodies? Is your noble baby more valuable than our babies? We work in the field until the child is dropped. We rest a few hours and are back in the field. Why should you be excused?"

May did not bother to argue any further. She simply turned her back to the commanding comrade and the others and walked away from the field.

She returned to the cave, lay on the bed, and listened to Kwanjin's voice coming from far away. "My poor husband. As a boy, patriotism lured you into a deep sea called communism. Maturity and experience opened your eyes, but you were already too far from shore to swim back. Then I came along, also drawn by the force of naive optimism. I became a lead ball chained to your ankle, matching the ball on your other ankle that is your mother. Soon another small lead ball will be born . . ." She turned to bury her face against a pillow to conceal her sobs.

When she had first arrived in Yenan, she never hid her emotions, whether they be joy or sorrow. But she had learned. Now she knew of the Team of Long Ears. If they heard her cry, they would report her to the authorities, and she would be called to a meeting and forced to confess her reason for daring to be unhappy in Yenan.

May fell asleep. When she woke up, the sun was setting and her stomach was growling. The thought of the food in the mess hall made her want to vomit. She glanced at the small earth stove at the corner of the cave. She visualized a large bowl of hot-sour soup. She debated. Her craving won.

When Kwanjin and Leahi returned from work, they found three bowls of soup on a wooden crate which served as their table.

Kwanjin frowned. "The last time you cooked, they forced you to write a ten-page confession.

If you're caught again, they'll put you in hard labor."

Tears filled May's eyes. "I couldn't help myself. I wanted something sour so badly." She swallowed. "All right. I'll pour the soup out and we'll go to the mess hall."

Leahi stepped forward. "If a woman doesn't get what she craves for, the baby will be born with red eyes." She pulled May toward the table. "If they find out, I'll say I cooked it."

"You'll do no such thing, Mama," Kwanjin said. "Let's finish the soup and go to the mess hall, to pretend we have not yet eaten."

The soup was meatless. Besides vinegar and soy sauce, there were only cabbage leaves and a few grains of rice. No one in Yenan had much in her food cabinet. May had traded a silver plate, her wedding gift from Hawaii, with the Chairman's new lover for the limited items used in the soup.

While gulping down the soup, Kwanjin looked at May and saw her long hair. He had told her that she looked more beautiful with her hair long. She had let it grow to please him, even though it was against protocol.

"May, you really ought to . . ." he said, frowning, then stopped.

"Yes?" She looked at him like a child waiting to be scolded.

"Nothing." His heart softened. "I don't want you to get into trouble, that's all."

May smiled. The steaming soup brought redness to her tanned cheeks. She looked beautiful. "I received two letters today," she told him with a sigh. "One from Hong Kong, one from Hawaii, but still nothing from Beijing. I hope my family and friends are able to survive under Japanese rule. Michiko and Jebu are out of the hospital.

Aaron is on his way to Kwangchow and Shanghai. They sent me some books too. One in English, several in Japanese . . ."

She rattled on, and Kwanjin's heart ached. May was many steps behind him in understanding the party system. She had matured quickly in the past year in many ways. Unfortunately, her growth was the result of disillusionment and a difficult life. And still, she was not learning fast enough.

"May, you may be criticized for writing to your friends in foreign lands. And those books are forbidden . . ." He swallowed the rest of his words when she saw May's eyes tearing again.

They finished their soup and rushed to the mess hall.

In autumn, when Chairman Mao heard the rest of China calling his men uneducated peasants, the leader was upset. "We must educate our soldiers. I assign Comrade Li to teach them to read and write."

Kwanjin thought hard. The soldiers didn't have any time for learning in a classroom. As soon as they were trained to march and taught to use the most primitive weapons, they were sent into battle. However, they had to walk a long way from Yenan to the Japanese occupied towns, and during the lengthy march they were usually bored.

Kwanjin gathered all the old people in the cave city. "Cut me many squares of cardboard, then punch two holes on one edge of each square, and tie a thin rope about two feet long through these holes."

Next he collected all the people who could write. "Use the darkest ink, write the simplest words, one on each square of the cardboard."

After that he assembled all the people who could draw. "Below each written word on the cardboard, draw a picture that tells, most obviously and unmistakably, the meaning of that word. And then give the cardboard squares back to the old people, and they'll cover the squares with transparent oil paper."

When the cardboard posters were made, he explained to the soldiers. "Each of you pick up a poster and put the loop over your head so that the cardboard will hang against your back, showing the written word and picture." He demonstrated slowly, making sure that they could follow. "When you are marching, look at the back of the person in front of you, study the shape of the word, and associate it with the picture. When you rest, try to use either a stick or your finger to copy that word on the dirt ground . . . you'll take turns to be the first in line."

He repeated his instructions many times, until the men knew what he wanted.

When he didn't receive any enthusiastic reaction from the soldiers, he added, "Just think how proud your family will be when the war is over and you are home again—you'll be not only a hero but also a respected person who can read and write."

One of the soldiers gave him a puzzled look and asked loudly, "But aren't all the reading people and writing people the bad ones? Are they not the enemies of us peasants? We were told the other day that after the Japs are destroyed, we'll turn our spears toward the rich and learned people. Why do we want to study and become our own enemies?"

All the trusting eyes watched Kwanjin, waiting for him to answer. Sweat broke from his forehead when he groped for the right words. He finally managed to utter, "Well, you won't learn too much this way . . . just enough to make your

families proud, but not enough to become the enemies of the people."

Like the grass-shoe/cloth-shoe idea, the posters
were adopted by other party leaders, and soon
the Eighth Route Army soldiers were seen marching everywhere with flash cards on their backs.

Late autumn, in their cave home, May and
Kwanjin lay in bed whispering to each other.

May said, "In spite of your endless hard work
and many clever inventions, you are still a junior
party leader. You have not been promoted for a
long time."

Kwanjin sighed. "I know. Wong Chung continues to turn down my request. Many other party
officers don't do much, but have received one
promotion after another."

"Perhaps we should bring our complaint to the
weekly meeting."

From the other side of the sheet draped over a
rope stretched from wall to wall came Leahi's
hushed voice. "My children, think carefully before you do anything. Even I know that the party
doesn't like any comrade who complains."

May giggled. "Mama hears everything," she
said. She held her husband tightly and stopped
talking.

When May fell asleep, Kwanjin continued to lie
awake and think. He wouldn't care so much
about a promotion if he were unmarried. But he
had May, and together they were soon having
a baby. He would like a larger cave, more food
coupons, and to have May excused from field
work. What he wanted most was the freedom for
May to cook, to let her hair grow, to write to
people outside Yenan, and to read the books she
enjoyed. The higher-ranked party members and
their families faced less criticism and fewer re-

strictions. To be one of them, he must get a promotion.

The meeting took place in the mess hall. After all the higher-ranked comrades made their speeches, Kwanjin asked permission to speak.

"I've entered my request for promotion to Comrade Wong three times, but three times I have been denied. I now ask the party to give me an explanation."

Many heads turned toward Wong Chung. Wong was both embarrassed and angered. He had turned down Kwanjin's requests on his own, without consulting any senior members. Now he must find a way to back up his decision.

Wong Chung stood, cleared his throat. "I am surprised that Comrade Li dares to ask for promotion. According to his record, he ought to be demoted."

Wong Chung paused, looked around the cave, then continued. "Li Kwanjin went to Beijing and brought back a dozen new recruits. He married one of them, kept her in safety, and sent the rest to the front. While half of his recruits died in battle and the other half ran back to their imperialistic homes, in Yenan Li Kwanjin and his lover began to create for themselves a feudalistic environment."

Wong Chung began with May's wedding gown. "Ever since then, our female comrades have tried to dress up for weddings, because they are poisoned by Comrade Hu's bad example. Comrade Li is responsible for the behavior of his lover."

Wong Chung then talked about the letters mailed and received by Hu May, sometimes addressed by her imperialistic correspondents as Mrs. Li Kwanjin. "The letters are not only to and from her friend in Hong Kong but also to people all over the imperialist nations. She receives gifts

from them, and some of the gifts are books that
contain poisoning thoughts, written in English
and Japanese, the languages of our enemy countries. There is no doubt that Comrade Li shares
these books with his lover."

Wong Chung concluded his statement with
May's cooking privately for her family and letting
her hair grow. "When the mess hall is good
enough for our Chairman, it ought to be good
enough for Comrade Li and his family. And when
our Chairman has made it very clear that a
woman should not wear long hair, Comrade Li
shouldn't encourage his lover to disobey that
order."

Without asking for permission, May stood up.
"Every crime mentioned by Comrade Wong was
committed by me. My husband has nothing to do
with any of them." Her face was white, her voice
trembling. Kwanjin tried to make her sit and
hush, but she would not stop. "I thought communism meant equal rights for women. If that is
true, then I'm responsible for my own actions."

From the center of the cave, Chairman Mao
stood from his chair. All the whispering voices
died away. The Chairman's words echoed clearly
throughout the cave. "We have heard from Comrades Li Kwanjin, Hu May, and Wong Chung.
We have enough knowledge to make a decision
about Comrade Li's promotion or demotion. The
meeting is over and you may all return to your
duties."

The winter wind blew through the night, sweeping the yellow sand into the air, keeping the fine
grains dancing high. The cave homes had no
doors. The women drilled holes over the entrances, nailed bamboo sticks to the rocky walls.
They then hung thick quilts from the poles to

keep the sand, wind, and chilly air out. But the cold wind managed to enter the caves from beneath and around the quilts, scattering sand all over the sleeping people.

"Autumn has turned into winter, and still you haven't been promoted," May said, shivering in the dark.

"Well, I haven't been demoted either," Kwanjin said, then pulled May into his arms. "Let me keep you warm."

They lay silently in each other's arms for a while, then May asked, "Kwanjin, do you think the Communists will take over China?"

"I don't know," Kwanjin answered in a whisper. "In north China the Eighth Route Army has killed far more Japanese than the Nationalist Army. The people are leaning toward our party. But our men are dying quickly. They move from one village to another, but before fighting the Japanese, they often alienate the local people. Only when luck is on our side does the whole town join our fighting men. But most of the time the villagers are afraid to side against the local lords, who are for destroying us." He paused. When he spoke again, his words were barely audible. "May, why the sudden concern? I thought you had lost your devotion to communism, since they have been picking on you for everything you do."

"I'm concerned because . . ." May put her lips next to her husband's ear and whispered, "Have you ever thought about leaving the party?"

Kwanjin didn't answer, but turned restlessly in the dark.

Still, May's soft voice continued to reach Kwanjin's ear. "After the baby is born and I'm strong enough, we can take Mama and the baby away from Yenan."

"Leave Yenan . . . ?" Kwanjin finally asked. "For where?"

"It's a big world outside these caves." Excitement made May raise her voice. "Beijing, the rest of China. Hong Kong, even overseas."

"But how can I make a living? I don't know how to do anything other than be a party member."

"We can live with my parents for a while until you find something."

"I will do no such thing!" Kwanjin pounded a fist on the bed. The bamboo frame groaned. May glanced at the thin drape, then took her husband's fist and held it tightly to keep it still. She didn't know why Leahi was so quiet. Usually, when the young couple made any noise they were not supposed to make, Leahi would cough first, then throw out a few questions.

"We will not discuss this further, not now," May whispered. "We have to wait for the right moment anyway. In the meantime, you and I had better not hold our breath for a promotion. I think it's time that we realized we are, as is every party member, living at the mercy of all the comrades— from the Team of Long Ears to the senior party officers."

May shivered again. Kwanjin held her tighter and used his own body to warm hers. She stopped shaking. His body heat was transferred to her, and hers to him. He began to burn with desire.

He turned from her to get undressed, and she undressed herself. The bed groaned loudly, but still no sound came from Leahi. Kwanjin took May in his arms like a musician caressing his beloved instrument. He began to play a love song composed with passion. At his touch, May closed her eyes, forgot all restrictions, hummed with her heart. When they reached the ultimate moment of pleasure, the musical notes emerged from her heart and escaped her lips. As she cried out, Kwanjin, too, moaned.

They slept together like two silkworms sharing a cocoon, for a few hours shutting out the outside world.

It was almost six when they left their cave. The pale face of a three-quarter moon appeared briefly in the dawning sky, but was soon covered by the gray flying clouds. The sun was nowhere to be seen. Kwanjin and May raced to the mess hall, with the wind howling around them and the sand beating on their faces. They ate some thin rice gruel for breakfast and then went to Kang Da—the University of Anti-Japanese and Anti-Imperialism.

The students were all children of ranking party members. They were safe from being sent to fight the Japanese invaders. These young people began their day's work in the cave classroom. They wrote with pens made from chicken quills and did arithmetic on abacuses that were peach pits strung on wires. They practiced calligraphy by using their fingers in shallow boxes of sand, and then spent the rest of the day farming and doing construction work.

May taught beside Kwanjin, and then worked with him and the students on the farm. She looked up from the hole she was digging in the rocky ground. She was both tired and bored to the bone. She wished that she and Kwanjin were in a home of their own, planting useless but beautiful flowers in the garden.

She dropped her hoe when she heard people shouting and screaming. She stood up when she saw Kwanjin running toward the other side of the

field, where two groups of people had gathered
face-to-face.

"Kwanjin! Wait for me!" she called, and followed him. When they neared the distant hilltop,
they realized the reason for the commotion.

People in Yenan had debated for several months
about the need of a pagoda. Half of them wished
to worship Buddha; the other half were strongly
against idol-worshiping. Last night the foundation of a pagoda had been built by the worshipers. This morning the nonbelievers had seen it
and begun to knock it down. When the builders
rushed to the site, they formed a circle around
the foundation, using themselves as a wall to
shield the unfinished pagoda from the destructive
hands. The nonbelievers picked up rocks and
aimed them at the worshipers. Several people in
the circle were hit in the head or face and were
bleeding badly, but the protective circle remained
unbroken.

May and Kwanjin saw at the same time that
Leahi was among the people protecting the pagoda. "Mama!" They yelled and ran faster.

"That's where Mama was last night!" Kwanjin
said as he ran. "No wonder we could do everything and she never made a sound."

"Look at the ones protecting the pagoda," May
said, moving quickly toward the circle. "They are
all as old as or older than Mama."

Kwanjin broke through the angry mob and
stood in front of Leahi, using his own body to
protect her from the flying rocks. He yelled at
May, "Don't come near! You can't afford to let
them hurt our baby!"

Leahi shouted from behind Kwanjin, "May! Go
away! I started to build the pagoda so that the
Great Buddha will give my grandson a good life!"

A young comrade among the attackers

laughed. "Old fool! There is no Buddha. Your grandson's future lies in the hands of Chairman Mao!"

Kwanjin stepped toward the young man. "Don't you dare call my mother an old fool," he said, then waved his arms at all the attackers. "Go away. As a junior party leader, I order you to leave these people alone."

Wong Chung appeared from behind the crowd. "You had better reconsider your order, Comrade Li," he said, glaring at Kwanjin. "I outrank you, and my words override yours."

Kwanjin swallowed hard. "Comrade Wong," he said in a determined voice, "these people didn't build the pagoda on party time. They did their chores during the day, then worked on the pagoda throughout the night. They didn't use any building material that belonged to the party. They used rocks and sand they dug from the ground."

Kwanjin turned and took his mother's hands, then raised those hands to show Wong Chung and the others. "Look! This old woman's hands are bleeding. Her nails are worn from digging. She didn't bother anybody by wanting a pagoda on a hilltop that's useless for anything else. Why do you want to hurt her, and the others who are just like her?"

Wong Chung lifted his chin, answered with a superior air, "Chairman Mao objects to the worship of idols. Those who disobey our Chairman are traitors to the party. Besides, when these people work all night, their strength is gone during the day, and the quality of their work will be affected. Also, they'll eat more if they do double work, and that's definitely affecting the rest of us."

Hu May saw Kwanjin's body shaking in fury. She thought, then raised her voice. "Kwanjin,

why are you arguing with Comrade Wong? The
Great Buddha has heard his words." She pointed
a finger at each of the attackers. "The Great Buddha is looking down from heaven at every one of
them, and when his home is destroyed, he'll
know who is responsible. He'll deal with them in
his own mysterious way. Kwanjin, let's take
Mama home."

Besides Kwanjin, Leahi was the first to know
what May was doing. Leahi turned to face the
pagoda and bowed deeply, then spoke loudly.
"Merciful Buddha in heaven, please forgive me
for not building you a home on earth." She
pointed at Wong Chung. "His words have more
power than the words of my poor son, and he
doesn't want you to have a home." She then
pointed at the others the way May had. "They
don't believe in you either . . . not until you show
them your power."

The others in the circle caught on quickly and
also started to bow to the Buddha in heaven while
pointing their fingers at Wong Chung and the
other attackers. Wong Chung's face became scarlet. The young attackers couldn't hide their fear—
a fear that was thousands of years old, rooted in
the hearts of all Chinese.

The Buddhists left the hilltop. The others left a
few minutes later, leaving the foundation untouched. Wong Chung called the officers to a
meeting in his cave, but didn't invite Li Kwanjin.
The meeting lasted a long time, and Chairman
Mao was asked to attend toward the end.

The worshipers gathered in Kwanjin's cave,
waiting patiently. Finally the meeting was over
and Wong Chung came to Kwanjin's cave.

"You win." Wong Chung glared at Kwanjin
and spoke through clenched teeth. "The fools can
continue with their pagoda."

Everyone cheered, including Leahi and May. Kwanjin was the only person who heard the rest of Wong Chung's words: "Li Kwanjin, you have openly declared war on the party. You had better be very careful from now on!"

17

As White Stone lay sleeping in the moonlight, Sung Hwa checked out of the hotel, holding a suitcase, and walked through the quiet streets toward the riverbank.

The Pearl flowed on one side of him, and the rice paddies stretched into the distance on the other side. It was difficult to imagine that war and the Japanese were only a few miles away.

Sung Hwa looked up at the moon, sending a silent prayer to Buddha. He had never used to believe in any supreme power, but Melin had turned him into a different person. He prayed for himself and Melin, then asked the Buddha to protect the villagers. His heart was filled with love and happiness, and he couldn't stand the thought of misfortune falling on anyone.

When he arrived at the river, the moon paled away. The eastern horizon was gray, and the birds left their nesting trees. He found a large stone with a flat top, dusted it with his handkerchief, then sat, waiting for Melin, glancing at his wristwatch now and then.

Melin had stayed in her mother's room until the night was deep, holding Yoto's hand, confessing her guilt for the sake of easing her own conscience, knowing that Yoto was sound asleep.

"But, Mama, it's all right. Hwa and I will be

married in a day or two," she had whispered to
her snoring Mama, blushing at the memory of her
blooming from a tightly closed bud into a fully
opened flower. "Mama, my fate is better than
Suelin's. She has often hinted to me about the
pain and agony she experiences each time her
husband touches her, and says that it is to be
endured by all Chinese wives. Mama, you and
Suelin ought to be happy for me. With Hwa, I
felt almost no pain, because my love for him has
made everything wonderful."

She had walked away from Yoto in slow steps,
crying and turning her head.

"Dear Mama, I'll leave you in just a few more
hours, and only Buddha knows when I will see
you again. Please stay healthy and happy, Mama,
and I'll come back with my husband as soon as
we can," she had muttered.

She had closed the door to her room tightly,
then packed only a small suitcase light enough
for her to carry to the riverbank. She didn't take
much, except a change of clothes, plus the sandalwood Buddha from Hwa and a few pieces of jewelry from her Mama. She had then lain in bed
staring at the window, imagining her happy future, waiting for the moonlight to fade.

When the first glimpse of gray appeared in the
eastern sky and the birds began to sing from the
tall trees in the garden, Melin quickly dressed,
then washed her face and smiled at herself in the
mirror.

"I am already Hwa's bride, but now I'll become
his wife," she said excitedly, and watched her
own image blushing.

She picked up her suitcase and was ready to
open the door when she heard her father
coughing at the other end of the corridor.

"Why is Baba up so early?" she mumbled in

surprise, and stood still. "Could he have just come home from the bed of some singsong girl?"

Ma Tsai-tu's footsteps stopped at Melin's door. Melin quickly kicked her suitcase under the bed. Her father knocked. She held her breath, hoping that he would change his mind and go away. There was no reason for him to come to her room at this hour of the day. He had never visited her in the past eighteen years; why should he visit her now, at the most crucial moment of her life?

"Melin, Melin!" Her father knocked harder, calling her name.

She opened the door, and saw him all dressed for traveling.

"Are you always up so early?" He glanced from her white wool skirt and yellow sweater to the yellow jade butterfly in her hair. "And always dressed so nicely at dawn?" He knew very little about his daughters, and decided that Melin had a strange habit of rising early.

"Baba . . . you never get up before noon . . . is something wrong?" Melin asked in broken sentences.

"We are going to Shanghai," Ma Tsai-tu said casually, then added, "Just you and I."

Melin nearly fainted. "When?" she asked, holding on to the doorknob.

"Now," her father said, then clapped his hands for the maid.

Melin couldn't speak as she listened to the maid's footsteps approaching. Her father had never taken her or Suelin or Yoto to Shanghai or anywhere else before; why must he choose this day for such an unusual event?

The maid stood waiting and Ma Tsai-tu said to the woman, "Pack a suitcase for Sheo-jay, and don't forget to include her most beautiful clothes and expensive jewelry." He turned to Melin.

"Since you're already dressed, I'll be back in only a few minutes and then we can leave for the train station."

Melin regained some of her wits. "Baba, I don't want to leave Mama when she's sick," she said weakly. "Can we go to Shanghai some other day?"

Ma Tsai-tu was not used to having his daughters bargain with him. He stepped forward until his face was so close to Melin's that she could smell his breath, foul with wine and tobacco. "Let me tell you once more, Melin. We are going to Shanghai today, this morning. We're not going because of some sudden impulse, Melin. Your Baba doesn't do things on impulses. You'll see the importance of this trip later, but I don't need to explain anything more to you until then."

Ma Tsai-tu glared at Melin with eyes that glowed with the authority tradition granted to all Chinese fathers. Melin lowered her eyes and bowed her head. Her eyes burned with tears and her body shook with fear and frustration.

Just before walking away, Ma Tsai-tu said, "I'm going to leave word with your Mama's maid that you and I are going to Shanghai." He grinned at his daughter threateningly. "If you are not ready when I return, your Mama will become sicker, I promise."

Melin knew what he meant. When he was unhappy with the children, Ma Tsai-tu would take his anger out on Yoto. Melin visualized her mother's sick face on the pillow, but in her mind she could also see Hwa waiting at the riverbank.

She gathered all the courage she had. "Baba, I don't feel well today. I don't think I can travel . . ." Her protest trailed away as Ma Tsai-tu raised a hand. Melin closed her eyes. She waited for the blow, but it never came. Holding her breath, she opened her eyes a little, looked, and saw her father lowering his hand with effort. He smiled at Melin instead, and when he spoke, his voice had a forced gentleness. "Be a good girl and go with Baba. Baba never asks you for anything, and now he wants your company on a very pleasant trip. You can't disappoint your poor Baba, can you? After all, Baba is getting old, and only Buddha knows how many more pitiful years Baba has left in this cruel world."

The best weapon possessed by a Chinese parent was neither a stick nor a whip, but a sorrowful look and a few begging words that reminded the young of the coming death of the old. Ma Tsai-tu used his weapon effectively, and Melin was beaten completely. All she wanted now was to find a way to let Hwa know.

Ma Tsai-tu left, trying to conceal the triumphant smile on his face. The maid had started to pack when the father and daughter were having their discussion, and now came to her Sheo-jay for approval. "I can't find the other suitcase, Sheo-jay," she said, "so I picked this one. Would you like to look at the clothes I picked?"

Melin shook her head. If fate were kind to her, she wouldn't need any of the things the maid had packed. If the Buddha in heaven knew how much she and Hwa loved each other, she and Hwa would be together soon.

The graying sky soon became pink, and several fishermen appeared. Very few of them paid attention to Sung Hwa. Most were eager to start sailing, hoping for a profitable day. As the fishing boats moved down the stream, the sun rose slowly. A group of young girls came with baskets filled with dirty clothes, and they looked at Sung Hwa, giggling as they did their laundry.

Sung Hwa stood up. He looked at the narrow path that led to the main road, then looked at his watch once more. Melin was late. He hoped that none of these girls would recognize her when she came. If one of them should run to the Ma house and report the scene to her father, and if her father should rush to the train station immediately, there would be trouble.

The village girls finished their chores and were gone. The sky had changed from pink to red, and now the sun blazed from a blue canopy, sparkling off the rippling Pearl. Sung Hwa looked at his watch, then picked up his suitcase and walked toward the road. The morning train would be leaving in only thirty more minutes. If he met Melin halfway down the road, they still could make it.

He stopped abruptly, remembering clearly that they were supposed to meet at the riverbank. He rushed back. He strolled back and forth along the river with the suitcase in one hand, pulling his neatly combed hair with the other. He soon heard the train whistling, pulling into the station of White Stone.

Maybe she's waiting for me in the hotel! he thought. *Maybe I remembered it wrong!*

He ran without stopping back to the hotel.

Melin grabbed a sheet of paper and a pen with her trembling hands. She must write Hwa a letter. Her thoughts were many, each taking a different direction. How could she make sure that Hwa would receive her note? Could she trust the maid? Should she go wake up her Mama and ask Mama to go to the hotel to talk to Hwa? No. Mama didn't even know of the existence of Hwa. It would take forever to explain the urgent situation,

and the sudden shock could bring Mama another
stroke.

Suddenly she thought of something. She went
to the maid and took the woman by the shoulder.
"You listen to me carefully! You must go immediately to the high school and tell my principal
that—" She heard her father's voice coming from
the corridor, calling impatiently.

"Melin, are you ready? The train is leaving in
thirty more minutes!"

"What did you say, Sheo-jay?" The woman
hadn't heard Melin clearly. "Go to school? I don't
go to school. I'm too old to learn anything! The
principal? Yes, I know Mr. Chew. We are distantly related."

Melin raised her hands to pull her neatly
combed hair, stamped her foot, and screamed
soundlessly.

Her father appeared at the door, followed by a
male servant carrying his suitcase. "Ready?" Ma
Tsai-tu asked. Without waiting for his daughter
to answer, he told the servant to pick up Sheo-
jay's suitcase and bring the luggage to the wagon.

"Was anybody here looking for me?" Sung
Hwa asked the hotel clerk.

The man stared dumbly, then shook his head.

"Are you sure?!" Hwa yelled at the man.

The man nodded.

From near the hotel the train whistled loudly as
it pulled out of the station. The rumbling sound
increased its rhythm, then gradually faded away.

Sung Hwa asked the clerk to give him back his
old room. He dragged his suitcase up the stairs,
locked the door, and sat on his bed. He leaned
his elbows on his knees, dug his fingers into his
hair, and then moved his hands down and sank
his nails into his face.

"Melin," he called softly at first, then screamed, "Melin! Why didn't you come to the riverbank?"

Melin sat by the window in the enclosed car, watching her hometown disappearing in front of her eyes.

"Silly child," Ma Tsai-tu hissed at his daughter from the seat opposite hers, then dragged deeply on his cigarette. "Shanghai is not the other end of the world. Why are you crying like your heart is broken? You'll be back to your dear Mama's old bosom in just a few days!"

Melin sobbed so hard that she was choking. Her hands were cold and her body stiff. She had never felt so helpless and near madness in her life. Her desperation had peaked when she looked all over the station with a last hope of finding Hwa.

If he shows up here, I'll run to him and throw myself into his open arms, she had said to herself. *I'll tell Baba that I'm already Hwa's bride. Hwa is much bigger and stronger than Baba. He and I will simply walk away . . . and then later we'll ask for Baba's forgiveness, of course.*

But Hwa was not at the station and now she didn't know what to do. The thought of Hwa losing faith in her was like a sharp knife, driving itself into her heart.

"He can't think that I've broken my promise . . . he simply can't think that way!" Unconsciously she uttered these words while sobbing.

"What did you say?" Ma Tsai-tu asked immediately, narrowing his eyes in suspicion. "He? What he? Who is he?"

Melin thought quickly. "I . . . promised Mr. Chew that I'd go to school to help him with some papers. He'll think of me as a bad student."

Ma Tsai-tu relaxed. "That old fool!" He then closed his eyes. He hadn't had enough sleep, and he needed to rest before facing the big task waiting for him in Shanghai.

As her father napped, Melin cried until the train reached Kwangchow. The wheels slowed down, and the comforting rhythm brought her wishful thoughts. *Hwa is smart . . . Hwa knows what to do . . . he will do something . . . something . . . something . . . !*

Melin felt a little better. Her father opened his eyes. She told him that she needed to go to the rest room to wash her face. Her eyes brightened with the sudden hope that if the rest room were far from their car, perhaps she could get off in Kwangchow without Baba knowing, and then try to contact Hwa from there.

Ma Tsai-tu opened the door of the compartment and pointed at another door. "Our private toilet is right here."

He yawned, then grinned broadly at Melin. "You are more precious to me than you realize, little girl."

Melin's hope of escape had been burst by Baba, but she washed her face and didn't cry anymore. She had faith in her Hwa. He would do something clever, and sooner or later they would be together.

"Tai-tai, there is a young gentleman at the door. He asked to see Melin Sheo-jay. When I told him that our young Sheo-jay has gone to Shanghai with her Baba, he acted like a Great Buddha had stricken him with a lightning stick. When he recovered and was able to talk, he asked to see you," the maid said to Ma Yoto. "He said it's very important."

"What's his name? And why is his business so important?" Mrs. Ma asked. She was sitting be-

side the window, looking at the winter plums
blooming in the walled courtyard.

The maid gave her mistress a card. "His name
is on it. He said that he must talk to you about
Melin Sheo-jay."

"Since Melin is on her way to Shanghai with
her father, why would a stranger want to talk to
me about her?" Mrs. Ma glanced at the card. Her
eyes froze on the family name.

The maid went on. "I think he is the young
man from the Land of the Gold Mountains. They
say he has stayed in the White Stone Hotel for
months."

"Sung! The Land of the Gold Mountains!" Ma
Yoto pressed a hand against her heart. "Tell him
I'll be right there."

Yoto walked into the living room, took one look
at the young man, and knew he was Sung Quanming's son. Except for the clothes and the haircut,
he was the duplicate of the man she had loved
many years ago and still couldn't forget.

She fell into a chair, breathing hard, staring at
the uninvited visitor. He stood, bowed, and re-
seated himself. The maid served tea and retreated
to a far corner of the room that was shielded by
a tall screen. She stood silently and listened to
every word that passed between her Tai-tai and
the stranger.

Sung Hwa introduced himself and began to
talk. He started with his decision to visit his father's hometown. He went on to his meeting
Melin, including the important part played by Mr.
Chew and without avoiding anything except what
had happened in the hotel room the other night.
He had become Chinese enough in the past
months to know that he must not let Melin's
mother know that aspect of their relationship; his

good judgment told him that it would be too much for an old-fashioned mother's delicate heart.

"Melin and I love each other. She doesn't want to marry the man you and your husband chose for her. She and I want to be married. We were supposed to meet this morning and go away together, but she didn't show up. I don't know what happened, but I know it has nothing to do with her changing her mind about becoming my wife . . . she will never change and nor will I. Your maid told me at the door that she has gone to Shanghai with her father. I can't understand it. She and I meet every day and every night, but she never mentioned any plan for a trip."

Sung Hwa leaned forward, poured out his questions quickly, one after another. "Mrs. Ma, why does Melin have to go to Shanghai? Was she forced to go, or did she go of her own free will? How long will she be there? Where is she staying? I must send her a telegram and tell her that I'll be on the next train, which leaves White Stone tomorrow morning. No matter what, I'm taking her with me from Shanghai to Hong Kong, then Hawaii and the United States." He looked into Yoto's eyes and waited for her to answer, holding his breath nervously.

Yoto picked up the teacup with her quivering old fingers, narrowed her aged eyes to study Sung Hwa through the rising steam. She felt the pain in her heart increasing. Her daughter had lied to her because of Sung Quanming's son. The two young people were in love regardless of the never-fulfilled love between the two old ones. Was the Great Buddha kind or cruel? Should Melin be congratulated for her good fortune or protected from harm?

At dawn Tsai-tu had left word with her maid that he and Melin were on their way to Shanghai, staying in the Cathay Hotel on Nanjing Road. He had told the maid that they would be back in a week or so, but nothing else.

The hot steam ascended steadily from the cup, transforming into the thin layer of smoke that had once filled the temple in White Stone during the Lantern Festival. A girl named Kao Yoto looked through the smoke and saw a handsome young man named Sung Quanming. Her heart was captured by him, and because of that, she was cursed for life. Now, as a mature woman, she must act carefully to prevent her daughter from suffering the same fate.

Yoto lowered the teacup. The steam disappeared; the smoke faded away. "Are you in love with my daughter? Do you truly believe that my daughter can be happy with you in the white devils' country?"

Sung Hwa was surprised by the sudden hardness in the old woman's voice. "Yes, I'm very much in love with Melin. She means everything to me, and it's going to be this way until I die," he answered, his voice tense. "I can assure you that your daughter and I will be happy wherever we go. I have a lot to offer her, and she has my love, my life, and everything I will achieve in the future . . . with her love as a reason for me to strive, I'll achieve a great deal."

"Love?" Yoto's voice softened. Perhaps Quanming had loved her at one time. She smiled a little. "Did your father tell you much about this village? Did he mention any . . . name?"

She held her breath. If only Quanming had told his son that his first love was a girl in White Stone. Or perhaps Quanming had said that there was a warm spot in his heart reserved for someone very special in his hometown. Then, of course, Yoto would help Quanming's son.

"No." Sung Hwa shook his head, confused by Yoto's odd questions. "My father didn't seem to have any fond memories of White Stone. He never talked much about it. But perhaps he didn't think I would understand. We were close only when I was a young boy. He left Mama when I was a teenager. He moved to Hawaii and married an American woman."

Yoto slammed down the cup. It made a loud sound, spilling hot tea all over the table. "When did he leave your mother?"

Sung Hwa gave the year, and Yoto tasted the bitterness in her mouth. She swallowed hard. So, the rumors were correct. Quanming had moved to that barbaric island where people were half-naked all year round. He was contemplating divorce when he had revisited White Stone years ago. Divorce was rare in China, but Yoto certainly could have acquired one if only he had asked her to go with him. But when she had wandered to his house in tears, he was dreaming of a barbarian woman!

"How could your father prefer a white cow over a good Chinese woman who loves him so deeply!" Yoto cried.

Sung Hwa couldn't hide his surprise. "How do you know Mama loves Baba? She never even admitted it to me and my sister, although we sensed it."

Mrs. Ma didn't answer. Her eyes were narrowed, her lips a tight line. She was thinking hard, looking for a quick way to get rid of Sung Quanming's son. Her precious Melin must be saved from Sung Hwa, like a butterfly saved from the toying hands of a heartless boy.

Yoto pushed her hands against the arms of the chair, lifting up her heavy body. "I'm happy for you, Mr. Sung . . ." Yoto paused.

She was proud of the fact that she might have aged, but her brain still worked fast. Lies formed quickly when they were born of a good Mama's need to protect her naive daughter. "Melin will be in the Land of the Gold Mountains very soon, with her Baba, looking for a house to buy, a place for the Ma family to live."

She forced a sincere smile on her round and many-chinned face when she saw the doubt and surprise in the young man's eyes. She cleared her throat, then continued. "China is lost, and we have nowhere to run except to escape the country altogether. My husband and I have prepared for this trip for a long time, but in a Chinese home the parents never discuss such important decisions with the children."

Sung Hwa nodded, stunned but listening.

Yoto said, "Since Melin has learned some English from school, and is much more clever than her three brothers, and because my husband doesn't know any English at all, he decided to take her with him on this trip. Where are you from? San Francisco? Yes, that's where they are going first. My husband wants to investigate that place, then go to other large cities, to find a new home for all of us."

Sung Hwa smiled. Yoto's words made sense. Melin had not stopped loving him or changed her mind about the marriage.

Encouraged by her success, Yoto made her performance even more touching. She smiled warmly and her eyes turned moist with tears. "Melin is such a good child. She loves her mother so dearly. I have been sick. If she had known that she was going to another country, she would never have agreed to go. So we didn't tell her until this morning, and mentioned only Shanghai."

Yoto glanced at the screen, saw the maid's feet,

and added carefully, "To keep Melin from knowing our plans, we hushed them in front of the servants. That's why the maid doesn't know anything."

The screen moved a little as the maid shook in anger. The woman was proud of the fact that she knew everything that took place in the Ma household. She knew what her Tai-tai was doing, and she didn't like the game that was being played on her beloved Sheo-jay. She had heard this young man confessing his love for Sheo-jay, including the important role played by Mr. Chew. Now she understood why Sheo-jay had been so happy recently. There was nothing the maid could do, however, since she didn't want to call her Tai-tai a liar. She needed her job. But she would go to her cousin Chew later to tell the clever principal everything and ask him to do something for his favorite student, Melin, and Melin's young man.

Yoto looked tired. Sung Hwa stood up politely, thanked her profusely.

Leading the way to the door, Yoto advised, "The only sensible thing for you to do is to go back home. Does Melin have your home address? She does? Good. As soon as she telegraphs me from San Francisco, I'll telegraph her back to inform her that you and she are in the same town. Why, she'll be so happy. She will contact you directly, I'm sure. You just go home and wait for the good news, Mr. Sung."

At the door, Sung Hwa became an American momentarily and kissed Yoto. Tears welled up in her eyes as she felt the trusting young man's warm lips on her cold cheek. She was about to call Sung Hwa back, but then quickly changed her mind.

The next day Ma Yoto sent a male servant to

the local hotel. He came back and reported that Sung Hwa had left on the first train. Mrs. Ma breathed with relief.

Only after the servant had gone did Yoto whisper to herself, "Quanming, I don't believe your son loves my daughter any more than you loved me. May the Great Buddha prove me right, or I'll eternally blame myself for making the cruelest mistake of my life."

18

AARON STOOD at the hotel window, waiting for Diana to return. She had told him that she must make some kind of arrangement for traveling.

On the street down below, Kwangchow began its first day under Japanese rule.

Vegetable, fish, and meat peddlers were the first to set up their stands along Main Street. Housewives and maids soon came to the market carrying shopping baskets, buying their families' daily needs.

The door opened. Aaron turned. Diana stood there, looking tired but smiling.

Aaron pointed at the street. "Only a few hours after what happened to those people, life goes on as usual."

"People have to eat and live," Diana said. "Are you ready?"

Aaron went to pick up his packed suitcase. "Where is your duffel bag?"

"We can't take anything with us."

"Why?"

Diana pointed at his Eurasian face and then at her own Caucasian one. "We attract enough attention without looking like two travelers. We need to sneak out of Kwangchow, remember?"

Her tone of voice bothered Aaron. "You don't need to talk down to me. Of course I remember.

I also remember we are not taking the train because it may be dangerous."

Aaron sighed. He didn't agree with the idea of giving up the train ride, since it was still available. Besides, Diana was so vague about how they would get to Shanghai without the train, but his pride kept him from asking. He merely murmured, "How can we get along without our things?"

"We'll rough it." Diana patted her slacks pockets. "I've hidden the brooch. We have the money and checks your father gave us. When we reach Shanghai, we'll buy what we need." She added with a smile, "We may even buy more jewelry."

Aaron hated to leave his things. But he wasn't going to tell Diana. Last night, when they had sat side by side behind the window, she had seemed to be as frightened as he. He had felt close to her then, almost considered her a sister. But now her superior air had returned, and he resented it. He gave his suitcase a kick to relieve his anger, then led the way out of the room to show that he didn't care.

On the street, Diana bought a few steamed buns from a peddler. "Eat as much as you can." She gave half of them to Aaron. "I don't know when we will see food again."

Aaron followed her example and ate the buns as they walked away from Main Street, through many narrow alleys. "From what I can see, the people in Kwangchow are very calm." He pointed at a woman hanging out wet clothes and a man riding a bicycle to work. "Like nothing ever happened. Perhaps they are used to being invaded."

"Everyone is scared, but life goes on," Diana said, taking large bites of her bun. "You're right about their being used to invasion." She counted the forces that had raided Kwangchow in the past

century. "The Manchurian soldiers, the British
Army, the Tai Ping rebels, the Boxers, the Nationalist troops, the many warlords . . ."

They were beside a fenced yard filled wtih
noisy chickens that were trying to run away from
a woman holding a large cleaver. Diana pointed
at the chickens. "China is this fenced yard. The
Chinese are the chickens. This woman, her husband, children, and in-laws all may come and
grab a chicken, then chop its head off. The chickens live from day to day. They scream and run
when the cleaver is over their heads. They eat
with good appetite again when the threat is
gone."

Aaron frowned. "I don't like the comparison.
Not all of us are willing to be chickens." He
looked around and said, "I don't see any Japanese. Where are they?"

"Settling down in their headquarters. They will
be out this evening, eating and drinking in restaurants, buying things. The nicer ones will pay, the
others will demand to have everything free.
When night comes, they'll either rape some
decent women or look for flower girls."

She explained to Aaron that the Japanese called
all the young girls who could be bought for a
night's fun flower girls. "The rich of Kwangchow
are busy now. They want to get on the good side
of the Japanese by offering them money and entertainment. The high-priced flower girls will be
hired by the local rich to charm the Japanese officers. The less expensive ones will be visited by
the soldiers."

"You can't know for sure," Aaron said disbelievingly. "You are as new to a Japanese-ruled city
as I am."

Diana shook her head. "No, I'm not."

Aaron stood still in the alley. "Diana, if you

don't tell me more about yourself, I'm not going anywhere with you."

"Please, Aaron." Diana looked at her watch. "We have no time to waste." She pulled him along. "I'll tell you as much as I can, I promise."

They came out of the last alley and began to walk toward the country. Diana talked as she walked quickly. "When I was ten, my parents took me to the northeast plain to establish a mission in the capital of Jilin province that is called Eternal Spring. We liked the people and they accepted us. I went to school there and had many friends. Life was peaceful and lovely for a year, then the Japanese moved in. The Nationalist troops couldn't protect us, nor could the Communist soldiers. Actually, we suffered at the hands of all three of them—the Japanese, the Communists, and the Nationalists. In 1931, when I was fourteen, the Japanese Army took over Manchuria. We watched those close to us being raped, tortured, and killed. My parents and I were spared because the Japanese didn't want to upset the British government. We continued to live in Eternal Spring for another year and learned to swallow our anger when we saw the cruelest persecution being applied to human beings by the hands of other human beings. In 1932 the Japanese made Eternal Spring the capital of their puppet Manchukuo regime and changed its name to Mukden, using it as a base for moving military forces into north China. My parents were transferred to Hong Kong that year. I continued my schooling there, and three years later I graduated from high school. I came to work for your father."

"No wonder you know so much." Aaron looked at Diana with a new understanding and respect. "That's why you could watch those people die without covering your eyes."

They walked silently for a while, past a rice field, and started on a narrow path.

"Aaron," Diana said, pulling his arm, "I ought to tell you something else."

As they moved on a winding road that stretched through the countryside, Diana continued to talk. "The Nationalist party is divided in two. The right wing, led by Chiang Kai-shek, is only for the rich. The left wing, led by a man named Wang Ching-wei, is for the poor and the middle class, but not as violently against the rich as the Communists. When Dr. Sun Yat-sen died in 1925, Chiang and Wang had an equal chance to become his successor. Chiang had the warlords and landlords on his side and won the leadership. Wang lives in Chiang's shadow, but still has his followers. Wang is a good man. He and his supporters want the privileges of the rich to be curbed, the farmers and laborers fairly treated, the freedoms of the citizens protected. But they disagree over the abolishment of tradition, religion, and private enterprise. In other words, they want China to become a better place for the majority, without turning it into a Communist country."

Aaron interrupted. "That sounds much better than either the Nationalists or the Communists. Well, Chiang is moving to Chungking in the southwest. Mao is in Yenan, the northwest. Where is Wang Ching-wei? Is he also too far away to help the Chinese people?"

Diana shook her head. "No. Wang and his men are right here."

Aaron's eyes widened. "Here?" He looked around the deserted country road.

Diana smiled. "You will meet some of them in a few minutes . . . you've already met some of them without knowing it."

Aaron's jaw dropped. "The man in the train station!"

Diana nodded. "And the newspaper vendor."

Aaron stared at her. "And you . . . are you one of them also?"

They could see a graveyard at the end of the road. Diana hastened her steps; Aaron followed.

"When this trip is over, I trust you'll never tell this to anyone," Diana said. "Your father doesn't know. No one does. When your mother came to New Territory to see me, she ran into a few of them. But she didn't know who they were either."

Diana told Aaron that her parents had become involved with the left-wing Nationalists the year after they arrived in Hong Kong. Two of the LWN leaders were wanted by Chiang Kai-shek to organize a strike in Hong Kong against the British factory owners who underpaid their workers. They were members of Diana's family's church and were also their friends. Her parents sheltered them in the mission house. When they talked about their dreams and the dreams of their colleagues, her parents realized that they, too, shared the same dream. Diana smiled proudly. "Unlike most of the British people, who look down on the Chinese, my parents have always felt a part of China. It didn't take them long to decide to join the LWN."

Aaron asked curiously, "And you?"

"Unlike my parents, I'm not very religious. But exactly like them, I feel I am Chinese. I began to work for the LWN when I was eighteen, soon after I started to work for your father. The people your mother saw in my apartment are underground workers. They bring things to me, then I pass the things out from the jewelry store."

"What kinds of things?"

Diana hesitated. "Mostly information, once in

a while medicine, and sometimes small weapons." She smiled at Aaron teasingly. "Are you afraid to be with me now, since you know I am a spy?"

Aaron shook his head. "Not at all. How often must I remind you I am not a child? I may not have your experience, but I've not exactly lived in a sheltered world. I've seen the invasion of Beijing. We barely escaped on the train. I suffered the loss of my beloved sister . . ." He couldn't continue any further. He lifted his chin stubbornly. "Anyway, I would like to join you and your friends and work for the LWN."

"Ha!" Diana laughed again. "Your parents will kill me."

"But I feel so useless." Aaron hit his thighs with his fists. "I felt like a coward when I watched the Japanese take over our city and slaughter our people. I felt even worse when you said most of the Chinese are like those chickens. Now I find out that even you and your parents are helping China—"

He screamed as a big man jumped out of the shadow of a tree and pointed a gun at him and Diana.

"It's the Moon Girl and her friend," Diana said calmly, then quickly gave Aaron a name: "Rich Boy."

The well-built middle-aged man studied Diana and Aaron carefully, then put away his gun. He introduced himself as Tea Drinker. "Scholar told us you've requested transportation to Shanghai," he said, and walked toward the graveyard.

Diana and Aaron followed. "Why the funny names?" Aaron whispered. "And why 'Rich Boy'?"

"It's better to call one another by assumed names. For instance, if Tea Drinker was caught and tortured, he could only say that my friend is

Rich Boy, so Aaron Cohen will not be involved,"
Diana explained. "I'm sorry if you don't like your
name. I couldn't think of anything else right
now."

"Why 'Moon Girl'?" Aaron looked at Diana unhappily. "That's much better than 'Rich Boy.' "

"In English, 'Diana' means 'moon goddess.'
Since I'm in China, I prefer to be humble. Instead
of a goddess, I'm just a girl." Diana stopped
when she saw a small old truck parked behind a
huge willow.

A man stepped out of the truck; Aaron recognized him as the slender young man Diana had
talked to in the train station. Diana now introduced him as Scholar.

Scholar gave Diana a key. "Don't forget to de-
liver the magazine in Shanghai," he said, and
walked away with the Tea Drinker after wishing
Diana good luck.

Aaron didn't know that Diana could drive. He
sat beside her, looked at her profile. Her eyes
were intent on the bumpy road, her jaw was
firmly set. Wind blew in through the open window, tossing her short hair. She was no longer a
sales clerk or a buying agent in a jewelry store.
She was an LWN spy! He was suddenly proud
and excited to be such a woman's friend.

"Now I remember the movie magazine. What's
in it? Whom are you giving it to?" he asked
eagerly.

"It goes to a bookstore in Shanghai. But I can't
tell you more." Diana changed the subject. "You'd
better take a nap."

Aaron was not sleepy. He was nervous and
afraid as they headed north, zigzagging around
and through rice fields and woods. Several times,
when they spotted Japanese troops in the distance, Diana drove into the deepest bushes to

hide until the road was clear. The pace of their journey was slow, the seats of their truck uncomfortable. They longed to reach Shanghai and leave all their worries on the doorstep of Diana's parents' home.

They met many refugees fleeing the villages near Kwangchow, heading on foot toward nearby towns. They picked up as many people as the old truck could carry. When night came, they parked in a thick bamboo grove and offered the truck to the old people and the babies as a bed. They slept on the ground. Aaron cuddled close to Diana and looked up at the night sky.

He thought of his parents in Hong Kong. If they had known his trip was going to turn into a spy mission, they would never have let him come. He thought of Yin. If she knew he was sleeping so close to Diana . . . He smiled. Yin was a good old-fashioned Chinese girl, never possessive or jealous. He yawned. Yin had no reason to be jealous anyway. Diana might as well be an older sister to both him and Yin. He curled up against Diana's lean form and slept soundly.

They resumed their journey at daybreak, still heading north. By midmorning they began to see people coming from the opposite direction, carrying their belongings and babies, holding on to their families.

"These people are coming from the direction of Shanghai," Aaron observed, "but they are in worse shape than those going there. I wonder what is going on."

Diana stopped the truck and jumped out. She grabbed a weak, shuffling young man. "Where are you from?"

"Whangpoo River," the man mumbled.

"That's in Shanghai!" Diana shook the man. "What's happened there?"

"It's lost to the Japanese." The man shivered. "Hundreds and thousands of people have died. The Nationalist Army fought hard this time, but they were defeated anyway. The Japanese were angry at losing so many soldiers. They took their anger out on the people . . ." He began to cry.

Diana asked urgently, "Do you know if the Japanese invaded the International Settlement?"

The man shook his head. "I am a fisherman. I was born on the banks of the Whangpoo River. I don't go to the International Settlement. That's where there is a sign nailed to the gate of the public park that says, *No Dogs or Chinamen Allowed*." He sobbed harder. "Now my Whangpoo River is filled with bodies . . . my parents, my brothers, and my wife."

Diana stopped and questioned everyone they passed on the road. They all said the same thing: Shanghai had fallen utterly to the Japanese.

From a great distance, they could already see black smoke rising from the bombed-out buildings, and low orange flames burning over many piles of debris. The sun was setting over the Whangpoo River, casting a red glow on the destroyed sampans and ships.

They passed a ditch filled with human bodies in soldiers' uniforms and civilian clothes, either riddled with bullet holes or decapitated. Thirsty flies gathered on the pools of blood. Hungry dogs waited for their chance.

Diana couldn't make much progress. The dead were being carried away, the wounded collected by ambulances and pushcarts. The survivors wandered around, aimlessly looking for shelter and food.

They saw Japanese soldiers everywhere, herding the captured Nationalist soldiers, kicking and beating them, patrolling the streets, evacuating buildings, and climbing up on rooftops to take down Chiang Kai-shek's large portraits.

They saw a half-naked woman run out of a house near the railroad track. A train was coming and she headed for it. The whistle shrieked. She ran faster and threw herself right in front of the wheels. Both Aaron and Diana screamed when the train crushed her. A crowd gathered around the broken body. Diana tried to detour around them, only to come up against another group surrounding an old man kneeling on the sidewalk. Two Japanese soldiers took turns slapping him. His white beard was covered with blood. Behind him an old woman lay either in a faint or dead in front of a ransacked store.

Aaron seized Diana's arm. "Please, Diana, let me do something for these people. Let me join your organization."

Diana didn't answer. Aaron felt her arm tremble. He looked at her face and realized how selfish his request seemed. He squeezed her arm gently. "We'll be in the International Settlement soon. Don't worry, Diana, your parents will be all right. The Japanese would not dare harm any British missionaries."

Diana stopped at a bookstore. She told Aaron to wait, then went inside with the movie magazine she had carried from Kwangchow. She came out a few minutes later without it. They then headed for the Internationl Settlement.

Night fell on the street near Diana's parents' home. A French restaurant was open; the mirrored walls and brightly lit chandeliers could be seen through the large uncurtained windows. A Russian bakery had its door opened wide; large dark, round loaves of bread were displayed on the counter. A German clock shop had many beautiful grandfather clocks for sale. An Italian eating place sent out loud music from its red-curtained window.

"Just like Kwangchow," Aaron said in disgust as they turned into a dimly lit alley crowded with people walking or sitting in front of the dark apartment buildings, small stores, and a little church. "The woman with the cleaver is gone, and the chickens are eating with good appetite again."

Before Diana brought the truck to a full stop, a white-haired Chinese woman stood up from the doorstep of the church and came rushing toward them.

"That's the maid my parents brought from Hong Kong," Diana said, turning off the engine. "I wonder . . ."

"Don't come near this place!" The old woman flailed her hands violently. She pointed at the church, then pushed Diana back into the truck. She tried to lower her voice as she spoke quickly in Cantonese, looking over her shoulder now and then in fear. "Japanese soldiers are inside your parents' house, arresting everyone who enters. They said your missionary father and mother were spies, hiding some young men who dared to resist the Japanese Army. Your parents were executed in the church courtyard this morning."

Diana screamed and tried to lunge out of the truck. The woman kept her firm hands on Diana's arms and raised her voice. "Your parents and I knew you would come. I risked my life waiting for you. Did I risk being murdered for nothing?"

A faint sound emanated from the church door. The woman let go of Diana, turned, and ran away. Tears streamed down Diana's face. But she hesitated only a second, then started the engine and put her foot on the accelerator.

19

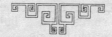

MELIN AND HER father heard about the fall of
Kwangchow and Shanghai when the train stopped
in Ningpo, a small town south of Shanghai.

"Of course we're not going to Shanghai now,"
Melin said, glad that she could go home to her
Hwa.

Her brief hope was dashed by her father's calm
words. "Shanghai's change of hands won't take
long. We'll wait." They waited for two nights in
a hotel in Ningpo. During that time Melin tried to
escape but failed. On the third day it was confirmed
that all the battles had been fought; Chiang's men
had left defeated. They traveled on.

"I counted on this to happen and I'm glad it
happened so soon," Ma Tsai-tu said. "Now we
are spared the sight of the bloodshed." He had
calculated the fall of Shanghai, and planned to
wait in the International Settlement with Melin
until it was safe to leave the district. He wanted
to be in Shanghai as soon as the Japanese took
over, to present them a beautiful welcoming gift.
He had gambled with his safety and his daughter's because he was a lucky man and usually
won.

In the Shanghai train station they were met by
two men in dark robes, who complained about
the two-day delay.

"My business associates." Ma Tsai-tu introduced them to his daughter without giving any names.

Melin instantly disliked both men. They measured her with their eyes, glancing over her from head to toe and back again. They exchanged looks with her father, as if speaking in a silent code about things she did not understand.

Motor cars were everywhere. Ma Tsai-tu hired one, and sat with the driver, leaving Melin in the back seat between the two men, who guarded the doors as if she might try to escape. They gazed at her as the car moved along the street, and she fidgeted uncomfortably, pulling her skirt down to cover as much of her ankles as possible. She stared ahead at the ruined streets of Shanghai.

The war was over. The Japanese soldiers seemed to be leaving the Chinese alone, unless there were signs of resistance. In the restaurants, theaters, hotels, and stores, the Japanese, Chinese, and Europeans coexisted in peace, at least on the surface.

They stopped at the Cathay Hotel. The two men escorted Melin and her father into the fourteen-story building, rode the elevator with them, then waited outside the suite on the top floor. A chambermaid and a valet were assigned to each suite. Melin waited for them to unpack for her and her father.

As soon as the maid and valet left, she asked, "When will we go home?"

Ma Tsai-tu ignored her question. "I'm hungry," he said, leading the way. "My friends are waiting for us."

The dining room was on the eighth floor. The night was young, and the place was almost empty. Two Englishmen were entertaining a few of the city's new rulers—half a dozen Japanese in uniform. One Chinese sat with them, serving as an interpreter. They all turned their heads toward

Melin as she and her father and the two men
entered.

"Ah, what a coincidence!" Ma Tsai-tu's two associates waved at the interpreter. "Our friend is
here. He is quite a brilliant Chinese, speaking
many languages. Maybe he will introduce us to
his Japanese bosses sometime."

Melin and her father took a table while Tsai-tu's
associates went to talk to the interpreter. From the
corner of her eye Melin saw them glancing at her,
and then several of the Japanese officers turned
to look at her. She shivered and tried to hide behind her father, but at the same time, Ma Tsai-tu
stood up, smiled at the Japanese, and bowed.

Melin turned her head to avoid the eyes of the
Japanese. She looked out the wide window and
had a full view of the city.

Without waiting for his friends to return, Ma
Tsai-tu ordered dinner and drinks. While waiting
to be served, he indicated the city of Shanghai
and said to his daughter, "Look at the people.
Each is an insignificant dot, but to every individ-
ual he is the center of the universe. We must try
our best to hold on to our delicate existence,"
Tsai-tu said enigmatically.

Melin waited for her father to go on, but her
thoughts were occupied by Sung Hwa. What was
he doing at this moment? Had he done whatever
he must to discover her whereabouts? Would he
appear soon to take her away from her father, to
end this ridiculous trip, and to go toward the
bright future that they had planned together?

Her father said, "The Japanese have taken
Kwangchow already. In a few days they'll have
all the surrounding villages, including our White
Stone. It won't be a pleasant time, I'm afraid."
He looked at his daughter. "I don't have to list

the horrible consequences. But you know what I'm talking about."

Melin nodded. "There is still time for us to run away, Baba." Her eyes brightened. Perhaps her Hwa could rescue her and her family!

Ma Tsai-tu shook his head. "The whole of China is in trouble. The only place safe is overseas. But we don't have any connections there."

Melin remained silent as Tsai-tu went on. "We must find a way to protect ourselves when the Japanese soldiers take over White Stone." He reached across the table, took his daughter's hands in his. "And we can only be saved by you."

"Me?" Melin's eyes widened.

"Yes."

"How?"

Ma Tsai-tu wouldn't answer. "Finish your dinner, Melin. I'll tell you soon enough."

The two men returned, exchanged a pleased look with Ma Tsai-tu, then all three of them nodded and smiled. Melin ate quickly. She wanted to return to her room as fast as possible. She prayed for this whole trip to be over quickly.

The three men didn't seem to be hungry. They waited for her to finish eating, then accompanied her back to the suite. The two men waited by the door like guard dogs while Ma Tsai-tu entered the suite with Melin. He walked her to her room, lingered at the door.

Tsai-tu leaned against the door frame, his arms folded in front of his chest. He took a deep breath and began to talk. "My daughter, I'm sure you remember the Japanese officers in the restaurant."

Melin nodded.

"Well, they like you very much. They've told my business associates that they would like to know you better."

Melin gasped and dropped her jaw. She raised a hand to cover her mouth.

Tsai-tu pretended that he didn't see Melin's expression. He continued to talk. "You are very beautiful, and the Japanese are lonely . . . most of them are here without their families." After a pause he continued very calmly, "I have arranged everything with the help of my go-betweens. The Japanese looked you over in the dining room, and they have agreed to accept my offer. They'll be here any minute now. Try to please them in every way, my child, and meet their every demand. If you play the Mah-Jongg tiles cleverly, when the Japanese take over White Stone, the Ma family will be spared."

Melin felt sick and weak and confused. She sat on the bed, looked at her father innocently. "But, Baba, how do you want me to please them?"

Tsai-tu laughed. "Did your foolish Mama not tell you anything at all?"

Melin blushed. She remembered Hwa's room in the White Stone Hotel. Her Baba couldn't mean that!

Tsai-tu went on. "You were supposed to marry your cousin, but he wouldn't be of any use to you or your family now. I'm not asking you to give to these officers any more than you would give to your husband. The difference is that instead of one husband, you'll have many." Tsai-tu sighed. It wasn't easy for a father to talk to a daughter on certain subjects. "Melin, just pretend you are a man, and then you'll agree that having more than one mate can be great fun."

Someone knocked on the door. Ma Tsai-tu started to answer it, then stopped and looked at Melin with a tenderness that had never appeared in his eyes before. "Melin, please don't hate your Baba. If Baba had a choice, he wouldn't think of using you. But there is no other way. Your brothers can't do much. Your sister is married. Your mother has a bad heart. And I . . . I'm really scared. The Japanese can take everything from us, chase us into the street, then burn down our house. They can rape you, torture your brothers, and make me and your Mama suffer. We could all die in the most cruel ways. Really, Melin, the whole family's fate is in your hands."

With a thumping heart Melin watched the tears roll down her father's face. Each tear was a reminder of the old tradition: a child belongs to his parents, not to himself; when the parents are in need of help, the child must oblige regardless of the price.

In her mind's eye, Sung Hwa appeared, overlapping the image of her crying father, calling to her in a voice many times stronger than tradition.

"No! Baba! You can't ask me to do this!" She stood up and began to scream. "Take me home! Please take me home! I want to go back to White Stone! He is waiting for me . . . !"

She stared in horror as her father opened the door and two Japanese officers entered the room, walking toward her in long strides.

"Hwa! Save me! Don't let them do this to me! I'm yours, Hwa!" she shrieked.

The officers' laughter was louder than her screams.

PART III

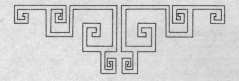

20

THE FULL AUGUST moon brightened a narrow path in the garden, leading to the gazebo hung with red paper lanterns. Servants emerged from the kitchen, moving in a procession of silhouettes, carrying covered plates.

Aaron looked down from the balcony, searching for Yin, and found her walking between two maids, toting a large platter of moon cakes.

He smiled. He and Yin would soon marry, but she was still unwilling to give up her servant's duties. He remembered Diana's words about his future bride: "She is your sanctuary in a world of catastrophe."

How correct Diana was, Aaron thought, and sighed. "A world of catastrophe." He repeated her words. The devastating scenes he had seen in Kwangchow and Shanghai had planted strong ambition in his heart. After returning to Hong Kong, Aaron felt he understood his country and wanted to do something for it. But what about his parents and Yin? He wished he were as brave and independent as Diana.

Diana had cried all the way out of Shanghai. But the tragic death of her parents had not taken away her alertness. All the way back through the ravaged country she had managed to keep herself and Aaron from being stopped by the Japanese. When they returned to Hong Kong, she had reminded Aaron that what he had learned about her must remain a secret from his parents. She told David and Meiping that her parents had been killed by looters, and asked for a month's leave from work. She had not been seen during that month. When she reappeared, she looked thinner and paler, but otherwise seemed recovered. She had never talked about her work outside the jewelry store, but Aaron was certain that she continued to run missions for the left-wing Nationalists.

Aaron watched Yin move gracefully through the gazebo. The moon shone on her loose black pants and wide-sleeved white blouse. Her swift steps indicated that she wore her soft cloth shoes. Yin was never comfortable in skirts or high-heeled shoes.

Aaron had fallen in love with Yin when he was a boy, perhaps on the night he insisted on rescuing her from the street. As he and Yin grew up together, his love for her flourished and was fortified by her love for him. He was eighteen now, and Yin a year younger. He wanted to marry her, and his parents didn't disapprove, just like they never objected to anything he set his heart on.

"But they are selfish too," Aaron murmured. "Once married, they know I'll not ask for another dangerous trip like the last one. And being as humble as she is, Yin will never ask for a home of her own. She and I will always live with my parents, and soon they'll have many grandchildren running around the house."

Aaron looked up at the moon. The wind was strong. Soft clouds sailed quickly, covering and uncovering the glowing moon. *The moon is hiding behind the clouds, and I will soon hide behind my married life.* Aaron shook his head. *I'm my parents' only*

child now, and I will soon become Yin's husband. I
have no right to risk my life!

He left the balcony to join the festivities.

On December 7, 1941, Aaron and Yin left Hong
Kong for a village near New Territory. She had
asked him to take her home, to invite her grandparents to the wedding, regardless of how they
had treated her and her mother.

Their train was delayed and they didn't arrive
in Kowloon until late that evening. It started to
rain. They went to a restaurant, ate supper, and
waited for the rain to stop.

Yin looked out the window and said, "It is too
late to go to my grandparents' house, and besides, we'll be soaked when we get there."

A modest hotel was attached to the restaurant.
"Let's stay here for the night," Aaron said. "Then
go to your village in the morning."

Yin blushed. For four years there had been only
kisses and caresses between them. They had
never spent a night together alone. Meiping had
given Rachel's room to Yin. In the Cohens' house,
Yin's room and Aaron's were only one hall width
apart, but Meiping's eyes were sharp and her ears
alert. The two young people loved, respected,
and feared Meiping. They never dared to upset
her, though at times their healthy young bodies
burned with desire for each other.

"Tomorrow is the eighth day of December.
There are only seventeen more days until our
wedding," Aaron whispered in Yin's ear.

His words echoed in her mind as they checked
into the hotel. Those same words increased in vol-
ume when she and Aaron were alone in the small
room. *Only seventeen more days before I'm his woman*
and he my man, Yin said to herself when Aaron

took her in his arms and started to undress her. *It doesn't matter even if I become pregnant!*

He peeled her clothes off gently, then took off his own in a hurry. They stood naked facing each other, their garments piled around their feet. She looked at him timidly, then moved her curious eyes downward. She stared for a few seconds, then her face turned a bright scarlet. She closed her eyes and her lips began to quiver.

He felt his heart drumming at his throat as he took in her nakedness one part at a time. He hadn't expected to find a woman's ripe figure hidden under her loose peasant-style frock. Her breasts were full like mellow fruit, her legs two shapely pillars protecting a small deep and mysterious temple.

A moan rose from his throat and escaped his mouth. He picked her up and carried her to the bed. He laid her on her back and knelt beside her. He kissed her tightly shut eyes, then moved his burning mouth to her hot, moist parted lips. He sucked her and gently bit her, from her mouth to her throat, then from one of her nipples to the other. With fervent devotion he planted a kiss on the dark temple between her legs. She immediately parted her legs wide. His penis throbbed and ached. He climbed over her, took her breasts in his hands, kneading them with passion, and at the same time entered her.

"Aaron!" she cried, and opened her eyes the moment he penetrated her. The pain didn't make her push him away; she pulled him closer instead.

He rocked back and forth, and her pain was driven away by a pleasant sensation. Suddenly he tightened his muscles, lifted his head, and shouted out her name. He reached climax. He collapsed on top of her, spent and angry with himself.

She lay motionless, feeling empty and lost. She tried to recapture the pleasure, but it was gone.

He rolled off her, and she went to the bathroom to dry herself between the legs, pausing now and then to stare at the stained towel. She came back to bed, and he quickly covered her body with his own. She circled her arms around him, listening to him breathing hard.

"I'm sorry," he said, sounding ashamed and unhappy. "I was too excited."

He didn't tell her that he had visited the prostitution houses with his friends. He wished that he had made one more visit recently, so that desire wouldn't have fired up inside him and exploded so easily.

"I love you," Yin said, tightening her arms around his body. "A man must never apologize to his woman. That's what we are now—a man and his woman. Please don't say sorry. Never, never."

Her soothing voice and gentle words made him feel manly and strong. Without trying, he was growing big again. He was surprised. It had never happened in any of the prostitution houses, even when the girls were pretty. He was on his knees once more, kissing her and fondling her breasts, and before long became one with her for the second time.

This time the fire kept burning and the flame stayed high. He felt like an experienced guide, taking his beloved girl through her virginal trip to an enchanted land. He watched her climbing the high mountain of pleasure. He waited for her to near the peak. He teased her and tempted her until she reached the point of no return. When she moaned beneath him, he was proud of her enjoyment. When she lay exhausted, saying his name in a hushed voice, he beamed like an emperor.

"It's going to be this way for the rest of our days!" he promised her. "And we shall have one hundred million days together!"

Aaron dreamed of chasing Yin through a valley blooming with flowers of all colors. She ran ahead of him, turning now and then to throw him a brilliant smile.

"One hundred million days together!" With each smile she repeated the same words he had said before they drifted off to sleep in each other's arms.

"One hundred million!" she said, then suddenly disappeared, the dream ended, and Aaron found himself lying at the bottom of a black ocean.

"*Due-na-ma!*" he cursed in his mother's words while struggling to swim to the top of the heavy water.

He quickly discovered that he couldn't move. He opened his eyes in the darkness and saw that he was buried in hard concrete, the collapsed ceiling, the fallen roof, the splintered furniture, the broken window . . .

"What the hell!" he cursed in his father's language while kicking and struggling.

He felt pain as his legs were cut by fragments of wood and his hands scratched by pieces of metal. He kept fighting his way out, until he was standing beside a pile of debris with blood dripping down his naked body.

"Yin! Where are you?" he shouted.

"Aa . . . ron!" Her voice came from underneath the largest pile of broken concrete.

He tried to make his way there. After only a few steps he heard a loud whistle coming from outside the window. The whistling sound ended with an explosion. The ground shook. More things began to fall around him, and a heavy dust filled the air.

"*Yin!*" He screamed her name.

He couldn't hear her over the noise from outside, the voices wild with the fear of death.

"The Japanese have bombed us!"

"Their soldiers are moving in!"

"The whole town is on fire!"

A red glow brightened the room. Aaron felt the heat, heard the crackling sound of wood burning, and smelled the smoke. Terror filled his every cell, giving him a strength that he had never possessed before. He raced to the source of Yin's voice and started to heave the concrete and lumber aside.

"Yin!" he called as he worked, straining to hear her answer.

"Aaron . . . I . . . it hurts . . ." Her voice was weak and filled with pain. "I . . . can hardly breathe."

"I'll get you out!" He didn't stop digging. He had no idea that he was crying and that his hands were bleeding. He paid no attention to the bombs falling and buildings collapsing, guns firing and people screaming. "Are you there? Yin!"

Her voice was frail like a thin thread. "Is Buddha p-punishing us for what we did before . . . before we are married?"

"Don't be ridiculous!" he yelled, lifting the last piece of concrete off her. "We *are* married! It's the Japanese and their death machine!"

He saw her naked body bruised and covered with blood. He knelt and took her face in his hands. He lowered her head to look at her closely. The fire was burning closer. The red light shone on her, giving her eyes a strange sparkle and her face a mysterious glow. She smiled at him slowly, and the sparkle became brighter, the glow intensified.

"Aaron . . ." She lifted a hand, opened her mouth. "I love you."

"And I love you!" he said, then froze.

All of a sudden her eyes became dull, her face darkened. A thin trail of blood dribbled from the corner of her mouth, and her hand dropped lifelessly to the ground.

"Yin! My Yin!" Aaron shouted, cradling her in his arms and pressing her against his heart. "My love! My wife! I can't let you go! You are my life!"

Around them, more bombs hit the ground and the city crumbled. He paid no attention to the piercing sounds and the quaking earth, but held her tightly and felt the warmth gradually leaving her body. He continued to hold her until she was ice cold. By that time the fire in the area had burned out, and the ambulances were zooming by. He stood up, holding her, hugging her tightly, and crushing his face against hers. Her body remained soft in his embrace, her eyes halfopen, and her lips slightly parted.

"Let's go home, Yin." He carried her out of the rubble, walking on bare feet over the hot ashes without feeling pain.

Standing on the street corner, he ignored all the people and cars, the ox carts and buses. He kept lowering his head to kiss Yin's eyes and lips, trying to close them.

"Sleep, my love, close your eyes and sleep," he whispered. "Hush, my bride, you need to rest. Whatever you want to say to me, you can say it when you awaken."

21

THE HOUSE WAS in Pearl City, not far from Pearl Harbor. The structure was Japanese in style, with a westernized kitchen and bathroom. There were two bedrooms and a large den, and a study with wall-to-wall bookshelves.

"For your law books," Jebu said, pointing at the built-in shelf, grinning like a young boy who has succeeded in surprising and pleasing his mother.

"How can we afford it?" Michiko asked, looking around wide-eyed. "We have a two-year-old son to raise, and my tuition is high."

"Uncle Quanming gave me a raise and lent me the down payment." Jebu put his arms around Michiko. "I knew that you wanted a home of our own. I've been looking hard. We can move in during the first week of December, and celebrate Christmas here."

Michiko held Jebu and sighed. "You're so good to me. I don't deserve you. I've been studying too hard to be a good wife. I'm sorry."

"Stop apologizing." Jebu held her away from him to kiss her on the lips. "Don't you know that I'm proud of you for studying so hard? Someday I'll have an attorney for a wife. What does it matter that you don't have much time for me and Genkai right now?"

He kissed her again, harder this time. There

was limited privacy for a young couple living with
the older generation. Their lovemaking had always been accompanied by the presence of Kiko
and Heroshi in the next room. Because he and his
wife were now all alone in an empty house, Jebu's
passion soared.

There was no furniture. Jebu dropped himself
to the floor covered with *ta-ta-mi*, the Japanese
straw mat, pulling Michiko with him. He kept his
mouth on hers as he undid her sash. Her outer
kimono came off easily. She had on two more
layers of long robes, each secured with a tight
waistband. He removed the robes one layer after
another. His clumsy and impatient fingers became
tangled in the silk strings and he cursed.

"*Due-na-ma!*"

"What's that?"

"I don't really know. I learned it from Uncle
Quanming. He says it when he is upset. The
sound of it makes me feel good."

"You are such a child, Jebu, and I love you so
much!"

Jebu was too busy to talk any more. He had
never undressed a woman before. At the home
they shared with his parents, lovemaking was a
quiet ritual which began with his waiting for
Michiko in their darkened bedroom, listening for
the screen doors to slide apart. She would come
to him quietly on her bare feet, her body per-
fumed and her hair down, her multilayered kimono replaced by a thin garment that was already
untied and would slip off at his slightest touch.

He finally removed all the garments from Michiko. Her naked body lay curved and white on the
colorful fabric, like a perfect piece of coral art
against a multicolored background. But coral was
hard, and Michiko was soft. He kissed every inch
of her softness, from her ears to her neck, then

her breasts, her abdomen, and her legs. He kissed her toes one by one, then went back to her thighs. He wouldn't leave her lovely thighs. He took her hair in his mouth, pulled it gently. She tried to push his head away, but when he started to tease her with his tongue, she changed her mind. She pressed his head down and began to moan.

Jebu continued to please her with his tongue, until her body tensed up into an arch and she cried wildly. He left her for a moment, breathing hard, and quickly undressed himself. He knelt over her and entered her.

"Michiko, you are my life. I'll do everything I can to make you happy. I love you more than I love my own life!" He never stopped wooing until he lay beside her on the mat, sated and out of breath. "That was great!" he gasped. "I can see that it's necessary for a young couple to have their bedroom far from their aged parents. Genkai is already two, but that was the best lovemaking we've ever had."

When he recovered, he turned to rest on his stomach, leaning on his elbow to look at Michiko. "Open your eyes, my love," he cooed softly, then laughed. "The saying goes that when a woman keeps her eyes closed through lovemaking, she is thinking of somebody other than the man in her bed."

Michiko opened her eyes quickly, and opened them wide.

Jebu laughed harder. "But of course the saying is wrong." He looked at her beautiful face. "My Michiko doesn't want to look at me when we are doing certain things because she is still my shy little flower." He kissed her lips, then rested his head on her naked breasts. He heard her heart pounding. He smiled. "My Michiko is showing

me her love with her fast-beating heart," he murmured, holding her tight.

Michiko used all her willpower to force herself
to be as lighthearted as her husband. She would
never tell Jebu the reason she had closed her eyes.

During their lovemaking, while her desire glided
high, there had been a dark premonition soaring
over her like a black bird flapping its wings. The
last time she had felt this way was the night she
stood in front of her school and waited for Jebu.
She and he had been attacked by three angry Chinese men that same night.

Michiko closed her eyes once again to block the
invisible black bird away, knowing it was still
there, lingering over her and Jebu.

They moved into their new home on Friday,
December 5. They spent all of Saturday un-
packing. Genkai woke them at dawn on Sunday,
crying and throwing a fit.

"I'll take him to the beach so you can study for
your final exam," Jebu said to Michiko. "I won't
bring him back before lunch. I'll pick up food so
you don't have to cook."

Jebu dressed the boy and himself in matching
kimonos made by Grandmother Kiko. They were
blue, with the Yamada family's crest embroidered
on the lapels. Genkai continued to cry, so Jebu
took from his neck the white coral Buddha given
to him and Michiko by Grandfather Heroshi and
let Genkai play with it.

Jebu carried his son in his arms. He kissed
Michiko at the doorway and smiled at her with
his boyish smile. "See you at noon, my love," he
said, walking toward the road.

Michiko stood waving, smiling at the two boys
who meant everything to her. She wanted to tell
Jebu to stay home, that she didn't care if she

failed every question on her final examination. She didn't call Jebu back because she knew how proud he was of her good grades, and it was truly impossible to study with Genkai crying in the house.

Jebu stopped at the road, took the boy's fat little hand, and waved it to Michiko, yelling, "Say good-bye to Mama! Tell Mama we'll be good boys. We won't come back to bother her until lunchtime, so Mama can study hard and become a big successful lawyer!"

When they were out of her sight, Michiko closed the door reluctantly, wanting to go after them and join them for a picnic. She forced herself to sit in front of her textbooks and tried her best to concentrate.

"I'm studying hard for the two of you, my dear husband and son," she said to her international-law book. "I do want you to be proud of me."

Michiko studied hard. When she looked at the clock again, it was a little after ten o'clock. She stretched, thinking how lovely the Hawaiian winters were. December 7, but warm like summer. Her arms stopped in midair when everything in the house began to move.

At first Michiko thought she was back in Japan and in the middle of another earthquake. The house shook, the floor rumbled, the cups and dishes fell from the cabinets, the books flew off the shelves. She ran toward the door and held on to its frame, trying her best not to fall.

She heard the many explosions, one followed by another. She ran out of the house and raced into the street. She saw smoke rising from the direction of the harbor. She heard a low droning coming from the sky. She looked up and saw airplanes flying low; she could see the red circles on the planes. It was then that she heard the sirens piercing through the air and saw people running madly in every direction.

She grabbed her next-door neighbor and screamed at him, "What happened? Does the siren mean it's an air raid? Who is attacking us? The Japanese?"

The man shook her off violently. "My wife and children are on the beach!" he yelled as he ran. "That's where the explosions are!"

"The beach! The harbor!" Michiko shrieked. "No!" She joined the dashing crowd, making her way toward the ocean.

Jeeps driven by officers raced past her. Trucks loaded with soldiers nearly ran over her. Military personnel charged forward with weapons in their hands. Civilians pushed and shoved and bumped into one another. She was knocked down several times before reaching Pearl Ridge Park. She got up each time, kept her eyes on the opposite side of the park where the shoreline lay, curving to Pearl Harbor.

In the middle of the park she stumbled. Instantly she felt people's feet on her back, their weight crushing her and pinning her to the ground. Some of them tripped over her, and more fell. They piled on top of her; she couldn't breathe. Lying there, she remembered that many people died this way during the earthquakes in Japan. She struggled, but it was useless. She yelled, but her voice was drowned by the cries of others.

An explosion came at the end of a screeching long whistle. The ground vibrated beneath her, the world turned black, and she lost consciousness.

When Michiko came to her senses, she could no longer hear anybody howling close to her. There were no more pounding footsteps. All the wailing and running were now muted and far away. No more new weight was added to her back, but those piled over her were becoming heavier. Something dripped on her; perhaps it was rain. She thrust and jolted with newfound strength until she was able to crawl out from under them.

Those who had fallen over her were either dead or dying. A crater about ten feet deep and thirty feet in diameter gaped in the middle of the park, only a few yards from her. Shrapnel, hundreds of fragments of it, had sprayed the park, pelting tree trunks and human bodies. The large pieces had severed people's heads, arms, or legs, while the smaller segments pierced through their hearts, stomachs, and intestines. She was covered with the blood of the people who had lain on top of her. Their bodies had shielded her from death.

She pressed her hands against her ribs. They must be bruised, because they hurt terribly with each breath she took. The pain reminded her that she was alive and must find her husband and son. She staggered on, stepping over the dead and avoiding the grabbing hands of the wounded.

"I'm sorry, but I can't stop to help you," she murmured.

She walked along the shore. The beach was littered with human torsos, some mutilated and motionless, others crawling and limping and leaving long trails of blood on the sand. The tide washed against the coast with its unchanged rhythm, throwing bits of cruising and fishing boats upon the land. The water was covered with oil and fragments of metal, sailor hats and military supplies, and other items from the sinking battleships in the harbor.

Michiko didn't pay attention to the continued explosions. She walked past several burning huts without stopping. The cries and moans vanished from her ears. When the siren penetrated the air once more, she heard it only vaguely. Her mind concentrated on finding a man and a small boy in matching kimonos. She could see, hear, or feel nothing else.

Jebu's blue kimono caught her attention at the entrance to the harbor, near the water and at the foot of a plumeria tree. She ran to him and saw that the tree was slashed in two. The white juice ran slowly down the gashed trunk. Red flowers fell all over the ground, like a blanket woven with soft red petals, covering Jebu so that he wouldn't be chilled in his sleep.

Jebu slept on his stomach like he always did. But there was a deep gash on his back, piercing through his body.

"Jebu! My husband!" Michiko dropped to her knees, put her hands on Jebu's handsome face, and turned it sideways.

He was soft and warm. But he neither opened his eyes nor uttered a word. Michiko lowered her head, kissing his lips, shaking his shoulders. "Please look at me. Please talk to me. Why won't you kiss me back? My husband!"

As she shook him, she saw Genkai lying under him.

"My son! My baby! My life!" Michiko was mad with grief, her tears blinding her eyes, her voice hoarse with sobbing.

She quieted suddenly when she heard a soft whimper, turning into a loud cry.

Michiko moved Jebu completely off Genkai; Jebu's tight grip on the baby came loose. Genkai fell out of his father's embrace and landed on the grass, screaming.

"My baby! My boy!" Michiko picked up her son and hugged him to her.

Both of Genkai's hands gripped a gold chain. At the end of the chain dangled the white coral Buddha that Jebu had taken off his neck and given to the baby to play with. The Buddha with the sad face had been designed and carved by Heroshi himself, carrying a message from the heart of a loving father: *I will stay with you every step of your life, and I will shield you with my own body to protect you from harm.*

22

A POLE STOOD beside the Ma compound's door, a Japanese flag at its top, flapping in the winter wind. Two soldiers guarded the entrance, holding their bayonets, glaring at the villagers who dared to linger.

In the setting sun the people of White Stone hurried on. Only when they were far from the soldiers did they risk talking.

"What a shame! The ancestors of Ma Tsai-tu have to be crying in their graves!" said one man. "An army headquarters in name, a whorehouse in reality!"

"Who knows? If his ancestors were as shameless as he, they might be celebrating," said another man. "I hear that this has happened in many villages—the landlords invite the Japanese officers to set up headquarters in their homes in exchange for protection. In the past five years the Japanese have done all sorts of evil things to us, but they've left the Ma family alone."

"Maybe you're right. We've all suffered in one way or another, but the Mas are unharmed by the occupation." The third man shook his head. "Perhaps the virtue of a worthless daughter is not too high a price to pay."

Behind the massive walls that surrounded the courtyard the garden lay in the twilight, quiet and peaceful. The only sound came from the lotus pond, where the water was deep and the goldfish were restless; they jumped and splashed, unconcerned about breaking the silence.

Melin stood on the curved bridge over the pond, wearing a thin white robe. The wind tossed her long black hair all over her face, but she didn't seem to care. Her face was white and smooth like porcelain, and, like porcelain, it showed no emotion.

"Sheo-jay! Where are you?" With the call appeared a woman in a maid's uniform. She looked around the garden, found Melin, and rushed to her. "Sheo-jay! Standing in this cold wind with almost no clothes on! You'll catch your death if . . ." The woman stopped. In a time as troubled as this, no unfortunate words should be spoken. She put her hand on Melin's arm, pulling gently. "Sheo-jay, please come with me. It'll soon be dark, and the party will begin. You need to get dressed and paint your face."

Melin didn't resist. She let the maid guide her away from the pond, moving docilely.

"Tonight's party is terribly important," the maid rambled on. "The cook is very nervous. He doesn't know if his sushi and sashimi are good enough to please the new commander. The master warned us that this commander is harder to please than all the previous ones." The woman sighed. "Why do the Japanese commanders come and go? In the past years there have been at least a dozen of them, and each has a different taste . . ." The woman's words trailed off and she looked at Melin with pity.

The cook really didn't have a right to complain. After all, he needed to please only the palates of the invaders, while Melin's duty was to please them in bed. "Sheo-jay"—the maid put an arm around Melin's bony body—"you're shaking. And you are so thin! You need to eat more, you know, and take better care of yourself.''

They were about to enter the house when Melin suddenly stopped. She looked up at the darkening sky, searching for the moon. But the sun was not completely gone, and the moon was nowhere to be found. "The moon should be bright and full, and all the loved ones should be together.'' Her whispering voice was not stronger than a sigh. "Hwa, when will I be together with you?''

The maid shivered. Her Sheo-jay had started to behave strangely since coming home from Shanghai, and had not been right since then. Why did she mention that young man again? He had been tricked by Tai-tai to leave White Stone in a hurry and return to San Francisco. Sheo-jay had rushed to the telegraph office and warned him to stay away from White Stone. She then lived for his letters until last winter, when the Japanese outlawed all communication to and from America. The poor girl! Her parents should do something for her, instead of making her sacrifice herself for the rest of the family.

"Sheo-jay, I'll draw you a tub of hot water, and you'll feel better after the bath,'' the maid said gently, guiding Melin into her room.

Beside the steaming tub, Melin stood and let the maid take off her robe. Her naked body was thin, but nevertheless the body of a woman. Her once small breasts had grown larger, her nipples darker, her hips fuller. She was unashamed of her nakedness, not the way she had been as a shy girl. When she was in the tub and the maid ran a soaped sponge over her thighs, she trembled only slightly.

A memory flashed into her mind, like a star twinkling from a cloudy sky. Its faint glow was only an indistinct speck that soon became unclear and then vanished tracelessly.

The first pair of hands had belonged to one of the two Japanese officers in Shanghai. The hotel room was guarded by the two men in dark robes who were supposed to be her father's business associates. Her father was the one who had opened the door for them, although with tears rolling down his face. They immediately pushed her father out of the room, and kept him on the other side of the locked door. She screamed and struggled when they approached her, but was unable to fight two men. They undressed her, then one held her, and the other entered her brutally. When both of them were through, they left her there and walked out the door. From the bed she saw her father standing in the hall, bowing, asking them to join him for a drink and discuss the "protection" of his home and family. The men had made her bleed badly, in spite of the fact that her virginity had already been given to Hwa that one beautiful night they shared in White Stone.

Melin closed her eyes. The hot water was melting away her memory, soothing and comforting her, almost like the opium. She leaned her head against the edge of the tub, lowering herself deeper into the water. Deeper . . . deeper, just like her addiction to the bitter dark juice of the poppy.

In the Cathay Hotel, when she was crying and yelling and trying to throw herself out the window, her father had prepared the opium and brought the pipe to her mouth. She had turned her head left and right until she was too tired to refuse. She had inhaled, and the opium had produced its effect almost immediately. Her hysterics turned into submission, her anger dissolved, and her pain was relieved. She no longer wanted to kill herself for something as unimportant as giving her body to some strange men. She had drifted into a world of twilight that existed between the lands of dreams and reality, where anguish was unfelt and tears unshed. She had stayed in that foggy world for the rest of the days in Shanghai, and then had floated out of the hotel and reached the train, almost levitating her way home.

The first time she asked for the pipe, the moon was full. She had looked at it through the window, and recalled the promises she and Hwa had made to each other. The thought of him waiting on the other side of the wide ocean was like thousands of knives stabbing her in the heart. She couldn't bear the ache, so she sent the maid to her father.

In the past five years there had been many terrible incidents as a result of the occupation. With each one, Melin needed a little more opium to help her through the torment.

A Japanese officer slapped her for failing to please him in bed. A new commander used his belt on her because she couldn't carry out his bizarre demands. Her cousin, the man she was engaged to marry before she met Sung Hwa, charged into her bedchamber and saw her with three men. He was drunk and took them on—he was shot and killed in front of her eyes. Her mother, who had begun to act peculiarly since Melin's Shanghai trip, seemed suddenly to realize what had become of her daughter. She suffered another stroke and nearly died. Many of Melin's friends from childhood were accused of being spies, arrested and tortured, then executed in the town square. . . .

"Sheo-jay," the maid called, "it's time to get dressed, and I've set up the opium table."

Melin stepped out of the tub, dried, and wrapped herself in a silk robe. Next to her bed, on a low table, an opium pipe lay waiting and a small lamp was lit. She stretched out, picked up a silver stick, opened a porcelain jar. She dipped the stick into the jar, brought out a small chunk of the tarlike substance, then placed it on the low flame. The opium bubbled up, and the room was filled with a strange fragrance. Melin placed the brown bubble on the pipe, lighted it, and inhaled deeply.

Soon the color appeared on her cheeks, and a glow returned to her eyes. She jumped up, agile and full of life.

She shouted for the maid to help her get dressed. "I want my new red dress. The one that's long and tight and good enough for a bride . . . a virgin bride!" She giggled like a child.

The maid dressed her, then applied heavy makeup to her face. Melin was only twenty-three, and it was still possible to bring back her striking beauty with a generous amount of powder, rouge, and lipstick. When she looked once again like a painted doll, the maid started to labor over her hair, using many pins to hold up the long silken strands, according to the Japanese fashion.

Melin was restless. She twisted in the chair, then reached forward and took from her large dresser drawer a pen and a sheet of letter paper.

The maid asked with a sigh, "Why bother to write? You can't mail anything anyway."

Melin looked at the woman in the mirror, smiling brightly. "Who knows? Maybe the war will be over tomorrow. Maybe I'll be able to mail all the letters to him in one big box as a surprise. And maybe he'll come back to me unexpectedly, and I'll show him these letters as proof that I've thought of him every day."

The glow in her eyes intensified, and the red

on her cheeks became brilliant. "And maybe when we are married, we can read these letters together, in our own home, in America, far from White Stone. He'll laugh at all the silly words I wrote, and I'll hit him without mercy!"

Still giggling, Melin bent over the pad. She wrote quickly, telling Sung Hwa, in line after line, that everything was beautiful and bright.

. . . I hope the war between America and Japan will be over soon, so I can at least hear from you again, and you from me. And I pray each day to the Great Buddha, for the Japanese to leave China. I'll be able to come to you then, my love.

I can't say that the war has harmed anybody in my family. Baba gave the west wing to the Japanese for their headquarters, but we stay in the rest of the house, and never see any of them. Tonight is the last full moon of the year, and in just a few more days everyone will be celebrating another new year.

Remember my oldest brother, Kiang? Three years ago he raped a village girl, so her father and brothers threatened to kill him. Kiang ran away to Shanghai, met a girl there, and married her. Now the brothers of the raped girl have been killed by the Japanese, and the father is very sick, so that at least Kiang is able to come home now with his wife and their two-year-old baby, a girl called Qing. When we are married, my love, I want to have many children . . .

She stopped writing when she heard her father's voice at the door. She put the sheet back into the deep, wide drawer that was half-filled with letters, then waited without turning around.

The maid added a few more final touches to Melin's hair and then left. Ma Tsai-tu closed the door and came closer. In the past five years he had aged a great deal. When he looked at his daughter, his eyes darkened with guilt and pain.

"Melin . . ." He stood behind her and placed his hands on her shoulders, looking at her in the mirror. "I . . ." He had trouble speaking.

"Yes, Baba?" Melin's face was exquisite in the paint, her eyes dazzling from the opium. She waited patiently for him to continue, showing no hate or contempt.

Tsai-tu sighed deeply. "I've come to warn you that this man, the new commander, is a very difficult person. You must be very careful, so he won't become angry and . . ." His voice trembled and he stopped.

Melin finished the sentence for him easily. "And beat me up? Don't worry, Baba. I was silly and stubborn then, but I'm clever and compromising now. I'll do whatever they want. You needn't worry, Baba, really."

Ma Tsai-tu nodded, then kissed his daughter on the forehead. His affection startled her. She looked into his eyes and saw tears.

"Baba," she asked, "are you ill? Is Mama sick again?"

"We're fine. Your Mama has withdrawn to a dream world and stays there. Your brothers are playing around, your sister is fighting with her husband, and I'm living well." Tsai-tu gave a sarcastic laugh, then swallowed hard. "None of us are inconvenienced by the occupation of White Stone. Thanks to you, my dear child."

Melin didn't answer. She stared into space, unseeing. There was a long silence.

"My daughter," Tsai-tu finally continued with difficulty, "I want you to know that I despise myself for being a coward. I do love you, Melin. You are my flesh and blood, and you remind me so much of your mother when she was young. I love her too, but I can't help being what I am. I'm afraid to suffer. I don't want to lose the house and the family fortune. I don't know how to protect my family and myself except . . ." His voice ended in a sob.

"Please don't repeat yourself, Baba," Melin said calmly. "You've already given me all these reasons. Remember? A few years ago, when we were in Shanghai?"

She stood up and held her father for a moment. Briefly her faraway look disappeared and her eyes glistened with tears. But she blinked the tears away and recaptured her look of oblivion. "Baba, let's go to the party. We mustn't keep our invaders waiting. Our lives are in their hands. They order, and we obey."

They left the room, walking slowly down the hall. They could hear the blaring cheers and laughter coming from the living room, and the loud conversation in both Chinese and Japanese. Melin murmured softly, " 'To live in misery is better than to die in glory.' I believe in the saying. Do you, my Baba?"

23

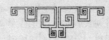

THE WINTER OF 1942 arrived harshly in San Francisco. The December wind was cold, the dark clouds low, the morning mist thick and heavy. Sung Hwa walked through Chinatown wearing a long gray coat. On the left lapel he wore a large button with white background and red letters that read "I Am Chinese."

He looked around and saw the same button worn prominently by many others. An old man met his eyes, smiled, raised a hand to the mandarin collar of his pajama suit, touched his button, and murmured, "Well, in a time like this, better wear a button than let the white devils mistake me for a Jap."

Sung Hwa kept going. He passed the stores, noticed the signs written in both Chinese and English, placed in every window: "This Is a Chinese Shop." He reached Clay Street, stopped at the Yung Fa Restaurant.

The Chinese in San Francisco continued to raise money for the defense of the United States, and the fund-raising was headquartered in the Yung Fa. Sung Hwa had a check in his pocket. He must make his donation before the program halted for the holidays. He found the small restaurant overly crowded. Every table was filled, every chair taken. The couple who owned the place and their young son were standing at the far end of the room.

"We have raised over eighteen thousand dollars for the Red Cross campaign," said the aged man with broad shoulders.

"And we have collected almost thirty thousand dollars for the Defense Bond," said the aged woman in a Pearl River dialect that reminded Sung Hwa of the way people talked in White Stone.

He remembered the year he had rushed home from White Stone, thinking that Melin would be in San Francisco. Two telegrams and several letters that had traveled faster than he, waited for him in his room. The one from Mr. Chew explaining Yoto's treachery burst his dream. Melin's telegram followed almost immediately; it was long and insistent, warning and begging him to stay in America. He didn't decide to listen until he opened her other letters, one after another. They repeated the same words: "Trust me. I love you. Don't come for me. When the war is over, I'll come to you. Everything is just fine here except that we are not free to travel. If you come, we'll both be in danger in White Stone. Please be patient and wait. . . ."

Her letters stopped when war broke out between Japan and the United States. He had not heard from Melin for over a year now, nor could he mail his letters to her. But his love for her was just as strong as before. He knew that as soon as the war was over he would go to her, marry her, and bring her back to San Francisco. His future happiness depended on America's winning the war. Contributing to the Defense Fund was only a first step. After this, he had much more to do. He gave his check to the woman and headed for the door.

Outside the restaurant, he ran into several white Americans visiting Chinatown, probably shopping for exotic presents and looking for a place to eat. They smiled at him and even nodded when he greeted them with a hello. Hwa sighed at the change of attitude since the bombing of Pearl Harbor. He had not heard them calling any Chinese "heathens," "mice-eaters," or "chinks." They seemed to want the Chinese people to know that America and China were linked together now, to fight the Japanese.

On the sidewalk, a group of Chinese surrounded a young man who was translating the American newspaper into Chinese. Everyone was laughing. Hwa paused to find out what was so funny.

"This newspaper is trying to teach Americans how to tell a Chinese friend from a Japanese enemy. According to it, the Chinese eyes slant upward, the Japanese eyes downward. The Chinese are thin, the Japs fat. The Chinese have straight legs, the Japs are bowlegged. The Chinese have high foreheads and long chins, while the Japs' faces are short . . ."

Sung Hwa shook his head and resumed walking. He passed many restaurants and stores that were closed because their waiters and sales clerks had gone to higher-paid jobs offered by businesses which had lost their white employees to the draft board. He recalled reading in the paper that in Los Angeles three hundred Chinese laundry workers had left their hot irons and washboards for construction jobs, and in San Francisco most of the cooks and waiters had become shipyard workers.

Sung Hwa had, through all his growing years, heard people in Chinatown complain about being unable to get out of the dump. Now the war had

opened a door for them. He knew that once the
Chinese entered mainstream American society,
there would be no way to keep them out. When
the war was over, the Chinese would never return to being merely laundrymen and cooks.

Sung Hwa reached the building of the recruiting offices. The various branches were located on
different floors. He approached the receptionist at
the entrance and asked for directions to the U.S.
Marine Corps. The young lady gave him his answer with a warm friendly smile.

"I bet you're Chinese," she said teasingly, looking at the button on Hwa's coat lapel. "What kept
you from coming earlier? All your brothers have
been here already. Did you know that as of today,
twenty-two percent of the Chinese male population in this country have entered the war? You
people sure are braver and more patriotic than we
thought!"

Hwa said to her half-jokingly, "Remember that
when the war is over and my brothers are asking
for equal opportunity in jobs!"

Hwa was the next in line to speak to the recruiting officer. He sat on a wooden bench. While
waiting, he remembered the argument he had
had with his mother. A-lin had tried her best to
stop him from joining the Marines. She had cried,
cursed, screamed, pleaded, and threatened. When
all failed, she had pretended to have a severe pain
in her heart. But Hwa knew that her intention
was good—she loved her son and was afraid of
losing him.

Hwa's attention was captured by the exchange
between the recruiting officer and a young Chinese man who looked more like a boy.

"How old are you?" the officer asked, looking
at the young man's button.

"Nineteen."

"Of course, but is that your Chinese age?" The officer measured him with his eyes. "It's hard to tell you people's age. You all look like kids. I've just learned that you Chinese count your age in a different way, and when counting it your way, you can be two years younger than you say you are. I don't understand it, but I was fooled by several of you boys who were sixteen or seventeen."

"I'm really nineteen."

"We'll see." The man narrowed his eyes, trying to see through the boy's winter coat. "You'll have to pass a very strict physical examination, you know. How much do you weigh?"

"About one-ten."

"That's what they all say." The man sighed. The qualifying weight was 105. Most of the young Chinese weighed less than that. They drank gallons of water before the physical, and some would eat bunches of bananas before stepping on the scales. "Well, what can I say? Your spirit is admirable."

The young man received a stack of forms to fill out. He smiled on his way to the doctor. He, too, had only just eaten a very big meal.

Sung Hwa stepped up confidently to be questioned. He was tall for a Chinese, and didn't need to worry about the weight requirement.

An hour later, when he walked out of the recruiting office as a U.S. Marine, he raised his arms high and waved them proudly. "Melin! Now I'm really fighting for us!" he shouted as he danced on the sidewalk. "With one more man fighting for the USA, we will win the war one day sooner, and you and I will be together one day earlier!"

24

THE WIND SCREAMED over Yenan, muffling the conversation among three people who stood on top of a hill at early dawn.

A young girl looked at Li Kwanjin and Hu May with fear in her eyes. "Comrade Li and Comrade Hu, how did you know I wanted to leave the commune?"

Hu May put a hand on the girl's arm. "I've been watching you for quite some time. The party is doing to you what they did to me—picking on you, criticizing you, and forcing confessions out of you . . . humiliating you in every way they can because you are from a wealthy family and your ways are different from theirs. They don't credit you for the fact that you've given up your home and family for Yenan. They disregard your dream of saving China through communism." May sighed. "I saw my own anger on your angry face. I read my fear in your frightened eyes. I recognized your decision to leave as clearly as I've recognized my own."

May stopped and looked at Kwanjin. It seemed a long time since that winter night when she whispered to him her wish of leaving Yenan.

Kwanjin read May's thoughts and took her hand. They both shivered as they considered all that had happened since then.

In the beginning, regardless of his disillusionment with the party, Kwanjin had continued to fear the world outside Yenan; he didn't know how to make a living out there and refused to be supported by May's family. His fear was driven away, however, by the party's rejection of his request for promotion—finally they had decided not only to demote him but also to punish May.

May and Kwanjin were stripped of their teaching opportunities and given constant hard-labor assignments. Their food coupons were reduced to half. They and Leahi were moved from their original cave to a smaller cave shared by two other families who were also being punished. Ten adults and three children lived in one cave, and no one dared to talk to the others for fear his words would be repeated.

During the day, Kwanjin and May farmed, chopped stones, and carried heavy loads in the rock quarry. They dug ditches, cleaned the outhouses, scraped and washed dishes in the kitchen. At night they forced themselves to stay awake and worked on their confessions, which were read once a week loudly by Wong Chung to everyone in the meeting hall.

"I seduced Comrade Li into marrying me so that I would be spared from going to the front." Until May had eventually written these words, Wong Chung had continued to claim that her confession was unacceptable.

"I encouraged my lover to wear silk dresses and let her hair grow long so that I could enjoy the beauty of a woman as did the feudalistic landlords." Kwanjin had finally dictated what Wong Chung had wanted him to say, to save himself from being ordered to rewrite the confession once again.

One day, in the rock quarry, when May was in the last month of her pregnancy, she had fainted from hunger and exhaustion. She had woken up in the arms of Kwanjin, his face filled with worry. The other workers were far from them, so Kwanjin had dared to whisper, "I'll never forgive myself for bringing you to Yenan. If we can escape to Beijing, I won't mind sweeping the floor in your father's silk shop."

When the baby was born, the party named him Li Enlai, after Chew Enlai, the party idol at the time. Enlai was taken to the nursery when he was two weeks old, in spite of the objections of Leahi, Kwanjin, and May. In the nursery, more than thirty babies were cared for by two women who were tired and bad-tempered. Enlai was allowed to come home only on the weekends. When Kwanjin and May went to visit their son and watched a comrade teaching the older children that children of the new China must love Chairman Mao and the Communist party instead of Baba and Mama, their hearts ached. Every Monday morning, when it was time to bring Enlai back to the nursery, Kwanjin would clench his teeth and squeeze May's hand tighter.

Wong Chung had only recently freed Kwanjin and May from their work in the rock quarry and returned them to a private cave to be shared with Leahi. But their food coupons had not been increased, and their ranks were still among the lowest in the party. May and Kwanjin had not changed their minds about leaving Yenan, but they knew it wouldn't be easy.

The girl looked from May to Kwanjin. "Will the two of you really help me to escape?"

Kwanjin and May answered at the same time, "Yes, we'll do our best."

Kwanjin then added, "May and I would have gone with you, but the two of us plus our son and my mother will make too big a target." He paused to look around, then leaned closer to the girl. "You must do us a favor."

"Anything, comrade, anything," the girl answered eagerly.

"Since you are going back to your home in Kwangchow, I want you to take my mother with you," Kwanjin said.

"Comrade Leahi?" The girl stared at Kwanjin.

"Yes," Kwanjin said in a hushed voice. "They didn't punish her on my account. They are not keeping a sharp eye on her the way they do us. Her escape will be much easier than ours." Kwanjin continued sadly, "I'm guilty of bringing Mama here, just like I am of bringing May. Mama is in her mid-forties now, but still healthy. Once away from Yenan, she may yet have a good life."

May put her hands on the girl's shoulders, looking at the girl pleadingly. "All you have to do is get her to Kwangchow. I have a friend in Hong Kong. He'll take over from Kwangchow, and help both of you in whatever way he can."

"It won't be an easy journey through the war zones to Kwangchow," the girl said thoughtfully. "Our own guerrilla soldiers, the soldiers of the Nationalist Army, and the Japanese will all give us trouble." She smiled at Kwanjin and May. "But, yes, I'll take Leahi with me. And we'll make it."

There were four people in a cave that had been made into an office. Wong Chung and another senior officer sat behind a desk. Li Kwanjin and Hu May stood facing them.

"It's impossible that your own mother left Yenan without telling you first!" said Wong Chung, glaring at Kwanjin.

"She didn't." Kwanjin looked at his feet to avoid Wong's eyes. "The party taught my mother to believe in women's freedom and sever family ties. She no longer asked her son to make decisions for her. When she wanted to leave, she just left."

Wong Chung knew that Kwanjin was mocking the party doctrine. Everyone knew Leahi listened to her son's every word and never decided anything on her own. He turned to Hu May. "And you want us to believe that you had nothing to do with your mother-in-law's betrayal?"

May nodded firmly. "Yes, Comrade Wong. I would have reported my mother-in-law's disloyal behavior if I had known."

Wong Chung narrowed his eyes to look from Kwanjin to May. Someday he would make both of them sorry for lying to him now. He said coldly, "We can't accept the assumption that a simple countrywoman in her mid-forties would decide to leave Yenan without some help from either of you. But since we can't prove anything yet, we'll keep her case open. One of these days we'll find the answer. Whoever is responsible for her disloyalty to the party will answer for it."

The other officer fingered through a stack of paper on the desk. "Comrade Hu's background is very unfortunate. She has friends in foreign places, and she likes to learn foreign languages and read foreign books. Perhaps she is more responsible for this whole thing than is Comrade Li."

Kwanjin said quickly. "No! You are wrong. Leahi is *my* mother. If someone has to be responsible for her behavior, then it will have to be me."

"No!" May shouted, and held her husband's hand in front of Wong Chung and the other officer. "My mother-in-law has always been closer to me than to her son. If anyone has put wrong ideas in her head, I'll have to be the only guilty one."

Wong Chung said slowly to Kwanjin and May, "Both of you are being very foolish. The party never forgives the guilty. We will soon find out the truth."

The same questions were asked many times. Kwanjin and May repeated their denials. Several hours later Wong Chung and the other officer were tired. Wong stood up to conclude the interrogation. "Comrades Li and Hu, all I can say is that Li Leahi's desertion has endangered both of your positions in the party. By refusing to cooperate, you have made the situation even worse. You are testing the party's tolerance. I'm afraid one of these days I'll have to tell you that you've pushed it too far."

Kwanjin and May walked along the mountainous ridge. The hills rose and fell in the moonlight. The night was deep, the people in the commune asleep. The wind was soft for a change. The dust swirled only near the ground, and the commune looked almost like a normal village.

"Is there any way to steal our baby from the nursery?" May asked. "Can we just take him with us and run?" She thought about the world outside Yenan, where babies belonged to their parents and it was not considered a crime for mothers to stay home and take care of their children.

Kwanjin had no answer for her. All he had were more questions. *How can we contact Mama? Has she arrived in Kwangchow? Will we ever be with her again somewhere, someday?* He asked May to reassure him once more that her friend Aaron Cohen would take care of Leahi.

"Yes, he will," May answered him firmly.

They sat on a flat rock and looked at the other side of the hill, where a tall pagoda stood shimmering white in the light of the full moon. Regardless of the disapproval of the hard-line party members, the majority of the people in Yenan had won the right to their pagoda. It had taken them four years to finish building it because they had to fight the war at the same time, and the construction could take place only when they were off-duty.

May and Kwanjin stood up and walked through the rolling hills, passing cave after cave.

They reached the pagoda and stood at the foot of the high structure.

The full moon shone on the pagoda, shrouding it with a silver armor. It towered over them like a giant, timeless, immense, and indestructible. The longer they looked at it, the smaller and more insignificant they felt.

To May's surprise, her husband dropped to his knees. He looked up at her pleadingly and she joined him. She looked into the pagoda and saw a large statue of Buddha carved by an amateur artist in the commune.

Moonlight poured in through the open window, illuminating Buddha's face. The face was happy, but the eyes were filled with grief. The moon was playing tricks, giving the statue a wisdom that both Kwanjin and May knew didn't exist.

"Great Buddha," Kwanjin prayed, "please help my family."

"Yes, my Great Buddha," May prayed alongside her husband, "please show us a way."

25

SINCE YIN'S DEATH, Aaron's parents had learned to accept that their baby boy had become a man.

When Aaron went out, he no longer asked for Meiping or David's permission. When he joined Diana Moore for further buying trips, their consent was merely a formality. When he closed his door and refused to be disturbed, they simply had to stay out of his way.

Aaron didn't like to shut his parents out, but he had no choice. To keep his parents out of his secrets was to protect them from trouble.

This day, he had no secret documents to deal with. He had received only three letters this morning, all from his friends.

Looking at the three letters, for a brief moment Aaron smiled like a boy. The letters were from people he had met many years ago, when both Rachel and Yin were alive, China had not yet been invaded by Japan, and he was indeed only a boy.

He couldn't remember if it was Michiko who had said that no matter what happened in life, their friendship would continue. He sighed. Sorrow had visited all of them since the day in the Park of the Sun Altar. But they had never stopped writing to one another. What had happened to one of them, had been shared by the others.

He opened the first letter; it was from Hwa.

Dear Aaron,

I am having my basic training here in the boot camp in Parris Island, South Carolina. The sun is boiling hot. The drill sergeant screams at us all day long. We are told that we are the lowest creatures who ever walked the face of earth, and he is doing the impossible to make us Marines.

I am writing to ask a favor. As you know, since the war broke between Japan and the United States, people living in the part of China under Japanese rule can no longer contact people elsewhere. I have not been able to communicate with Melin, and it's driving me crazy. I know Hong Kong has also been bombed by the Japanese, but still the peninsula is a British colony. I wonder if you could go to White Stone?

If only you could see her and give my love to her personally, I'll be eternally in debt to you, my dear friend.

Please ask my Melin to be brave. Tell her that I am fighting the war for her, and she must, in her way, fight a winning battle for me.

I don't dare to dream that you could get her away from White Stone to Hong Kong until the war is over. But if that should be possible, my friend, we'll name our first son after you. . . .

Aaron put down Sung Hwa's letter, recalled the tall, handsome man he had met in Beijing. At least Hwa's beloved was only in a small village that had fallen into Japanese control, instead of an unknown world that could only be entered after death. Of course he would try his best to contact Hwa's girl.

He opened Michiko's letter, and his heart ached as he read the tearstained sheets. When he finished he stared into space, dwelling on a question raised by many wise men but answered by none: could the death of a physical body terminate the existence of its spirit?

He couldn't believe his Yin had ceased to exist. He believed that she had moved her lovely spirit from her destructible body to an indestructible world. Now Michiko said that she believed the same thing about her Jebu. Aaron wondered if in the world beyond, the spirits contacted one another. If they did, would Yin and Jebu be friends now, like he and Michiko?

He shook his head and opened the letter from Hu May.

When he finished reading it, he left his room and went to the garage to start his car, which had been given to him by his parents on his last birthday. He smiled when he remembered the arguments between him and Diana when she taught him to drive. He whispered as he pulled out of the driveway, "Diana, you taught me not only how to drive but also how to live after Yin's death. I stood on my feet when I remembered your courage in accepting your parents' death. I dried my tears only because I followed your example."

He drove down the curved road that led to Hong Kong. The city had not recovered from the bombing. Destroyed buildings had not been rebuilt. Burned structures remained deserted. The poor used cardboard and metal sheets to put up temporary shelters. Naked children walked on bare feet among the ruins and swarmed toward Aaron's car when he slowed down.

Aaron rolled down his window, threw a handful of coins at the children, then drove on. He reached the business district and stopped at a jewelry store that bore the name Cohen's.

"Good day, young Lau-ban, Miss Moore is in the office." A sales clerk bowed to Aaron.

Aaron nodded, and glanced around the store. People were buying jewelry, regardless of the war. He looked at the carefree faces of the customers, and thought of the faces of those beaten, raped, and killed. *China is a giant ying-yang sign,* he thought as he ascended the stairway in the back of the store. *The rich contrast the poor, like day contrasts night. When half of the Chinese are laughing, the other half are crying. When half are living, the other half are dying.*

Diana answered, "Come in."

She smiled at Aaron from behind the manager's desk, looking beautiful in a yellow blouse and brown slacks. "What can I do for you, Rich Boy?" she asked teasingly, her brown eyes gleaming with mischief.

He pretended to frown, but actually no longer resented the name. It made him see the graveyard in Kwangchow, where an old truck parked and two rugged men stood watch. It reminded him of an adventure that had planted the seed for a new life. "Are you ready for another buying trip, Moon Girl?" He called her by the name that was much more beautiful to him than "Diana."

Diana's eyes brightened. "You've been contacted?" Aaron had been working for the organization long enough to be contacted directly. His parents had noticed that, like Diana, he had befriended many strange people, but they had never interfered.

"Not anyone from the LWN," Aaron said. "But two old friends. One of them has asked me to go to Kwangchow and check on the safety of an old lady named Li Leahi. Another begged me to go to White Stone to see his girlfriend, Ma Melin."

Diana nodded. "No problem. We have contacts in both places. Let's get our road permits."

Two days later, Diana and Aaron's road permits were ready. Each permit was a piece of paper which bore the owner's picture and reasons for traveling; it was granted by the Sino-Japanese government.

"Where would we be without the Sino-Japanese government?" Aaron asked Diana in the train on their way to Kwangchow. Because of the requirement for road permits, very few Chinese were able to travel, so they had four seats all to themselves.

"We'd be in much worse shape than we already are," Diana answered. Soon after Japan had conquered the major cities of China, they had offered Wang Ching-wei, the leader of the left-wing Nationalist party, a position as head of a government which they claimed would fly the Japanese and Chinese flags at equal height. Wang had accepted the offer, knowing that the Japanese would simply eliminate those who refused to cooperate. He had hired the LWN members as government officials. He had chosen Nanjin as his capital, using it and Shanghai as bases for many secret anti-Japanese organizations. Diana and her friends had joined one of those organizations very early. After Yin's death, Aaron had persuaded Diana to include him in.

Diana continued, "Without the Sino-Japanese government, even more Chinese would be arrested. The torture would be more severe, and certainly more death sentences would be carried out."

"I hope the Japanese will not poison Wang like they did so many others," Aaron said. Many prominent Chinese who had openly disagreed with the Japanese had died suddenly after attending dinner parties hosted by the Japanese. "Without Wang, fewer road permits would be given to the Chinese. As a result, you and I would not be able to travel."

Traveling meant they could bring much-needed medicines to the Communist guerrilla fighters, and let them know the locations of the Japanese troops stationed all through China. It also meant sneaking small weapons in briefcases that were supposed to contain jewelry, and making escape possible for those whose secret mission had been discovered by the Japanese.

A man boarded the train and sat next to Aaron. Aaron and Diana stopped talking.

In the train station in Kwangchow, all passengers were lined up by Japanese soldiers. Aaron went to the men's line, Diana the women's.

"Road permit?" a soldier asked.

Aaron showed it to him.

"Raise your arms," another soldier ordered.

Aaron had gone through the body search many times before, but still felt insulted. With his hands over his head, he stood still. The soldier felt every part of his body, searching for anything that could be a weapon. Aaron turned to look at the women's line, and saw another soldier doing the same thing to Diana. He hated the man for laying his filthy hands on her, who was to him a sister, a friend, a teacher, a partner . . . and much more.

"You may go now," said the soldier.

At the end of the line there was a Japanese flag. All the Chinese had to bow to it before leaving the station. Aaron bent slightly with his teeth clenched.

"China dog! Stop!" a soldier yelled, pointing

his bayonet at a man who had tried to slip away without bowing to the flag.

The man was in his early twenties, probably a college student. He stared at the soldier stubbornly, held his head high.

The soldier ordered him to bow; he shook his head. The soldier raised the butt of his rifle and smacked it against the man's head. He fell to his knees. Two more soldiers came to join the first one. They thrust at the man with their bayonets, keeping him kneeling. Each time he tried to stand up, they kicked him down. He glared at them. They hit him in the face until it was covered with blood and he could no longer open his eyes.

"Take him away!" an officer ordered.

As the man was dragged into a military police car, the crowd moaned, "Jail . . . wooden shoes . . ." Aaron shivered. The Japanese prison guards had invented a special way to torture the Chinese by nailing a person's feet to two wooden boards. The prisoner was then forced to stand and rock back and forth. The wooden shoes were not removed until the blood drained away and the prisoner died.

"Don't worry, Rich Boy." Diana tugged Aaron's hand and whispered softly, "Scholar is working out of Kwangchow jail. He'll do his best to spare this man." Since Aaron had joined the team, he, Diana, Scholar, and Tea Drinker had worked closely together.

Diana and Aaron walked from the station to Main Street and stopped at a movie house.

Neon lights brightened the night, glowed on the people in line. In the past few years motion pictures had become the most popular entertainment in China, and business had been unaffected by war. Movie actresses were worshiped by the public; when they appeared in theaters for the openings of their pictures, people waited for hours to catch a glimpse of them.

A dark car appeared. The crowd roared, shouting the name of a famous actress. A beautiful young woman emerged in a glistening gown, smiling and waving at her fans. She was followed by a big man dressed like a bodyguard; the man was Tea Drinker.

Aaron and Diana pushed their way toward the actress and her protector. He was taking each sheet of paper handed to him by the crowd and examining it before giving it to the actress to autograph. Tea Drinker didn't show any recognition of Aaron and Diana when he saw them.

Diana took from her slacks pocket a small piece of folded paper and gave it to Tea Drinker. The big man pretended to give it to the actress, but kept it instead. When he gave Diana a piece of paper that was supposed to contain the actress's autograph, it was a note he had slipped out of his sleeve.

The actress, whose family had suffered under the Japanese rule, was now an LWN member. The Japanese conquerors treated all beautiful young entertainers as their playthings. She attended their parties frequently, and afterward was often taken to one of the high-ranking officers' beds. She had sharp ears, attentive eyes, and quick fingers. Tea Drinker had just passed to Diana a piece of information the actress had gathered. It was the location of the next meeting to be attended by all the high-rank Japanese officers.

On the piece of paper Aaron had prepared for Tea Drinker he had written the name of Li Leahi and described her as an escapee from Yenan, perhaps accompanied by a young girl. He asked that the underground network check on all newcomers to Kwangchow to find out if Leahi was all right and if she needed any help.

Tea Drinker had returned to Diana a piece of paper that contained a list of pawn shops, antique stores, and private homes that Aaron and Diana should scout for jewelry but actually pick up some medicine, and even weapons, that were in need of transport.

Diana and Aaron spent the night in Kwangchow, sharing a room in the hotel next door to Fong's Pawn Shop. They had been sharing a room now whenever they traveled, to give the appearance that they were indeed brother and sister from an average home that needed to save money. They revisited the Fong couple, who still remembered them, and bought a few pieces of jewelry, although the couple were not involved with the LWN. Later Aaron slept on the floor as he always did, and Diana on the bed. The next morning they traveled to White Stone.

They went first to the dormitory of the high-school principal, and were greeted by a man who introduced himself as Mr. Chew.

"I have some nice jewelry waiting for you," said Mr. Chew. "Except for the Ma family, the landlords are not doing too well. They are forced to sell their precious stones, and have asked if I know any buyers."

Mr. Chew, a college graduate from Shanghai, had been an LWN member for years. He was known by the people of White Stone as a person with many out-of-town friends. The villagers looked at his two non-Chinese visitors with interest but were not overly alarmed. When he, Aaron, and Diana were alone, he listened to Aaron's request and sighed.

He led them to the Ma house. On the way, he told them he had introduced Melin to Sung Hwa.

"It was love at first sight," he said. "Melin's maid came to me after Sung Hwa left White Stone, and told me what Mrs. Ma had done." He went on to tell them about Melin's Shanghai trip and the life she had been forced to live since. "If you could take her away from White Stone, it would take some time to get her off the addiction. But then she will be her old self again, and I'm sure she can recover in the care of Sung Hwa." He smiled for the first time. "What a beautiful couple they made."

In front of Ma Tsai-tu's house, two Japanese soldiers pointed their bayonets at the three visitors and asked in accented Chinese, "What do you want?"

Mr. Chew bowed deeply. "I want to see my former student, Ma Melin."

One of the soldiers said, "She is our commander's flower girl. She does not visit with common village people. Her father won't allow it."

Mr. Chew bowed once again. "May I see her father, then? Maybe he will change his mind."

One of the soldiers went reluctantly into the house. Aaron, Diana, and Mr. Chew waited. They looked at the Japanese flag and the sign that said "Imperial Army Headquarters," then exchanged glances.

The soldier at last returned. "Mr. Ma said for you to wait here."

Ma Tsai-tu took his time. When he finally appeared, he came through the door and closed it quickly behind him. "What do you want?" He frowned at Mr. Chew. "I have no more children in school. I have no intention of donating any more money."

"I didn't come for your money. I wish to visit Melin." Mr. Chew bowed politely at Ma Tsai-tu.

"I have some out-of-town friends whom Melin may like to meet."

Ma Tsai-tu glared at the two strangers. "A white woman and a mixed-breed man!" he hissed at Diana and Aaron. "I don't believe the Imperial Army commander would like to see them at his headquarters."

Diana pulled Aaron forward and said with a smile, "Mr. Ma, my brother and I are friends of a good friend of your daughter's. If the Imperial Army commander doesn't wish to have us in his headquarters, perhaps you can let your daughter visit us elsewhere. We can wait for her in Mr. Chew's place."

Ma Tsai-tu narrowed his eyes, looked at the three people carefully. Something told him this white woman was not telling the truth. He hadn't known Melin had any friends who knew foreigners. "Who is this friend of yours who is also my daughter's good friend?" he asked, then glanced quickly from one face to another, gauging them for lies.

Mr. Chew, Aaron, and Diana looked at one another quickly to decide who must answer. Their hesitation lasted only a few seconds, but long enough to increase Ma Tsai-tu's suspicion. He listened to the name given by the principal. He was almost certain it was a nonexistent name. He was instantly cautioned: why would the honest Mr. Chew tell a lie just to bring two strangers to his house to see Melin?

Ma Tsai-tu smiled at the three visitors. "I'm sure Melin will be glad to see her good friend's friends. But she is sleeping right now, and will not wake up until late." He looked at his watch. It was not yet noon. He thought fast. "How about meeting her tonight?" He turned to Mr. Chew.

"I'll tell her to come to your place tonight, let's say about eight?"

Ma Tsai-tu didn't intend to let Melin see anyone at all. It was best to keep her away from the outside world and constantly drugged with opium—the less aware she was, the better she could serve her purpose. He walked across the courtyard, stopped on the bridge over the pond, and looked at his watch again. "Eight hours is long enough for me to check on many things . . ." he murmured.

First he would check on the name given to him by the principal. Melin's maid would know the names of all Sheo-jay's friends. If that name didn't belong to any of them, then it was proof enough that Mr. Chew was plotting something.

Next he would give Mr. Chew's name to one of the Japanese officers and suggest they check out the man thoroughly. If a spy was caught with Tsai-tu's help, the Japanese would reward him generously.

Mr. Chew had two extra bicycles besides his own. He, Aaron, and Diana tried the three bicycles out that afternoon.

"I remember seeing Melin riding one," Mr. Chew said. "When she hears that you'll bring her to Sung Hwa, she'll follow you to the end of the world!" He drew a map for Aaron and Diana, showing them the best way out of White Stone. "Melin wouldn't have a road permit. You must keep her away from all checkpoints." He sighed. "Let's hope she is not too drugged to ride a bicycle."

Mr. Chew cooked a simple meal for them. They ate and waited for night to fall. Looking at the darkening sky, the principal said thoughtfully, "Right now it is the darkest hour for China. When the Japanese are defeated and the Nationalists and Communists melt into one, then China will see daylight again." He talked about the left-wing Nationalists' goal, "Neither the rich nor the poor will rule alone. Both will share the power. The feudal system is not all bad, nor is communism. The only ones who ought to be extinguished are people like Ma Tsai-tu—" He stopped abruptly.

Aaron and Diana asked him what was wrong. He raised a hand for them to be quiet. He thought for a long while, then said with a frown, "Ma Tsai-tu may be setting up a trap. He promised to let his daughter meet us too quickly." He looked at the bicycles. "The two of you should take two bikes and wait for Melin outside White Stone. I'll stay here and bring her to you on the third bicycle."

Diana and Aaron couldn't argue Mr. Chew out of the arrangement. They hurried to finish eating, then left the principal on their bikes. When they reached the country road, night had fallen. They waited at the end of a rice field under a canopy of silver stars. They were excited about bringing Melin with them to Hong Kong. "She can live in our house," Aaron whispered. "Mama will take good care of her until Sung Hwa returns home from the war—"

They heard gunshots coming from White Stone. The empty terrain between the field and the village allowed sounds to travel clearly. From the shouting and screaming they knew that the Japanese soldiers had fired at Mr. Chew as he tried to ride away from his surrounded house. They then heard police dogs barking and soldiers running, heading in their direction.

"What—?" Aaron asked.

Diana answered by jumping on her bike and beginning to pedal.

When they were miles from White Stone and no longer heard their pursuers, they stopped to rest. A new moon appeared from behind the clouds, gleaming on their angry sweating faces.

"Ma Tsai-tu tricked us!" Diana said, breathing hard. "How stupid of me!"

"And me," Aaron said, trying to catch his breath. "Mr. Chew realized it could be a trap and saved our necks." He shivered in spite of the sweat that soaked his clothes. "What do you think will happen to him?"

"I'm not optimistic," Diana said, and jumped back on her bike. "We have no one in the White Stone jail."

Aaron followed Diana silently, and decided not to tell Sung Hwa what had really happened tonight. *I'll write to him and say that I did try to visit Melin, but her father wouldn't let me see her. I'll say that her principal knows she is well, but he knows nothing else. No man should tell another man that the girl he loves has become a whore,* Aaron said to himself as he pedaled on.

Diana and Aaron stayed in the same hotel in Kwangchow before going back to Hong Kong.

In the middle of the night someone knocked on their door. Aaron answered it and Tea Drinker entered quickly, wearing dark clothes and a grim expression. "I've found out about the woman you asked me to check on," he told Aaron. "Li Leahi arrived in Kwangchow safely. She then went to a nearby village called Willow Place. She is living there now, in a fishing hut near the riverbank. The villagers say that every day she walks along the Pearl River and rests under the willows, and seems to be content."

When he finished, Diana asked him if anything was wrong. Tea Drinker looked at Diana and his large frame began to tremble. "They . . . arrested . . . Scholar." The big man sobbed be-

tween words. "They took him . . . to the Torture
Tower . . . in Shanghai. His identity was revealed
. . . when he tried to help the man who was arrested in the station for not bowing . . . to the
Japanese flag."

Both Aaron and Diana had heard of the Torture
Tower in Shanghai. It was said that the floors and
walls in every room were stained red by the blood
of Chinese women and men, that, once taken
there, no one would come out alive.

After Tea Drinker left, Diana and Aaron stood
by the same window again and looked at the
night streets of Kwangchow. The Japanese had
put up new lampposts at the mouths of many
narrow alleys. It had been arranged that each
lamp shone prominently on a large billboard that
advertised a headache medicine called Jen-dan.

"Scholar, my friend, my buddy. How you must
be suffering right now . . ." Diana sobbed quietly,
her willpower crumbled, her perseverance gone.
She was for the first time a fragile woman crying
helplessly. "And Mr. Chew . . . and all the others. Will the people ever be free?"

Aaron put an arm around Diana. He stroked
her with one hand, raised the other to point at
the Jen-dan logo that was a man with drooping
mustaches. "We all know the Japanese put up a
Jen-dan sign at the entrance of every dead-end
alley to prevent their army from retreating into a
wrong lane. The Japanese are preparing for street
combat because even they are not sure whether
their occupation will last. Yes, my Moon Girl, the
night will be chased away by sunlight, and the
people will be free someday." He kissed her gently on the cheek. "Please don't cry anymore, my
Moon Girl."

26

SUNG HWA was on his way to Hawaii, to wait for the order that would send his platoon into battle.

All the young Marines were quiet during the journey. Reality hung like a dark cloud over their heads: the training was over. No more war games. The Japanese were waiting for them in the Pacific islands, hiding behind every tree and inside every cave, aiming to kill them or capture them and torture them to death.

Every Marine had his own way of ignoring that oppressive cloud. Hwa's way was to think of Melin's beautiful face. "I will not be killed! I will live to win the war. I'll go to White Stone to marry my Melin!" Hwa repeated these words to himself frequently. He shivered each time he imagined Melin's sorrow in the event of his death. She wouldn't be able to survive the pain. For her sake, he must stay alive.

Lying on his bunk bed, Hwa folded his hands under his head, stared at the bunk above him, and thought of Melin. He had been so disappointed when Aaron's last letter arrived. His only relief rested in his knowledge that Melin's family—her father—would protect her from harm as long as White Stone was not totally destroyed by the Japanese.

Hwa's hatred for the Japanese was so deep that he pictured himself wringing the neck of every one he saw in the Pacific islands. He shook his head when he remembered that Michiko was a Japanese but also his friend. Being a U.S. Marine, Hwa knew that there were only eight thousand Japanese left in Hawaii now, since President Roosevelt had approved the evacuation of twenty-one thousand Japanese from the Hawaiian islands. He smiled at the thought of himself in his Marine uniform hugging Michiko in her kimono.

He looked forward to that reunion, but first he must see his father, Sung Quanming. He felt a premonition of dread as the ship sailed closer to Oahu.

"Hwa-hwa!" Quanming stared at the strapping young Marine.

"Baba." Hwa felt a lump in his throat. He had not been called by his diminutive name for years. Many pleasant pictures flashed through his mind. The backgrounds varied, but at the center were always a young father and a small boy. Hwa blinked his tearing eyes and saw his white-haired father opening his arms. He hesitated a moment before throwing himself into Quanming's embrace.

They stood with their arms clasped tightly around each other for a long time. Hwa felt his father's arms shaking, and Quanming heard his son's heart drumming. When they let each other go, they smiled with embarrassment as they dried their tears.

"You are the best-looking Marine I have ever seen!" Quanming stepped back to look at his son. "Dark, strong, handsome." He laughed as he looked up at Hwa's face. "When did you grow so tall?"

Hwa also laughed. He had not laughed so heartily since he left White Stone. "Perhaps you have shrunk, Baba. I only remember looking up at you, never glancing down like I'm doing now."

Quanming realized that they were still standing outside the door, with his Polynesian servant watching curiously. Laurie was on Maui island for business. Otherwise she would have corrected Quanming and invited Hwa into the living room a long while ago. Quanming smiled as he thought how happy Laurie would be when she knew that Hwa had finally come to visit them.

He took his son's arm and guided Hwa into the house. "Come in, and welcome to your Baba's home. You will make it your home too, I hope. How long will you be in Hawaii? Please say that you'll stay here until the war is over."

Hwa shook his head. "I can be shipped out at any time. We were told that we will not be here longer than two weeks."

Quanming's voice filled with worry and disappointment. "Two weeks . . . such a short time. Then you'll be shipped to the Philippines, Guam, or Okinawa, where some heavy artillery is waiting to devour my boy."

They sat in a spacious living room filled with sunlight, facing a balcony overlooking the Pacific. The servant brought them drinks in two tall glasses. They sipped the rum-and-coconut concoction and told each other the things they had mentioned in their infrequent letters. Quanming told his son about the hardships he had had to conquer in the establishment of his business in Hawaii, and Hwa told his father about the prejudice he faced in the U.S. Marine Corps from the whites who decided that the Chinese looked just like the Japanese enemy.

Quanming asked about Guai and A-lin, then sighed. "Your mother didn't invite me to your sister's wedding. When you wrote to me that she was getting married, I sent her a check, but she never cashed it."

Hwa opened his mouth to ask about Laurie as a return courtesy to his father's inquiry about Guai and A-lin, but the words wouldn't come out. He had forgiven his father for leaving him, but not the woman who had lured his father away. He knew he was being childish, but couldn't help it.

Hwa's lack of feelings for Laurie was quickly detected by Quanming. The father decided not to be hurt. A son could never sympathize with a father's love for a woman other than his mother; it seemed to be a universal rule. Quanming felt better when he thought of Laurie's sweet smiles. No one could resist her once she smiled, and he knew Laurie would smile at his son.

"I've told you about Ma Melin, the girl I'm going to marry." Hwa's voice was filled with tenderness as he mentioned Melin's name. "I hope the next time I come to Hawaii she will be with me, and we will be on our honeymoon."

"There are many Ma families in White Stone," Quanming said thoughtfully. "I used to know one . . ." He tried to remember the name of the man he had met only once. "Ma . . . Tsai . . . something."

Hwa almost dropped his drink. "Ma Tsai-tu is my Melin's father!"

Quanming stared at his son. "Then Melin's mother is Kao Yoto." He remembered the last time he had been in White Stone. In the Mas' house he had been introduced to two young girls. The older one was beautiful, the younger one a child with a bright smile and two long pigtails.

"That's right. Melin's mother is named Yoto, a tricky fat old woman who lies well . . ." Hwa told his father what Yoto had done.

"I can't understand it," Quanming said, shaking his head. "She tricked you into leaving her daughter after you told her you were my son?"

Quanming recalled the days when he and Kao Yoto were young. They had met in a temple bright with glowing lanterns, and later walked among the many statues of Buddha. They held hands while the smoke rose from the incense burners around them, and kissed as the flames flickered from the red and white candles on the altar. But then Yoto had decided to marry a rich man chosen for her by her father, and Quanming had come to the United States. When he returned to his hometown, Yoto was already the mother of five children, and during the brief meeting he and she had never exchanged one word.

"Baba, is there a way for you to get Melin out of White Stone?" Hwa knew that his father could do almost anything.

Quanming thought for a long time. "I'm afraid not, my son. I left China when I was young and powerless. Whatever power I have gained since then still can't be extended into my homeland." He paused, then asked, "Hwa-hwa, how do you feel about the Japanese?"

Sung Hwa hesitated. "Well, I like Michiko and Jebu, and I am very sorry about Jebu's death." He paused, then squared his shoulders and lifted his chin like a good patriotic Marine. "I hate all the other Japanese. They invaded China, bombed Hawaii, and have killed many Chinese and Americans. Most of all, they occupied Melin's village and separated her from me."

"You're talking about the Japanese military, but not the Japanese civilians," Quanming said slowly. "There is a big difference—like the difference between the Chinese warlords and me."

Hwa shrugged. "As a U.S. Marine, my duty is

to fight the Japanese. According to my sergeant, all Japanese are vicious creatures." He began to relay to his father one of the many stories told by his sergeant.

On the Pacific islands there were bamboo forests. When an American was caught by the Japanese, he was tied spread-eagle and facedown over a field of bamboo shoots that grew about twelve inches every twenty-four hours. The tied man would watch in horror as the sharp, tough shoots grew nearer to him, and eventually pierced into his body. Many American soldiers were found dead, run through by bamboo and wearing the most agonized expressions on their faces.

Quanming sighed. "Hwa-hwa, are you free tonight?"

"I have a two-day pass. I don't have to go back to the base until tomorrow night," Hwa answered. "My only other plan is to visit Michiko after leaving you."

"I'll go with you to see Michiko. She is like a daughter to me and Laurie. After that I'll take you to visit some of my other Japanese friends. They just may change your opinion about the Japanese . . ." Quanming paused when he saw that his servant stood at the door expectantly. "Excuse me, Hwa, I'll be back in just a moment."

Hwa watched his father follow the servant to the garden to talk to the middle-aged man in a Hawaiian shirt. He saw his father frown. Quanming then returned, fretting, hitting his palm with his fist.

"Hwa-hwa," Quanming said to his son, "I'm afraid we can't wait until tonight to visit my Japanese friends. Something has come up and I must go to them immediately."

*   *   *

Michiko was taking a nap. She heard the knocking in her sleep.

"Jebu, go answer the door . . ." she mumbled. She opened her eyes and saw that, where Jebu should be sleeping, slept Genkai.

She stared at her son and remembered that Jebu was dead. A lump rose to her throat. Her heart contracted. Nothing would ever erase the pain. The knocking became louder.

"Michiko!" Quanming called.

Michiko grabbed a kimono and ran to the door.

"I'm sorry if I've wakened you, but this is urgent," Quanming said as he looked at her bare feet and thin kimono.

Michiko stared at the man behind Quanming. She frowned at his uniform, then looked at his face and screamed. "Sung Hwa!" She flung her arms around Hwa's neck. "You've come to Hawaii! And you're with your father! I am so glad. Jebu would be so happy too." Tears filled her eyes when she remembered their meeting in the Park of the Sun Altar . . . when Jebu was alive.

"My son receives a much warmer welcome than I, but I suppose an old man shouldn't complain," Quanming teased Michiko, then became serious immediately. "Michiko, I've got two seats on a boat that will sail tonight."

"Tonight! And why only two?" Michiko covered her open mouth with her hands.

Quanming said quickly, "You, your parents, and your in-laws must decide which two of you will go first. Genkai can be the third, since he won't occupy a seat."

Sung Hwa watched Michiko staring at Quanming, remembering his father's explanation on the way to Michiko's place.

Quanming had told Hwa that more and more

Japanese were being sent to the detention camps in California; they would receive notice in the mail one day and were often forced to leave the next morning. But there were also fishing boats leaving Hawaii every day, and a few of the captains were willing to enter the Sea of Japan when paid adequately. By smuggling onto these fishing boats, a few Japanese were able to return to their homeland. The price had gone up steadily for these limited passages. Quanming had tried to use his wealth and influence to put his Japanese friends on these boats, but had not been successful until now.

Quanming had further explained to Hwa that Hawaii contained seven islands; one called Niihau was privately owned. A large fishing boat would sail from Niihau that night, captained by a man known to be experienced at breaking through the blockade. Quanming had told Hwa that they must put two of their Japanese friends on the boat tonight because it could be their last chance to escape deportation.

"I . . ." Michiko looked from Quanming to Sung Hwa. "I don't know. May I take Genkai to see my parents and in-laws?"

Quanming nodded. A few minutes later, Hwa, Michiko, and Genkai were in Quanming's car, on the way to the Yamadas'.

As he drove, Quanming looked at the child in Michiko's arms. "I hope you will choose to go, Michiko. But since your culture and mine are similar in many ways, I know the young will have to give first choice to the old in a situation like this. I can't influence your decision, but no matter which two of you go first, please take Genkai. The detention camps would be a terrible place for a child."

"This is so unfair," Michiko said, lifting Genkai

and looking at him by the moonlight that poured
in through the car window. "He is an American
. . . or at least a Hawaiian. He was born right
here on this island."

Quanming nodded and sighed. "Hawaii is not
yet a part of the States. Even if it were, it
wouldn't help Genkai. All Japanese, from babies
to old people, whether born in the United States
or not, are classified as enemy aliens."

Michiko kissed Genkai, then held him close to
her heart. "It's ridiculous to call my little Genkai
an enemy alien. He is nobody's enemy. His father
was killed by a Japanese bomb." She leaned her
cheek against the baby's and began to rock him
gently.

Sung Hwa listened from the back seat. It pained
him to hear Michiko so distraught. He knew that
those in charge of the camps would be the kind
of people who would classify children as enemy
aliens. If Genkai should be taken to one of the
camps . . . Hwa didn't want to imagine.

Quanming and Michiko introduced Hwa quickly
to the Yamadas, then told the news to Heroshi
and Kiko. Sung Hwa studied the old couple carefully, but couldn't find them any more dangerous
than Genkai.

Heroshi sat cross-legged on the *ta-ta-mi*, looked
calmly at Hwa's U.S. Marine uniform, then at
Quanming and Michiko. "My son's physical form
was destroyed and buried in this country. His
spirit floats above this island. The parting between us is only temporary. When I die, his spirit
will come to meet mine, and then guide me to
the world of eternity." He turned his aged eyes
to the window, looking at his rock garden. "My
spirit and his will soar freely toward the temple
of the moon." He looked back at Quanming and

sighed. "If I left for Japan, his spirit would not find mine, and we'd be parted forever."

He smiled, bowed deeply to Quanming and Sung Hwa, then continued. "Not only my spirit but also my body is refusing to go back to Kyoto. Like a bonsai, my roots in the old pot were dug up many years ago, and I have rooted myself in a new bonsai pot here. No, thank you, my dear friend. I'm not leaving this island. They can send me to a detention camp, but the camp will be somewhere in America, my new homeland."

Kiko also bowed to her guests before she spoke. She said simply, in a voice much bigger than her small frame, "My place is beside my husband."

Quanming drove across the island to the west end, arriving at the sugarcane field in Waianae. He brought Hwa, Michiko, and Genkai into Michiko's parents' house and told the Ikedas about the boat leaving tonight.

The Ikedas grabbed the chance immediately and firmly.

"It's too bad that there isn't one more passage available, Michiko," Mrs. Ikeda said to her daughter. "Your husband is dead. A young Japanese widow should not stay in a foreign land. You should come home with us. We still have many relatives in Hiroshima. Maybe a kindhearted old widower will want you . . . if you are lucky, and if you behave properly."

Sung Hwa was amused by the difference between Mrs. Yamada and Mrs. Ikeda. All human beings were unique individuals, he concluded. His conclusion was further confirmed by the words of Mr. Ikeda.

"According to my opinion and the opinion of many other wise men, within a very short time the Japanese will win the war and conquer all of Asia and the Pacific. America, the paper tiger, is torn and in big trouble." Mr. Ikeda took Genkai's small hand and wouldn't let it go. "I have no son. Genkai is the only grandson I'll ever have." He looked at his daughter with sorrowful eyes. "Since you cannot come with us, you must let us take Genkai to Japan. We'll bring him up properly. I will teach him how to become a brave and honorable samurai."

Michiko shivered. She took her son's hand from her father's grasp. "I don't want Genkai to know anything about hara-kiri . . . or anything else about the way of the samurai. No, Genkai is staying with me."

Quanming left the Ikedas to pack, warning them to be ready when he returned for them that night. In the car, Michiko was still upset. Quanming invited her to go home with him and Hwa.

Michiko was silent for a long while. Then she said, "It is the Japanese way to see our relatives off on a long journey. My in-laws will want to say good-bye to my parents, I'm sure. And I'll have to take Genkai as well. The night wind will be cold. I need to go home first, to get a sweater for Genkai."

Quanming drove to Michiko's home and waited with Hwa in the car. They waited for a long time.

"Women!" Quanming mumbled. "What can be so complicated in picking up a baby's sweater?"

Neither Quanming nor Hwa noticed the tears on Michiko's eyelashes when she came out of the house holding Genkai, his little sweater, and a rather large bag. They didn't see her hands shaking either. When she said nothing in the car and was speechless in Quanming's house, they thought it was natural that a daughter would be sad to see her parents starting a dangerous voyage.

Quanming and Hwa had much to talk about. They didn't pay attention to Michiko when she didn't eat anything while Hwa and Quanming had dinner. They saw her pacing before the window holding her baby, but they didn't see her shoulders trembling ever so slightly.

They had no idea that when Michiko had entered her house a while ago, she had found lying on the entrance floor three U.S. government letters dropped by the mailman through the mail slot.

At midnight, seven adults and one child met at the north shore of Oahu island, exchanged a few hushed words, then climbed into a small boat. The two strongest men began to paddle immediately. When they were far from the shore and could not be heard by anyone, they turned the motor on and headed toward Niihau at high speed.

Quanming and Hwa had paddled hard. They sat back now, waiting for the cool breeze to dry their sweat. Looking at the ocean and the people around him, Hwa realized what he had gotten himself into—a U.S. Marine helping a group of Japanese to escape. He observed the Japanese around him, studying their faces revealed by the moon: Michiko, the sad young widow; Genkai, the innocent little boy; Kiko, a heartbroken mother; Heroshi, a father waiting for death to reunite him and his beloved son. The Ikedas were just an old couple chased back to their homeland by the hardship of the sugarcane field and the threat of the detention camps.

Hwa suddenly asked his father, "Will the American government really put these people behind barbed wire, thinking that they helped to bomb Pearl Harbor and may harm the U.S. war effort in the future?"

Before Quanming could answer, Michiko spoke.

"That's right." Michiko's voice was strong and clear. "This afternoon I received three notices, one for each of our families. I kept them until now, because there is nothing we can do, and I didn't want to upset all of you until I had to."

Michiko held Genkai in one arm and used the other to reach into her kimono and take out the letters. "They were all mailed to me because I filled out the yearly reports for the immigration office."

She handed the three sheets of paper to Quanming. "The evacuation notices are not only for me and Genkai, my parents, and my in-laws but also for Jebu." She continued bitterly, "They don't even know he is dead. They are still afraid that he may be a dangerous 'enemy alien.' "

Quanming squinted his eyes to read the notices in the moonlight. "The day after tomorrow!" he cried. "They expect you to board a ship at dawn! How can they do this? How many of us can be ready to leave our homes on such short notice?"

Michiko said, "It's obvious that they don't consider the Japanese normal people with needs and feelings." Her voice trembled as she continued, "The way they worded the notice made me realize how they see us, and how they will treat us in the camps."

She looked at Quanming, tears rolling down her cheeks. "Uncle Quanming, I've changed my mind about keeping Genkai with me." She held her baby close and turned to face her parents. "Please take my son to Japan with you. But please don't force him to become a samurai if he doesn't want to . . ." She cried too hard to continue. She took the bag off her back, put it together with her parents' luggage, then regained some of her composure and said, "I packed for him . . . his clothes, his toys, and my heart." Her voice broke again.

The boat seemed to have slowed down with the weight of Michiko's sorrow. No one spoke as she set Genkai on her lap and parted the child's kimono collar. A white coral Buddha hung from a gold chain, radiant in the moonlight. "Please let him wear the Buddha always. Jebu used to wear it around his neck all the time. He gave it to Genkai on the day he died. If he hadn't, maybe he would have lived and Genkai died. I believe the Buddha is a lucky charm for Genkai, and I also believe it carries Jebu's eternal love for his son."

Michiko put her hand on the gold chain and looked at her parents. "I've shortened the chain to fit Genkai's little neck. . . . I hope by the time he needs a new chain, I'll be with him."

Heroshi shut his eyes. Tears slipped from under his closed eyelids. Kiko cried silently, clutching her husband's hand. They refused to believe that their grandson was soon to be out of their sight and that they and their daughter-in-law were going to a prison camp.

Mr. and Mrs. Ikeda were more than happy to take Genkai. They nodded their promise to their daughter, although they would never stop Genkai if he should choose to become a samurai and the situation should demand he take a sword in his own hands and cut out his intestines.

Quanming wanted to take Michiko in his arms and hold her the way Laurie would do. He wished that Laurie were here instead of on Maui island—Laurie would know how to comfort the poor girl.

Sung Hwa shared a part of everyone's agony. He sank his teeth into his lip when he realized that in a few days he would be fighting with soldiers who were, underneath their uniforms, the same as these people on the boat.

They reached Niihau near dawn. In the house of a friend of Quanming's they rested for a short while. A large fishing boat could be seen floating offshore, waiting for the final passengers to board it before setting sail for Japan.

A fast motorboat at last arrived for the Ikedas. They boarded it eagerly, then reached their arms toward Michiko, who stood on the dock holding her baby. She couldn't let him go. Heroshi and Kiko wished their in-laws a safe journey, then took turns saying good-bye to their grandson. Both seemed to have aged a great many years in the past hour.

Quanming parted Michiko's locked arms by force, taking Genkai from his mother's embrace. "I'm sorry, Michiko," he said, his voice hoarse. "But I have to do this. The ship must sail before first daylight." He handed the boy to Mrs. Ikeda.

The small boat left the shore immediately. "Genkai!" Michiko screamed, and ran into the water, chasing after the boat. Her kimono floated around her; she looked like a drifting flower. "My baby! My love! My life!" She raised her arms toward her son, and then she fell.

The boy didn't cry until then. He reached for his mother and wailed. His voice was drowned in the roar of the motor and the rumbling sea. When a high wave came, the small boat disappeared behind it. When it reappeared, it had joined the fishing vessel. After a while, even the large ship was but a small black dot moving toward the far horizon.

PART IV

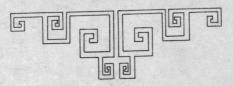

PART IV

27

Autumn 1944

IN HONG KONG, outside Cohen's Jewelry Enterprise, a car stopped with a loud squeal. Aaron jumped out quickly and charged into the manager's office without knocking.

Diana frowned. She and a well-dressed Caucasian man were sitting at her desk looking at a tray of loose diamonds. She explained the intrusion to the man. "This is Aaron Cohen, our young Lauban, my boss's son."

"I need to talk to you!" Aaron ignored her unpleasant tone. "It's important."

Diana asked the man apologetically if he would excuse them for a few minutes.

As soon as the door was closed behind the customer, she exploded. "Rich Boy! You are behaving like a spoiled brat! I thought you had grown! It's not going to work if you act like this—"

Aaron didn't let her continue. "Wang Ching-wei has died," he said in a trembling voice.

Diana gasped. The leader of the LWN had been in perfect health the last time he made a public appearance, and that was only a month ago. "A plane crash? A car accident?" she asked disbelievingly.

"Stomach ulcer," Aaron said. "It suddenly de-

veloped right after a dinner party hosted by one
of his Japanese friends."

"That must mean either that the Japanese want
to put an end to his operations or that the war
is almost over and the Japanese have started to
eliminate the most powerful Chinese in the Sino-
Japanese government." Diana told Aaron to sit
down, then left the office.

She returned with her assistant manager and
gave him the tray of diamonds to take to another
room to continue the deal with the buyer, then
closed the office door.

"What will we do?" Aaron asked.

"Nothing but wait," Diana answered. "A change
will come soon. I'm positive Wang didn't die of
an ulcer. If he was killed for helping the Chinese,
then the Japanese will put their own man in his
place, and all policies will be different from what
they are now. In that case, the LWN members
had better lie low for a while."

She paused in thought, then continued. "I believe the war must be nearing its end, and the
Japanese are preparing to retreat. Wang knew too
much, so he had to be eliminated." She looked
at Aaron sadly. "The LWN organizations are not
strong enough to fight either Chiang or Mao. All
we have are people with courage and dreams. No
matter which party gains control of China, we'll
be living at their mercy."

Aaron tried to make sense of it all. "But either
party should be kinder to us than the Japanese,"
he said. "After all, China will be ruled by its own
people again."

Diana stood up, walked to a window, and
looked toward the far sky. "Wang Ching-wei was
a great man. He never saw his dream come true,
a dream of seeing China led by a party milder

than the Communists and less corrupt than the Nationalists."

Aaron joined her. Fast-moving clouds gathered in the western sky. A storm was forming. "In the west, both parties will be busy now," Aaron said. "The Nationalists must be practicing their victory march in Chungking, and the Communists will be doing the same in Yenan."

In Yenan, the large cave used as a mess hall was buoyant with the air of victory.

"The Japanese are losing the war! We'll soon have them completely defeated!" Wong Chung shouted, waving his hands high in the air. "Our guerrilla fighters have done well! Our Eighth Route Army soldiers are all heroes!"

Kwanjin whispered to May, "That man has some nerve! Even a fool knows we didn't do much more than the Nationalists to fight Japan."

Wong Chung turned and focused his eyes on Kwanjin. "What are you saying, Comrade Li?"

Kwanjin stared at him defiantly.

Wong Chung refused to look away from Kwanjin, his hatred written clearly in his eyes. The party had not been able to prove either Kwanjin or May's guilt in having helped Leahi to leave Yenan. But because both Leahi and Kwanjin had joined the party many years ago on Wong's recommendation, Wong was blamed by his senior officers for having failed to keep a tighter rein on his junior members. A black mark had been added to Wong's excellent record, and he swore to make Kwanjin pay.

"Only cowards talk and at the same time are afraid to be heard," Wong challenged Kwanjin. "Comrade Li, are you a coward?"

"No." Kwanjin accepted his challenge immediately. "I am from the Pearl River. No one raised

on the Pearl is a coward. I said that—" May
placed her hand on Kwanjin's arm like a steel
vise, effectively cutting off his reckless words.

Everyone in the mess hall who saw May's action laughed. Wong Chung waited for them to
quiet down, then raised his voice. "Our Comrade
Li is not a coward. He is only henpecked!"

Kwanjin pushed May's hand away and glared
at her in fury.

"I did it for your own good, and you should
know it." May's voice was barely audible. "Have
you noticed the way he has been looking at you
since your Mama left? It frightens me . . ." She
tried to describe Wong's animosity toward her
husband. "It's like a mad dog crouching behind
you, waiting to lunge at your throat." She
shuddered.

Wong Chung had to turn away from baiting
Kwanjin when the senior officers began to discuss
the party's best strategy when victory came.

One of them said, "When the Japanese leave
China, we should hurry to all the major cities before Chiang Kai-shek gets there. We should send
our people into Beijing, Nanjin, Shanghai, and
Kwangchow to spread the Communist solution.
We must capture the people's hearts before they
have a chance to listen to Chiang's lies."

Another officer agreed. "We should send those
with homes in the big cities back to their families.
They will talk in favor of the party, and their relatives will join them. If our plans are carried out
successfully, by the time Chiang's men arrive,
people will only spit on them."

Under the table, Kwanjin and May squeezed
each other's hands.

"Are you glad I stopped your big mouth?" May
whispered to her husband, smiling at him with
new hope shining in her eyes. "My home is in

Beijing, and the party needs me to broadcast in its favor. You and Enlai are coming home with me, of course." Her face glowed as she thought of the future. "Our dreams will come true. We'll have a home of our own. No more commune for us or nursery school for our son."

Kwanjin used all his willpower to lower his excited voice. "I'll be able to tolerate Wong Chung now, because we'll soon be let out of this cage to fly free and never look back!"

The birds resting alongside the banks of Arizona's Gila River were frightened by the piercing siren. They flapped their wings in a chirping complaint and took flight.

Michiko looked out the window at the birds while getting dressed in a hurry. Her skirt was tattered, her blouse a rag. The camp didn't provide a uniform, and she was too embarrassed to remind Quanming and Laurie that instead of chocolates, nuts, magazines, and books, she needed clothes.

The siren lasted for one full minute. By the time it stopped, the other seven women in Michiko's room were also up and ready.

The camp contained over a dozen barracks, each about twenty feet wide and 120 feet long. Each barracks was partitioned into six rooms, and each room was assigned to a family. The single people like Michiko and Iko shared rooms, eight to a room, sleeping on four bunk beds.

The desert sun was brutal even in the morning hours of autumn. In front of the barracks the detainees stood at attention, sweating and waiting for their barrack guards to call the roll.

No one flinched or frowned as each number was called. They had been held captive long enough to have grown accustomed to not being treated as individuals. Besides, the guards didn't want to bother with pronouncing Japanese names.

"Four-twenty-one!" called the armed guard, a thin little man in his mid-forties, holding a clipboard.

"Here," Michiko answered without expression.

The guard went on with the numbers listed on the sheets of paper clipped together, and Michiko remembered how she and the others had at first resented being deprived of their family names. But that was just after they had arrived on a crowded train in 1942. It was now September 1944.

They filed into the cafeteria at seven o'clock sharp. The large room was like a dusty oven. The wind blew in through the open windows, carrying the desert sand, adding a layer of grit to the floor and other surfaces. The carrots in the salad were cut into flower shapes, and the cabbage resembled the flowers' leaves. The kitchen workers were fellow detainees doing their best to give the simple food a Japanese touch, telling the others not to lose faith.

But the adults ate with their heads bowed or their eyes staring into space, and the children whispered their questions and curbed any small amount of joy they might feel regardless of the confinement.

"Iko," Michiko said to the woman sitting next to her, who slept on the lower deck of her bunk bed, "you must eat more than that. We all need to keep up our strength for the day of our freedom."

Iko was in her thirties, but looked much older than her age. She shook her head and pushed her plate away. "I'll never see freedom again."

Michiko wanted to say something more, but a female guard was blowing on her whistle, telling the children to line up for school. Education for the young had not been ignored in the camp. The authorities had sent books, and assigned the detainees with teaching certificates to conduct classes under the guards' supervision.

After the children were gone, the adults lined up and filed out, going to work. The younger men headed for the farm, where they worked hard to grow their own vegetables in the arid soil. The older men worked with the women, on jobs that didn't require much physical strength.

Michiko walked in the bright sun, crossing the compound, enclosed by barbed wire fences. She passed the schoolrooms, and could hear the children pledging their allegiance to the American flag, then singing the national anthem. Iko's son and daughter were among them.

"When Kitaro and Sumiko sing the American national anthem, they always wonder why they are not free like other Americans," Iko said, walking beside Michiko. "They were born in this country, and have never seen Japan."

Immediately Michiko thought of Genkai, who was now five years old. About a year ago Quanming had received a letter from Mr. Ikeda, enclosing a picture of Genkai. Since Laurie had forwarded the letter and picture to Michiko, she had carried Genkai's picture in a folder next to her heart all the time. She often looked at the picture and remembered what her father had written: "Genkai is healthy, strong, honest, proud, and brave, just like a samurai."

Michiko also remembered what Quanming had added at the end of Laurie's letter: "To be a samurai is better than to live behind a wire fence." Those words had helped her to believe that she had made the right decision in giving Genkai to her parents. If she hadn't sent Genkai to Hiroshima, he would be in the camp school now, just like Iko's children. His memory of the world beyond the wire fence would have diminished by now, and he would not know any place but the prison camp.

Michiko squinted her eyes in the blazing light, looking up at the soldiers in the nearest high watchtower. Their bayonets glistened, making her feel cold in spite of the burning sun. She looked away from them and glanced at the other side of the fence. The desert was endless, the Gila River shimmered, and the birds were gone. Michiko imagined herself flying with the free birds, heading west of the Gila River, passing over California, and crossing the Pacific Ocean, all the way to Hawaii without making a single stop.

Her eyes fell on the area beside the Gila, where a small cemetery was growing in size. Many detainees were buried there, among them her in-laws. She wondered if their spirits were finally freed, and if Jebu's spirit had come to guide his parents. She looked at the river once more before entering the leather shop.

Wooden tables and long benches filled the shop from one end to the other. Women and older men worked here ten hours a day, six days a week, making leather purses that were sold expensively outside the camp, and receiving fourteen dollars a month for their labor.

Michiko worked on a half-finished purse with a design of roses indented on both sides. She pressed hard with the tool, making indentations in the leather. Her fingers were callused, her nails broken. Her hands were rough and the pearl ring on her finger looked as pitiful as its owner.

"Each pearl is for one of the four happiest years of my life," Jebu had said when he gave the ring to her on their fourth anniversary.

Now Jebu was dead, Genkai thousands of miles

away, her in-laws buried, and the ring that had resembled a four-leaf clover was totally misshapen. Two of the pearls were gone, lost during Michiko's turn to scrub the toilets. The bent catches on the empty settings looked like the claws of a dead animal clutching onto nothingness.

Iko saw Michiko staring at her finger, followed her eyes to the ring, and sighed.

Michiko glanced at Iko, feeling sorry and angry for the woman.

Iko and her husband, Sada, had two children. The four of them plus Iko's aged parents used to live in New Jersey on Sada's dairy farm. Sada was Japanese-American. The Selective Service drafted him, and he became one of the thirty-three thousand Japanese-Americans who served in the U.S. armed forces, in the Nisei combat unit.

Sada was killed. Soon after his death, the dairy farm was taken away and the whole family was sent to the camp in Arizona.

Michiko smiled at Iko, trying to cheer up the woman. "Well, if the ring was not battered, I probably wouldn't have been able to keep it this long," she said. The guards were not allowed to rob the detainees, but there were ways for them to make life impossible until the desired items were offered as gifts.

Michiko continued to talk as she and Iko both bent toward their work. "The missing pearls can be replaced once we're out of here. You and I will recover, forget these terrible years, and go on with our lives . . ." Her voice broke.

"Michiko, are you ill?" Iko asked with concern.

"I . . . Sometimes I feel that I've reached the end of my rope. I can't stand this camp any longer. I want to get out of here. I want my freedom so badly I could scream," Michiko said, drying her tears.

"We all feel this way, Michiko, every one of us," Iko said. "Sometimes I see myself living in a cave, far from light and air. I'm dying, but I can't run from the cave. . . ."

The cave was occupied by the Japanese, and the Japanese wouldn't come out.

In the autumn of 1944 the U.S. Marines encountered strong resistance in a small village in Guam. They lost many men, but still couldn't force the Japanese out of a cave that was too high for the flamethrowers to reach.

Sung Hwa volunteered to go behind the hill and climb above it in order to lower a whole case of explosives on a long rope. The fuse was already lit when he began to swing the rope back and forth. He let go of the rope as the explosives swung inside the cave.

He ran as fast as he could. Before he was back to his squad, he heard the explosion and felt the ground shake. The cave was destroyed with all the Japanese buried in it. Sung Hwa was promoted to corporal and praised for his bravery by his colonel.

"I'll remember your name," said the colonel.

Guam was secured, and Hwa's unit was sent to Okinawa. They landed on the north end of the island and took control of the airport on the first day.

Like in Guam, when the rest of the infantry moved on, the demolition team looked for land mines. Hwa used his bayonet to poke into the ground at an angle. When he touched something suspicious, he would clear the area, place a charge on it, then run as fast as he could. He had about five seconds before the explosion to reach a safe distance and drop himself flat on the ground.

Sung Hwa cleared almost two hundred mines

in three days, and one of those mines saved the very same colonel's life.

"I owe you a favor," said the colonel, who remembered Sung Hwa's name. "When you need one, come to me."

Sung Hwa remembered the colonel's promise.

28

August 1945

IN SHANGHAI, at ten o'clock each night, the city went dark. The Japanese in power shut off the electricity so that the American pilots couldn't find their targets. In the past year the bombing had become a nightly routine. American planes arrived every night, dropping bombs aimed at Japanese factories and military bases but which fell on Chinese homes and other civilian buildings as well.

"We must assist the U.S. Air Force," Aaron said to the others, "since we know it's the Americans who are winning the war for us."

There were over a dozen of them, gathered in a small fourth-floor apartment near a large factory. The windows were covered with double-layered curtains made in accord with the Japanese order—the black layer facing the streets, the red facing inside. Strips of rice paper were glued to each window to keep the glass from shattering when bombs fell nearby. On a wooden table stood an oil lamp less than five inches tall; its low flame flickered behind a thick red glass shade. Like the curtains, lamps of this sort could be purchased with Japanese approval on the streets of Shanghai.

"How many of us have flashlights?" Diana asked.

Only three people raised their hands; the rest had torches made either from wood or from newspapers rolled tightly.

"We'll have to make do," Aaron said, looking at his watch. It was nearly midnight. "The air raid should start any minute now." He wished everyone Godspeed, and the group left the apartment.

He and Diana watched as the others moved discreetly into the streets. They then climbed the stairway to the rooftop.

A low wall enclosed the flat roof. Diana and Aaron leaned over the wall, and in the light of a half-moon they saw dark shadows moving quickly, surrounding the factory next door. When each form had melted into the darkness, Aaron and Diana relaxed a little. They sat on the concrete ground with their backs against the wall and waited for the sound of a siren.

"How much longer do you think the war will last?" Aaron asked.

"It will be over any day now," Diana answered.

"We've been saying that since a year ago, and have been doing this for just as long . . ." Aaron's voice trailed away in the night wind. He didn't want to think about the friends they had lost while helping the U.S. pilots find their targets.

Diana heard Aaron's unspoken words. She counted their lost friends. "But their lives were given for the destruction of many buildings and factories important to the Japanese," she reasoned. "Their sacrifices are bringing the war closer to its end."

A siren pierced through the night air, rose to its highest pitch, then descended quickly. It was immediately followed by a second, then a third. Before the last siren died away, searchlights brightened the sky, and the Japanese ground force was ready to shoot down the enemy.

Around the factory, patches of light appeared, each representing a Chinese communicating with the American pilots. On the rooftop, two torches began to burn. Aaron held one, Diana the other. They watched the night sky and listened for the hum of engines. They waved their torches in wide arcs as the first plane made its approach.

More planes appeared and flares were sent down, each a glowing red ball, falling slowly, revealing the hidden buildings to the pilots in the sky. The first bomb exploded and shook the building Aaron and Diana were on. They stood tall and straight in the ear-shattering noise, guiding the unseen pilots with their twin torches.

Suddenly Diana heard Aaron scream.

She looked and saw him doubling over, his torch dropped to the roof. As she ran to him, she noticed for the first time the sound of gunshots underneath the exploding bombs. They were coming from the street and spraying everything in sight. Diana flung her torch down and stamped both of them out. She hunched next to Aaron and saw the pain on his face and blood on his right shoulder.

"Is the wound deep?" she asked, her voice strained but under control

He shook his head.

She put Aaron's left arm over her shoulder, and her right arm around his waist. She used herself as a crutch and helped him to move to the roof's trapdoor.

They hurried into the stairwell, neither taking a last look over the low wall and down at the street.

They knew what had happened without seeing their friends lying dead or dying on the ground.

In the apartment, Diana lit the oil lamp and

checked Aaron's wound. "The bullet is still in there." She frowned. "We'll have to get you to a doctor."

"No," Aaron said. "We can count ourselves lucky if the soldiers don't search this apartment from door to door. We'll never reach a doctor at this hour without being caught. We must wait at least until morning." She touched a wet cloth to the wound and he flinched at the pain. "Diana, do we have any liquor in this place?"

She left for the kitchen and came back with a bottle of cooking wine. Aaron drank from the bottle. They didn't speak for a while. No words were needed to express what they both knew: Aaron must bear the pain through the long night.

The wine numbed Aaron's senses a little and he had stopped bleeding.

As he lay on the cot and Diana lay beside him, his left arm touched her bare skin. She had removed her dark camouflage clothing and wore only her underwear. When she sat up to check on his wound, the lamplight shone on her sun-golden skin.

"Rich Boy . . ." She followed Aaron's eyes and scolded him gently with a smile. "You are being a bad boy, but thank God you're not hurt so badly after all."

Aaron felt his face burning. "I never noticed you as a woman, Moon Girl . . ." He looked from her long slim thighs to her small rounded breasts to her familiar face. "And you're such a beautiful one."

They fell asleep just before dawn. With the first light came another commotion in the streets. They were about to run when they noticed that the shouting was not in Japanese.

"The Japanese have fled!" someone cried. "We are free!" It sounded like every Chinese in the entire city was drunk with joy.

29

MR. IKEDA WORKED in Kure from Monday morning until Saturday noon, and lived in a dormitory for men that was provided by the shipbuilding company.

He returned to Hiroshima every Saturday afternoon, where he spent the night and the next day in a rented small house with a vegetable garden.

Every Sunday night Genkai would ask the old man, "Am I going with you? Or am I staying with Grandma?"

In the past six months Grandma Ikeda had been sick often. It had become too much for her to take care of a six-year-old boy. The factory owner didn't mind Ikeda's grandson staying in the dormitory, and the other lonely men in the dorm welcomed a well-behaved child's laughter.

When Genkai stayed in Kure, he went to the local school. When he stayed with his grandmother, he went to the Hiroshima school. He liked both of his first-grade teachers, and was happy in both places.

During the first week of August 1945, Mrs. Ikeda felt unwell. Genkai had stayed with her the previous week, but she hadn't even been able to get up to cook for him. When her husband came home for the weekend, she asked him to take the boy with him Sunday night.

On August 5 a messenger came from the hospital in Hiroshima, arrived at the shipbuilding factory, and asked for Mr. Ikeda. "Your wife was taken to the hospital by your landlord. You'd better come to the hospital with me immediately."

"But my grandson is here in school . . ." Mr. Ikeda hesitated.

Ikeda's friends promised to take care of Genkai until the grandfather could return from Hiroshima.

On the sixth of August Genkai went to school as usual. At 8:16 A.M. he was concentrating on mathematics.

The windows began to shake, and then the sunlight disappeared. He couldn't see well enough to write the numbers, and then heard a faraway thunder, like an approaching storm.

The rumbling intensified and the ground vibrated, and all the children said there was another earthquake.

The teacher dismissed the class and told them to remain in the schoolyard. When Genkai went out of the room to stand on the playground, he looked in the direction of his home and saw thick dark dust rising and swirling in the shape of a huge mushroom.

Sung Hwa put down his glass of beer and picked up a notepad.

His platoon had been in Guam for over a month now, waiting for orders to land a big attack on Japan. Until the order came, he spent much time sitting outside his tent either writing letters home or looking at the palm trees and the eternal blue sky, daydreaming about the peaceful days to come and his long-delayed reunion with Melin.

He began to write a letter to his father. After only a few words he heard wild cheering from a group of men in his unit.

He ran to them, and was told that they had

heard over the public-address system that an atomic bomb had been dropped on Japan that morning, and the war was at last over.

All of Yenan was celebrating their joy.

"The war is over!"

When Kwanjin and May heard the news, they were on their way to the nursery to visit their son. They looked at each other, then clung together in a tight embrace.

"We'll be home soon!" They laughed and cried as they held hands and ran toward the nursery.

"Does it mean I can stay with you all the time now, Baba and Mama?" asked the six-year-old Enlai.

Kwanjin picked up the boy and lifted him high into the air. "Yes! You and Baba and Mama will live in a real home in a big city!"

"Will I still go to school?" Enlai circled his arms around Kwanjin's neck.

"Yes," May answered. "You'll go to school in Beijing. Elementary school, high school, and then Beijing University."

Enlai's eyes opened wide with fright. "Will they have teachers who smile once in a while? Will there be other kids like me?"

Kwanjin held his son tightly to his heart, pressed his face against the child's, and closed his eyes. "Yes, Enlai. You'll have teachers gentle like your Mama . . . not quite as beautiful, I'm afraid. And you'll have lots and lots of friends. Your life will be very different, my son, but so much better than the life I have given you here."

Kwanjin felt May's elbow jab his side and opened his eyes. He saw Wong Chung standing only a few feet away, holding the hand of a little girl. It was obvious that Wong had heard Kwanjin's words.

"Are you celebrating a little too early, Comrade Li?" Wong Chung grinned at Kwanjin, then ran the tip of his tongue over his lips, as if they were parched from thirst.

The desert seldom received enough water. When it rained, every drop was swallowed quickly by the sand.

The detainees absorbed the rain also. When they reached the cafeteria, they were drenched, their threadbare clothes glued to their bodies. They ate dripping wet.

When the lunch hour was half-over, a commotion rose from the small dining room attached to the cafeteria, where the guards ate while being entertained by a radio.

"What happened?" Iko turned her head toward the dining room. "They are on their feet laughing and shouting!"

Those who sat nearest to the guards heard the news first. It spread quickly, and the cafeteria was soon an ocean of cries—cries of joy and cries of anguish.

Many of the detainees pushed their food aside, jumped up, and hugged one another, laughing. "The Americans dropped an atomic bomb on Japan! The Japanese military is truly defeated! They will surrender now and we can go home!"

Others remained seated, their faces ashen, their jaws slack, their voices trembling as if their world had come to an end. "Hiroshima? The entire city has been destroyed? Everyone there must have been killed. Those who didn't die immediately have to be suffering the greatest horror imaginable!"

The room turned black before Michiko's eyes. Her fingers lost their grip on the water glass, and she slipped slowly to the floor.

Guam, August 15

Sung Hwa and the other men stood at attention and listened to the colonel. "Yesterday, Japan agreed to an unconditional surrender. The signing of the peace treaty will take place in early September. On August 28 we will leave for Japan, to participate in the keeping of the peace. When all is secured, we'll go back to America, and you will be discharged in San Diego."

Sung Hwa was proud and happy to have won the war, and impatient to be discharged. But he felt terrible about Genkai and the Ikedas' being in Hiroshima. He still remembered clearly the night he and his father took them to the fishing boat.

On August 27, just before leaving for Japan, Sung Hwa received a long telegram from Sung Quanming.

My son, I am asking a favor. I know that your unit is among those going into Japan. Please look for Genkai and the Ikedas. Their home is in Hiroshima, near Hiji-yama Park. The boy is six. He has a scar on his left thigh. He might be wearing a white coral Buddha around his neck. Please search for him. I pray you find him alive. Otherwise, confirm his death. Please. We must know. Michiko will be coming home any day now. I have faith in you, my son.

Sung Hwa read the telegram many times. He knew that it was not easy for his father to use the word "please" to him, yet the word had been used three times. A Chinese father was too proud to plead with his son, and Quanming was among the proudest of them all.

Sung Hwa knew it was time to remind his colonel of his debt.

*   *   *

On August 28, 1945, three weeks after the atomic bomb was dropped, the detainees were still not allowed to leave Gila River. On August 14 Japan had agreed to surrender, but so far the Emperor had not yet signed the surrender agreement, and the U.S. government couldn't officially consider the war over. More prisoners died in those three weeks, because of either old age or illness, and Iko was one of them; she died on August 25.

Michiko stood at the gravesite, looking from her in-laws' graves to the grave of her friend, holding the hands of Iko's children, the boy to her left and the girl to her right.

"Mama said you'll take care of us. Will you really, Aunt Michiko?" asked Kitaro, the eight-year-old boy, looking up with an old man's worry on his young face.

"Yes," Michiko answered weakly. "I promised your mother."

If she hadn't made that promise to her dying friend, she might have lost her sanity by now, knowing that most probably Genkai and her parents had died among the 130,000 people killed in Hiroshima.

The warden's words began to ring in her ears again. "The heat rays had a temperature of more than three thousand degrees Celsius! People in Hiroshima were charred alive. Those who died instantly were the lucky ones."

Iko's seven-year-old girl, Sumiko, pulled Michiko's right hand. "Aunt Michiko, I'm hungry."

Michiko forced herself to function. "I'll find something for you to eat," she said, then walked like a robot to the mess hall and pleaded with the kitchen workers for some food for the children.

She sat beside them to watch them eat, thinking that she would never see her Genkai eat again. She took Genkai's picture out of her inner pocket to look at it. Genkai was smiling happily, his eyes bright with a small boy's mischievousness.

Her eyes moved from the picture to the table, stopped at the dark crisp skin of the cold baked chicken. She could see her Genkai's soft skin scorched by the atomic bomb's heat. She tasted bile in her mouth. Holding the picture, she rushed out and vomited.

As she leaned against the wall and cried, Kitaro appeared.

"Aunt Michiko, please don't be sick. If you're sick, you may die like Mama, and then my sister and I will have to go to an orphanage . . . the white people will treat us Japanese children very badly, I know." The boy's voice was calm, but his eyes were anxious.

Michiko put away Genkai's picture, wanting to crawl into a dark hole and die. But Iko's children's needs were like the many strings attached to the limbs of a puppet, pulling her and forcing her to go on.

She smiled weakly and said, "I'm not sick . . . I'll be all right. Don't worry, and don't be afraid. You're too young to worry and to fear . . ." She couldn't continue. She began to cry again. Was there anyone to comfort Genkai like she was comforting Iko's boy? She knew that her parents were not much use in giving tenderness to a child. She had counted on compensating Genkai with her own loving care as soon as the war was over, but now she might never have that chance.

She went to the bathroom to wash her face and rinse her mouth. When she came out, both Kitaro and Sumiko were waiting for her.

Kitaro said, "The warden was looking for you. He wants you in his office. You have a telegram."

The telegram was from Laurie and Quanming.

Received your letter. Please be strong. Trying to have you released soon. Bring your friend's children to Hawaii. We'll be waiting for you. Hwa is on his way to Japan. We've asked him to go to Hiroshima to look for Genkai and your parents. Do not lose faith.

Michiko pressed the telegram to her heart and cried until Sumiko and Kitaro tugged on her sleeves.

"Be strong and do not lose faith." She heard both Laurie and Quanming's voices and visualized their welcoming arms.

She forced herself to smile at the children.

Sung Hwa arrived in Japan on August 31, and the moment his colonel granted him permission, he took the train to Hiroshima.

He found himself among thousands of natives of Hiroshima who had survived the bombing and fled. Now they were returning to search for anything left of their lives. He saw them going into the remaining houses that stood like skeletons, and heard them crying when they couldn't find anything or anybody untouched by the bomb.

It was almost four weeks after the bombing, but corpses of the newly dead were still piled high in many places. Hwa saw three large fires blazing and roaring in the autumn wind, cremating bodies. Beside each fire were gathered many people, some with their heads bowed, others staring into the flames. A few women and children cried, but most of the men bit their lips and clenched their fists, trying to conceal their emotion, in keeping with their tradition.

About a dozen Japanese soldiers scattered around the burning fire, digging holes to bury the unburned remains. They looked at Hwa in his uniform, then quickly looked away. From their expressions Hwa could tell that they already knew that their emperor would be signing the surrender agreement the next day. They were ashamed of losing the war and resented the presence of a Chinese in the uniform of a U.S. Marine. Hwa walked away from them, reached a large tent, and was greeted by a strong stench and the agonized groans of many people.

The tent was a station put up after the bombing, to keep the wounded until they could be taken to hospitals elsewhere. There were not many hospitals in Hiroshima to begin with, and now, except for the Red Cross hospital, they were all destroyed. People were lying on the ground, on mats, sheets, oil paper, or newspaper. They were packed so closely that Hwa had to walk carefully to avoid stepping on them. If they had not been moaning, he would have thought that many of them lying in blood-soaked bandages were dead—he had not known that human beings could continue to live in such horrible shape.

Their hair was either matted with filth or singed off, their bodies were disfigured, their faces so badly burned that he couldn't see their features. He saw a little girl with two pigtails that were burned to a crisp and stood stiff like two horns. He saw a naked young boy whose body and face were covered with festering red blisters.

"Did we do this? Or did the Japanese military leaders?" Sung Hwa moaned, feeling sick with guilt and sorrow. "They started the war and we ended it. But look who is paying the price!"

He scanned every face in the tent, while trying to remember those of the Ikedas. That night in Hawaii, he had not seen them clearly, and now he couldn't bring their images to mind.

He checked out every child carefully. With their

hair burned away and clothes substituted by bandages, it was hard to tell the boys from the girls. He looked for a gold chain and a white Buddha. He didn't find any child wearing it. He shook his head when he remembered Quanming's detail of the scar on the left thigh—not many children had any unscarred limbs.

Their charred lips were unable to speak, but their eyes were able to express their torment. As Hwa searched, he met many pairs of pleading eyes.

"Let me die! Please! I can't take the pain any longer!" yelled the eyes of a man.

"Where are my loved ones? They are not suffering like me, I hope?" asked the eyes of a woman.

"Mama! Help me!" begged the eyes of a frightened boy.

"Mama and Baba, did I do something very bad, to be punished so severely?" wailed the eyes of a dying girl.

Sung Hwa left the tent. He walked past the burned-out city hall and arrived at the emergency food-distribution center. Several men were giving out rice balls. Two women were ladling out cold tea. He saw several children in tattered clothes, with petrified eyes and ash-covered faces, but none of the boys had around his neck a chain with a Buddha. He took out of his pants pocket a candy bar and a pack of chewing gum, gave them to the children, and wished he could do a million times more for these people.

Outside the food-distribution center he saw a young boy pushing a handcart that carried a badly burned young woman. In the woman's tightly clutched arms was the body of her dead infant.

"Please let me help you," Hwa said, taking over the handles of the cart. The boy studied his face for a few seconds, then nodded and stepped ahead to guide the way, walking in long strides with the air of the head of a family.

They paused at a burned house. Hwa thought it was the boy's home, but the child only stopped to look among the ashes for some usable boards from a broken door. He gathered the boards and brought them to Hwa, said something that Hwa assumed meant he should keep an eye on the boards. As Hwa waited with the woman and the dead infant, the boy returned to the house and found a hammer and some nails. He brought the things back, squatted beside the cart, and began to hammer the boards into a small coffin. Hwa helped him. When the coffin was finished, the boy carried it with both hands and led Hwa to an emergency open-air crematory.

Many people with homemade coffins waited in line. The boy loosened his mother's arms, took the infant's body, and placed it in the coffin. Hwa waited with them. When it was the small coffin's turn to be cremated, the boy bowed and Hwa bowed with him while the woman in the cart remained unconscious. Hwa glanced at the boy's face and saw tears glistening in his eyes. Those tears never did fall; the boy kept them back with willpower. His chin lifted and his shoulders square, the boy carried himself like a brave and proud samurai.

Once again the barefoot boy in tattered clothes led the way and Hwa in his Marine uniform followed, pushing the handcart. They passed many bodies lying along the sides of the deserted streets. They went across a curved bridge and saw cadavers floating in the river. There were also white paper lanterns floating in the water on wood boards, with small candles burning inside. The Konji characters painted on these lanterns seemed to be people's names. Hwa guessed that the lanterns were burning for the dead, guiding their spirits to a world free from war.

The boy led Hwa all the way across the city to the Red Cross hospital. While helping the boy locate someone who could assist his mother, Hwa met an American missionary nurse.

The middle-aged woman looked exhausted. She told Hwa that with four hundred beds, this was Hiroshima's largest and most modern hospital. They used to run things smoothly and in perfect order, but the past four weeks had been sheer hell. She admitted the boy's mother and placed the woman on a bed, pushing her through a corridor with both Hwa and the boy following alongside.

"I wish we could find a room for her," she said, indicating the many beds which lined the corridor. "But I'm afraid we'll have to fit her in wherever we can." She looked at the woman and whispered to Hwa, "I don't think she will last through the night anyway."

Hwa glanced at the people lying on the beds in the corridor. He saw the once-white wall beside the beds now stained with blood. The wounded had dipped their fingers in their own blood, then made marks on the wall.

"Why do they do that?" Hwa asked, aghast.

"They are writing their names," the woman explained. "Their faces are burned beyond recognition. They don't know when they will lose consciousness. They are worried that if their families come to look for them, they won't be able to find them. If their beds are moved away or if they should die before they're found, at least their families will know that, at one time, they were here."

"I'm looking for three people . . ." Hwa quickly told her about Genkai and the Ikedas. "How can I find out if they are alive or dead?"

The tired nurse shook her head. "Look over this hospital, then search the city. See if the house is still standing. You can also try the child's school and the grandparents' work places. There is no record listing the names of the dead and wounded. Not yet. If you come back in a year or two, maybe there will be such a record."

The nurse began to speak to the boy in Japanese. Hwa interrupted her by giving her half of all the money he had, and asked her to use it for the boy and his mother's needs. He then asked for directions to Hijiyama Park, rested his hand briefly on the boy's thin shoulder, and walked away.

He searched the hospital but didn't find Genkai or the Ikedas in any of the beds. They were not in the morgue either. He left the hospital, and was certain now that he wouldn't be able to find them before the day was over. He headed for Hijiyama Park, thinking that they were probably dead. He saw many searchers wandering the streets, stopping at the scattered bodies, examining the corpses, turning them over, and peering at the unrecognizable faces.

"Do I have to do that?" he asked himself, and decided that after looking around Hijiyama Park, he would have to begin checking the corpses of small boys.

He reached Hijiyama Park and saw the houses in ashes. Among several clusters of homes, not even a chunk of a roof beam was left. He saw a small boy squatting among the rubbish, digging through the remains. The boy heard Hwa's footsteps and looked up. He met Hwa's eyes but showed no emotion on his dirt-covered face. Hwa smiled at him, but the boy frowned. Hwa waved at him, but he didn't wave back, only bowed his head and returned to his digging.

Hwa was tired. Beside him, a large rock stood covered with black dust. Hwa wiped it with his handkerchief and sat, watching the boy in a ripped kimono shoveling and poking with his hands, working diligently. When Hwa was about to leave, he saw that the boy had found the blackened remnants of a tricycle and a pair of half-melted skates, both bent as if a giant hand had twisted them out of shape.

They were obviously once the boy's favorite toys and were now completely ruined. Hwa expected to see the boy cry. To Hwa's surprise, the boy clutched them in his arms and carried them from the site dry-eyed. He walked past Hwa without giving him even a glance.

But beneath his torn kimono a gold chain glittered and a white coral Buddha stared at Hwa with sad ancient eyes.

Sung Hwa told the whole story to his colonel, then repeated his plea.

"I owe you only one favor, but you are asking two." The colonel shook his head. "You ask too much."

"Not really, sir," Sung Hwa said, maintaining his most respectful tone. "The two favors are closely related."

The colonel frowned. "Your being discharged here instead of returning stateside, and my taking a Japanese boy to Hawaii?"

"Yes, sir."

"I fail to see the connection."

"Well, sir . . ." Hwa wanted to try again, but the colonel waved at him to stop.

"I'll not bargain with you," the colonel said, leaving no room for further discussion. "I'll allow you to be discharged here in Tokyo, but you'll have to take the child to Hawaii yourself. I don't want to be caught with him holding my hand when my wife comes to meet me. What will she think? Anyway, it's against regulations for the boy to travel with us. But after you're discharged, well, that's different."

Sung Hwa saluted the colonel and left the office. On his way to the barracks, he smiled. He and Genkai could fly in a military plane to Hawaii—a trip that would last only a few hours. After giving Genkai to his father, he would take another military plane to Shanghai, where a large division of the American Air Force was currently stationed. A short train ride would bring him from Shanghai to Kwangchow, and then to White Stone.

As he neared the barracks, he heard his buddies laughing and Genkai giggling. In the past few days Michiko's boy had become a pet to the Marines, and had discarded the samurai attitude imposed on him by his grandparents, along with his ragged kimono.

Quanming greeted Hwa and Genkai at the military airport. He picked up Genkai and looked at Hwa with tears in his eyes.

"I thank you." His voice quavered. "Michiko doesn't even know the good news yet."

They walked from the airport to the parking lot, and Quanming explained that when Hwa's telegram arrived, Michiko had already left Arizona for California and Quanming had no way to contact her. Quanming stopped at the car and looked at Hwa with a broad smile. "But what a surprise we'll have for her! Her ship is arriving in just a few more days."

When Hwa didn't get in the car with Genkai, Quanming looked at his son. "You're coming with us, aren't you? You will spend a few days in our house, go to the pier with us, and then stay a little longer? I do want you and Laurie to have a chance to know each other."

"Baba." Hwa put a hand on Quanming's shoulder. "Another plane is taking off in an hour. Melin has been waiting eight years for me, and I must not keep her waiting any longer."

Hwa walked away from the car, turning many times to wave to Quanming and Genkai.

Michiko stood on deck between Iko's two children, all three of them wearing new clothes purchased in California with money Laurie had wired to Michiko.

Kitaro was proud of his new suit, Sumiko happy in a pink dress. Michiko couldn't bring herself to wear any color other than white; it was the right color to mourn Genkai.

Michiko searched the pier and saw Laurie and Quanming. Their white hair gleamed in the Hawaiian sun, contrasting with their tanned skin. She raised a hand to wave at them, and then through her tears she saw between them a child wearing a blue kimono.

Michiko squinted her eyes to study the child's face in the brilliant sunlight, and found herself looking at a mixture of herself and Jebu, a face that she had looked at millions of times in a picture.

Her heart was beating at her throat, and she heard herself scream, "Genkai! My Genkai!"

30

"THE CHANGE HAS COME, but not for the better," said Diana, sitting beside Aaron's hospital bed.

"But it will improve, won't it?" Aaron asked hopefully.

The room was filled with fresh flowers, sent by friends and Aaron's parents, who had flown to Shanghai and stayed in a hotel near the hospital.

The bullet had been removed from Aaron's right shoulder. He couldn't raise his right arm up straight, but the doctor said he would be able to eventually.

Diana didn't answer. She avoided Aaron's eyes, gazing at her hands for a long while. When she finally looked up, her beautiful brown eyes were sad. "The city of Shanghai is a circus. You can stand on the street and watch the grand parade of one bizarre group after another."

Diana tried to describe what she had seen since Aaron's operation. "As you know, there are always looters and thieves at a time like this. Merchants have raised the prices on everything. The rich are celebrating, the poor can barely survive. The Japanese have not yet all gone, but the Americans have already landed. They are wide-eyed strangers in a strange land. Except for the aged officers, the rest are young soldiers visiting the Orient for the first time. They give out chewing gum and candy bars and throw coins to all the beggars. Some of them think all Chinese girls are barmaids, the others mistake our prostitutes for princesses. You see many uniformed American boys riding on rickshaws and pedicabs with Chinese female companions, but none of them know what they are getting into."

"Never mind the American soldiers," Aaron said impatiently. "Are Chiang's men back?"

"Not in the city, but gathered nearby," Diana said. "The Americans have decided that the Nationalists should rule China. They helped to airlift Chiang's soldiers to the outskirts of all the major cities. They're waiting for the right moment to make an impressive entrance." Diana shrugged in disgust. "The high-ranking officers are already here, of course."

Aaron didn't understand Diana's uncharacteristically low spirits. He leaned closer to her. "What are you hiding from me, Moon Girl?"

Diana shook her head. But Aaron saw her swallow hard, and noticed her clenched fists on her lap.

"All right." Aaron raised his good arm and pushed away the blanket. "If you won't tell me anything, I'll just have to see for myself." He swung his legs over the side of the bed.

"No, you don't!" Diana stood up to push Aaron back to bed.

He saw her eyes. "Why are you crying?"

Suddenly Diana collapsed. She sank back to the chair and covered her face with her palms.

"Please, Diana, what happened?" Aaron left his bed, sat on the arm of her chair, and pulled her toward him.

Diana dropped her hands, looked up at Aaron. "Do you remember Tea Drinker?"

Aaron stared at her tear-streaked face and nodded.

"And the movie actress we saw in Kwang-chow? Who relayed so much information to us?"

"Yes. Tea Drinker worked for her. What about them?"

"They died this morning."

"But how? I thought the war was over!"

Diana was calmer now. "The Nationalists started to arrest the Communists and the LWN as soon as they arrived in Nanjin and Shanghai. Those who worked for the Sino-Japanese government have gone into hiding. A few were arrested and sentenced to either death or life in prison. Tea Drinker and the actress were only two among many. The trial was informal, the execution carried out immediately."

Aaron held Diana tightly, pressing her to his chest, and ran his fingers through her short hair. He could just see the dainty actress and the big man working together, like a little daisy blooming beside a giant oak tree.

"What kind of world are we living in?" His voice was filled with anger. "Is there no justice?"

"In China, no. Never." Diana's tears were replaced by anger.

"China is four thousand, six hundred years old. Her billions of people have suffered through all those years, persecuted by each successive ruler," she said. They lamented not their own fate, but the death of their dreams.

Aaron suddenly felt tired to his bones. "I'm only twenty-two, but I feel four times that."

"And I'm twenty-eight." Diana smiled up at Aaron. Her face looked like a flower after a spring rain. "I am tired too, but I'm afraid we can't afford to rest."

"What do you mean?" Aaron hoped that she wouldn't mention anything about fighting another battle. "When I was a boy eight years ago,

I loved China. I wanted to understand it and improve it. As a man now, I suppose I still love China, but my passion has cooled."

He looked at Diana apologetically. "I'm sorry Moon Girl. Count me out of your next action." He touched her cheek. "You too have done enough. Will you please stay out of the line of fire for a while?"

Diana laughed. She stood up, and held his hand as she guided him back to bed. "I'm afraid I can't count you out of my next action, Rich Boy. We must fight side by side for life," she said calmly.

She told him that from a dependable source of information she had learned that both she and Aaron were on the undesirable list of the Nationalist government. "As soon as you can leave the hospital, you and I will be on the run."

She tucked him under the blanket, sat beside him, and held his hand. "You, I, and the others like us are only shooting stars. We may light up the dark skies of China, but our illumination is brief, and shooting stars must fall to the ground. Tell me, where would you like to fall?" She listed many countries.

The ship sailed out of the East China Sea and moved into the Pacific Ocean.

In his cabin, Aaron stretched out on his bunk, looking out through the porthole. A wave rose, splashed the glass, left it dripping with salt water. "Mama's tears!" Aaron sighed.

Aaron would rather have fought ten more useless battles than make his mother cry. But he had had to tell his parents the truth.

"My son, the spy!" Meiping had screamed at first.

"My baby boy, running for his life?" The tears had come next.

"I'm a senile old man who doesn't even know what is happening under his own nose." David's words had pained Aaron.

"You're not senile, Papa," Aaron had argued. "It's just that Diana and I are very good at maintaining our cover."

When the Cohens accepted the inevitable, they helped him to decide where to go.

"San Francisco, where I met your mother," David had suggested.

"Yes," Meiping agreed. "But first stop in Hawaii and visit Quanming and Laurie. They will be thrilled to welcome Meiping's boy."

Aaron heard a knock on his cabin door. He got up slowly, careful not to touch the sling on his right arm. By the time they arrived in California, his shoulder should be healed.

Aaron blinked his eyes several times at the sight of Diana in a pale green dress adorned with white lace. "You, in a skirt? And high-heeled shoes? Pearl earrings too? Is it perfume I'm smelling?"

Diana looked a little embarrassed. She entered the cabin and turned around for Aaron to examine her thoroughly. "Before boarding the ship, your mother insisted we go shopping in the French Territory of Shanghai. She supervised my packing too. All my old slacks and practical shoes are gone."

"You are beautiful," Aaron said, unable to take his eyes from her.

The cabin was small. She had to walk around him in order to get away from his intense gaze. Her foot tripped over his and she fell into his arms. "I'm sorry," she said. "Did I hurt your shoulder?"

Aaron held her firmly with his left arm so that she couldn't get away. "You didn't hurt my shoulder. You did everything but hurt me."

Their eyes met. She blushed. He kissed her on the forehead. "Thank you for being my friend," he said.

"I'll always be your friend," she murmured.

He ignored her comment and kissed her on the cheek. "And thank you for being my sister," he said, then kissed her on her other cheek. "And my partner."

"You don't have to thank me . . ." Her voice died in her throat when he kissed her on the mouth.

He moved his lips away from hers only long enough to say, "But most of all, for being my love." And he kissed her again.

A large wave tossed the ship up. When it came down again, the eternal ocean caught it tenderly and rocked it in its strong bosom. Aaron and Diana lost their balance and fell on the bunk.

"I *must* have hurt your shoulder this time." Lying next to Aaron, Diana gently touched his bandaged wound.

"Never mind my shoulder." He lifted her face with his left hand and forced her to look into his eyes. "Do you love me?"

"I . . . don't know," she said reluctantly. "We are friends, partners, brother and sister . . ."

"But I love you," Aaron said, surprised that she was avoiding the issue—it wasn't like her at all. "My love for you keeps growing and changing, like a bud becomes a flower, then a fruit. I can't separate them anymore because they are all one. You're still a friend and a sister, but my love is in the fruit stage now . . . I love you as a man loves a woman."

"What will be the next stage?" She laughed

softly, trying to joke about it. "When people finish eating a fruit, do they usually throw the pit away?"

He detected a trace of sadness in her voice. He studied her eyes carefully and found a touch of worry. He became suspicious. "Diana, what is it?" He loosened his embrace.

She was still unwilling to answer his question. "How could you love me?" She tilted her head to one side, looked at him doubtfully. "You loved Yin . . . may still love the memory of her. I am so different from her. I am not an obedient girl. I won't think of you as my master." She looked away from him and lowered her voice. "And I am not young."

He had found the answer. "So that's it!" He grabbed her again, this time even tighter than before. "The age difference bothers you. And I thought you were clever." He kissed her quickly. "Do you know how much older my father is than my mother? Twenty-six years! If two people can be happily married when he is that much older than she, why can't they be a perfect match when she is only six years older than he?"

She stared at him. "Marriage? You want to marry me?"

"No, I want you to jump into the ocean to have a swim with me!" He shook her gently. "Of course I want to marry you. But not until I hear you say that you love me."

She shook her head slowly, then answered softly, "I don't know the exact moment I fell in love with you, but it's been a long time."

Tears filled her eyes as she continued. "Maybe it happened when you slept beside me on the hard ground along one of those country roads outside Kwangchow. Maybe it was when we knelt behind the window and watched those people massacred and we trembled in each other's arms. Or it could have been on the rooftop when we guided the American airplanes to their target."

She reached up to kiss him on the lips. "I was very sad when I discovered I loved you like a woman loves a man."

"Sad? Why?" He kissed her passionately, and only let her have her lips back so that she could explain.

"Because I didn't think you would ever love me the same way. Through the years I've been warning myself . . ."

She changed her tone of voice to pretend she was giving herself a stern order. "Be prepared! Any day now, he will come to you and tell you that he has found a girl and they will soon be married. You must congratulate him, and be ready to become their children's old aunt!"

"My silly Moon Girl!" Aaron had heard all the answers he needed to hear for now. They had the rest of their lives to talk. Right now he wanted only to kiss her more.

31

"I CAME HERE to save China, but I didn't accomplish a thing." May looked at the empty cave. "Eight years are gone, and so are all my dreams."

"I was here long before you, and I've wanted to save China since I was only a child," said Kwanjin from the entrance. "My dreams were harder to kill than yours, but the party managed to do it anyway." He picked up their simple luggage. "Let's go."

"That's right, Mama, let's go," said Enlai, pulling May's hand.

They walked toward the foot of the hill, passing one cave after another. Many people watched them with envy. The party had begun to carry out its plan since the war ended: each day several of Yenan's residents were sent back to their hometown with a mission. In front of one of the larger caves stood Wong Chung's lover. The woman glared at the Li family. May felt sorry for her. Wong didn't have any relatives outside Yenan, and people like him had no excuse to leave.

The wind blew fiercely. Yellow dust quickly cloaked everyone's clothes. May, Kwanjin, and Enlai were no longer wearing their baggy uniforms. "If you don't dress like a comrade, you'll convince people more easily," said Chairman Mao, who often wore a scholar's long robe to

have his portrait done. Following his order, those
leaving Yenan had dug into their bags and found
their old civilian clothes.

May had on an old blue cotton dress. Once
back in Beijing, she would go to her father's shop
and pick the best silk for a new wardrobe. She
would also have new clothes made for her husband and son. She looked at Enlai's shabby outfit
and sighed. When she glanced at Kwanjin's dark
pants and white shirt, she remembered the first
time she had seen him in the Park of the Sun
Altar.

She caught her husband's hand. "I love you,"
she said softly.

"I love you too." He gave her an instant reply,
then looked at her curiously. "Why the sudden
emotion?" During the stressful Yenan years they
had all but stopped expressing their love with
words.

May shook her head. "I don't know. Maybe
because you're wearing the same thing that you
had on when I met you for the first time." She
smiled at him tenderly. "You walked tall and
proud between those two brutes. Your handsome
face was angry but fearless. The wind was tossing
your hair over your forehead and flapping the
sleeves of your white shirt . . ." She squeezed his
hand tightly. "Maybe that magic shirt has the
power to make me fall in love with you all over
again."

Kwanjin squeezed her hand back. "When we
reach Beijing, I'll find a job. I'll work hard. And
when I have enough money, do you know what
I'll buy?"

May shook her head.

"A gold chain with a locket, just like the one
you traded with the police for my life."

"Oh, Kwanjin!" May stopped walking. She looked at her husband with tears in her eyes.

"Mama, Baba, please hurry!" Enlai called impatiently. "I can see the truck now!"

Beside the parked truck stood a few other families. Those leaving today were to bring their luggage to the truck that would take them to the train station later, then return to the mess hall for one final briefing from Wong Chung.

Kwanjin and May wished that they had been excused from the boring lecture like the children had been.

Wong Chung repeated everything that had already been repeated numerous times. As he rattled on, he kept glancing at Kwanjin with a smirk, as if he were greatly pleased by a secret victory. Kwanjin and May were used to Wong's peculiar behavior. They were glad that soon they would never have to lay their eyes on the man again.

When the truck driver sounded the horn to remind them that the train wouldn't wait, Wong Chung spoke faster. "Don't forget that many of our comrades have already been arrested and killed in Shanghai and Nanjin by Chiang's men. You have to avenge them. You'll speak for communism, and convince the people of Beijing that our party is the only party that can save China. You'll get your reward when China is ours. We'll destroy both the left- and right-wing Nationalists, and rule China forever—" He stopped when the horn blew once again.

As they filed out of the hall, Kwanjin and May were thinking only that, once in Beijing, they would erase Wong's face and voice completely from their memory.

"Li Kwanjin!" Wong's voice was piercing. "Stop right there!"

Kwanjin and May stood still. "What now?" Kwanjin cursed with a frown, turning slowly to face Wong Chung.

May held on to Kwanjin's arm. "The driver is blowing his horn again. Enlai is waiting for us," she whispered urgently. "What can this man want now?"

"Go to Enlai," Kwanjin said, trying to remove May's fingers from his arm. "I'll be joining you in just a few minutes."

"No!" May raised her voice and tightened her grip. "I'm not leaving without you!"

Wong Chung stood before them with a humorless smile on his face. "I see that the lovebirds are having a little disagreement," he said. Those lingering in the mess hall laughed uncertainly. "Perhaps I can help solve the problem." He took a few steps toward the door, then stopped to wait for Kwanjin and May. "I'll walk you both to your truck."

Kwanjin and May exchanged puzzled glances. They had no choice but to follow him. They saw Wong Chung nod his head to two men in charge of security, who instantly fell in behind them. So Wong Chung was now important enough to have his own personal bodyguards, Kwanjin thought. "You don't have to bid me any private good-byes, you know, my former teacher," he said to Wong sarcastically as they continued walking.

"That's not exactly what I have in mind, my former student," Wong answered as he reached into his shirt pocket and took out a sheet of folded paper. "I received a letter from Willow Place just yesterday." He looked toward the truck and narrowed his eyes at the sight of Enlai waving for his parents to hurry up. "It was written by the town's letter writer and addressed to you, Comrade Li."

Kwanjin and May stumbled slightly as they moved on.

"It's a thank-you letter," Wong Chung said slowly. He looked over his shoulder to make sure that the two security men were still following. "Let me read it to you." He unfolded the sheet.

Kwanjin tried to grab the letter as he came up beside Wong Chung. "Since it's a letter from my mother to me, I don't see why it should be in your hands. I can read it myself."

They were at the truck now. Wong Chung gestured for the two men to come forward. They pried May's hands from Kwanjin and pushed her aside; then each took hold of one of Kwanjin's arms.

"Baba!" Enlai screamed from the truck.

"What do you want with my husband?" May had regained her balance and tried to stand beside Kwanjin once more. She was shoved so roughly this time, she went sprawling to the dirt.

Kwanjin's face was white with anger. He tried to free himself from the men but couldn't. "You have no right to keep me from going to Beijing!" he yelled at Wong Chung. "My family and I are going there on a party mission. Detaining me is in disobeyance of Chairman Mao's order!"

Wong Chung answered quietly. "I never do anything against the Chairman. Nor do I ever do anything without a proper reason. That's why I wasn't prepared to reprimand you until this moment."

Wong Chung began to read the letter. He skipped to where Leahi described her happiness in Willow Place. "Coming home to my beloved village was all your doing, my son," Wong Chung read deliberately. He looked up from the letter to see Kwanjin's ashen face, then went on. "Ever since you were a boy, you believed in your party.

I'm glad you finally let your Mama know that you love her more than communism." Wong Chung folded the letter and put it back into his pocket. He would place it in Kwanjin's file later as evidence of Comrade Li's betrayal. "We've been looking for proof of your involvement in your mother's disloyalty since she abandoned the party. I'm very pleased that the proof has fallen into my hands just in time." He looked at May. "It's too bad that your mother-in-law didn't thank you too."

Wong Chung turned to the two men. "Take him away!"

The men began to drag Kwanjin. May screamed. Enlai cried loudly from the truck. The truck driver, who had been blowing the horn intermittently, now started the engine.

"Wait!" Kwanjin said, and something in his voice made the two men stop.

Kwanjin looked at May. In his eyes there was love, promise, pleading, and many other complicated emotions. "May, please go with Enlai."

May shook her head. Tears streamed down her face and she couldn't speak. From the truck, Enlai cried louder, and the driver was ready to move.

"I've never asked you to do anything for me," Kwanjin said quickly, looking fiercely into May's frightened eyes. "I'm asking you for the first time now. Please listen."

May stared at her husband, sobbing hard, trembling uncontrollably.

"Please, May, go to the truck and take care of our son."

The driver blew the horn one last time, and the wheels began to move slowly.

"Go!" Kwanjin screamed at May, and stamped one foot on the ground.

The people in the truck could not stand any

more of what they had been watching. Since freedom was within their grasp, some of them became brave. Three women jumped off the moving vehicle and ran to May. They grabbed her and carried her back to the truck with them.

The truck picked up speed toward the road. May wanted to jump off, but several people pinned her down. Enlai held her and screamed and cried. He didn't know anything except that Baba had missed the ride.

May craned her neck to look back. She saw Kwanjin exactly as the first time she had seen him—between two armed men, walking tall and proud, his handsome face angry but unafraid.

32

MA TSAI-TU walked toward his daughter's courtyard carrying a jewel case.

The war was over. His Japanese protectors had
left China as war criminals. But he had nothing
to fear. It seemed that with the help of the Americans, Chiang Kai-shek would be the next in
power. Chiang had always been in favor of the
rich, and Ma Tsai-tu certainly was that.

Because of Melin, his family was unharmed, his
home untouched, his fortune undiminished. In
addition to his many acres of land, he still possessed most of the fishing boats in the village,
owned several shop buildings, and controlled a
number of lucrative loan operations. The fishermen, merchants, and farmers of White Stone
wouldn't dare mention his collaborating with the
Japanese, since they must continue to make a
living.

"I'm going to thank my precious daughter for
what she has done," he said to himself.

He found her in her bedchamber, sitting beside
the window, resting an elbow on the windowsill,
holding her head with her hand. Her face was
half-turned, her profile chalk white. Her long hair
cascaded over her naked shoulders, reaching to
the small of her back. She was covered only from
the waist down by a loosely wrapped towel.

"Melin, please get dressed," he said, looking away.

Melin turned her head slowly to face her father, but didn't respond. Her eyes met his, and he shivered. His daughter's eyes were two large black holes surrounded by dark gray circles. Her lips were colorless, and her mouth curved downward. Her cheekbones seemed almost to pierce through her pale skin. The sun shone on the hand that held her chin; blue veins traced its back, and the bloodless fingers trembled visibly.

"Melin, I brought you something," Tsai-tu said, showing her the jewel case.

Melin didn't answer. She stared at her father with her uncomprehending eyes.

The maid came out of the inner chamber carrying a load of soiled clothes. She had just helped Melin with the bath, and finished cleaning the bathroom.

"Give your Sheo-jay a smoke of opium, then dress her!" Ma Tsai-tu ordered the maid. He left the jewel case on Melin's vanity and walked out of the room.

When the father returned an hour later to look at his daughter, he breathed with relief.

Melin's paleness was disguised by heavy makeup and her stringy hair was twisted into a bun and adorned with jeweled combs. Her thinness was concealed by a long gown, and her hands no longer trembled. Her bright red lips parted into a smile, and she was able to focus her eyes on her father.

"Good morning, Baba," she said, showing no memory of his earlier visit.

The father's heart contracted. He waved away the maid, brought the jewel case to his daughter, and the two sat on a lounge chair with the case between them. Ma Tsai-tu opened the case, keeping his eyes on Melin's face, waiting for her to gasp, to smile, perhaps even to laugh.

Melin looked expressionlessly at the rubies, jade, sapphires, and diamonds, mounted on rings, bracelets, necklaces, and earrings. "Are they the private collection of the last commander?" she asked, her voice flat.

"Yes. That man robbed these from our people, but he was searched before leaving China. He asked me to keep his treasure for him until it becomes possible for him to reclaim it." Ma Tsai-tu laughed. "It seems that the Japanese are taking their defeat as only a temporary situation. They all declare that their country will regain its strength soon, and when that day comes, they will possess the world."

Tsai-tu shook his head. "I'm not a fool. Of course I promised him, knowing that Japan is permanently defeated and he'll never be able to come for these things."

He pushed the case toward Melin. "They are yours now, every single piece."

Melin didn't look at the jewelry. "Why?" she asked, keeping her eyes on her father.

"Well," Tsai-tu answered with difficulty, "I want to give you a gift, a reward, a gesture of gratitude, for what you've done . . . for me, for your Mama, and for the rest of the family."

"Maybe you should return them to their original owners. Or give them to Mama," Melin murmured, picking up a ruby ring, turning it, watching it sparkle in the sun. "Maybe these things will bring her back to the real world."

Ma Tsai-tu sighed. "Your mother is happier in her dream world, where she is once again young and beautiful." He shook his head and stood up. "She is with her favorite granddaughter—your older brother's daughter, Qing—playing like a child."

The change in Yoto had occurred when Melin returned from Shanghai and found Sung Hwa gone. Melin had seen the guilt on her mother's face, and felt that Yoto was tortured by a great uncertainty. The later realization of Melin's role with the Japanese officers had brought another stroke to Yoto. From then on she had begun to block out the existence of her daughter, until she no longer seemed to know the face of her once-favored child.

Ma Tsai-tu stopped at the open door. "Melin, do you have any plans for the future? I mean, since your cousin was killed, do you have anyone else in mind for a husband?"

Melin didn't answer. Nor did she look at her father. She continued to toy with the ring.

Ma Tsai-tu laughed softly and said, "No matter what has happened, when it comes to the subject of a husband, you are still shy like a virgin. Well, don't worry, my daughter. You are only twenty-six, and very rich. I'll find you a husband. Within a year you'll be married. A year after that, you'll be a mother. Everything unpleasant that's happened in the past years will then be forgotten."

The opium kept Melin going through the day. She joined her family for lunch, and visited with them in the afternoon. When evening came, everyone went back to his own room to rest for dinner, and Melin returned to her bedchamber to write a letter to Sung Hwa.

Sitting at her desk, she stared at the blank paper. After his name, she was unable to put down a single word.

It had been so easy to lie when the war was going on. She had known that she was helping her family, and that knowledge had given her endurance. The ending of the Japanese occupation had freed her, but also taken away her resolve.

"I'm so tired, Hwa," she whispered, dropping the pen. "Too tired to write, to lie, to . . ." She stopped when the maid tapped on the door and entered.

"Sheo-jay, forgive me, but I called you many times and you didn't seem to hear me," said the woman. "The opium is ready."

"Put it away," Melin said without moving.

"But, Sheo-jay!" The woman hesitated. Through the years she had watched Melin's addiction, and knew well the horrible withdrawal symptoms.

"Do as I say," Melin ordered in a low but firm voice.

When the maid was gone, Melin locked the door. She undressed herself slowly in front of the full-length mirror, until she had nothing on.

Her eyes swept over her slouching shoulders, bony ribs, and skinny legs, then returned to the area between her navel and vagina.

The shiny ridge of a red scar stood out from her white skin, extending eight long inches. She rubbed her fingers over it, and remembered the past spring.

She had gone to the hospital in Kwangchow to see a doctor. Before the trip, she was bleeding badly from an abortion performed by a village woman. After the trip, she no longer bled, but was marked permanently by the scar.

"The color will fade, and the ridge will become smooth. Eventually the scar will be unnoticeable, although you will never become pregnant again," the doctor had said.

Melin had never let anyone see the scar. When she was with the Japanese officers, she kept the room dark.

She had never told anyone about the outcome of the operation, and that was why her father still thought she could become a mother.

"I can't keep you from seeing this, my Hwa." She stared at the scar and imagined it growing in size, deepening in color. "And I know how much you want children. You'll hate me, Hwa, you'll hate me so much!"

She dressed again, this time in slacks and a loose blouse. She then opened two dresser drawers. From one she took out stacks of letters tied with pink ribbons. They were from Hwa; the last one was four years old. From the other drawer she emptied out all the letters she had written but was unable to mail. She untied the ribbons and mixed her letters with his. She gathered them in a tray and carried them to her bed.

On the nightstand a sandalwood Buddha stood staring at her. She took it and held it close to her heart for a moment, then also dropped it to her bed.

The maid had put away the opium pipe, but left the oil lamp burning. Melin picked up a letter and brought it to the low flame.

"All the love we had for each other, my Hwa," she said when the corner of the letter caught fire.

"And the dreams we had for the future," she whispered, dropping the burning letter into a brass spittoon.

"Good-bye, our promises and hopes," she said as she burned the next letter.

"Good-bye, our life as man and wife," she said with the third.

When the ashes piled high in the spittoon, she picked up the sandalwood Buddha and brought it to the flame. The wood was more than eight years old and very dry. It caught fire and burned quickly. She watched the Buddha's feet flaring while holding its head, then laid the Buddha down gently on the ashes.

"When Hwa gave you to me, he said you would protect me. But you didn't. I guess I'm only a worthless girl and don't deserve your protection," she said, staring at the Buddha blazing in the spittoon. She then burned the rest of the letters and let the hot ashes fall on the remains of the Buddha. "With the ashes of our love lying all around you, you can have a pleasant trip back to your heavenly temple in the moon."

When the maid came to call Melin for dinner, she said from behind the locked door that she was not hungry. The entire household was used to Melin missing her meals, and nobody worried.

The night was deep, and the crescent moon was high. Melin stood at her window, looking at the blue-black sky and many stars scattered around the new moon.

She left the window and stood briefly in front of the mirror to look at herself once more. The glow from her morning's dosage of opium had faded. She saw a weary face with haunted eyes and sunken cheeks, and when she looked at her lower abdomen, she felt the red scar burning through her clothes.

She left her room without looking back.

She walked slowly from one courtyard to another, saying silent good-byes to her family.

Suelin had brought her husband and children home for a visit. Melin could hear the couple arguing fiercely.

She moved on to her oldest brother Kiang's room and heard him and his wife fighting about unimportant things.

She paused outside the living-room window,

where her father and her two other brothers were having a nightcap and talking about the singsong girls in Kwangchow.

She went on to her mother's window and stopped there, debating whether to go in and embrace her mother one last time. She heard her mother's voice, talking to the granddaughter.

"I'm so happy to have you sleep with me, my sweet," Yoto said to the five-year-old in a high-pitched childlike voice. "We'll get up early and ride on the horse wagon to the countryside. We'll fly two large kites at the foot of the mountain, and look at the white stones shining high above. The ghost of a rich lord roams there, you know, carrying in his hands his bleeding head . . ."

Melin sighed. Her mother had used the granddaughter as a substitute for her daughter, and couldn't tell any difference between the two.

"I love you, Mama," Melin said softly. "Baba said I sacrificed myself for the family. I'm not sure if my brothers and sisters were worthy of my sacrifice, but you certainly are, my dear Mama."

The crescent moon illuminated the garden, showing Melin the way to the lotus pond.

She stood on the bridge, and was surrounded by a symphony of cicadas, crickets, frogs, and nightingales. She listened for a while, then leaned on the railings of the bridge, gazing at the moon's reflection on the dark water.

Through the years, she had tried to refuse letting more men into her bedchamber, until her father convinced her that it would be the end of the Ma family. She had also tried to face reality without the help of the opium, until the pain had become totally unbearable. She had begged some of the Japanese officers who seemed to genuinely like her to give her a road permit to travel, but none of them listened to her.

She left the bridge and walked to the edge of the water, where large rocks were piled high to form a crouching lion. She climbed to the lion's back, glanced up at the moon one last time, then dived into the pond.

The reflection of the moon shattered as the water splashed loudly. The night symphony ended as the musicians were frightened into silence.

When the cold water closed over her head, Melin suddenly realized that it was not yet too late. She wanted to live. She began to fight her way upward, but the roots of the lotus plants were long and strong. Like ropes, they tangled around her ankles and arms and imprisoned her fragile body. She kicked and thrust wildly, and soon her limited energy was gone.

Her lungs were about to burst, so she opened her mouth and let in the water. She choked, and felt the unbearable pain fill her burning chest.

Hwa! she called, but there was no sound. The last thing she saw was the crescent moon shining above a blanket of water, millions of miles beyond her reach.

Epilogue

ON A WINDY MORNING, Sung Hwa arrived in White Stone.

He grabbed a porter at the train station. "Find me either a wagon or a rickshaw, and hurry," he said, giving the man a large bill.

The porter pocketed the money, then shook his head. "Sorry. All wagons and rickshaws are hired out for the day by a rich man." He looked from Hwa's uniform to his face, decided it was useless to tell a stranger the rich man's name. "But I may be able to find you a bicycle for rent."

The bicycle stand was only a short distance away. The porter chatted as he led the way, asking if Hwa was familiar with the spiritual marriage. When Hwa said no, the porter wanted to show off his knowledge to this ignorant foreign Chinese.

"When a young girl dies a spinster, her parents will arrange a spiritual marriage for her, so that her spirit won't wander alone in the other world. The groom is, of course, the spirit of a bachelor, whose living parents can't bear to see their son lonely in the world of the dead—"

Hwa interrupted him impatiently. "Where are the bicycles? I'm in a hurry."

"We're almost there," the man said, then continued with his story.

"The dead girl's parents hold her funeral and

spiritual wedding on the same day. This way the bride will be greeted by her groom, and he can introduce her to all the other spirits he already knows."

They found the bicycle stand, but the owner was not there, and all the bicycles were locked.

"He has gone to watch the funeral and wedding procession, I'm sure," said the porter with envy. "You'll find everyone in White Stone standing alongside the road to the graveyard. It must be quite a sight! This lucky spiritual bride's father is so rich he is willing to spend a fortune on a worthless daughter. He hired all the wagons and rickshaws to carry her portrait and dowry."

Hwa had already waited eight years. He couldn't wait one more second. He still remembered the way to the Ma house. "Melin, I'm coming!" he said, and left the porter gaping.

He ran into the procession on the country road that stretched toward the graveyard. Tall trees with thick foliage stood to one side, where the Pearl River flowed. To the other, wildflowers and weeds grew high. On a quiet day the wind could be heard traveling through the trees and weeds, but now the weeping wind was overpowered by the voices of the people.

A wagon was piled with a paper bed, sofa, dining table, and chairs. Hwa heard people say that when these were burned, the fortunate young couple would have a well-furnished home in the spiritual world.

Another wagon was loaded with paper robes and gowns, hats and shoes, for a man, a woman, and young boys and girls. People around Hwa praised the thoughtfulness of the bride's parents, who had provided clothes not only for their daughter and son-in-law but also for their grandchildren.

A rickshaw was pulled slowly, carrying a larger-than-life portrait of a young man. Two large wooden panels covered with white paper stood on either side of the picture. In black ink and bold strokes the man's name was written on one, his father's name on the other.

Hwa heard the crowd's approval—the groom was the bride's cousin and had been engaged to her, but the young man had been killed in the war before their wedding could take place.

In weddings for the living, the bride walks humbly a few steps behind her groom. In a marriage of two spirits, the bride's portrait is carried by a rickshaw which follows respectfully several yards after that of the groom.

A villager let his child sit on his shoulders so the boy could have a better view. They moved in front of Hwa, standing between Hwa and the bride's image.

Hwa could see only the writing on one side: *Beloved Daughter of Ma Tsai-tu.*

"My poor Melin has lost her sister," he said to himself, then vaguely remembered that Melin's sister was already married. *Why the spiritual wedding for a married woman?* he wondered.

Hwa moved to a better position to read the other name.

Ma Melin. It was written clearly in large black characters.

Hwa was certain it was a mistake. He blinked. The snakelike lines danced all over the paper, then regathered to form the very same name: *Ma Melin.*

With a bewildered expression on his face, Hwa pushed several villagers aside. He reached the bride's rickshaw and followed the procession closely.

Melin's eyes looked out of the picture to meet the eyes of Hwa, her face beautiful and illuminated with love. Her lips curved in a soft smile; he thought he saw them part to whisper: *Hwa*.

"Melin?" Hwa moved closer to her. He held his breath and waited for her to tell him that he was deceived by his eyes.

A gust of wind swept across the country road and disappeared into the woods, leaving the trees rustling and the weeds stirring restlessly. Hwa cocked his head and listened intently, then called a little louder, "Melin?"

The villagers whispered and looked at one another. They hushed when Hwa cut into the funeral procession as an unwelcome member. They fell totally silent when Hwa stopped the rickshaw puller and pushed the man to one side.

"Melin?" Hwa raised his voice and stepped up to the rickshaw. He raised a hand. Slowly and gently he brushed his fingers over Melin's forehead and then her cheek. When he touched her lips, the procession stopped and the spectators stood motionless. The Ma family members opened their mouths when they saw the outsider pick up Melin's portrait.

Hwa held the portrait at arm's length so that Melin could look at him clearly.

"Melin, I'm back," he said, then brought her closer to his heart. "I'm sorry to have kept you waiting," he said softly.

He was totally unaware of the crowd's murmur, or that it had turned into a loud roar. He didn't notice the several male servants coming toward him.

"The fools arranged a wedding for you. Why didn't you tell them you are already married to me?" He clutched the picture to his chest, embracing Melin tightly, and turned to take her away.

A man seized Hwa's shoulder; two others tried

to snatch the picture from him. Hwa struggled against them, keeping Melin out of their reach.

"Melin, shall we tell them you are my wife?" he asked hysterically, shielding Melin, protecting her from the rest of the world.

The sighing wind returned. It moaned in the trees and sobbed in the weeds, then whispered in Hwa's ears, granting its consent.

Hwa raised his voice. "Melin is my wife!"

Everyone glared at him.

The wind blew harder and Hwa shouted once more, "She is mine!" The three men fell back in confusion.

With Melin's picture in his arms, Hwa turned slowly, challenging the Ma family and every villager, daring them to disagree.

Together with the wind's lamenting cry, Hwa bellowed, "Melin and I married each other in our hearts, spirits, and souls! For eight years I have been Ma Melin's husband and she my wife!"

The mighty wind carried Hwa's shrill wail to circle above White Stone. The wind took his words and soared high, flying from an earthly village toward the temple of the moon.

Author's Note

When we were working together on *Children of the Pearl*, my first book in English, my editor asked me why I wanted to write it like a history textbook. Fiction is wide open, she said. You are free to make the story your own.

Being a Chinese, my wings are chained. To soar freely is a new experience; to write without being confined by ancient rules is not easy.

Only a few of the historical events have been modified—the order of the fall of the cities, the time of death of certain historical figures, and so on. I have not exaggerated any of the tragic brutality of the period; indeed there were worse things that happened to my own family that I could not bring myself to write about.

Thank you, dear Audrey, for showing me how to break the chains. And thank you, John Paine. Without your guidance, I could not have told this story.

About the Author

Ching Yun Bezine was born in northern China in 1937, just before the Japanese invasion which forced her family to flee to Shanghai. There her father's shipping business flourished and she grew up surrounded by luxury and waited on by servants. But when the Communists came to power in 1949, the Yun family fled once again, this time to Taiwan. Ching obliged her parents by becoming a lawyer (her brother is a doctor) and by entering into an arranged marriage to a Chinese physician she did not know. Twenty-five years old and pregnant, Ching left her husband and emigrated to the United States, where she has lived ever since. While struggling to survive as a single mother in a foreign land, Ching earned her bachelor's and master's degrees in fine arts and wrote fourteen best-selling books in Chinese, published by Crown Taiwan. In 1973, while working toward her Ph.D., Ching Yun met Frank Bezine, an American psychologist and educator. They were married one year later in Hawaii. With *Children of the Pearl*, published by Signet in 1991, Ching Yun Bezine made her English-language writing debut. *Temple of the Moon* continues this epic saga of East meets West, and the career of a remarkable author who brings her unique experience and fresh new voice to American fiction.